Woven on the Wind

Also by the Editors

Leaning into the Wind: Women Write from the Heart of the West

Also by Linda Hasselstrom

Feels Like Far: A Rancher's Life on the Great Plains
Bitter Creek Junction
Bison: Monarch of the Plains
A Roadside History of South Dakota
Dakota Bones: The Collected Poems of Linda Hasselstrom
Land Circle: Writings Collected from the Land
Going Over East: Reflections of a Woman Rancher
Windbreak: A Woman Rancher on the Northern Plains
Roadkill
Caught by One Wing

Also by Gaydell Collier (with Eleanor F. Prince)

Basic Horse Care
Basic Training for Horses
Basic Horsemanship: English and Western

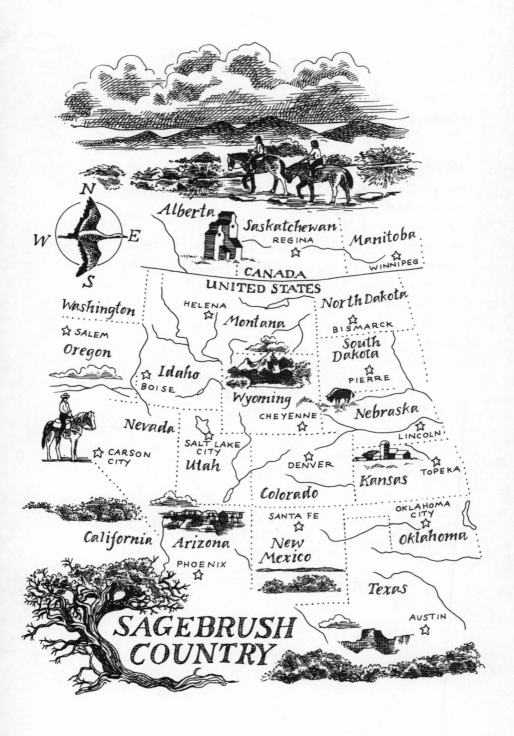

SAGEBRUSH COUNTRY

WOVEN ON THE WIND

Women Write About Friendship in the Sagebrush West

Edited by

LINDA HASSELSTROM,

GAYDELL COLLIER,

and NANCY CURTIS

For Jean — Hope you enjoy this chorus of women's voices.

Nancy Curtis

Gaydell Collier

Linda M. Hasselstrom

HOUGHTON MIFFLIN COMPANY

Boston   New York   2001

For information about permission to reproduce selections from this book,
write to Permissions, Houghton Mifflin Company, 215 Park Avenue South,
New York, New York 10003.

Visit our Web site: www.houghtonmifflinbooks.com.

Library of Congress Cataloging-in-Publication Data
Woven on the wind : women write about friendship in the sagebrush
west / edited by Linda Hasselstrom, Gaydell Collier, and Nancy Curtis.
    p.   cm.
ISBN 0-395-97708-8
1. Women—West (U.S.)—Literary collections. 2. Female friendship—
Literary collections. 3. American literature—Women authors. 4. West
(U.S.)—Literary collections. 5. Friendship—Literary collections.
6. American literature—West (U.S.) 7. Female friendship—West (U.S.)
I. Hasselstrom, Linda M. II. Collier, Gaydell M. III. Curtis, Nancy.
PS561.W63 2001
810.8'09287—dc21   00-053880

Printed in the United States of America
QUM 10 9 8 7 6 5 4 3 2 1

Illustrations by Leslie Evans

Credits begin on page 312

Dedicated to the women of sagebrush country,
whose stories, told or untold, weave us together

Contents

꿏

II 🦌 Leaves Speak for You: The Nourishing   103

III ❧ New Flowers Unfolding: The Promise   197

Introduction:
Voices Woven of
Wind and Sage

"Friendship," Ralph Waldo Emerson wrote, "like the immortality of the soul, is too good to be believed."

Because friendship touches us so deeply—far beneath the glibness of words—it is difficult to articulate. Is real friendship too good—too difficult, too precious—to be explained or understood? Many women think so.

Friendship can be simple or complex, conventional or surprising, as tough as it is tender. Friendship sometimes develops between the most divergent personalities—old and young, cultivated and uneducated, unsophisticated and worldly—defying conventional logic. Harmony between two women may be expressed by gifts, phone calls, letters initiated by every possible occasion—or it may mean sitting together in silence. Friends may talk over every detail of their lives, or they may hardly speak as they make jam or plunge down a river on a raft. And yet, in spite of all the comfort and joy friendship can bring, it also may lead to some of the most painful moments in life. Friendship involves trust, and trust betrayed is devastating. Because of these myriad ironies and layers, deep friendship may never be easy to understand or discuss, but it is certainly powerful and enriching.

For *Woven on the Wind*, we asked women to write about their friendships and relationships with other women. This task proved more difficult in many ways than our aim in our first collection, *Leaning into the Wind*. Many women told us, "It's easy to write about the land. But how can I write about my friends?" We wondered whether these relationships might be less important to Western women, many of them the epitome of independence. We feared that many women might find friendship indefinable or consider a good friendship too important to risk by trying to write about it. How *do* women view their relationships with other women? We discussed the question and our own relationships driving together down miles of Western roads, concluding that we didn't know the answer ourselves. Still, we were determined to find out—or at least to try.

We solicited manuscripts from the entire Interior West, an area including all or parts of sixteen Western states and two Canadian provinces. For this new collection, we asked women to consider how friendships are established and maintained over the distances of space and time inherent in Western rural life.

We decided that nonfamily relationships should be our main focus and that, since eulogies are best delivered in person, we'd emphasize friendships with living women. We wanted the writing to cover an infinite variety of relationships rather than being confined only to the safe and sugary ones. Life's relationships are not all rose petals. Sometimes they rot or stink, taste bitter as gall, or dry up and blow away. We reasoned that by encouraging women to explore relationships that become contentious as well as those that turn into lifelong connections, we might help other women learn how to sustain the best kinship, how to help build the communities of strong women that can be so important to us all.

Sagebrush, the predominant plant in the setting for these writings, suggested itself as an icon. Just as sagebrush symbolizes the West, we believe it captures the heart and life of this book's central theme: women's friendships, no matter how they are expressed. Sometimes misunderstood and vilified, sometimes glorified and praised, sagebrush impresses us with its diversity, its hardiness, its practicality, its symbolism, and its loveliness —like the women in these pages.

Sagebrush (*Artemisia*, including sagewort and wormwood), sometimes poetically or mistakenly referred to as "sage," should not be confused with true sage (*Salvia*, of the mint family), the herb that flavors many dishes. Sagebrush authority Kendall Johnson, professor and head of the Department of Rangeland Ecology and Management at the University of Idaho, tells of the college student from New Zealand who "did not know the difference and chose to flavor a stew with sagebrush instead of sage, with astonishing results." Although, in the pages that follow, we sometimes take the privilege of literary license to speak of "sage," we're referring to sagebrush.

Sagebrush plants are as diverse as their environment. Generally, we think of big sagebrush—*Artemisia tridentata*—as representative of the West's signature genus, and it is the most prominent. But there are many species, subspecies, and varieties of the genus *Artemisia* endemic to the West, as well as to similar steppelike climates around the world. So, too, we might say that the women in these stories are diverse, coming from native or far-flung origins, sinking roots and thriving, being fed themselves and at the same time nourishing others from this challenging and varied land.

Sagebrush grows in desert valleys and high above treeline in the mountains, in sunbaked arid soils as well as on ditchbanks and streams. The plants grow on isolated windswept ridges, in dense patches like islands, or regularly spread over the earth as far as the eye can see—a soft gray-green blanket thrown over the landscape. The women who wrote these stories come from isolated Nevada ranches and the Idaho high country, from Arizona deserts and the high plains of Saskatchewan—from every country corner of this sagebrush sea.

It is this ubiquity, as much as its other qualities, that suggests sagebrush (particularly big sagebrush) as a symbol for these women of the West. At a book exhibit, an East Coast editor asked us whether sagebrush was the same as tumbleweed—Russian thistle that dries and breaks off from its roots, then rolls with the wind. "Far from it!" we exclaimed. She was correct, however, in that both plants represent the West, both in fact and myth, historically and in the present. As an image suggesting the idea of the West, sagebrush is liberally scattered throughout movies, photographed for book jackets, even adopted as a symbol for movements such as the Sagebrush Rebellion—disagreements between ranchers and federal agencies over management of the land.

Hardiness is part and parcel of diversity and versatility. As a genus, as a species, and even as individual plants, sagebrush adapts to its environment in a mind-boggling variety of ways—just as these women have found endless ways to cope with the challenges of their lives. Big sagebrush has both deep and shallow roots, to take advantage of water that percolates deep into the ground and the sprinklings of summer rain. Some plants may flower in summer, others in fall, to take best advantage of weather conditions. Seeds and seedlings often proliferate, although some species may spread through sprouting from the roots. The leaves themselves are variable, adapting to the stress of drought, to a landscape that is often downright hostile. Sagebrush is tough. Sagebrush is a survivor. Sagebrush is resistant to man's attempts to control it—traits suggesting as well the indomitable spirit of Western women.

Perhaps surprisingly, sagebrush is one of the West's most useful plants. Because of its beneficence, adaptability, and practicality, Kendall Johnson has a sympathetic view of its "multiple dimensions," calling it "Mama Sage." This view contrasts with that of people who seek to control sagebrush by burning, plowing, or using chemicals. Many sagebrushes provide nourishing forage for deer, elk, pronghorns, and livestock. Although cattle might not find the leaves palatable if other feed is available, the plants provide excellent emergency fodder in winter. Sagebrush also provides shelter and nesting sites for sage grouse and other birds, as well as for small mammals. It provides windbreaks for larger animals and holds moisture in the soil as it helps prevent winter snow from blowing and evaporating in the wind. Its roots provide a host for the vibrantly beautiful but partially parasitic Indian paintbrush.

Most Indian tribes in the West learned to use sagebrush almost as completely as they used the native bison, making from its leaves, bark, roots, and stems clothing, medicines, sleeping mats and blankets, cleansers, torches, brooms, tinder, towels, shoes, and ornaments. The chewed root was used as a charm for love or hunting. Its smoke, believed to exorcise evil, is still used as incense in religious services and ceremonies.

Early inhabitants of the West depended on the sagebrush around them in many ways, incorporating it into their lives and revering its "Mama Sage" character—that strong but nurturing spirit that also typifies the rural women who populate the following pages.

Beyond all their diverse qualities, the sagebrushes are beautiful, their scent pungent and refreshing. The soft gray-green or silver-green leaves and the rounded, cushionlike appearance of some plants contrast with the distant browns and tans of the rangeland and the bright detail of a flower. The comfortable ordinariness represents the spirit of hope and the bond of love found in Western women and their writings.

In *Leaning into the Wind,* the women wrote of their relationship with the land, a subject that came close to more hearts than we ever imagined. Love of the Western landscape even touched readers—both women and men—generations removed from their ancestral soil, who responded to the deep, universal need for rootedness, groundedness, wholeness.

In *Leaning,* the women incorporated their relationships with animals, men, seasons, and work into their feelings for the land, but they seemed to skirt their relationships with other women. Yet as we traveled the West promoting that first anthology, our own friendships deepening and broadening as we met many of the writers represented in the book, we were intrigued by the subject of women's bonds with one another.

We believed that putting together *Woven on the Wind* would be more difficult, but we received nearly a thousand manuscripts from many hundreds of women. From these we chose the pieces that best supported the theme so well represented by sagebrush. We began work on the first collection confident that the women of the West would shape the book. They have shaped this one as well, and each piece included here represents many others that we could not include. We are extremely grateful to all those who sent their stories to us. Their eloquence inspired us as we edited and created an introduction for each section of the book. We quoted or paraphrased their words where appropriate in section titles and within the introductory material. For example, Sharon R. Bryant's account of how her daughter's spirit "dances with whirlwinds" and "soars with the raptors over peaks" is a description that might apply to many of the women whose writings follow. And when Nedalyn D. Testolin speaks of a friend, she might be portraying many Western women: "She's beautiful. She's like the sky and the grass and the rain and the sage, all in one."

To write deeply and honestly about friendship is not easy, and in some cases it is impossible. But the women whose words fill the pages of *Woven on the Wind* found many ways to express a range of connections. And despite bitterness or loss, as a whole these relationships—these friendships—wash over us with the fresh scent and healing pungency of a sagebrush wind.

LINDA HASSELSTROM,
GAYDELL COLLIER,
and NANCY CURTIS

Woven on the Wind

I

My Feet Set Down Roots: The Grounding

Woven on the Wind begins with writing by Western women who have set their roots deep in the soil, drawing nourishment from the earth as well as from "women remembered." Life in this arid country has taught these women to stay "close to the wind, earth, creeks, grasslands," learning from the land and from each other.

Hardy and versatile, women have always been part of the West, but they were often invisible to the mythmakers who did, and still do, view the West as a male fantasy. "The joys of a woman's life" were "not mentioned in books, not found in the universities or corporations." Ignoring the lively truth, or taking for granted women's triumphs and talents, official historians and literature professors often acknowledged only the "antiseptic remains of history." But the truths endured, "growing quietly in the hearts" of women scattered throughout the West.

Sagebrush, too, was often ignored or overlooked. Until Kendall Johnson began referring to "Mama Sage," little homage was paid to sagebrush, and even less to Western women. Philip Fradkin says that sagebrush has come to dominate the plains "by pure ordinariness" and persistence, another apt description of women. Many biologists now believe that sagebrush is as essential to Western ecology as women are to humanity — that without sagebrush, the entire ecosystem would collapse.

For a while, women "pretended not to notice" being forgotten in formal accounts. Keeping busy with their households and other tasks, they kept an "undulant silence," accepting the idea that women were "supposed to want other things."

Hiding the truth doesn't make it disappear. News stories about drug use, alcoholism, and other ills make it clear that the West is not immune to the problems of the larger world. But even poor soil, even the greasy, hardpacked clay we call gumbo, can bring forth beauty — "gorgeous flowers in gumbo" — just as many of the stories in these pages grew from difficulty.

Telling our stories helps us realize how similar we are and creates connections between women "with wind-chapped cheeks and wrinkle lines" who may never have met. Just as sagebrush, deeply rooted, shelters other plants and feeds an abundance of wildlife, so these stories can provide comfort and community for others, both in the West and elsewhere.

Stoic acceptance was the first rule of enduring hardship of any kind in many Western families. Tradition taught Westerners never to argue, never to complain, because "the more it hurts / the bigger the pearl." In joy or sadness, we sang or wept "without saying a word," learning from some of our elders that "lonely is a state of mind." Our silence sanctioned and helped promote the creation of a Western myth that had no place for the reality known to women. Each woman who has written her story has taken a stand, saying, "I chose to break my silence."

Writing of friends, mothers, teachers, and others, ordinary women have recorded a rich and varied legacy of other women from the past. In poems and essays, "in quiet words we speak," each woman tells how her "feet set down roots," how she drew strength from others, learning to survive in spite of isolation and loneliness.

Even as the editors compiled and shaped this manuscript, we knew that some tales would remain untold and found another striking parallel between women and the sagebrush outside their doors. Beneath the outer bark of sagebrush root hides a slender white filament called the heart thread. Only by peeling away the root's tough husk — or opening up the dark shell of a woman's silence — can we find the translucent heart. To learn how other women have illuminated our spirits, we must know their stories. If "we share our lives," we will remember the women who inspired us, and their light can "never dim, flicker, set, or be extinguished." But if our "deeper feelings are mostly inaccessible," we cannot move toward a deeper understanding of one another.

The heroines in this "tapestry of tales" are often humble women with little to leave as souvenirs. We may find a thread to follow in objects as common as faded photographs in a tin box or as startling as a wooden leg in the attic. Although we may no longer see "their faces flashing in the sun," their wisdom enriches and inspires us. Through these pages, they live on to cast their light over a larger circle.

"Rooted to the earth," the women who inhabit the following pages have grounded us and given us the courage to go forward. "Tapping into ancient rhythms," their stories set their roots deep in our hearts, showing us how to thrive and how to nourish.

JANE WELLS ⭐ My Heart Still Grins

It was the time of day when the sun hesitates to call it quits and ranchers feel honest if they've given their best and relieved if they haven't. The big barn doors were latched open, and horse traffic was calm and easy. I sat on the back of an old flatbed used for feeding, still warm from the sun, savoring an after-dinner cup of coffee. A friend who boarded her horse with us introduced me to her guest, another woman with a sincere smile and kind eyes. Offering them refreshment, I left for the house to pour a glass of iced tea, brew a cup of herbal tea, refill my coffee, and set out cookies baked that afternoon. It was important to me that our anticipated visit be as relaxing as my hospitality could provide. I hoped the barn cats would not try to sip our drinks and the dogs would not beg for cookies, but I never suggested we visit in the house.

The three of us found places to perch in front of the open barn doors. We wore matching outfits of sweat-stained jeans that were worn and faded, thin cotton shirts covered with horse hair, dusty boots, and hairstyles never featured in fashion magazines. Oh, we were a sight as we got comfortable on overturned feed buckets.

We talked of things that define us: a new colt, a sweet mare, where we came from, how we got here, hinting about lost loves and tears shed but long since dried on our pillows. There was bittersweet, but no bitterness.

All the while, the bright light faded into softer colors until our edges became subtle outlines. Still we talked, quieter now as the night sounds came and the animals settled down.

My friend, with her goofy sense of humor and delight in living, jumped up and announced the grand finale. She would play a song we just had to hear. Finding the tape in her Volkswagen with the back seat removed to make room for her dogs, she filled those empty spaces inside and those shadows outside with crazy music — a country song with a Cajun beat. Oh, it was just perfect: "Mad Cowboy Love."

We danced without moving, we sang without saying a word, and we laughed out loud to be part of this night and each other. It was a celebration. Three women, three friends, sharing the best of times, and I knew, without any doubt, that this night would count mightily toward reckoning the good and the bad.

JUNE FRANKLAND BAKER ❧ June and I, Singing

Given the same name, we were friends,
not copies. After high school
the sweet accident of our name
darted across the country between us,
like the swallow last evening above my lawn,
first I've seen this far from the river bluffs,
blur of momentum, only its tail
victorious signature over the grass.

I remember the dip and rise of "La Golondrina,"
tale of that swallow separated from home
we sang as a duet, a cappella.
As we paced the sidewalk, practicing,
our voices lifted over the schoolyard —
at first in unison,
then taking leave, each to form
its own pattern through the air.

KATHLEENE WEST ❧ Thinking of Rain in the Dry Season

Those summers when the Skeedee ran dry
and the corn burned white and the dust sealed
my father's face from smiles,
Aunt Bakie drove out from Omaha after church.
It was almost as if it had rained.
She brought marshmallow peanuts,
jellied orange slices,
and the Sunday funnies.

Her name was Amelia,
but she'd always been Bakie.
I quizzed her for explanations, leaping
over her parcels and weaving around her
as if she were a Maypole.
Perhaps she fell into the flour bin as a child.
Or was enchanted by a hungry witch
and forced to bake bread and strudel in a tower.
And the curse blighted the land,
not to be lifted until she escaped.

My questions ignored, she opened the packages
and turned the steamy morning to a holiday.
Balancing rhinestone sunglasses over her bifocals,
Mother agreed they'd stop the glare in the hayfield.
She posed in the fireweeds by the windmill,
flinging her hands over her head.
Then she and Aunt Bakie snorted and nudged each other
like two horses in forbidden wheat.

I jammed my hands into my pockets
and kicked up dust,
but Aunt Bakie tossed a scarf over my clipped hair
and told me to lean over the water tank to see
my beauty. My reflection floated from me,
an uncertain mermaid swaying in the water.
I ripped the scarf from my head, waving it
like a standard, and ran
from the smell of moss and wet stones
to Mother and Aunt Bakie.
They stood on the hill beyond the house,
their faces flashing in the sun like two mirrors.

It's all about friendship Mary Hadley

MARY HADLEY 🦌 No Room for Strangers

I first met Pat and her children at a California beach picnic four days before
our families moved to Nevada. We needed to evaluate each other, although
it was too late to change our minds. Like partners in an arranged marriage,
we wondered whether we could stand each other every hour, of every day,
of every week. Could her children live by my children's rules? At the time, I
didn't realize all eleven of us would crowd on top of each other in the same
ramshackle house.

Both Pat and I had agreed with our husbands' plans to move. My husband, Bob, had been foreman on a cattle and avocado ranch, and Pat's
husband, Cliff, was a government welder who had grown up with horses
and livestock. Both men eventually wanted their own ranches. In January
of 1956, when my father-in-law invested in an abandoned Nevada cattle
ranch, we agreed to move a thousand miles to bring it to life.

While our children played on the beach, Pat and I measured each other
against our shared dream, clasped hands, and vowed to succeed. We
would not see each other again until we arrived at the ranch.

After two long days of travel, Bob and I drove into the high desert valley. Snow-covered sagebrush spread unbroken, with no sign of man's plow,

fence, or power line for fifty miles to the Nevada-Oregon line. The distance hurt my eyes.

We drove below tall mountains, passing only a few narrow dirt roads with wooden mailboxes. In the middle of nowhere, a whole town crowded into one small building: post office, gas station, bar, mercantile, grocery, and owner's home. Fifteen miles farther, we turned at a mailbox and drove the last five miles into the foothills.

The deserted ranch slept against the mountain on a creek-fed meadow. Dark shadows lowered as we drove through the creek to a small house under giant cottonwoods.

Bob clicked the light switch, but nothing happened. "I knew it was too quiet," he said. "No generator means no electricity, no water." He tried to light the oil space heater, then threw the matches down in disgust.

Exhausted, I surveyed the kitchen while my three-year-old son and four-year-old daughter held my legs and the six-week-old baby slept in my arms. Whoever lived here before had abandoned the place, leaving ossified food, dirty clothes, and an unmade bed. Bob drove us seventy miles back to Winnemucca, settled us warm and safe at the hotel, and returned to fix the Witte light plant. The kids and I sprawled on the beds too tired to cry. I bathed the two older children, and we shared a hamburger and milk shake. After a few bites, they both fell asleep.

Bob returned in time for breakfast and drove us the seventy miles back to the ranch house.

The kids and I inspected every corner. My head barely cleared the light bulbs in the ceiling. The kids ran to each low window to look outside; no one had nailed an inside wall over the house's ribs. The kids rolled on the warm Masonite floor, laid directly over the dirt like thin wall-to-wall carpet. I cleaned, cooked, and rocked the baby. The kids listened to my stories about the mountain and the creek and how they'd learn to be buckaroos. I held to my dream, afraid of reality.

That afternoon Pat arrived with Cliff and four kids, ages two to seven, to share our house and our dream. While the kids squealed and circled like colts, Pat took off her coat and rolled up her sleeves. "What's for supper?" She lifted the kettle's lid and stirred the beans. We worked as a team — I measured, she stirred. No need for a boss when two women work as one.

In the morning, Bob left for Oregon to buy stock cows. Cliff fixed the frozen water pipes and planned a kitchen for the big bunkhouse. The change between sea level and five thousand feet left Pat and me breathless. We laughed and fought for the only excuse to rest. Pat leaned against the doorway with my baby cradled in her arms. "I should do that," she said, "but I have to hold the baby." When the baby cried for her bed, Pat and I sat knee to knee on facing chairs and drew oxygen into our lungs.

The fourth day, two mothers and seven kids traveled seventy miles to the store. The ranch paid for canned goods by the case lot and eggs by the half crate. We left our list with the store manager and shopped for snow boots, warm coats, and gloves for the kids. The stair-stepped children fit together like meshed fingers. We counted them in and out of stores. We never lost a child, and when we picked up a few stray preschoolers, Pat cut them from our bunch as we passed through the door. Our kids marched through town like ducklings and rode home on a bench of grocery boxes.

Camping in the house with beds in the living room and with nothing in its proper place, Pat and I thought the same thoughts. The closest mother tended the child in need. Our dreams became a reality, but our life was a great adventure.

We brought a milk cow, freezer, and sewing machine to a place where radios played only when the night sky bent far-off airwaves low enough to hear. Only the *Snake River Stampede* played country music by day for lonely ranch wives. Television and clothes dryers were only memories.

On the fifth day, eight hundred mother cows and one newborn calf arrived by train. Bob trucked the cows to the ranch while Cliff spread hay in the meadow. Pat and I cooked, baked, and kept track of kids in the two-acre meadow surrounding the house, inseparable in most of our work and all of our play.

Buckaroo outfits work on horseback with long ropes. Bob and Cliff team-roped each pregnant cow and eased her down to brand her. When the cows calved, they hid their newborns in ditches and left for the feed ground. After coyotes fed on unprotected calves, the cows set up cooperative daycare.

Bob left for the Denver Stock Show to buy bulls while Cliff fed hay. Our children learned about cold snow, open spaces, and "leppy" — orphan — calves that waited at the back door for a nipple bucket.

Pat's first-grader attended a one-room school with one teacher and seven students, where the community watched old movies once a month. Everyone brought babies, grandmothers, and refreshments. We partied when they changed the reels, and little ones slept behind the screen on cots.

After Pat moved her brood to the remodeled bunkhouse, the kids still ran in a herd at one house or the other. Pat fed our Indian buckaroo dinner and supper; I did breakfast. All deliverymen and passing cowboys stayed for a meal that became a social gathering with two cooks and all the kids at my house. Pat told visitors, "No need to earmark — my kids have brown eyes, and Mary's have blue." But when they ran in one kitchen door, dashed the length of the room and out the other door, and sped past the dinner table and back to start again, they made a continuous line.

On March 15, we opened the meadow gate to a green valley — after the spring rains and the smells of sage, damp earth, and grass filled our souls. Without fences, the cows calved on the open range between the Oregon state line and the Southern Pacific railroad tracks one hundred miles away.

The mother cows arrived at their cooperative daycare near the ranch gate at the same time the afternoon school bus stopped at our mailbox. Each day the same ten calves lay in a circle, and a different cow stood watch. As the cows approached, each calf raced up and down the road and around its mother. Pat and I laughed at the familiar emotion.

Adversity welds people together in more than friendship. Like sisters, Pat and I traded cooking, children, and time to buckaroo. We loved the open, lonely country, where strong, resourceful women earned respect by initiative and dependability. We found that distant neighbors gathered like family when needed and that lonely is a state of mind.

SHERRY SCHULTZ SHILLENN 🦎 *Dear Judy*

I'm writing this for you because these past ten years have been difficult for us as friends. How did I know when we first met sixteen years ago that I would end up owing you, thanking you, for what has become of my life? How did I know your friendship and sensible ways would be the frail thread that connected me to reality, community, and family?

Remember when we first met in 1983? I moved to town and met you through church friends. You were recovering from knee surgery at home. I came by your house with a small chocolate cake and a card, stayed awhile to fetch and carry and to tidy up. By the end of that afternoon, we'd become pretty good friends, or so I thought. The real test of our friendship was a long six years down the road.

Our lives were filled with jobs and husbands, housework and vacations, a new baby boy for your collection of sons, and three daughters at my house who were just itching and aching to baby-sit. We began a ritual of walking several miles at 5:00 A.M., rain or shine, wind or darkness, past vicious dogs or transients sitting by the road. We had to do it. We were getting fat at our desk jobs, and there was no other time of day we could fit visiting or exercising into our schedules. Our talks became the strength of our days, and we logged thousands of hours of conversation, becoming the sisters neither of us had.

In 1989 I began a decline into a darkness that was both gradual and sudden, unexpected and yet predictable, knowing what I know now. It began with the departure of my first-born for college and my strange fear of walking past the door to her empty room, continued with my stresses at work — a disastrous boss, a frivolous lawsuit against our office staff — my lumpectomy, my hysterectomy, my absent-mindedness, the nightmares when I could sleep at all. I had crying spells when my feet touched the floor most mornings and anxiety and panic attacks when I pulled into my designated parking spot at work. I sought comfort in church and family, coworkers and mental health professionals, my doctors, my pets, my husband, my prescriptions, and you.

The seasons went by. The downward spiral was unstoppable. I quit my job. I alienated my children. I found only hypocrites seated in the church pews and choir loft, places where I had always found solace and refuge. I quit answering the phone, getting dressed, attending my children's basketball games, concerts. I began pulling out my eyelashes. I lost my keys, my shoes, my list of things to remember. I forgot to feed the dog and cat. I forgot my husband's birthday, my parents' anniversary. I didn't even care. Clinical depression is an ugly thing.

Through it all, we kept on walking every morning. You must have hated what I'd become. You must have been so sick of my sickness, so completely tired of prompting me and coaching me and encouraging me and crying with me when I felt so lost. And then the bottom fell out. Your husband got a transfer, and my last, best friend moved away.

Since being there physically was impossible, you kept me sane with frequent flowers, scores of books, marathon phone calls, and visits. You scolded me and laughed at me, made peace between my children and me when all other efforts had failed. I swear, you alone must have kept my husband from leaving me. You taught me how to journal and to look for one good thing in my world every day. You helped me filter through the small stuff and save my energy for the big stuff, like Erin's wedding, so I wouldn't make a fool of my family or myself. You've kept me from going under and going to pieces so many times I've lost count. You've never given up on me, your "friend from the dark lagoon."

The only thing you've ever asked in return was that I try to use my gift of writing for this book. It's just one day before the deadline, and I haven't the heart to let you down.

Love,
Sherry

AGNES L. WICH 🦌 *Letter to a "Friend"*

Dear Liz,

Over the years, I've probably written this letter at least a hundred times in my head, but only just now on paper.

I must admit, a certain anger, and a little pain, drove those compositions. I just didn't get it. How could my best friend — the one I grew up with, the one whom I had shared all those trials of adolescence with — not understand my joy? How many hours must we have spent talking about boys, sharing our heartaches, planning our future?

I saw the disappointment in your face. Disappointment in my choice. My husband-to-be was just a farmer. You tried to be polite, but I saw through it. After all, I grew up with you! You even suggested, a mere two days before my wedding, that I shouldn't get married. You said I should continue to work and live on my own and buy all those things I probably always wanted. But, as I explained to you, all those things were not what I wanted.

The very worst thing, though, was when you came to visit us hardly a year later. We didn't have much, yet I had tried so hard to make our small, aging farmhouse attractive and comfortable. I received no compliments from you.

I heard only the gloating about your exciting job at the university and the many wonderful trips you had taken for business and pleasure. You were so worldly! I should have been jealous. Funny thing, though, I wasn't.

We enjoyed a pleasant visit, you and I and my husband and your latest beau. I tried to show you the farm, especially beautiful that time of year. Newly budded trees, fields colored a pale green by the newly sprouted corn, the backdrop of snowcapped Rockies. You didn't even notice, or at least you didn't let on. That would be admitting an acceptance of my chosen life.

What really took the cake, though, was what you said as you left that day. My husband had already returned to the field, so you took your opportunity. "You know," you started out, "there's more to marriage than talking about the weather and the crops. You two don't really share — in a deeper sense, I mean. You're missing out on so many things. There's more to marriage — there's more to *life* — than *this!*"

I was speechless. How *dare* you walk into my home and make a judgment about my marriage and my life? You attacked the most precious and private part of me, and yet, ironically, you knew nothing about our life together. You chose to pass judgment on an afternoon tea.

It was, perhaps, a good thing, as I look back on it now. I would meet many more like you, with preformed stereotypical ideas about farm and ranch life. It's just that I never thought the first would be you.

We've been married twenty-two years now. I only wish you could have been here to see "all that we've missed out on." My life has been more of an adventure than you could have possibly dreamed. No, we never went on fancy trips. Nor did we ever get rich. And things were never easy. There's always lots of hard work waiting to be done.

But I wouldn't have changed a thing. I've been surrounded by the very essence of "life" day in, day out. What a gift! We have been blessed by the beauty we've seen daily at our doorstep: the deep golden moonrise on the hills to the east, the majestic orange sunset over the Rockies, the multitude of wild animals — deer, fox, raccoon, coyote, skunk, and the thousands of geese that "graze" in our field. Can you imagine the feeling of watching the old ewe give birth to twins or bottle-feeding a baby pig? Or the sound of a thousand toads on a summer's night? Have you ever watched your children run through a field unhindered by streets and fences, nurture a sick calf, or play with a lamb?

I could go on, but still you probably would not understand. It's interesting, though, that many like you think we rural women live some kind of backward, submissive life, acquiescing and dutiful. This lifestyle has given me *wings* to pursue my dreams, to get my degree, to unearth and regain my soul.

So, I thank you, Liz, for that tip-off twenty-two years ago. It helped prepare me for what was to come and challenged me to seize every opportunity to champion women and our rural way of life.

I hope this letter helps lay my anger to rest. I have carried it, festering in my heart, for far too long. I can only hope that you have enjoyed as great a life as I.

Your friend,
Agnes

HELEN APPLEGARTH McCONNELL ❧ Goldie

When I think about women and friendship, a memory leaps to mind from when I was about five. On a hot summer day, my mother, with my baby sister and me, had gone to town. Coming home, we got stuck in the sandy road and walked to a neighbor's house. It was very hot, and I was tired. Why couldn't Mother carry me, too? I was thirsty, and, worst of all, my long cotton stockings were getting full of stickers and my shoes were full of sand.

When we got to Goldie's, she sprang into action, getting us cool drinks and wet washcloths to bathe our hot, tear-streaked faces. Then that dear lady sat on the floor in front of me and picked the stickers out of my stockings!

How do girls learn about women and friendship? By watching their mothers, of course. And when their mothers' friendships spill over to them, the influence is lifelong.

DIANE J. RAPTOSH ❧ The Rapture

Let's both take our shirts off, cross hearts, and hope not to stare. Sit over here. This flat rock likes splitting sunlight with us. Let's lick air like lizards on the count of six, since that's how old we were last year. Now lean back, and let's pull off our shorts. If you're quiet as that hawk, you can hear a runt heart leap in your wrist. We have as many in our skin as worms. Whoever tells a soul about this will get blisters all across the *m* of her top lip. So take off your underwear, and I will, too. Let's sit still as concrete lions turned snout tip to whisker. Let's lip-kiss so fast we'll forget what we did, but harder than you'd like to kiss your mom. Now swear on Stripe's cat spit your gut for forgetting's real good. If you can't, that red-tail's not circling just to watch us, those hyacinths aren't blueberries on a stick, and besides, remember, no other girl from Miss Rose's homeroom will ever like you like this.

SHANNON DYER ❧ Girls' Night Out

I'm the first to arrive. I couldn't wait, closed the feed store five minutes early, barely kissed my kids good-bye. I drove with the windows down, Aretha Franklin screaming about respect — unusual behavior for a woman just shy of forty. But tonight I can forget who I'm supposed to be and be who I am.

In our unincorporated town with little more than a post office and lumberyard, I pull up in front of a battered, paint-stripped, sloop-porched bar and café. Centrally located between our ranches, it gets little business — ensuring some privacy if we get loud or silly.

I pick a back booth so I can watch the door, and order a beer. Before I get more than a few sips, Sharon comes in, her grin as wide as mine. You'd think we hadn't seen each other in months or years instead of a day or two. But this night is special.

She orders a soda and slips into the booth, already teasing me about being overanxious. Sharon wears a green golf shirt and cardigan; her makeup and hair are perfect, conservative, classic. "I had to wait for the boys to get out of the hay field. Someone showed up to see some bulls, so Jerry was busy with that. I fed the little kids. I didn't know whether I was going to get away or not." Sharon's got four kids, a predicament that would do me in. She slides across the table a newspaper clipping about a religious Web site, and we are quickly caught up in a discussion about the horrors of raising teenagers.

Sharon and I are imports from cities to this open, hilly range and to cattle ranching. We lived on the same dorm floor at a university with twenty-two thousand students. We hated each other. To our relief, we passed out of each other's lives. To our horror, we became engaged to ranchers we met at school and ended up living within a few miles of each other in a county of fewer than a thousand people.

Since our husbands had been friends all their lives, Sharon and I were duty-bound to get along. Seventeen years later, with an accumulation of six kids and one ranch lost and bought between us, we have developed a deep friendship full of humor and trust.

When Mickie comes into the little café, she orders a draft beer and exchanges a few words with the bartender. She's laughing before she gets to the booth. Native to the hills, she didn't grow up in this neighborhood. She and her husband spent the first years of their marriage on the rodeo circuit. She loves horses, cattle, her husband, and her three sons, though maybe not in that order. A tiny woman, she is prematurely gray, with vivid blue eyes that dance with humor or occasional anger. Soft-spoken, she has definite opinions and isn't shy about stating them. She's carrying a Thomas Merton book. "Is Margaret coming? I need to return this."

Sharon scoots over for Mickie. "She said she'd be here." We laugh, knowing Margaret may or may not show up, and if she does, it will be later. Margaret, a relative newcomer who's been in the hills only three years, came to settle affairs on the family ranch when her uncle died and somehow never got away. Raised in Los Angeles and educated at Wellesley, Oxford, and the London School of Economics, she has made the most dramatic adjustment to life here. Unlike the rest of us, Margaret didn't marry a man already wed to the land.

This is Girls' Night Out. We hate the demeaning title, but it sticks. If we were too concerned with politically correct verbiage and nonspecific gender roles, we wouldn't be living out here. I don't remember how it started. Probably way back when our kids were too little to be left without a baby sitter and we were too broke to afford one. Back in those days, getting out of the house or off the ranch sometimes felt like the only way to hang on to what little sanity we had left. For whatever reason, these infrequent get-togethers, when we leave husbands and kids to fend for themselves, have become a tradition.

Calling four women together for an evening might sound simple, since out here there's no competition with cultural performances, restaurants, late shopping hours, or movie theaters. But the planning takes mediation and lots of negotiation. Because we are a resourceful, determined lot, and because this time with each other is important, we work it in. We come together to share our insights and questions, to delve deeply into God, the spirit, the Bible. We also talk about husbands — some baring more than others. It would be easier to list topics we don't discuss, if I could think of any. Our coming together is like a stream-of-consciousness release from the restraints of normal society.

Margaret shows up after Mickie and I have switched from beer to coffee. We've covered prayer and the latest school gossip and speculated about the effects of NAFTA on cattle prices and whether the Ranchers-Cattlemen Action Legal Fund's latest scheme will be effective. Sharon and Mickie exchange information on paying children salaries for ranch work and the resultant tax consequences. Our sides ache from laughing, our throats are raw, and our cheeks are sore from constant smiling.

Margaret, vivacious and quick-witted, has long, "Hollywood blonde" hair she flips behind her shoulders when she makes a point. She pulls out a battery-operated candy dispenser and hands it to me for my youngest daughter's birthday. She gives Mickie a videotape for her son. Then, sitting down, she tells a funny story about carpenters working on her place. Margaret is seeing a well-respected and much-beloved rancher — in the blush of a new romance while the rest of us celebrate anniversaries counted in decades. We tease her about her beau, in his mid-seventies.

Tomorrow my husband will ask what we talked about, and aside from one or two details, I won't be able to answer him. Not because I'm sworn to keep any confidences, but because this evening's real meaning goes beyond words. What do we talk about? Life, in its excruciating detail, as only women can talk about it.

With this group, I don't have to be strong. I'm not required to give the impression that I know what's going on, that I'm independent or smart. We've known each other so long we share inside jokes years old, and a word or gesture can send us into peals of laughter. We know one another's eccentricities, faults, and strengths. Despite that knowledge, we accept and trust each other.

Our choices are limited here. We form friendships that we expect to last for the rest of our lives, that must be built with understanding and flexibility to withstand any storm, bend to any amount of sunlight. Out here, our friends aren't categorized. There aren't the people from church, separated from the mothers from school and the ladies I see at work, or the wives of my husband's friends. They are all the same. I may have seen the same woman Friday night, be on a booster club committee with her Tuesday afternoon, and teach church school with her Wednesday. I might have visited with her husband at the feed store on Thursday, heard a story about her son on Friday.

We are sisters in the truest sense. We share the cycle of this land, tied together by location, circumstance, history, and relationships that entangle business, personal, familial, and political aspects of our lives. Kahlil Gibran says not to seek your friend only with hours to kill but with hours to live.

So while I live daily with these friends, several times each year we meet for an uninterrupted evening of soul baring.

After midnight, heading home, I laugh out loud, remembering conversations. Tomorrow I'll go back to being mom, wife, bookkeeper, cook, committee chairman. But this night and others like it remind me that I am more than the roles I fill, as rewarding as they are.

JOYCE BADGLEY HUNSAKER ⁂ Something of the Earth

She came from a hard place. "If your godfather hadn't gone down on the *Titanic*," her mother once told her, "our lives would have been much different."

As it turned out, an abusive childhood led her to an early marriage that turned sour in the old timber and mining camps of the great Pacific Northwest. She learned in a hurry to rely on herself and not ask for favors. Oh, she was a scrapper all right. Her childhood had left its mark. How many times had I seen her draw herself up to full height — five feet even and ninety-seven pounds soaking wet — then silently stare down an angry, cursing, six-foot man? How many times had I seen those ebony eyes narrow and those leathery fingers wag at someone who needed to be told in no uncertain terms "just how the cow ate the cabbage"? Plenty. I thought she was completely magnificent. She was a survivor. She was Aunt Maybelle.

The first summer she said "Come and stay with me awhile on the mining claim," I thought I'd died and gone to heaven. None of my friends had aunts who knew how to pan for gold, or lived in a log cabin on their own claim and cooked pancakes on a wood stove, or collected arrowheads and fossils, petrified wood and odd rocks, and could tell you the stories of each. None of them had aunts who were part Sioux. None of them could shoot a gun.

"Here," she said, shoving a pistol at me one day. "There's rattlesnakes that need killin' down by the outhouse. You better learn how to hit what you're aimin' at." Then she taught me how to skin the snakes, and we marveled together at the beautiful scale patterns on their backs. She kept the rattles and made earrings out of them. They sounded their telltale warning buzz whenever she walked or shook her head. "How appropriate," my dad said with a grin.

Aunt Maybelle had helped raise him after their mother died. After Dad was out on his own, she became a pilot, flew bombers in World War II. Ferry pilots, they called them then, flying aircraft from the states to appointed stations so the planes could be put into action. She showed me a picture of herself in her uniform once — but just once. "It don't do to get too attached to the past," she told me. "Emotion don't hold. Livin' is for now."

She bought me my first pair of jeans. First boots, first fishing pole. She knew the names of stars, where to find the best wild mushrooms, how to make squirrels come up on the porch and take peanuts out of her hand. She made jellies and cobblers from wild huckleberries and kept a chicken coop for fresh eggs. She drove the Alaskan-Canadian Highway all by herself for years, from Oregon to Alaska, to spend time with her son and his family. She was fearless. She was independent, outspoken. She was The Genuine Article. I wanted to be just like her.

When she faced cancer and the removal of one breast, her comment was typical. "Don't have use for it anymore anyway," she said. Then the cancer took one lung. "Guess that's it for my smokes," she teased her doctor. Cataracts finally took both her eyes. Due to all those years of living outdoors and not wearing sunglasses, the doctors said. Even a succession of surgeries couldn't hold off the inevitable. Aunt Maybelle was blind. "I still got pictures in my mind," she told me. Yet there was a hole in her spirit. We both knew it but never spoke of it. "Emotion don't hold," you know.

The last tape-recorded book she heard before going into the hospital was a book I wrote. She had a neighbor dial me up on the telephone so she could tell me. "I think I'll keep this one awhile overdue," she said and laughed. "I want to get it fixed in my mind before my hearing goes, too!" The next day she fell and broke her pelvis. Infection set in, then pneumonia in her one good lung.

The respirator had to do her breathing for her. The wispy hair that had known so many flamboyant colors throughout her life was now as white as her hospital sheets. The wiry body that had taken her faithfully over mountains, into mines, across prairies, through forests, and down raging rivers was finally giving out. I couldn't imagine my life without her. I wondered how I'd ever say good-bye.

She jerked. Her brown fingers clutched the bed rail like claws. Her years of living in the open had tanned her already-dark skin to the color of tree roots. She always had that organic feel about her, that she was something of the earth, not just on it like the rest of us. Horses understood that. And deer and elk, trees and rocks.

The respirator made a wheezing sound, then a gurgle. Aunt Maybelle reached up with one hand. I caught it and held it to my cheek.

"It's me," I told her, and she nodded. "Do you need anything?" No. "Shall I just stay here?" Yes.

I pushed back her hair from her forehead and ran my fingers over the deep wrinkles of her face. I had to tell her now how much she meant to me, I decided, whether she wanted to hear it or not.

"Aunt Maybelle, do you remember years ago when we were at a Grange reunion with Dan and Blanche, remember?" A groggy nod. "I was a little girl. I had been being naughty or getting into some kind of trouble, and you had steamed over to reprimand me." Another nod. "That's when someone else came up to us and said, 'Maybelle, if you don't do something about that child, she's going to grow up to be just like you!'"

It was hard to tell if the change in her face was a smile of recognition or not, but I took it for one. "Well, I just wanted to tell you, at that moment I felt like I had been given the highest compliment anyone could ever give me." I squeezed her hand. "I still feel that way."

She squeezed my hand back. Then she fell asleep. Two days later, she died.

We scattered her ashes across the West she loved, the West she helped create, the West she ultimately became. A raven watched us silently until the ashes were gone. Then it took to the air, squawking. With teary eyes and choked voices, we sang "Tumbling Tumbleweeds" into the wind, then drove home to finish the chores.

Aunt Maybelle would have wanted it that way. The earth accepted her in a way I envied. She didn't always get along with people, but the rest of creation recognized and embraced her.

STEPHANIE PERSHING BUEHLER ❧ Sisters

My sister flies in from the city
like some exotic bird,
red coat, shimmery blue pants.
At home now,
perched on my old kitchen table,
we peck reminiscently.
I sit, stirring instant coffee
into my favorite chipped pig mug.

While I am off at work,
she cleans my refrigerator
and preens over nine jam jars,
hidden in the dark, sugar-crusted.
I re-counted after she left;
there were only eight,
plus one jar of apple butter.

DEB CARPENTER ❧ Love and Light

I toddled down the hallway to my bedroom for a nap.

"I love you, Debbie."

The hall was dark, and as I turned to face the voice, my little eyes blinked to adjust to the well-lit dining room. My mother sat at the end of the tunnel-like hallway, surrounded by daylight.

I was three or four at the time and don't remember my answer, or even if I responded. But I do remember my awe and newfound awareness. My mother loved me! I'm sure that wasn't the first time she had said it, but it was the first time I was fully aware of her message. It startled me with its impact, but as I grew older, that message was the one source of light I knew would never dim, flicker, set, or be extinguished.

EVA POTTS WELLS BURTON ❧ Without a Doubt

Now that my mother is gone, I finally realize her influence on my life. I probably would never even have thought about it had not my oldest daughter pointed out the influence I have had on *her* life. Recently, she asked, "Were you happy as a girl? Were you happy in raising your family?"

I don't ever remember asking myself, "Am I happy?" I just did what needed to be done, as my mother did before me. I'll never know if my mother was happy. My mother and I never talked about feelings. I received very few hugs or kisses from her. I don't remember that she ever said to me, "I love you." I don't recall ever seeing my mother cry. I always called her "Mother."

Did she love me? Absolutely. Did she influence my life more than anyone else in my seventy-plus years? Without a doubt.

PEGGY SANDERS ❧ If . . .

She killed herself.

May 26, 1962, the day after being diagnosed with lupus erythematosus, she took a .410 shotgun and shot herself to death. This followed two years of severe drought on the irrigation project where she lived, where the Angostura Dam was, that May, too low for farmers to get any water for their crops. The "experts" even went so far as to say the dam would never again be full. Most people called her Oleta; I called her Mom. I was ten years old.

If, if, if only she hadn't died, she would have seen the rain that started to fall two days after her death, and it rained and rained and rained. It more than filled Angostura Dam by the end of June.

If, if, if she had held on, the lives of my brother, my dad, and I would have been much different.

If, if, if she were alive, we would do the mother-daughter activities that I see my aunt and cousin do, my neighbor and her daughter do. I will forevermore be lonely for her.

SHEILA VOSEN-SHORTEN ➳ *Pearls from the Milk*

The Milk had always been a river to run to. Growing up as the eldest of eight children in an alcoholic home, I tried to create order. Today I skipped school to find in nature and Irene the rhyme and reason I needed in my own life.

I'd lived on the edge of Glasgow, Montana, of school, and of my peers for ten years. The river and Irene centered me. On hot days, the river's brown water, crowned by tiers of tangled willow and tall cottonwood trees, enticed me to plunge right in. I felt included in the simple lives of whitetail does as I watched them lead their fawns through evening's shadows and down the river's banks to drink. I wrapped myself in the tall grasses protecting me from the sting of mosquitoes singing in my ears. And there was the constant surround of cooing mourning doves.

Spending time on the river with Irene, who lived in an old homestead shack just one hundred yards from its banks, never left me feeling peripheral. My time with Irene left a mark on me, just as swimming daily in the Milk River stained dark brown bands across the grain of my toenails over the course of a summer.

This morning Irene stood on the muddy banks of the Milk River ankle deep in clamshells. I watched her rake in yet another clam. Looking down at my own bare feet, I remarked to her that my toenails were beginning to look like clamshells. She laughed in her high piercing cackle, knelt to pick out a clam that was still spitting water near my foot, pressed her knife blade between its tightened lips, and shoved downward until the shell lay open.

I felt sad for the brown-striped clam dying in halves under May's hot sun. Irene severed the pinkish muscle attached to the inside of the shell, stripped away the meat with her knife tip, and revealed the smooth white mother-of-pearl coating that was home to this clam. It didn't even bleed. She studied the cool hard inner surface and then, leaving it hinged, dropped the shell into the weeds.

Reaching up, Irene unclasped a chain from around her neck and held out a black cross. With great reverence, she touched each of the small irregular pearls set into wood. "Fifteen," she counted.

Irene lived alone. Every day after the spring floods had subsided and the warmth of the sun had shrunk the churning brown water back into its muddy, cottonwood-lined channel, she carried a long rake down the steep riverbank. She had fashioned the rake out of two six-foot pieces of bamboo and could reach nearly halfway across the receding river by the summer's end. In the shallows, where carp feed at the water's edge, Irene would set about gathering clams.

She pulled in a dozen or so using the rake and then waded into the coffee-colored water, stirring up fine silt with her bare feet as though she'd just added cream. Irene prodded with her toes, feeling for the rough edges of oval clamshells. Shedding my own shoes, I carefully waded in. The squishing mud slipped like wet ribbons between my toes. I felt grounded in such cool soothing contact.

While I was seeing with my feet, my eyes were free to observe my sixty-five-year-old friend bending over from her waist as she plunged her arms into the warm Milk and pulled her hands back out, clutching two large clams. Within minutes the side of my own foot chafed against an irregular edge, and holding my breath I gently flexed my ankle and traced the shape of a clam with my toes. Excitedly, I too plunged in up to my armpits, but the clam escaped my groping fingers, burrowing into the mud and out of reach. Irene's laughter proclaimed her "Queen of the Clams" and me her muddy subject.

Not all the clams grew pearls. In some, grainy irritations entered their inner domain as they fed off the bottom of the Milk River, and over time the grains became enveloped in real mother-of-pearl. This muddy river is far from being an ocean, nor is its silt made of the kind of sand that glossy pages in nature books describe as the beginning of beautiful cultured pearls later strung into necklaces for women who have never even considered digging for clams with their toes. Although the pearls that Irene found weren't perfect, the town jeweler took the time to set them nicely into a cross for this persistent woman, who had great patience with me.

The people in Glasgow called her the Cat Lady. She lived with six or seven cats in a three-room house belonging to a rancher on the edge of town. She paid no rent and fed her cats with her Social Security check. Irene believed that cats were reincarnated souls, and she took in all that she found on her porch stoop. One favorite cat that she'd buried near the tree shading the pile of clamshells later appeared to her as a ghost. She still placed flowers on his grave and talked to him when she felt lonely.

Myriad Manx, tiger-striped, and longhair tabbies rubbed against her legs, purring, as she dug for hidden treasure among the clams. Her cats didn't mind the rotting meat and mewed incessantly until she flung scraps of clam from the tip of her knife. I wondered whether I had ever been one of her cats.

Being with Irene made me think about things like life and death. I'd been thinking a lot about what was important to me. I was exhausted from trying to cook, clean, sew, counsel, and pray my brothers and sisters, my mother, and myself into the perfect family so that my father would not drink. The river's solitude and Irene's certain and simple life helped me sort things out.

At age sixteen, I continually sought ways to add deeper layers of beauty to the striated scars that had gathered in each of us over years of Dad's drinking. Our individual lives had become compressed into an enmeshed morass, and quite like the river clams, we lived on a bottom that had no boundaries. We fed off the dregs of self-consciousness and shame. Somewhere within our souls, there had to be a cool white iridescence that could envelop the pain and transform its ugliness. Surely, from all of the cutting, wearing, self-deprecating images we had taken into ourselves, there must be some pearls taking form.

I soaked in the quiet of the river and Irene's support. Mourning doves cooed, absolving me from my failure to make everyone in my family feel loved. My worries began to drop to the ground, and my pile of clams grew.

ANNE SLADE 🦌 Tea with Daphne

She is sleeping, propped up in bed,
the checkered afghan draped
around her thin shoulders.
She stirs, and momentarily her blue eyes focus on mine.
There is no recognition.

I show her the crocuses, tell her I picked them
in her pasture.
She turns toward the window,
watches the spray of sprinklers on manicured lawns,
the trucks passing on the road outside the hospital.

Someone is driving down the road.
You'd better put the kettle on for tea.
I walk down the hall to the nurses' station,
make the tea, and carry a tray back to her room.
You only brought two cups, that won't be enough,
and where are the cookies?

I pour, set her cup on the bedside table,
and tell her how I wish we had her oatmeal-date cookies.
No one makes cookies like hers.

A shy smile pulls at the corners of her mouth.
You rascal, you really think mine are the best?
I nod as she turns back to the window.
Leave the dishes in the sink, I'll do them later.
I take the tray back, then return to her room.

Where were you? Did you wash those dishes?
You don't know where they belong.
It'll take me half the day to sort them out.
I hold her hand. Her eyelids flutter.
I reach for my purse, lean over the rail
to kiss her velvet cheek.
Do come again.
Maybe we'll have those oatmeal cookies
next time you come for tea.

I drive back to the ranch, find her recipe,
and disregard every dire warning I've ever heard
about cholesterol.
I mix sour cream and butter with the oatmeal
as the dates simmer on the stove.
I can hear her voice.
Be sure to stir the dates, they burn real easy.
Keep stirring until they're thick.

CAROLINE PATTERSON 🐾 Preserving

Harvest time begins with a phone call. It is my mother. "Help!" she says. "I'm drowning in raspberries." Last year it was strawberries. The year before huckleberries, picked at the family cabin. "I'll be there tonight," I answer, and the annual season of making preserves begins.

Each year, in mid-July, my mother and I make jam in my family's home in Missoula, Montana — the house that my great-grandfather built above the Clark Fork River in 1904 when he won a lawsuit against the Great Northern railroad. This is one of our most intimate moments — usually we are shy with each other, and our feelings are more implied than stated — but as we busy ourselves with the berries, our tongues loosen.

I gather things: sugar and pectin from the store, dusty jars from the basement. By that evening, I am in the back yard of my childhood home, plucking hairy raspberries from the canes that sprawl over the fence in a luxurious tangle. My mother is on the other side, her metal bowl nearly filled to the rim. We talk easily as we pick, the conversation filled with current news and dreamy pauses. We nod at the boys tearing down the alley on their bike, roll our eyes at the neighborhood dogs who come by for a friendly pee. We pick until the sun burns red and the air cools and the bowls are full and we're ready to ignore any berries remaining on the canes.

The kitchen is bright, the counter filled with measuring cups and big canisters of sugar. My mother washes the berries, cleaning out stems and leaves, then mashes them into a pulp. I measure and remeasure the sugar and the berries. This seems to be one of the rituals of our jam making: everything has to be measured at least three times, because, as we talk, we forget the number of cups we have and have to start over again. At this point, our conversation is truncated, focused solely on our tasks. "Eight cups of sugar?" I ask. "No, six cups of *berries*," my mother says. "How many cups of sugar did I say I had?" "I don't remember," she answers, arm deep in raspberry pulp.

As the mothers call their children in and the hiss of tires on the street grows quieter, we grow silent. Measuring and mixing finally require all our concentration. Nothing about this is hard. Making jam is a matter of following a recipe from the pectin box or a card bearing my grandmother's stately script, but timing is everything. If we don't put in precise amounts at precise times, the jam will be too thin, and we'll call it syrup. Too thick, and it will be difficult to spread on cold winter mornings.

Finally, we have mixed the sugar and the berry pulp and the pectin, and they are slowly bubbling in the same kettle that my grandmother used to thicken chokecherry syrup and my great-aunt to make pear compote. My mother unloads jars from the dishwasher and places them, steaming, on the table. I am at the stove, stirring down the thick bubbles that rise up from the bottom of the kettle. The boiling makes a deep growling sound. My face is moist. My spoon cuts through the red syrup, sending out lazy waves, then the liquid closes over it again.

This is the point where the stories begin. As I skim pink foam from the kettle, my mother tells me about my grandmother, who baked tiny versions of the famous cakes she called "try cakes." About how my great-aunt, who picked pears each summer, canned them in a syrupy compote, and then, in July, wrapped the jars in tissue paper for Christmas. About how each month my great-grandfather gave my great-grandmother a day to do anything she wanted, which she called "going to California."

My mother tells me how my great-grandmother stood at the back window of this same kitchen and rolled out her pies on a marble-topped cutting board in her pantry. As I stir, I wonder what she thought about as the dough grew thinner and thinner. Did she wish she were back in Chicago? Did she wonder whether coming West had been a mistake? Or was she just happy for the blanket of sunshine reddening the tomatoes in the garden?

The stories continue as I ladle the thickening syrup into jars at the table. As I fill a jar, my mother dips tongs into a pan of boiling water and pulls out a lid and a ring. She caps the jar, screws down the ring, her hand gingerly touching the hot tin.

As we fill jar after jar, I feel a communion not only with my mother, but with all of the women who have stood in this same kitchen, their brows prickled with sweat, putting away food for winter: my grandmother with her grape jelly, my great-grandmother with her hulking crocks of sauerkraut. It is as if, by filling the same thick-pleated Mason jars, by walking the same floors, by using the same dented funnel that their jellies flowed through, I have called them up. It is as if, by repeating their movements, I have brought them alive and made them flow through me.

This is one of the rare moments where my life most resembles that of my female forebears. I have spent much of my life as my male forebears did: adventuring, developing my intellect, and pursuing my vocation. I have spent much of my life distancing myself from everything the women in my family seemed to represent: confinement in the home, unceasing nurturing, self-sacrifice. But tonight, as I fill one jar after another with jam, our lives are the same. I feel the same pleasure of harvest at the sight of the jars filled with our pickings; the same pleasure of knowing that, in some small way, I am prepared for the winter ahead. Somehow, by repeating their gestures, I slip underneath their skins and experience the world as they did: the small satisfactions of the well-baked pie, the sleeping child, the perfect needlepoint rose.

At last, all the jars are filled, and we are sitting at the table staring at our handiwork: twelve jars of raspberry jam. The gold lids gleam, the scarlet contents are speckled with seeds. My father and my husband wander in, sniff the sugared air, taste fingerfuls of jam, and wander out again. The stories have stopped now. Instead, we sip our tea or eat a cookie and listen to the chorus of pops or tinny rings that the lids make as they seal onto the jars. We stretch our legs. "Ready?" my mother says finally. Then we get up and do it again.

STEPHANIE PAINTER 🦎 Trinity

I

She drove on an asphalt cut through
prairie grass, the highway home
or a shortcut. I cringed as she took her hands
from the wheel, lifted her

camera, and shot clouds out of the sky.
The stop came so sudden, I fell

forward into the arms of the seat belt. She aimed
her camera lens toward the markers of a long-dead bull.

Then I saw: bones
against the fence. Vertebrae aged in the grass
and thistle: fleshless white sculptures waiting
for bone seekers. From the marrow

hollow I learned the shape of the bull
who lent the bones we stole
simply focusing through the bone tunnel.
Some fit nicely beneath the seat.

We could not take them all. A part of the bull
stayed behind, like words that we don't want to hear —
Good-bye. You were wrong. Your mother
is dead — ghost bushes visible at the fringe of mist.

Hard edges of this road float just
beyond reach like a woman with a secret, a woman
driving through a camera lens or
a woman riding with bones.

II
Not the evergreen dreams of lodgepole
or ponderosa pine — more the lacy and ethereal
fantasies of white-barked aspen or cinnamon-
whipped willows. A forest of deciduous

dreams that fades away like seasons then flowers
again. My mother walks into my studio empty-
handed. She stops several feet away, holds a hairbrush — old and blue — toward me. "Comb your hair," she says,

then dematerializes molecule by atom, the brush hanging
there like a Cheshire cat smile. Months later
she appears to hand me my diary. "Write
this down," she demands. And the day she hands me

the pantyhose she says, "Stephanie, for heaven's
sake, wash these." Often the advice seems sound
and answers a question I should have asked. But sometimes, the bowl of chili vaporizes before she says, "Eat,

eat, before it gets cold." Symbols scrape
the bark of my dreams — a blue hairbrush, my lost
diary, tepid food and dirty laundry.

III
You hear them again. Those words
that you don't want to hear — *Your mother is dead* —
ghosts visible at the fringe of mist.

Hard edges of this road float just beyond reach
like a woman whose tears
lubricate her lust.

When only a mother would
listen, you talk to the wall. There is no
mother, but there is always a wall.

Love might last forever, but
by then it has been salted with the bones of sad
and angry spites —

a separate passion for secret
places where you could find
an opening.

Then the soft pats centered
on the back — mother touch.

And then again, the wall.

MAY H. BAUGHMAN ᪥ Stella He

I attended school during the early 1930s in a little one-room country schoolhouse in the northeast corner of Colorado. There were approximately eight
students from the first through the eighth grades. I was in the second grade.

On the first day of school, we arrived to find a new teacher, dressed in
bib overalls, blue shirt, work shoes, and no socks, with funny-cut hair and
the strange name of Stella. She was probably about eighteen years old or so.
Since we children were all country kids, we were quick to size up someone
of the same background. This meant dirt-poor, without a lot of education,
but there to do the job.

But was it a man or a woman? It looked like a man, sounded like a man,
but had a woman's name. So naturally, from the first day of school, we

called it "Stella He." No amount of correction by our parents, that Stella was a woman, changed our name for it.

Stella He brought a bar of homemade soap to school and made certain we washed our hands before eating or whenever Stella He felt someone's hands were dirty.

Stella He taught us how to run sand through a window screen and get different grades of sand. Stella He taught us how to identify the different weeds. Stella He played ball with us, and he was good. He helped us collect different kinds of grasshoppers. He found things to do in that barren little yard.

When Stella He was talking to you and wanted to make sure he had your full attention, he faced you with his hands on your shoulders and a firm grip that certainly got your attention. But the punishment that had the big boys shedding tears was when you did something naughty and he told you that you had been caught but you denied it. He would say, "Do you think I'm blind?" Then you were taken to the front of the room and forced into his chair and told, "Now sit there and see what I see." Somehow that was so humiliating to sit there for an hour.

Stella He would tell each of us to bring a vegetable to school; he would bring a piece of meat. This was all put into a pot on the potbelly stove in our room. At noon we had a bowl of hot soup. The smell of his brew cooking was very comforting in a chilly room with the wind blowing or the snow falling. We had soup from the first cold day in the fall until the first warm day in the spring.

One beautiful spring day, Stella He drove horses and a wagon to school rather than riding a horse as usual. He took roll call, then said we were going for a surprise ride. We climbed in the wagon and drove off through the cow pasture to the house where he lived. Stella He had us each wash our hands at the pump in the yard. We followed him into the house, where his mother was making doughnuts.

We sat around the oilcloth-covered kitchen table with a big glass of milk, eating as many doughnuts as we wanted. His father and mother hugged each of us good-bye as we left to go back to school.

I honestly think I learned the basics of life from Stella He. Play hard, study hard, make do with what you are and what you have, and love is not always mushy.

C. L. PRATER ❧ Aunt Noi

If Aunt Noi knows you enjoy one of her Thai dishes, she will go out of her way to make it for you. After thirty years, she still does not know the English names for some of the ingredients she uses. I ask her the Thai names, which I can't say, and then forget them within the hour. The sauce she makes for jasmine rice is simple: fresh cilantro, onion, garlic, and Good Taste fish sauce, which she has to have someone drive her to the oriental market in Grand Island to get. We high plains relatives haven't yet acquired a taste for the hot peppers she uses, and, after thirty years, we're probably not going to, so she adds them only to her bowl. She has an interesting way of slicing vegetables, holding them scissorslike between her first two fingers and slicing them upward toward her forefinger.

I watched her cook this past Christmas, and we talked in between the chopping, rinsing, and traffic of five women in a steamy kitchen with the little ones running through. She married my uncle thirty-one years ago on Christmas Day in Bangkok. Her English is still hard to understand. At times she comes out loud and clear, blunt and to the point, like her famous, "Why you get so fat?" I asked her what it was like to come to this much colder part of the world so young, not speaking any English. She said, after a pause, with a sort of sad smile, "I cly, cly . . . Gamma say, 'Jim, why she cly?' You famly togeder, I no see my famly."

I remember one of the first Christmases after my uncle was discharged from the service, she shaped and polished all the women's fingernails — her way of making a connection since she couldn't talk to us. I was at that self-conscious-yet-invisible age — too old to be cute, not old enough to sit with the grownups. Good for getting the salt off the stove and keeping my little brother out of trouble.

"You turn, now," she said, motioning to me. I'm sure I probably looked behind me to see whom she was talking to. But she wanted to do my nails. I was amazed, impressed by her acknowledgment. She worked on my scruffy tomboy nails just as carefully as she'd done my grandmother's. In her eyes, I was not a child. It was one of the first experiences that gave me value as a woman.

JO-ANN SWANSON 🦌 The Oddest Daughter

In Memory of Tami, 1958–October 13, 1996

Where the wild
strawberries grew
the grandmothers are
both dead

by the time she was thirty-three
strange men tore soft curves

from old Highway 93
she hated that new flat avenue

when the black cherry bloomed
she came home to heal bruises
from the Oregon biker
who found Jesus
she left her two girls but
what else could she do?

that fall, chokecherries hung by frost
she was lost, at thirty-eight, nobody will
say so in this violet fairy tale
gone wrong, but maybe
she threw off her dancing
shoes, were they red, star-crossed?

threw them like fast horses
headfirst into the strawberry
beds and willows
took the slow road home
barefoot as Cinderella

drunk that night, she ran from
her hit-and-run, hair lit on end
like brambles under huckleberry
moon, stuck on the stark
center line, pleading, guilty, true

on that home stretch to Rollins
she'd done her dancing
at the Spinnaker and not
much music in Lakeside, by the way

by now the big brothers
all come home, brawny strawberry blonds
faces lit by inner sun
earned in thinning bids

the darker black cousins
who tore up Seeley Lake
lean as pickaxes, home

from heroin in Seattle and
pot in Frisco, all the big
boys home from the wars
her heroes now too reformed

she was the younger one
who worshiped the big boys
drew horses with long necks
photos show summers spent
in orchards and gardens
she wore a blue dress
that matched her eyes
dug potatoes that last week
from sandy, crumbling beds
and joked her name was MUD.

"She should've gotten
arrested," her brother
said later. "Instead."

Her red carriage was waiting
groaned warning over the hill
two weeks before delinquent
boys tossed frozen pumpkins
through windshields
she held home ground
begging a ride that carried
her legs two hundred yards
off the path to that
sandy strawberry patch

the cars sliced both
her legs
off at the knees
caved in her head

have you met
my ugliest
daughter, her
winking old father
didn't mean it but
always said.

CHERYL ANDERSON WRIGHT ᶻ⅍ Homemade Noodles

When I was eight years old, my mother became very sick. The doctor said that she must have her gallbladder removed. "How will we manage?" my dad asked.

Mom replied, "We'll have Mom come and stay to keep an eye on things. Cheryl knows how to do the washing and cooking and cleaning. With Mom here in case of trouble, she can manage just fine." So when Grandma came to stay, I became an eight-year-old housekeeper for my dad and three brothers.

The first day, Grandma asked, "What are you making for supper?" just as I had heard her ask Mom many times. I felt very grown-up.

"I'll make chicken and noodles and green beans and rhubarb sauce, if you will tell me how to make noodles," I answered, doubtful now that the time to cook alone had come.

"Well, you go wash up, and I'll tell you how to make noodles. You'll need to get them done this morning so they can dry before supper," Grandma said.

I washed really good with soap and water and returned. "Hold out your hands. Did ya wash good?" Grandma nodded solemnly. "Well, get a bowl and put four big handfuls of flour in it and then come show me."

She sat in the rocker in the sunshine. Her feet, gnarled and twisted from arthritis, were encased in brown cotton hose and corduroy house slippers. Her walker stood near to hand, but she generally preferred to ignore it and hobble from place to place. She wore a lavender print housedress of her own making and a bibbed apron, held to the front of her dress by two safety pins. Her pure white hair was braided, rolled into a bun on top of her head, and held firmly in place by three hairpins. Her black eyes shone with mischief and intelligence.

I took the bowl to her. "Better put in a couple more handfuls and then see what you got. I forgot how small your hands are."

When I returned, she said, "Looks about right. Now get a couple of eggs and put them in there with a sprinkle of salt. Then add two eggshells full of milk and stir it all up good."

"But, Grandma," I said, "how am I going to know how much flour to use when you aren't here to help me?"

She thought for a moment. "Go in on my dresser and get that tablet. Dump the flour out on a cloth and measure it back into the bowl. Then write how much you have. We'll start you a recipe book so you'll know how to cook when you get big. Might as well, beings you'll be doing a lot of cooking the next few weeks."

"Almost two cups, Grandma."

"Well, make it two cups then and write it in your book. Two cups of flour, a sprinkle of salt, two eggs, and two eggshells of milk. Then mix well."

I mixed up the noodles. "Now put some flour on the table and dump your dough out on it and knead it a couple of times, till it all sticks together in a ball," she said. "Then take the rolling pin and roll it out nice and thin."

I began rolling out the noodles, but I had a hard time reaching the table, so I pulled over a chair to stand on. I rolled and I rolled, but no matter how hard I pushed, the dough just seemed to come back to its original shape. Frustrated, I whined, "Grandma, I can't get this stuff to roll!"

Grandma chuckled and hobbled to the table. "Reckon you're still a mite small to get up the pressure you need." She took the pin and in seconds had rolled out a nice thin round. "OK," she said, "now sprinkle some flour on it and roll it up. Then cut it into thin, even strips and spread them out to dry. And when you get the noodles done, you might as well get that chicken on to boil."

When Dad and the boys got home, I had dinner waiting. The boys made fun of my skinny noodles, saying Mom always cut them wider, but Dad said, "Taste just fine to me. Maybe the best noodles I ever had."

Grandma gave the boys a look, and then, smiling, she said, "Tomorrow she plans to bake a pie."

CHARLOTTE M. BABCOCK 🐎 The Path

All the world can see the path worn across the grass that connects Ruth's house and mine — an aging umbilical cord. Ruth doesn't like it now, this matted, threadbare grass track. She fusses about it.

She blames our mailman for this track, the shortcut he uses from her mailbox to mine. She thinks she must point it out to him and ask him to use the roundabout sidewalk.

He's the best mailman we've ever had. I won't have it.

Ruth, how long have we neighbored here? Thirty years, you say? I make it thirty-four and some days. Have we ever used the perfect squared-off walks to share our hearts?

How are we connected, Ruth? I cannot count the trips this path is testament to, but you, memory fading like the twilight, have forgotten.

NORMA NELSON DUPPLER ✤ Secret Sin

Hagar was my grandmother, my godmother, and the weaver of a priceless oral history. She never wrapped anyone else in her tapestry of tales, because I was the only one who had time to listen when she had time to talk.

My close relationship with Grandma was directly related to my distant relationship with Mom, who had tried for six years to have a child before she got me. She wanted children, just not me. Although I was tolerable when small, once I learned to speak, her shame grew with me every year, because I wasn't a small, dark-haired, plastic-brained Barbie. So beginning at age two, I toddled over to visit Grandma. Mom seemed relieved when I left.

Hagar embraced this anti-Barbie barbarian and strapped herself in for the ride. In return I would have done anything for her. I even tried to be perfect for her. At two or three, I sat quietly, covering my ears, huddled beside Grandma, while the first minister I remember screamed at us. When I sat with Mom in church, I squirmed, fidgeted, and wiggled, and was spanked when I got home.

My most egregious sin at Grandma's house occurred when I was six or seven. I was playing with a plastic measuring tape from her sewing basket when I tore it in half. Terrified, I mended it with white adhesive tape. I never told because I was afraid to disappoint her, afraid my sin was unforgivable. After all, Mom couldn't even forgive me for being big for my age.

I kept my secret as I turned into a blond, fleshy Viking teen who did ranch work, worked cattle, and shot guns. I was a straight-A student, an artist. I sang solos or duets with Dad in church. I didn't smoke, drink, do drugs, or run around. Still, Mom wore the face of disapproval around me. In contrast, Grandma was never disappointed in me, so I did chores and drank coffee with her. When we were together, she spun the straw of life into golden stories.

Once, while I was setting her hair, white and thin with age, she said, "I had brain fever when I was a child. I lost all my hair, but most of it grew back." Before antibiotics, Hagar survived spinal meningitis. "I caught smallpox, but since I'd had cowpox, it wasn't a bad case." Grandma was tough. Grandma was a survivor.

Hagar immigrated at fifteen, working first as a house girl for some established Norwegians. "As soon as I got here, I caught typhoid," she said. "I ended up owing my employers my doctor's bills. I didn't know how I'd ever climb out of that pit." Later, she worked for the Nelson brothers. They'd lost their father, first settler in the township, and were orphaned two years later. Older sisters and unenthusiastic guardians raised the younger children. Grandma married Andrew, the youngest, an intellectual, state legislator, writer, and bossy husband. "He would invite the minister and family to dinner, or some of his political buddies, without ever telling me," Grandma said.

"Andrew hosted Barnes County picnics, which meant work for me," she said. He turned the farm work over to his sons as soon as they were able so he could stay in the house or politic. Meanwhile, Hagar chased and milked cows; separated the cream and cleaned the separator; fed cows, pail calves, and chickens; washed and sewed clothes; cleaned, canned, and cooked; and threw bundles for the threshing crews. Grandfather gardened. After he died in 1949, Grandma gardened, too.

Her lips set in a straight line, Grandma told me, "I had men who were interested, but I never wanted to marry again." After surviving a 1905 old-fashioned marriage, why would she want another?

Surviving her pregnancies was a nightmare. She dipped a sugar lump in her coffee and sucked it. "When Alf was born, the doctor had to use forceps to pull him out. Alf was born with a broken jaw and could barely nurse. I had toxemia with all of my pregnancies except your uncle Lynn, and he weighed thirteen pounds," she told me. "The only reason I lived after my seventh pregnancy was because I had a D and C." Even at twelve, I knew that a "D and C" was an abortion. "The doctor did it," she went on, "because of my sixth case of toxemia. My blood pressure was so high I was dying, and then I got blood poisoning from the D and C." She survived that, too, along with a goiter operation, glaucoma, a cataract, and heart problems.

"'No more children,' the doctor said, glaring at Andrew. Grandma looked me in the eye and said, "You know what that meant." She munched on potato chips and ate ice cream, musing, "I went up into the mountains with the cows and milked and made cheese when I was your age." My dad didn't let me milk, but some of my earliest memories are of going with Grandma to chase the cows home. By then, my father and Uncle Lynn did the milking, but Grandma got the cows so it was one less chore for her boys. She had to carry me the last distance, while I held a switch and said, "Shoo! Shoo!" from her arms.

When I was eight or ten, I took over chasing the cows in, because my boy cousins on the farm had failed. So just as Grandma fetched and stalled cows to make the work easier for her sons, I took over to make the job easier for Grandma.

Every night Grandma did fancywork, embroidering towels, pillow-cases, and tablecloths. With fine, soft yarn, she knitted green and yellow baby clothes for pregnant neighbors. I never had the patience for minute projects like that, but I admired her fancywork as much as she admired my drawings and paintings. Mom didn't even tape my paintings to the refrigerator. Grandma framed them.

Every summer I picked chokecherries for Grandma, and she taught me to make chokecherry wine. She trotted it out for company in shot glasses but never drank any herself. She'd drunk it once, she said, and gotten uncontrollable giggles. While we washed the purple from the utensils and our hands, she told how she helped neighbors give birth before doctors came to our area. One time, when she was helping a doctor with a birth, he had to leave for another patient before the woman had passed the afterbirth. "He told me I had to get the afterbirth out of her or she'd die from infection. I had to scrape it out with my fingernails. She never even got sick!"

Our relationship was not without conflict. When my young love was not only blind but also deaf, dumb, and stupid, I told her about a boyfriend. "He's a German. If you marry him, I'll disinherit you," she said.

"Go ahead," I replied. I knew no one was good enough for her children or for me. My boyfriend reminded her of her heartbreak when her daughter married young, but she adored my fiancé after she met him.

One time, when my husband and I visited Grandma, she was searching a drawer for something. "Where is that Ford?" she said.

My husband and I exchanged a look that said, "Oh, no, she's lost it!" I asked, "What do you mean?"

"Oh," she said, "I have a knife I named after President Ford because it's not too sharp but it's kind of nice to have around."

Unlike Ford, she stayed sharp. She worked and sang as she always had until a month before she died at ninety. Even at the end, I couldn't confess my sin to the woman who had shown me what a woman could be. When a stroke killed her two weeks after she was diagnosed with leukemia, I plunged into an abyss of grief, knowing she'd never wrap me in her stories again.

BARBARA M. SMITH 🦌 Ladies Aid

We drove down the lane in that farm car
singing with grasshoppers
to a cool church basement afternoon
the talk and laughter of women
the smell of cooked coffee.

Suddenly she turned into an unfamiliar place on the way,
a weed-grown approach, a narrow two-story farmhouse
unpainted, weathered the color of trout.
Jaw set, she pulled down her girdle,
mounted the steps, and brought forth a woman
in shadows and silence, untying her apron.

Her man came carrying a pitchfork.
"Where the hell you think you're going?"
Grandma stood straight before him.
"I'm taking her with me to the Ladies Aid. Let us by."
I watched from the window.
His wife looked at the dirt,
slight and hesitant in the face of fury.
Grandma held her hand.
But for the workings of insects,
there was silence.

"Bunch of goddamned nonsense," he said,
but he moved out of their way.
We circled the yard, drove on
with a sound like the gathering of bees
in the back seat.

SANDRA GAIL TEICHMANN ✹ Light

One spring in the late fifties, April's parents drove us to Santa Fe in their Hudson. April's father drove slowly so we could see rabbits in the sagebrush, yellow bloom in the cactus, maybe the writhe of a rattlesnake. He kept the windows clean so we could take in the whole of the blue sky arched between the peaked mountains and the flat tops of mesas.

At every historical marker along the highway, we stopped and got out. April's father filled, packed, and lit his pipe, while Claire, April's mother, read the past aloud: Francisco Vásquez de Coronado, Don Juan de Oñate, Don Pedro de Peralta, the great Pueblo Revolt driving the Spanish and their Christianity out of Santa Fe, Don Diego de Vargas, Billy the Kid, Teddy Roosevelt's Rough Riders, and cowboys driving cattle from Texas — Chisholm, Loving, and Goodnight.

In Santa Fe, April and I had a hotel room of our own, and we felt almost grown-up enough to go into the drugstore and buy a pack of cigarettes. Almost grown-up, but still too timid, too young for the cigarettes, we walked around the plaza, into the store, and past the display counter time and time again. Then in our room, we watched the silhouetted movements of couples behind the shaded windows facing ours across the courtyard and smoked cigarettes we stole from April's mother. Claire didn't know we were smoking, because she smelled of her own smoke. She may have missed some of her cigarettes. Even so, she left April and me alone, coming to our room only to suggest we pack our bags an hour before we left. As

I think about it now, she seemed to think we were more grown-up than we did.

Claire. She died last summer. Claire. Light. In that mountain town, she was the only person I knew who traveled to England; played bridge; read James Joyce; traveled to Ireland; was born in Ireland; traveled to Europe, to Hawaii, to Alaska. Claire rode on ocean liners and airplanes and trains, and when she needed money, Claire taught English in high school, substituted for regular teachers. She saved, and then she and April traveled, spent all the money, leaving April's father, Alex, at home, where he was pleased for the time with a young lover.

In a class Claire taught while Alex spent afternoons with this same lover, I learned to write "I should have" rather than "I should of." And I never forgot that.

I was riding on a bus through New Mexico to Mexico when I last thought of Claire. The bus lulled me through the night as it retraced the route we had taken in that Hudson Commodore and brought back this old story, melted time, mixed the days, left no fine lines.

As often as possible, I spent the nights and evenings after school with April. My mother didn't approve, maybe because Claire smoked cigarettes, didn't keep house, and didn't go to church every Sunday.

But I understood life better when I was around Claire, and I was missing her on that bus trip. She was blind before she died the previous summer. At the end, Claire couldn't read the books in her home library; couldn't write letters and journal pages; couldn't play bridge with her friends; couldn't paint the mountains, the rivers, and the skies with blue and green watercolors; couldn't walk through the soft spring air; couldn't see the trees in new leaf. But she did outlive Alex and did ignore the other women. And for me there was a certain grace in this civility. Rather than go to the nursing home, where nurses would have taken care of her, she died.

April's mother wore floral dresses — roses, red roses — dresses like those of the Indian women on the bridge and in Ciudad Juárez. Claire wasn't a beauty. Claire was fat and didn't even have two breasts. Her cotton bodice sagged, showing the scar of a bloody chest cut to the rib bones on one side. But Claire's talk was unlike any I heard anywhere else in that mountain community, in subject and in accent and in tone, a tone of interest in me, interest in herself, too.

But Mother said Claire talked too much. Claire would talk, but she'd also stop. She'd stop, and she'd make me answer questions, answer them specifically and fully, as if she were trying to find out something, know beyond the ordinary what I thought. She wasn't testing me. Claire wanted to know more than what she already knew, know more than the presence or absence of dust on the dishes in her cupboard. She seemed to want to see beyond the perfection of the painted or unpainted walls of her basement, beyond the edged borders of her grass growing into the weeds of the empty lot next door. She needed to know the extremes of temperature, the degrees Fahrenheit of the full sunlight at her kitchen window and the degrees Celsius at the iron settee in the shade. She wanted to know both and all, know beyond the swept or unswept length of her sidewalk curving from the steps of her house to the street, beyond the length of the street's curve to the grocery store at the base of the hill. She acted as though I might know something about what she wanted to know, and she seemed to know that I wanted to talk about places beyond, places distant, abstract, impractical, pure possibility. She acted as though there could be nothing — nothing — of more importance as she listened to me, the steam rising from her cup of tea.

Maybe Claire's kitchen stove wasn't so clean, but she had a pot of tea and a table to talk across, and in her daughter's room grit fell from rocks on the windowsill — not pretty rocks — rocks that only April liked the shape of, the shine of, the weight of. And all that was OK with Claire. A cat came in and out of the house as it pleased, and sometimes I, holding the cat, torn ears and ragged black fur, thought that Claire's house might really be dirty, infected with the cat disease Mother warned about. But I went to Claire's house anyway whenever I could and held the cat to me, to my neck, to my face, my ears, and I drank the hot tea that Claire poured for me.

As much as I cherished Claire, I remember my embarrassment when April and I, sixteen, maybe seventeen, had to put up with our mothers for the day. The four of us had gone to a university town for shopping and walking around the campus where April would study world history when she graduated from high school. At lunch in the cafeteria that day, I was conscious of Claire, her accent, how she asked questions of everyone.

"Is the food always so bad here?"

"In what subject is your major study here?"

"Where do your parents live?"

Claire's voice was loud and odd as it came full from the depths of the lopsided bodice of her printed dress to echo the questions in the white-tiled cafeteria of higher learning. She spoke louder until everyone stopped to watch and listen. And maybe it wasn't Claire who embarrassed me so much as the small-mindedness and timidity of my own mother as she held herself demurely and falsely behind Claire's vital presence.

Whatever it was, April and I escaped from our mothers to the ladies' room. We examined ourselves in the mirror. I, taller than April, worried about my too-large nose, wished it were shorter, turned up like April's. I worried that I was tall, too tall. I worried that I was skinny, flat-chested. And worst of all I worried that my elbows were bony and stuck out from my sides. My feet were too big, and I was ugly, outright ugly, I thought. And my hair, my hair never was right, what with Father telling me to keep it and my fingernails cut short, and Mother giving me a home permanent every three months. But most of all I worried I would be a copy of the meanness of my mother.

April didn't like herself much either. Red hair — no one had red hair — and worst of all the freckles. If she didn't use tanning cream to make herself evenly dark, she used lemon juice to fade the dark spots to a creamy white.

I was furious with Claire and my mother that day in that university cafeteria, not for the questions and the brogue, but that they had spoiled any chance that April and I might have been mistaken for students; might have been, if not beautiful, maybe intellectual. Claire had asked too many questions, made the four of us seem to know nothing — two mothers from some cow town and two daughters not nearly old enough to read Ginsberg or Plath. Yet I knew that Claire believed in my dreams, believed in all that my own mother tried to deny.

What mattered was what Claire wanted to know, what she thought and talked about. In Claire's presence or at home with Mother, I didn't know or care why I always wanted to be at Claire's house for supper, for breakfast, for all night, for my life. I only knew I had to be there.

ECHO ROY ❧ Prairie Ocean

She taught me more than how to read, write, and do arithmetic. Nina Mae Evans shared with me the pleasures of reading a good poem, sipping a cup of freshly brewed, sweetened hot tea, and soaking my feet in a horse trough on a hot spring day.

My first impression of Mrs. Evans was that she must be really old. To a six-year-old, pure white hair, a wrinkly smile, and a pair of round bifocals meant old. As my first-grade teacher and first experience away from my parents, Mrs. Evans didn't waste any time changing that initial impression.

Based in a one-room schoolhouse that sat in the middle of one of our pastures, Mrs. Evans taught me and a sixth-grade neighbor boy, George. The school had been placed halfway between our two sets of ranch buildings for convenience. Her living quarters were an even smaller one-room building we called the teacherage. I learned later in life that Mrs. Evans was sixty-seven when she accepted the position at Bates Creek School. She had tried to retire but was called back to duty when the district was unable to locate a teacher who wanted to live sixty-five miles from town and five miles from the closest neighbor, without electricity, indoor plumbing, or a car.

During my attempt to become a teacher, I've reflected back, remembering and realizing in the process exactly what a significant influence Mrs. Evans had on me. For instance, she had me memorizing and reciting poetry in the first grade. At age eight, I recited Rudyard Kipling's poem "If" in our 4-H talent show and won overall champion. I carry that poem with me to this day and have come to know that her introducing me to poetry probably served as the impetus that carried me into a writing and speaking career.

I remember getting to spend a night or two with Mrs. Evans when the weather wouldn't permit Dad to pick me up after school. I loved those evenings. We'd sit together by a potbelly stove, where she would read to me and I would read to her by the light of a kerosene lamp. We sipped sweet hot tea, and I remember her telling me she didn't mind getting old, but she hoped she would die before she got too old to make her own cup of tea.

It seemed Mrs. Evans always displayed a happy attitude, and for someone so old, she sure could run fast from base to base in three-man baseball. She was strong enough to push George and me on the merry-go-round and yet light enough to ride the teeter-totter with me. She took us on nature walks and told us about other parts of our country and other lands. One day we found a sandy bog hole near the windmill. We three lay down on the warm May ground and closed our eyes. We pretended we were on a beach and the miles of prairie were our ocean. We wiggled our toes in the sand and then soaked our feet in the horse trough. When Mom asked what we had done that day, I'm sure she was a bit confused when I said we'd gone to the Pacific Ocean and walked barefoot on the beach.

KATHRYN E. KELLEY 🦌 *That's What Neighbors Do*

Mom yawned over her breakfast coffee. "Tired, Mom?" I asked.

"Mmmm — a little. I was up most of the night," she replied.

"I didn't hear you. Why were you up?"

She named a neighbor lady. "She had a miscarriage last night, and her husband asked me to help her."

My young mind wasn't familiar with this problem, but I wasn't afraid to ask questions. Every country kid was familiar with animal reproduction, but human reproduction didn't get a lot of discussion.

"What did you do to help her?" I wanted to know.

"Mostly I kept her company. It didn't take long for the baby to come. When she had rested a bit, I washed her and made a clean bed for her. Then I heated some soup to strengthen her." In my mind, I pictured the drafty farmhouse bedroom, an old iron bed on worn linoleum, and kerosene lamplight. The soup would have been heated on a wood-burning cook stove like ours. She probably used cobs to make quicker heat for the late-night soup.

"Then what?" I persisted.

"Eat your oatmeal." Mom was still on duty. "Then we wrapped the baby for burial."

I pushed oatmeal around the bowl. I'd never thought about what happened to human babies that didn't live. Barnyard information didn't apply here.

"Where did you bury it?"

"Him. It was a boy. We buried him in the grove near the others. This was not her first miscarriage."

This was serious stuff. In the dark of night, while I slept securely in my bed, grownups were giving birth and burying the dead. No hospital. No doctor. No priest. They were too far away. Grownups helping with sadly difficult matters and going about routine business the next morning.

"Mom, why did he ask you to help?"

"Because that's what neighbors do," was her calm reply.

MARY PEACE FINLEY 🦌 Rosario

She leads me down the dirt street, then onto a trail that winds through banana trees and past small plots of beans and corn. She is thin — too thin. Some of her teeth are missing, but her eyes are lively and her smile warm.

We're going to thresh the dry red beans that have grown in her small garden.

Rosario's house is a tiny adobe structure with a tin roof and dirt yard. A crumbling outbuilding — a bodega — stands empty. It has no door. *"Me robaron todo el maiz,"* Rosario tells me. "They stole all my corn. All I have left is inside the house, and they'll have to kill me to get it." She means it. Her children peek from the door. Their noses are running, stomachs abnormally distended — not the chubby roundness of baby fat, but the mark of malnourishment. "The neighbor's pigs rooted out most of my bean crop. This is all I have left."

Tied bundles of dried bean plants hang over the ineffective barbed wire fence. Rosario spreads a piece of canvas on the dirt and hands me a stick. We thresh out no more than twenty-five pounds of beans. For a family with a disabled father, five children, and a mother who eats only beans, rice, and corn, these beans will not last long.

The oldest girl, Judi, glances at me and slowly smiles. She looks about six, but she is ten. Judi takes care of the house, her father, the other children, and the cooking while Rosario sews in the women's cooperative.

The threshing is finished in less than half an hour. We finger the discarded plants, retrieving a few overlooked beans. Rosario thanks me and pats my arms.

Later, I roll my skirt and blouse, half-slip, some hair ribbons and ponytail fasteners, three small teddy bears and two toy airplanes, rubber bands, pencils, and safety pins into a tight package. I wrap them in a leaf from an old calendar. I hope it won't be conspicuous. I hope she won't be insulted. I see her on the street, slip her the package, and she kisses my cheek.

The next day, Rosario finds me. This time she is the one who reaches out with a package — a weather-whitened plastic bag of dried red beans, the most precious gift I have ever received.

GINNY JACK PALUMBO 🐎 Elvira

"Elvira! Elvira!" The words rocked the pickup, matching the beat of the slapping windshield wipers. My friend and I laughed at the silly song lyrics.

Brakes squeaked. "You're famous, Elvira!" I said. Our old Chevy plowed into the bare yard of the Indian colony.

"Don't think so, Little Buddy. Damn mud!"

Elvira climbed down from the pickup. She tramped through the damn mud on short legs to her small house tucked quietly at the hem of Winnemucca. A tall dark boy waved from the shadows.

Every rough mile back to the home ranch I fought mud, reminding me of the spring day I'd met Little Buddy. That was Elvira's name for me, but I argued she was my Little Buddy.

"You're shorter than me, Elvira. You're Little Buddy."

"But I'm bigger around!" Elvira always won. "I'm one damn fat squaw!" She'd laugh, patting her plump tummy and speaking in chopped, rhythmic syllables typical of Paiute Indians from northern Nevada.

My boys attended a rural school near a Paiute Indian reservation. Elvira said she wouldn't live there. "Too much drinkin' on that damn res. Toby's related to a lot a them black devils," she said, laughing. "He's safer in town."

So Elvira and her son, Toby, lived next door to her ancient parents in Winnemucca. She hoped and prayed to wipe out, before it was spun, a web that ensnared too many young Native Americans.

Many years before, our husbands had ridden together on the buckaroo crew of a large ranch. Her old man was an aging white guy: short, square, smiling. My old man was tall and skinny, lean and mean. Their boy, Toby, played cowboys and Indians with our three blond sons. The men drank Jim Beam, sat in torn kitchen chairs reliving rides on rank horses, and boasted how they'd "die with their boots on." Months passed before Elvira trusted me enough to allow me, a damn whitie, into her fascinating "Injin" world.

We often walked the brittle brown hills of northern Nevada, where I'd trailed after my capricious cowboy. Elvira won me to her native soil by telling tribal tales. I can't forget Elvira's ground squirrel stew or berry gravy made from buckberries and wild elderberries, which grew on the banks of the Humboldt River and a dozen spilling tributaries.

We picked berries together one fall. We spread old blankets under the twisted bushes and slapped the branches with sticks, then sat and picked the litter from the fruit. Tossed out, too, were daily challenges: cowboys, kids, calves in the garden, gambling, the deadly witches' brew of alcohol and man.

"I hope Toby don't get in that damn drinkin' habit," Elvira said. To this day, I remember her dusky skin uncreased by the ever-ready grin.

Back at the small trailer furnished by the ranch, we boiled the tart berries, stirred in flour to make a gravy. Elvira then dropped blobs of the sweet mess onto wax paper to dry in the sun. The boys told their dads we made mud pies all day. They laughed.

Elvira's coal black eyes smoldered. "It'll taste damn good come winter."

Elvira and her old man quit that winter and moved to work on another ranch in a neighboring county. Spring came. We moved on.

Eventually, Elvira quit her old man, too. I struggled to keep in touch, but we moved again and again. Many dark days I missed Elvira's patient "Things'll be OK, Little Buddy."

Our kids saw Toby at school football games. His dad died of a heart attack during branding, died with his boots on. The four boys grew up, but Toby grew huge.

We finally returned to Winnemucca to visit. Sullen and silent, Toby towered over his mother. Elvira laughed, called him "Little Buddy," smiled the same smile under her black cap of short curls.

Three years later, I heard Elvira's name again. We had moved from Nevada to Idaho, but a friend called me long distance. "Elvira's dead! Toby shot her!"

Toby, drunk, high, or both, had demanded Elvira's "Indian money," the government check. She refused. Toby shot her with his hunting rifle. Indian Police found him watching TV, drunk, three days later — his mother dead in the next room. As I drove the long road to her funeral, the radio blared, "Elvira! Elvira!" Raindrops drummed on the roof of our old pickup, the windshield wipers slapping in time.

LINDA M. HASSELSTROM
❧ Six Artists at a Country Retreat

Five of us have just discovered
apple juice stains our fingers black.
No, I don't know why.
The air is spiced with laughter
thick as apple butter.

This morning the poet
noticed the tree in the yard
drooping with fruit.
The photographer pulled
herself aloft
to stand at the tree's heart,
shook branches while the weaver
danced below, catching apples.
Together they foraged through the grass
gathering the hems of their skirts
to carry the harvest inside.
The poet washed jars
the painter found hidden
in the pantry, behind pots and pans
in the dark hole under the stairs.

Now apple pulp
sizzles on the stove,
sticks our shoes to the floor.
Rude noises rise from the boiling pot.
Sucking a blistered thumb,
the photographer pokes twigs
among the coals in the old wood stove.
The poet tries to recall her grandmother's recipe.
Gesturing with a wooden spoon,
she's shocked by a memory so clear
the old lady seems to stand
behind her at the range.
If she could see us now, she'd say,
"My stars! It don't take six women
to stir one pot of apple butter!
You go pick more apples.
You three cut them up —
you — dump those apples
in a sink full of water.
The leaves and ants will float.
Keep scooping them off
while you cut out the cores.
Someone find more jars."

The novelist ransacked every drawer
but found no lids.
The weaver shows us

how her granny made do
without lids, covering jam with wax
when times were hard.
In a reverent circle,
we watch a viscous yellow flow,
the way she tips each jar
to coat the edges.
The scent of honey tells me
it's not paraffin but beeswax —
ten times the cost.
The painter who supplied it
shrugs — she found no other wax,
believes this morning's worth the price.
The sculptor, fingers clean of clay for once,
molds caps of tinfoil
to thwart the pantry mice.

The poet pours hot jam on a white plate
while someone butters toast.
Around the big oak table,
we spread preserves thick
and talk with our mouths full.
Licking our fingers, we tell each other
stories of our grandmothers' love,
how they hoped to live to see our babies.
Not one of us admitted
to our grandmothers why
we never would have children.

The other five have learned to hide
their love of women from the world,
disguise their passions,
refusing the rash company of men.
Radiation made my husband sterile,
but I am widowed now, finding ease
within this gathering of women.
The painter recalls how
her grandmother guessed she hated lox,
each year served a smaller morsel.
Now she recites a prayer for Passover.
The weaver tells us how
her granny shook her head
when she married a white man.

It didn't last. After that,
she followed the old lady's advice,
cast her eyes down around our kind.

Finished with our tea and toast,
we wash our cups, scrub the heavy pans,
wipe the jars clean, and set them neatly
on the worn white cloth.
Then we mount the stairs to work
that tells us who we are,
who we will never be.

I lift a stove lid to stare
into the dimming coals,
knowing my grandmother's name
is now as empty as her home.
Upstairs, by candlelight,
I plait words together,
creating poems I hope
will hold their shapes,
solid as the braid
she wore like a crown.

During the night, one of us
tiptoes down the steps,
stands in the warm kitchen
where the stove cools,
creaking like an old lady
tightening her black shawl
against the chilling dark.
She admires the jars
packed dark with harvest,
sweet with legacy.
Coals flare and settle
like dreams of distant
granddaughters.

LORRIE MYDLAND ⭐ Beverly

When you marry, you expect to acquire new relatives, and I acquired an unusual number when I married Gordon. But I hadn't expected to acquire
Beverly, about twenty-six years old and retarded. Mother Mydland had be-

friended her for years, and she helped with housework if the mood came upon her. Beverly first arrived at our home when I was gone. She washed my cashmere sweaters in hot water.

She sometimes could really help me with housework if I needed her. She loved to rearrange the furniture. When we were gone, we'd come back to find everything changed. All I would have to say to get her to put things back was, "Gordon doesn't like it this way."

She adopted me. She liked my clothes; she liked all my things. When she arrived, she'd go through my closets and say, "This is beautiful — when did you get it? Where did you wear it?"

She would look through my catalogs and magazines, read the prices, and say, "Would you pay thirty-five dollars for this blouse?" We'd discuss the material and its washability and come to some decision. We always had lots to talk about.

Beverly was always happy. She'd come in the door with a big smile. For Christmas she always managed to find the one gift that our son, Gabe, enjoyed the most. She gave me something fluffy and frilly, like baby doll pajamas, spending more than she could afford on all of us, and she was pleased to do it.

She was one great big happy girl. I seldom heard her complain, although she had much to complain about. Her father was old, cross, and mean-spirited. Her mother was blind and deaf.

She had started school, but the school sent her home. She seemed always to have a cold and needed to blow her nose even when she was grown.

Gordon's mother had taught her to identify and count money. I tried to teach her to read, but she was too old to be interested in children's stories. So I managed only to teach her to sound out words. I was always concerned she'd drink mouthwash thinking it was something else — or maybe not know what was under the sink.

When Gabe learned to read, he'd read to her. I would hear him say, "What is h-o-u-s-e?" She'd say, "You should ask your mother." He never knew she couldn't read.

When we were gone, she would come to our house, about two and a half miles from her home. Once she unlocked a window in a porch to get in. She made a chocolate sundae, leaving spots on the table, took a nap on our bed, and then went back to town. She was a great way to get rid of old Christmas cookies.

She often put things away so that I couldn't find them. When I said, "Where are Gabe's boots and warm clothes?" she beamed and rushed to get them. She knew how to keep me needing her.

One day after her father died, she said her mother wanted to go to the cemetery to see her husband's gravestone. On the day I took them and Gabe, the heat was terrible and the wind very strong. When we got to the cemetery, all Beverly knew was that her father was buried near a tree. Brookings Cemetery is full of trees. I probably was the only one of the four of us who could read. We walked and walked. When we finally found it, Beverly's mother got down on her hands and knees and placed her fingers on the letters of the headstone.

Gordon called Beverly "Your Little Flower." She was, he said, "a blooming idiot."

When I told Beverly we were moving to Pierre, she began to take things from the house, such as pictures I treasured — getting even with me for leaving. Our fourteen years together were over.

Many ladies had tried to teach her responsibility, how to dress, and how to talk. But when welfare told her she wouldn't have to work to have her own apartment and money, she began to have problems with the law. She bought alcohol for juveniles, stole a checkbook, wrote bad checks, and became immoral. When Gordon became a judge, he'd say to her, "Beverly, what would Lorrie or my mother say about this?" Finally, he sent her to the penitentiary.

One day I saw Beverly on TV, working on a penitentiary paper-cutting machine. She wore her big smile. Perhaps she had even volunteered to be on TV. I cried and cried. My happy little flower!

JEANNIE FOX ✸ Twinkle, Twinkle Little Star

I first see her sitting at the kitchen table in the women's shelter. She hides her face behind one of her hands. She doesn't want the children to see her face, afraid that it will scare them. I'm feeling the same as I try to find her right eye amid the swelling and discoloration. I see boot prints on her forehead. Days later, as the physical healing begins, I recognize the beauty beneath the disfigurement: high sculpted cheeks, dark brown eyes. That must have bothered him so, how other people looked at her. The marks show he tried to stamp out that beauty.

In the privacy of my office, she recalls how he bought drinks, forced her to take them, though she dumped some out when he wasn't looking. She felt the tension, knew the beating was coming. He was mad about her being accepted for the next semester at Oglala Lakota College. When he picked a fight with another man, she hid in the bar bathroom for two hours, hoping the fight would satisfy his rage or that he would simply go home, pass out, and sleep it off. Later on that wintry November night, she walked across the north Rapid City hills. With each step, she worried about her children, still in the house where his family lived.

She remembers being thrown down the basement stairs. "Bitch!" he cried, raving, demanding to know where she'd gone. "Who were you with, LaDonna?"

Yelling, hitting her, he held their six-month-old son. Their three-year-old daughter tried to shield her mother with her little body. As his fury continued, the child, trying to return the comfort her mother gives when she's sick or sad, sang "Twinkle, Twinkle, Little Star." Fading in and out of consciousness, LaDonna saw an elderly woman take the baby. The woman retreated upstairs, leaving him to finish his business. Tired, he took a cigarette break, then kicked her face with his work boots, saying, "You're going to die. Do you want it to be tonight or tomorrow?" Eyes closed again, she thought about her babies.

Hours later, when he wandered off in a stupor, she dragged her bruised and bloody body out a basement window and walked, didn't know where, until a Good Samaritan pulled over and offered her a ride. "Oh, my God," the driver said when she saw LaDonna's face. Within hours, she was at the shelter, her children retrieved by law enforcement officers. He was later arrested, but the rest of the family was not. She was not safe. Her fear was intense.

One night I get a call. She has missed curfew; she is drunk. Another woman in the shelter has been watching her children sleep. I go out in the dark night, intending to involve the usual authorities when I arrive. Instead, we talk. The alcohol has freed her to say things she dared not say earlier. She tells me about the threats. "His family is big. He can get me anywhere, even in prison," she screams. I wouldn't understand, she says.

For reasons of safety and professional distance, I have never disclosed my personal circumstances, but she's been through enough social service agencies, talked to enough white do-gooders, to know that I've had an education, that my children sleep in their beds in the house of a gentle father, that I've never known the struggle of poverty, racism, or physical violence. Mistakenly, she assumes I don't know the suffering of addiction or how alcoholism can devastate a family. Yet she talks.

She knows that as long as her baby son, the son of her abuser, is with her, she is a target. He becomes the price for her safety, her survival. She hands him over to the family and spends the next several months shuttling back and forth between the reservation and the hostile town, trying to better herself, trying to salvage a college education, working various jobs to show that she can take care of herself.

We meet occasionally and embrace. Unspoken communication passes between us as we look into each other's eyes. She tells me she caught a glimpse of her son the other day at the mall. He was well dressed and clean. "They take good care of him," she says.

She knows she is of more value to him alive, even though she is not yet even a memory in his infant mind. When I take my toddler to work with me, trying to create a nineties balance of career and motherhood, she comments on how the child has grown. We are both visibly pregnant again. Despite the differences in our skin, our experience, our existence, we are mothers, and we know love for our children.

She makes a sacrifice I am fortunate enough not to know. But I have caught her fear. I dream fitfully at night of the violence, feel the grief of a mother separated from her baby. And I know that this could be me. Shelter statistics prove domestic violence knows no boundary of race, age, even socioeconomic status. Yet my guilt can't keep it from happening to someone else.

So every week I sit at the shelter kitchen table facilitating the support group discussion, hearing the stories, in awe of the strength and resourcefulness of the survivors sitting with me.

SAUNDRA DEREMER ❧ Summer Friends

We were summer friends. During the school year, her parents taught in faraway places, and when school was out, they returned to the old family farm. I lived year-round on a family farm some twenty miles distant.

During the summer, we often went to the Hill farm after church for a languid dinner around their table, where Cherie's mother urged food on us until the bowls were empty and we were full. After the grownups retired to the living room for conversation, Cherie and I rambled through the orchard or played with the cats.

This was the rhythm of our friendship. We didn't attend school together; we didn't write letters to each other. During high school, her father died, but Cherie and her mother continued the summer pilgrimage back to the old farm.

I married and moved to another state. Cherie married and moved to a town only two hours away from me. We resumed our friendship and traveled between each other's homes with our children.

My husband died; hers left. I remained where I was; she returned to the old farm of her childhood, never to leave it again.

We phoned each other. I visited her when I went back to see my parents. Her house began to age. She acquired ten cats and six dogs. She didn't cook anymore. One night she called from the hospital to say she'd had a breakdown. She went back to the old farm, took on more dogs and cats, and lived out of her bedroom.

When my father was put in a nursing home, I called to tell her I could not go alone to see him in that place. She came with me and spent the day holding his hand and comforting him while I pushed him in the wheelchair, up and down the halls.

During the last year of his life, when his suffering was so intense and my helplessness so unbearable, I called her often in the wee hours of the night. She listened while I grappled with despair. At the funeral, she sat by the organ while I played his favorite hymns — the hymns she and I sang in the church of our childhood.

We still don't write. She won't. She hasn't been in my home in twenty years — the dogs and cats need her. But we talk in the middle of the night. This week I bought new bed sheets and was having trouble getting used to their coarseness. She also was having trouble with new sheets. Wrong color.

I ponder this friendship and know our shared past is the foundation for it, but it is her nonjudgmental attitude toward me and my unconditional love toward her that keep the phones ringing.

BETTY DOWNS 🦌 Learning How to Be Lonely

I stood at the door, my heart beating a tattoo against my chest. What would this strange lady do when she opened the door?

I'd spotted her the day we moved into the little town of Manville. The road construction camp where I lived with my husband was set up in a vacant lot across the street from her neat little brown house on a corner lot. I'd watched her working in her yard wearing jeans, a baseball cap covering her short-cropped gray hair.

I decided the best way to meet her would be to borrow a rake. I knocked lightly, then again. The door flew open to reveal a short, stocky, craggy-faced lady perhaps seventy years of age. I was startled as she took one look at me, grabbed me by my arm, and, shouting in what she later told me was her gruff sergeant's voice, said, "You come in here. You're one of the camper girls, and I want to talk to you." Thus began a wonderful friendship with Ione Stotts, a true pioneer of the West.

She led me into her dining room. "I used to do what you're doing," she said. "My husband worked in construction of the gas lines. I lived in a little camper and moved with the jobs. I used to cook for twenty men in that little kitchen. They ate in shifts. We lived in a tent when I was first married. Had a board floor for that tent. It was a good way to live." Her eyes looked beyond me as she remembered.

I visited her often. It didn't take long to tidy my little camper, and about coffee time I would find myself at her door eager to hear her stories.

Her childhood had been extremely lonely. Her parents were separated; her mother was a trumpeter in a traveling band. The large picture that hung on Ione's wall showed a petite, beautiful lady dressed in ruffles and lace, holding a trumpet. It was hard to believe that one so fragile-looking could mother someone as rough around the edges as Ione.

"By the time I was fifteen, I was in everybody's way, so they sent me to live on my uncle's ranch, where I herded sheep. For days all I did was walk and talk to the sheep. It suited me, and I learned how to be lonely."

She met her husband when he came to the ranch to break horses. She took me to that ranch one day on an excursion: gray weathered shacks that once were chicken houses, barns, and outbuildings circled around what had been a corral, where she stood reminiscing.

"I used to sit up there on the top fence watching him work with the horses. I was just a girl, but he treated me like a lady. When he left the ranch to go to the next spread, I went with him." Her eyes became dreamy thinking of it. This was the beginning of her nomadic life in a tent. She was used to living outside — the sheepherding had seen to that. "He taught me how to ride, and we became a good team. When he got the job with the gas company, we traveled all over. Our little girl was born, and she traveled with us. We both got tired of people, and we decided to do some guiding for hunters and fishermen. That's when the real fun began."

Just as her husband had taught her to ride, he taught her all he knew about hunting and how to live in the mountains. When he died, she had a little girl to raise, and all she knew how to do was keep right on guiding hunters and fishermen in the Wind River Range.

One morning over coffee, she told the story of her first guide job. She first met the men when they came in for supper that evening. Carrying their fish, laughing and swearing, they stopped dead in their tracks when they saw her.

"Why it's a goddamned woman!" one man exclaimed. In her gruff voice, she informed them she had heard every cuss word that had ever been spoken.

Soon she was seldom without a job, became expert at finding elk and deer, and knew the best fishing holes. One of her most renowned clients was the lawyer F. Lee Bailey. She said, "He was a gentleman and wore his pants just like I did." I don't think she was ever intimidated by anyone.

One morning Ione stopped at my camper and announced, "Get your coat; we're going for a ride." In her car, we drove out to the cemetery to begin the day at the spot where her husband was buried. A black figure of a cowboy astride his horse had been etched in one corner of a gray stone. Our next stop was a hilltop north of Manville. "You can see four states from here," she said: Wyoming to the west, Nebraska to the southeast, South Dakota to the east, and, she swore, western North Dakota. I never argued with her.

"This is where I come when I can't stand being around people any longer." We sat there a long time. Neither of us spoke. I'm not sure she had ever taken anyone to the top of that hill before.

She was the only woman I ever met who had found my underwear secret. Living in a camper, not always close to a place to wash clothes, I had discovered the joy of wearing my husband's soft, flexible, nonbinding underwear. One day when I was at Ione's, I helped her fold clothes from her clothesline, including men's shorts. "Do you wear these, too?" I asked.

"Do you?" she retorted in surprise. "I found out these are the best things to wear when you ride horseback."

Leaving my friend that fall was hard to do, but the construction job was finished. We kept in touch, even though she sold her place and moved miles away from the ranch to be closer to her daughter. I stopped to see her in 1985. She lived comfortably in a small trailer.

I was shocked when her daughter wrote that Ione had sat down on her davenport and with a sigh left this world. Her body lies beneath a gray stone in Manville, but I know her spirit is on horseback, riding to a rendezvous at the top of a hill where you can look into four states.

When things get tough for me, I put myself back in that moment and feel a fresh breeze of relief as I look out in my mind's eye at the blue, green, and golden expanse of four states surrounding me and feel a renewal of spirit — a spirit Ione would understand.

FAYE SCHRATER ❧ Dormant Seeds Sprouting

Dear Cathy,

Your letter arrived yesterday, and even after twenty-one years, I recognized your handwriting — that precise, almost Palmer penmanship that you and both our mothers learned. With some trepidation, I held the envelope, wondering if you had merely sent condolences about my father's death or if you had responded to my overture of renewed friendship.

You were one of Daddy's favorite people. When he died, I knew I had to write more than just a death notice. He often spoke of you, reminiscing mostly about the 1950s. He said all he needed was you, me, and his dog Tippy to trail three hundred head of cows and calves or five hundred steers twenty-three miles from the ranch to summer grazing at Bear Trap and back again in the fall.

Do you remember? For those few summer and fall days and a few days between when we checked the stock, we spent twelve to fourteen hours straight on horseback. Riding for my dad, we came home dusty and with sunburned noses, and earned five dollars a day. In my selective memory, we spent most of the summer riding those three miles from one house to the other or up into the hills along Otter Creek. Even though we sewed clothes for 4-H, attended local 4-H meetings and county and state fairs, washed endless piles of dirty dishes, and occasionally worked in the hay fields, what I remember are the hours on horseback. Working for my dad, we used saddles, but for fun we always rode bareback — you on The

Brown Mare or Paint, me on Skooks or Ole Blue. Mom called us her "wild Indians," a compliment meaning we were so at home on a horse we could ride with only a bridle.

You and I became friends in early March of 1952. My folks had moved five times that year, and Ten Sleep was my fifth school. Lonely and shy, I walked out of the March mud and onto the bus for the twenty-mile ride. You asked if I wanted to sit with you; I did. You were in the third grade and I in the fifth, but that difference shrank the next year as you jumped a grade. We were close friends for the next five years until my family moved across the mountains. I didn't see you again until you came to the university a year after I did. Two years later, we roomed together. After graduation, our lives diverged. I worked in a local hospital before going back to school; you married and settled in Colorado. I married and, after the Peace Corps, went east to work and attend graduate school. But always we wrote.

The summer of 1978, I visited the West, taking your address and directions, intending to see you. I couldn't find your house or even your name in the phone book. I drove away, embarrassed, uneasy, half-regretful, half-relieved.

I never could write and tell you how anxious I'd been about seeing you after all those years. I worried so that you wouldn't recognize the country girl, that you'd reject the Easterner, that I unwittingly sabotaged the visit. After twenty-six years of friendship, I was ashamed of not trusting you, but I could not write and explain.

In all the years since, I have thought often of you and that day when I drove away from a long and dear friendship. My dad always stopped to see you during his peregrinations north from Arizona. He kept me informed about your life, wondered why you and I weren't in touch. I could never tell him, and he never pushed it.

After I mailed the letter telling you of my dad's death, I wondered what you might write, had even begun to think you wouldn't write, even though only two weeks had passed. But you did. I wept over your expressions of affection and esteem for Daddy. You called him "the last of the gentleman cowboys." Your offer of friendship warmed a cold ache of longing and self-disgust I'd held for years.

Someone once said, "Friends are flowers in the garden of life." If that's true, Cathy, the seeds have long lain dormant. With attention and warmth, they may sprout and bloom again — an extraordinary gift from my father to the two of us.

With warm regards,
Faye

JANELLE MASTERS ❧ *Of Potatoes and the Wind*

Once when my friend Phyllis was out in Seattle visiting her son, a local journalist interviewed her for an article on rural women. Phyllis had lived in North Dakota all her life, and I guess the journalist thought she had found the archetypal rural woman. But when she found out that Phyllis habitually read four newspapers a day, the *New York Times* being one of them, she lost interest. When she learned that Phyllis was a veteran *New Yorker* subscriber, she gave up completely. Phyllis was clearly not what she expected. A woman from Rolla, North Dakota, should want to chat about potatoes and wind, not be able to discuss Tina Brown and the latest shakeup in the publishing world.

I first met Phyllis when I moved back to North Dakota from Florida seventeen years ago. I had gone bird watching in the early spring and was back in my little rented house in Rolla puzzling over my bird books, looking to see whether North Dakota really had mountain bluebirds. Not knowing any other birders in the state, I called Dr. Gammel. He said, "Why are you calling me when you have one of the best birders in the state living right there? Call Phyllis Hart."

On our first birding trip, she met me at the end of her long driveway. It had been a bad winter, and she didn't want me to chance driving through the melting snowbanks to her house. I sized her up: a lean woman of about sixty, I guessed, whose hair was gray and whose face was lined, yet whose walk was light and graceful. She held a bird book and a pair of binoculars. She smiled, got in my car, and sized me up, too, I suppose: a woman of about thirty, brownish hair and brown eyes, dressed in old blue jeans and a faded T-shirt.

We drove off as we would countless times after that. Images of those birding trips fill my head: A baby great horned owl on the ground, pretending it wasn't there, while Phyllis and I pondered how to "save" it; we soon scrambled to the safety of the car when we heard the warning snap of the parent's beak close by. The baby ferruginous hawks that we watched grow into vicious adults one summer; they would tear into pieces the rodents their mother brought them and then toss the chunks back like martinis. The roadkill owl we found that we just had to identify; we got out of the car and stood over it with our bird books open. We laughed later wondering whether passing motorists thought we were giving the smashed owl its last rites. "There are those crazy bird-watching women again, and look what they're doing now," I mimicked as we drove away, wiping tears from our cheeks.

Of course, there's a limit to how much one can talk about birds exclusively. We soon realized that we were both Democrats. "Sure," she said, "John [her husband] and I have been canceling out each other's votes for years." But she was not a party-line Democrat. She hadn't voted for the Democratic candidate for president for ages and usually wrote in Shirley Chisholm's name on the ballot. Once, after John had implied pretty strongly that Phyllis and I were extreme liberals, I gave her a bleeding-heart plant, and we both cackled as we planted it in the flower bed.

In a restless period, I moved from Rolla to Grand Forks, then moved from there to Oregon, then back to Grand Forks, then finally to the Mandan area, where I've stayed put for ten years. Wherever I've gone, I've received notes, postcards, letters, and cards from Phyllis in her distinctive small handwriting. In whatever tempestuous mood or phase I've gone through, I could always depend on those steady missives, giving me weather reports, bird counts, planet sightings, reading assignments. "Have you read *Miss Peabody's Inheritance* yet?" "Hasn't Venus been a sight to behold?" "I can hear the cranes but can't see them." "What do you make of the Republican onslaught?"

In addition to our common interests, Phyllis was at the center of one of the strangest small-world stories I've ever been privileged to participate in. North Dakota is often called one big small town. You meet one person, and he or she knows someone you know. But what are the chances that the man you met in Thailand and considered marrying would one day catch up with you in North Dakota, all because of ruddy turnstones?

One day in Mandan, my phone rang and on the other end was a voice I didn't think I would ever hear again. Ted and I had met in Yala, Thailand. We were both Peace Corps volunteers and had dated for a year before going our separate ways, he back to Detroit and me back to North Dakota via Africa. We kept in contact, rejoined each other briefly in Detroit, and made marriage plans. Then the whole thing fell apart, and I moved to Florida to lick my wounds. When I got that telephone call ten years later, I had been through many restless moves.

"This is Ted," the voice said. "Ted Adams."

"Good God," I said. "Where are you?"

"Phyllis gave me your number," he said.

Phyllis? I was shocked. I still am. How could this be? It turns out that Ted had become a physician and was working in Belcourt, six miles from Rolla. His girlfriend had been searching for turnstones with Phyllis and was talking about her doctor friend who had been in the Peace Corps in Thailand. Phyllis became curious, knowing I had once lived there, and the rest is history. Phyllis and I still shake our heads in disbelief over that one. For years after that, I thought of Phyllis as being the center of a great wheel, spokes leading out to God knows where, with her in the calm center, writing her communiqués, reading her newspapers, and thinking her thoughts, while the world spun madly about her.

One day last summer, I received a note from her written from the Mayo Clinic. Along with her review of a recent book and questions about my latest trip, she mentioned that she was there to find out why she had developed a distended abdomen with a mass forming on the left side. I folded the letter carefully and put it away, but the note gnawed at me. A couple of days later, I retrieved a message from my answering machine. Again I was shocked to hear the voice of Ted, now married and living in Minnesota. "Janelle, I thought you'd like to know that Phyllis just had surgery for ovarian cancer." The room grew cold, and the vision I had of Phyllis as the calm center was shaken.

I kicked myself into high gear and sent off a telegram: "The bad news is a drag. Am reading A. S. Byatt's *Insects and Angels*. We must discuss. Let me know when."

In between her visits to the doctor and my teaching schedule, we finally got our chance. On a magical fall weekend in Rolla, Phyllis and I again went birding. We counted thousands of snow geese, talked of the woes of the Democratic Party, discussed movies and A. S. Byatt, and pondered the ramifications of the information superhighway.

On a later visit, we sat together and sipped coffee. She was dressed in an oversize sweatshirt decorated with line drawings of gulls and sandpipers and wore a head wrap. She pointed out a *New Yorker* and said, "I've let my subscription lapse. There it is, Janelle, my last issue." When I looked surprised, she said, "Well, don't you think that forty-eight years of reading the *New Yorker* is long enough?"

Throughout the day and into the gathering cold of the evening, she was way ahead of me as we plowed through four newspapers. We even talked briefly about a potato soup recipe, and I believe we cursed the wind.

LEE ANN RORIPAUGH 🦌 *Pearls*

Mother eats seaweed and plum pickles,
and when the Mormons come knocking
she does bird-talk. I've never seen
an ocean, but I'd swim in one to look
for secrets. She has a big pearl
from my *oji-san*, says it will be mine
when she's dead. It's in a drawer
hidden with silver dollars. I hope
she doesn't buy a ticket, go back
to her sisters and leave me.

With stinging strokes, she brushes
my hair, pulls it into pigtails
that stretch my face flat. I walk
to school across sagebrush while

she watches from her bedroom window.
Once I found a prairie dog curled
sleeping on the ground and brushed
away ants on his eyes. Mother
saw me dilly-dally, told me not
to touch dead things.

I have a red box in my desk
with a dragon lid that screws on
and off. It smells sweet from face
cream, and I keep a *kokeishi* doll
inside for good luck. Wishing
for more colors in my crayon pail,
I make up stories about mermaids
and want a gold crayon to draw hair,
silver for their tails. But
we can't afford lots of kid junk.
I have piano lessons. She says
I'll be a doctor someday,
but I think I'd like to be a fireman
or maybe a Roller Derby queen.

One day when I was walking home
some boys on bikes flew down
around me like noisy crows.
They kept yelling *Kill the Jap!*
I ran as fast as I could but fell
in the dirt, got up and fell.
My mother came running to me.
She carried me home, picked out
the gravel, washed off blood,
tucked me into her bed, and let
me wear the ring for a while.

I wish I had long white skinny
fingers, gold hair, and a silver
tail. I'd gather baskets
of pearls. But my hair is black,
my fingers stubby. Mother
tells me they're not found just
floating underwater. She says
oysters make them, when there's
sand or gravel under their shells.
It hurts. And the more it hurts,
the bigger the pearl.

ROBIN LITTLEFIELD ✺ The Art of Living the Moment

"Rob! Rob!" Footsteps erupted in the hallway, and Mother burst through the kitchen door. Already grinning, I was eager to hear what she wanted. You see, I trusted my mother.

"LET'S GO TO THE DUMP!" She grinned back at me. She'd caught me off guard and knew it, and pounced on the situation for all it was worth. "We'll get ice cream after!" She clapped her hands together over her auburn head and danced about the kitchen.

Dumbstruck, I shook my head from side to side in rhythm with her steps. "Oh, no! No! No! NO! NO! I'm NOT going to the dump!"

But by the time she gathered her purse and keys, I was sitting in the pickup, garbage loaded, waiting for her. I still don't know how she does it, but every time, mere moments after my determined refusals, I am besieged with feelings of not wanting to be left behind.

Mom slipped into the driver's seat, a smile consuming her entire face. At that moment, I knew just how much she loved me. I pretended not to notice.

Dodging potholes, we bounced down the dirt road leaving the ranch, our little butts more airborne than not, while my mother gleefully navigated the old truck as if we were beginning some grand adventure.

True to her word, on the way home from the dump, we got ice cream. But it rarely ended there. Negotiating freeway traffic with her owl-sharp perception of detail, licking Jamoca Almond Fudge, she spotted a distant boutique. "Look, Rob! The Country Girl is having a SALE!"

These outbursts trained me to clutch the armrest with one hand and my ice cream with the other. Already U-turned, my mother sped back in the direction from which we'd just come. Sure enough, there'd be the Country Girl with SALE in red letters splashed across the window. I'd been thrust into these situations too often. I knew what lay ahead. Seconds after the old Apache rumbled to a halt, Mom was bounding across the parking lot. Like me, she was dressed in her going-to-the-dump finest: knee-high rubber boots, jeans, and an oversize flannel shirt. It was never enough for my mother to window-shop. She'd down the last of her ice cream, calling over her shoulder, "Hurry up, Rob!" as she disappeared through the door.

We'd be greeted at the door by the owner, adorned in her painted nails, knits, and diamonds. Once inside, we were swallowed up by the nearby city's socialites: excited women, all chattering at once, whom — because of my father's business — my mother always knew.

Once, however, our spontaneous shopping spree was forgotten in pursuit of another adventure that appeared unexpectedly in our path. We had just turned onto the county road leaving the dump when Mom slammed on the brakes.

"Robin!" She pointed. "It's a gopher snake!" Eyes bright, she clutched the wheel with both hands as she leaned across the dash, peering at the three-foot snake stretched across the road. "Quick! Go get him!"

"What?" My mouth dropped open for the second time that morning.

"Yes!" She exclaimed. "We'll take him home. Stuff him down one of those gopher holes in the artichoke patch."

My back stiffened against the window. "You're crazy."

"Hurry up!" She smiled. "There's a car coming. Want him to get run over?"

Slowly, I opened the pickup door and slid to the pavement. The snake was stretched full length across the middle of the road. I leaned over. His eyes were half-closed as he dozed on the sun-warmed asphalt. Cars now approached from both directions. So, with my legs spread, I straddled the snake and, like a traffic cop, stretched out my arms, palms out, both ways. The cars stopped, and I bent lower over the pavement. Although the snake was immobile, I could see that he was very much alive and now aware of my presence. I cupped my hands. My idea was to grasp him, simultaneously, just behind his head and about two-thirds of the way down his body. I hovered a foot above the ground. He was a moment away from my clutch. Without warning, the snake lunged several feet forward. I snapped upright. Teeth clenched and eyes narrowed, I glared at my mother. Her face, still careening out the window, glowed with anticipation. "Hurry now," she cooed, "before we lose him."

"Humph!" I muttered. "Before WE lose him." In a flash, I sucked in my breath, grabbed the snake at my preplanned points, and stood erect. The gopher snake, who hung two-thirds the length of my body, whipped his tail up around my forearm and recoiled in my grip. I was surprised at his strength.

I loosened my grasp to better support him. He relaxed and became still. With both arms held well away from my body, I carried him to the truck and stiffly slid through the open door.

Like a getaway driver, my mother punched in the clutch and shifted into low gear, and we lurched down the road. She bubbled with pride. "Oh, Rob, you were wonderful!"

"Uh-huh," I mumbled, never taking my eyes from the giant creature draped across my lap.

"Oh! I can't wait for Grannie to see him," she continued.

"Grannie?" I pictured my seventy-odd-year-old grandmother, who lived privately in her own dwelling on our ranch. She was a sweet, kindly woman. I failed to fathom the connection.

"Oh, yes." Mom beamed. "She was the one who found the gopher holes this morning."

When we pulled into the ranch, my mother sprang from the truck, threw open my door, and took off running. "Ma! Ma! We've got a surprise for you!"

From a distance, I could see my tiny white-haired grandmother, with a steadying hand on the rail, descend her steps and eagerly approach her youngest daughter. Arm in arm, they came toward me. Mom made my grandmother close her eyes. Haltingly, the huge snake entangled around my arms, I slipped out of the truck.

"OK, Ma, ready?"

Grannie's scream was heard throughout the valley. During my childhood, I had never known my grandmother, in any kind of crisis, not to wet her pants. This time was no different.

JUDITH MCCONNELL STEELE   The Women

I didn't know I loved the women
their tender wrists
banded by small watches
they wear even when they make love.
Thin straps wrapping their veins
telling them: This moment is now,
this moment is all.

I didn't know I loved the women
soft purses slung like precious babies
under their arms.
Carrying small moments of their lives
old photos, powder loose
in its case, keys
to their secrets.

I didn't know I loved the women
telling their stories
over hot cups of coffee
leaning close, elbows almost touching
on the hard Formica tables.
Tender secrets, stolen
from ordinary lives,
curling around their heads like smoke
from their smoldering cigarettes.

I didn't know I loved my mother
hanging out the wash,
snapping out pillowcases, hankies, undershirts,
pinning them to the line like pieces
of her story.
Humming "My Funny Valentine" through
the clothespins in her mouth.

I didn't know I loved my mother
sitting at her dressing table
clipping on gold earrings.
Putting on red lipstick, pink rouge,
white powder, black stockings,
putting on another life
telling me good-bye.

LILLIAN VILBORG ❧ Sigga

One year he left, and she was alone out there in the bush, with kids and a
herd of wild horses for company, occasionally a brown bear. And of course
the ubiquitous mouse and rat both in and out of the house. I was one of the
kids. Twelve going on thirteen going on thirty. I was the hired hand for two
months.

She was my mother's sister, four months pregnant that summer as we
milked twenty cows every morning, hoping the kids wouldn't wake up until we were finished. She let me milk the cows with big soft teats. Like
Speed, who got her name because she was so easy to milk. Speed was a
good milker, too — sometimes she gave over a pail. We milked in the barnyard no matter the weather. The cows stood patiently untethered waiting
their turn. We leaned our heads into their bristly hair, their soft bodies
smelling of earth and grass and dung, the milk pail held tightly between
our knees, the bottom resting on our boots, the pail pinging with the first
squirts of milk and then splooshing as the pail filled. Around the barnyard,
the brown cow pies were pancake polka dots on the black earth.

After we finished milking, the cows meandered lazily, relieved of their
full udders, out of the yard. We then had to separate the milk and feed the
calves. I turned the separator handle while she slopped the skim milk into
half-pail portions to take out to the calves. All the leftover milk went to the
pigs; she and I shared the weight of the five-gallon pail as we hauled it to
their pen. Together we lowered the heavy cream can into the well. I ran into
the house to check on the kids while she washed the separator and pails.

Twice every day. Morning and evening. Beginning with finding the cows. I never understood why the pastures weren't fenced there like they were at my grandfather's place. She'd put her intuition and her ears to work as she set out to find those cows, listening hard for the bell. They never came home on their own. Badly trained, some said.

Once, when she was out looking for the cows, a lightning storm came up that was so close you couldn't count to two before the thunder banged. I was home minding the sleeping kids, and the house shook with every bolt. I waited for her breathlessly, restlessly, and was dismayed when the dog came home without her, his skinny frame sticking out through his fur, which the rain had pelted into him. Finally, I saw her, hair plastered to her skull, clothes soaked. No cows. She couldn't find the cows. We didn't milk that night. They never came home that night.

Now I realize she was scared a lot that summer. She never let on. And there were times when she was very brave. Like the time she told Myrt she knew she was stealing money from the cream checks. I figured that took a lot of guts because Myrt was our only neighbor within ten miles. Myrt didn't take the cream into town for us anymore. And she quit sending her kids over to borrow stuff. In great indignation, she sent them with wagonload after wagonload of stuff she had borrowed in the past — flour, eggs, baking powder, glasses, pots, dishes. We were amazed that she remembered so many things. We piled it all up into a heap in the middle of the kitchen floor and laughed and laughed and laughed.

But it couldn't have been very funny being pregnant, having three kids under eight, and running a farm with a twelve-year-old girl as your main helper. Your only helper. What could she talk to a twelve-year-old about? Couldn't tell her how lonesome she was. Couldn't tell her how scared she was. Couldn't tell her that she didn't know what to do, didn't know how she was going to cope, no man, new baby coming.

She must have hated going to town. Hated the stares of the townspeople. Hated their whispers. Isn't it a shame? He's gone off with another woman. Younger. Someone who isn't too tired to go to dances, kick up her heels. Left her alone. And in her condition. With all those kids, too. She should never have married him anyway. He's not her kind.

One time, when we were going to town, the old '38 four-door dark blue Chevy didn't start because we couldn't find the key. She was sure that one of the kids had hidden it. And then it felt as if we were very alone. We were the last farm on the road to the lake, seventeen miles from town. It would take a long time to get into town on the green and gold John Deere tractor. That would never work. We had to find someone to hot-wire the car.

Once she screamed when she put her hand on a mouse while reaching into the cupboard for a dish. Almost hit the ceiling. I've been scared of mice ever since.

I slept on a cot by the window in the living room. After I was in bed — and all the kids, too — I saw her sit in her rocking chair in the kitchen.

While I fell asleep to the sound of the loons' lonely cries at dusk, she had a few minutes of quiet before she passed out from exhaustion. She sat in her huge kitchen in her log house, the heat of the day cooling through the screen door. She rocked as the moonshine filled the sky and the kitchen, the frogs set up their thrumming accompaniment to the loons and occasionally an owl. Not calling her name. And for just a brief bit of the day, her dog, Duffy, sitting beside her, she wasn't scared. She was filled with the quiet wonder of it all.

But next day it was back to the backbreaking work. Heating water for washing. Hauling water for washing. Washing. Hanging on the line. Ironing. Folding. Emptying the slop pail. Pumping drinking water. Water for dishes. Cooking. Washing up. Keeping track of the kids. Baking bread. Canning. Picking berries. Weeding the garden. Making beds. Sweeping floors. Going into town to shop. Taking in the cream. She took refuge in her garden, where the earth cooled her hands, its black heavy consistency cradling the potatoes, carrots, radishes, onions, turnips, beets; feeding the tomatoes, beans, peas, rhubarb, spinach, lettuce, Swiss chard, corn.

One day she left me alone on the farm with the kids and went into the city with my mom and dad. It seemed pretty serious. She was going to see a lawyer. Trying to find out what she could do. Before winter set in. Before the baby was born.

She must have hated him for leaving. But she never said anything. I kind of liked it just her and I, without his teasing to tears. I liked the quiet calm of it with her. When her little son said that his daddy wasn't a bad man, was he, I said no he wasn't a bad man, and my twelve-year-old heart bled for the boy. She just kept doing what had to be done, kept moving through the days. Every day a necessity, every day a chore, and some days rays of laughter and light.

Smelling the smells from the big lake, the weedy water smells. Feeling the heat hang on the air, the summer heat moistened by the waves. The dragonflies taking care of the mosquito population. No one taking care of the armyworms.

ELLEN VAYO ❧ Lupe's Song

we the ladies of the circle gather together
once a month   second Wednesday   7:30 P.M.
some of us droop into Lupe's old green sofa

a few of us cuddle into mismatched chairs springs creaking
the rest of us sit cross-legged on threadbare carpet
we always pray the rosary   one leads   the rest

gripping our beads bow our heads and together chant
holy Mary mother of God pray for us sinners
after the rosary we drink Carlo Rossi

from a crook-necked bottle and Lupe   hooked to dialysis
always sings some naughty little song
a few of us stare   blushing through splayed fingers

most of us just giggle
between sips and songs we plan
our annual bridge party   proceeds

to feed the hungry   clothe the naked
one Wednesday evening in early spring
Lupe decided against dialysis

we still meet once a month
still make plans to feed the hungry
clothe the naked   still pray

holy Mary mother of God
but Lupe doesn't sing anymore

LUCY L. WOODWARD ❧ The Lady Who Knew How to Live

I first saw Margaret Luster when she pulled her car up by our trailer, climbed out, and said, "Well, glad to see you got some clothes on. Charles said you were half-naked."

Our friendship began then, when I was a new bride, and it did not die with her two years ago.

I had quit my job in New York, stopped in Ohio for our wedding, and headed west with Tim. Sponsored by Gulf Oil, Tim was pursuing his Ph.D. in geology. We bought a secondhand sixteen-foot trailer and hauled it from Texas to Casper, Wyoming, stopping in a junkyard to replace "Betsy's" broken piston.

That summer we lived in the Red Valley, north of Arminto, an interruption in the gravel road out of Waltman, which was only a post office and convenience store. Tim mapped the Deadman Butte area; I was wife, secretary, chauffeur, cook, lover.

We purchased provisions in Casper, then Tim drove the Jeep north, pulling the trailer, and I followed. We maneuvered the vehicles through a muddy creek, up a steep bank, and across a valley to crumbling Baker's Cabin. Rocky hills encircled our valley; their colorful sedimentary layers challenged me to memorize the entire geologic section.

Before long, blissfully in love, I was driving us in the Jeep past coffin-shaped Deadman Butte to Grave Springs and Poison Spider Creek. I took down descriptions of rock formations, typing them by the Coleman lantern. I snapped photographs while Tim measured outcrop angles with his Brunton compass.

Lonely for another woman, I wrote Mother long letters. Our cat wasn't enough. One hot day, alone, wearing a halter and shorts, I was hanging laundry on the corral fence, near a rattlesnake skin tied there. Terrified of the blowing rattles, Kitty ran under the trailer. Then I heard another noise, a pickup chugging up the dirt road.

Afraid to touch Tim's gun hanging inside, I waited as the pickup stopped, motor still running. A man's massive, weathered face appeared in the open cab window.

"What are you doing here?"

"We have permission — from the L & L Sheep Ranch."

"I *am* the L & L Sheep Ranch." He looked hard at me. "Young woman, don't you know any better than to run around here half-dressed?"

"But . . . there's no one to see me."

"Don't you know this is sheepherder country?"

"Well . . ."

"You get back in there. Put on some pants and a shirt." He threw the truck into reverse, turned, and disappeared down the road.

I don't understand why, I thought. If the sheepherders choose to herd sheep, they don't like people. Don't see why there's any danger from them. I put on jeans and a shirt and soon heard another car approaching.

A woman got out and walked with a rocking gait toward me. Her friendly blue eyes danced beneath black curly hair, and her rosy cheeks glowed with health. She stood five feet seven, with a large barrel torso and narrow hips. I said, "Hello?"

In a husky voice, she said, "I'm Margaret Luster. That was Charles. We run the L & L Sheep Ranch for Milt Coffman. Charles is foreman. I'm his wife."

"Come in," I said.

She sat at our tiny table and looked around. "You two come to our place for supper. I'll be back later, and you can follow me to the ranch."

She saw me glance at her toothless bottom gum. "Can't make them lower dentures fit, but that's all right, gums hardened up. I eat apples, even corn on the cob. Big old ewe I was shearing kicked out both top and bottom. Stomped on my foot, too," she added, showing her outsize left foot. "Have to buy expensive shoes now, in two sizes."

She stayed long enough to tell me she was born in Cokeville, Colorado, in 1910. She had two sons, Bill, still in Casper, and Jim, a banker. A baby girl had died. When she married Charles, she managed the sheepherders.

We went to their ranch house that night for steaks, fried tough as rope. In a corner stood a rock-polishing outfit. In a basket by the rocking chair, I saw intricately tatted white doilies and wondered how she could tie such tiny knots with her thick, callused fingers.

"I like crocheting better," she said, pulling out a bunch of red and orange afghan squares. "My mother taught me before I was eight. She died in the 1918 flu epidemic."

"When you were only eight?'

"Yes. Mama ran to the edge of my father's grave. Gonna jump in with him. She was a big woman. Two men had to pull her back. She died two days later anyway."

Charles said, "Yeah, then her father's executor ran off with all the money. Them three little girls went to foster homes."

"And did fine," Margaret said. "Learned to work hard and do for ourselves. God helps those who help themselves. I worked hardest. Had to. *I* got *bad* families."

"That's because *you* were bad," Charles teased.

"That's right," she agreed. "I didn't like putting up with those people. I had better sense than they did."

We drove home beneath a vast star-studded night sky, awed by these realistic, enduring people. That summer, while I drove the Jeep and Tim worked geologic maps, Margaret kept in touch. I had found the friend I needed. I sensed that even with totally different backgrounds, we understood each other, shared a special knowing that broke through all artifice, born of our common love for the land and for hard work. I wanted to be like her — strong, cheerful, and brave.

When we needed a break, she'd have us over for supper. She loved making us laugh, revealing the absurdity in people and situations. A joke began with a sly, sideways glance. Her blue eyes sparkled, her mouth twitched, and out came the perfect comment.

Each week when I drove alone seventy-five miles into Casper for ice and groceries, I learned to trust my judgment, because that's what she did. I had much to learn. She taught me how to cut meat into steaks, a roast, and stew, assuring me that when the ice in the cooler melted by Thursday, there was always the cold "crick."

When we came back to work for Gulf in Casper the next summer, we saw her occasionally when she came into town. When our babies began coming, we often drove to the mountain pasture at Grave Springs for picnics with Margaret and Charles.

One day she called us and said, "Charles is dead. He took sick and died." When they lowered his body into the ground, she rushed sobbing into her boss's arms.

She moved into town. She had spent twelve hundred dollars on the funeral, two burial plots, and a tiny trailer. She borrowed fifty dollars and survived. She baby-sat for several families, including ours. I needed her mothering, and she needed us. I could count on her familiar "Hullo" over the phone. When I despaired, she listened to me cry. When we were too busy starting our business, she took time with our children. Once in her well-worn coat at a school play, she informed the bejeweled grandmother next to her that she was Tommy Woodward's grandma.

Two of her grandchildren died, and another was paralyzed. When son Jim died suddenly in Europe, much of her sparkle disappeared.

Nothing daunted her. One blowy winter, she resolutely set out in the pickup for Chicago to collect a newborn grandson whose parents could not keep him. She brought him back through a snowstorm, feeding him from the abandoned baby lambs' small bottles.

Margaret never complained, even when she nearly died after falling and breaking a hip while housesitting on a cold January day. When they got her to the hospital six hours later, her lungs were almost full of fluid. But when she overheard an intern say, "This one's dying," she decided not to.

In spite of the pain, her humor irrepressibly bubbled up. In the hospital, she would say she hurt down below in her "grone." Submitting to a bath, she told the male nurse such funny jokes about her grone that nobody got embarrassed. The doctors liked caring for her because she made them laugh.

She lived five years longer in her little trailer, always glad to see me. She died with oxygen piped into her nostrils and a feeding tube in her stomach. I had asked if she wanted us to ask God to take her home. She nodded, blue eyes bright. Outside, I wept only once. Never again, because she was soon safe in heaven with Charles and son Jim.

EILEEN THIEL ❧ Resolving Mrs. Wackerly

The honeymoon Gene and I had stolen from hay harvest ended at 2:10 P.M. on June 30, 1958. As soon as Gene left our newly rented farm to tell his dad we were home, I began sorting our belongings and arranging the kitchen cupboards.

The house was old, and the wooden floors creaked. Green light reflected through overgrown lilac and snowball bushes pressing themselves against the windows. Toward evening I switched on the electric bulbs, but they only enhanced the gloom, taking on the hue of green kitchen walls.

A peculiar scent became apparent, and I could not let go of the feeling someone else was in the house. Moving quietly from one room to the next, I checked each area. Satisfied I was alone, I turned to finish my work and nearly knocked over a woman about my own height, but in her seventies.

"I'm Mrs. Wackerly," she said. "I own this farm."

Everything she wore was brown. She seemed to blend into a solid pillar of uninteresting dust except for a dash of sunburned freckles and her hair, which was a blaze of fiery henna. She did not twitch a muscle when I bumped into her.

"I'm sorry," I said. "I didn't hear you knock."

"I didn't," she replied. "This is my place. I need to inspect the house to make sure my tenants don't ruin anything." Her eyes followed mine as they checked the status of the outside door. "And don't put a lock on the door. I'll tear it off and send you a bill for the repair."

By politely introducing myself to Mrs. Wackerly, I unwittingly established a pecking order. She would perpetually peck, and I would produce the order.

"One thing I want to make clear," she said, pointing to several appliances. "You are not to touch any settings. If you start twisting the dials around, they'll fall off, and if anything breaks, you'll have to buy me a new one."

I never learned to stand up to aggressive people. I had been painstakingly taught to be nice, so giving in to bullies was a hobby of mine. By the time Mrs. Wackerly finished with her list of rules, I would have shined her shoes just to get rid of her. Actually, I told her Gene would be glad to prune her orchard. When she left, a sweet odor lingered — a strange mixture of honeysuckle, onions, and baby talcum. In the future, it would be the clue that told me she had been going through the house in my absence again.

I don't think Mrs. Wackerly had allowed any changes on her rental farm since she stopped living there during the Depression years. And for some reason, she had nailed the front door to the house down tight. Maybe it was a memory she'd tried to cage.

The day I tried to scrub the age away from the kitchen floor, Mrs. Wackerly smelled wax through her binoculars and stood at my elbow before the floor was dry.

"Don't you ruin that floor now, dear, or you'll have to replace it." Her little round eyes sparkled at the thought. Leaving dust tracks on the still damp linoleum, she rubbed her hands together, agitated, like a chipmunk while she inspected the corners for any wax on the baseboards.

"This pattern is delicate, you see. You might scrub it off if you're not gentle."

Mrs. Wackerly decided she liked me and always called me "dear" as opposed to "that bitch who rented the house before you."

There must have been memories of more genteel days in Mrs. Wackerly's head. She invited me to share tea with her often. Once, under pretense of business, she commanded Gene to stop work and sip tea in her parlor at four o'clock. She never asked him again after he showed up in his work clothes and grease-stained hands.

She seemed to enjoy watching me in different circumstances — or maybe a better word is "torture" me with bizarre situations while she drew her own conclusions. But it was a mutual observation. While she acted out her role of tough manager, I simply learned as much as I could about her — why she was always angry and suspicious and where her mean streak came from.

In a year, Gene and I decided to rent a larger farm. By that time, Mrs. Wackerly had mellowed slightly.

"I'll miss you," she said.

"I'll miss *you*, Mrs. Wackerly," I lied.

"June, dear, call me June," she said, a little too late.

I often think of that miserly, mean old biddy with humor now. At the time I found her in my life, I was a misfit, a California palm tree trying to grow at forty-three hundred feet in the raw high desert winters of Idaho. During our relationship, I discovered her secret. She was lonely and afraid. I was, too. For that reason, I actually welcomed her voice. I'm sure this puzzled her, and she tested me often. I could never bring myself to yell at her, because of what I'd discovered about her and what I was learning about myself.

ELLEN WATERSTON ❧ Spun Sugar

Whipped Jell-O salads astride red doilies
Next in line to pies sassy with rhubarb and berries,
Carefully tined with the maker's initials.
Squares of perfection in chocolate formation
Foolishly follow lace cookies and powdered sugar cookies
Off the edge of the platter.
The coffeepot's bubbling frenzy promises fresh brewed.
And beneath the artificial tree,
Handmade gifts equal to the number.

Years the women have gathered like this
For the Ladies' Club Christmas dinner,
Each driving frozen dirt miles,
Past winter's yellow stubble,

Christmas earrings swinging wildly,
Baubled glasses readjusted, looking forward

To talk, as they always do, of children and grandchildren,
The new divan, or a doublewide for the hired man;
Gingerly skirting all mention of damaged machinery,
Downed fence, missing cattle,
Or borrowed hearts — returned broken or lost forever.

Spun sugar,
A guarantee of friends for the future.
Miles and miles they've traveled together,
So wise, or so tired,
That different ways of doing things
Seems just plain too far to go —
Instead, taking solace in spun sugar
Again this year.

KAREN N. MILLER ☙ *Capes*

The scissors slice across the scarlet satin in whispered confirmation. We are making the capes, bringing months of talk to life in Beth's basement: I will become a *crone* in a ceremony planned for September 20. Meredith carefully pins the pattern to her cedar-scented white wedding sheet. Judy lays out new black satin. Beth, still firmly in the center of the *mother* phase of life, cuts the red for the cape I am eager to shed.

I was born on my paternal grandparents' homestead in Jones County, South Dakota, and there — close to the wind, earth, creeks, grasslands, and two- and four-legged animals we kept — grew to adulthood. I chose a city-based career but brought my family home to the farm for a month every year until finally returning to South Dakota in 1983. I see the farm as the home of my soul and the souls of my children.

Our foursome — Beth, Meredith, Judy, and I — began as a support group for women who run their own businesses, yet we rarely talked shop. Rather, as the years passed, we spoke of everything else, of marital and family events, personal goals, spiritual struggles. We came to know one another's stories in rich and wonderful detail. Beth and I both believe that our similar experiences in childhoods on the prairie gave us values we are especially anxious to pass on to family and friends. She, too, returns often to her childhood farm in North Dakota to renew her spirit.

Gradually, our women's group became aware that in our focus on career success, we had neglected some of our heritage as women. We began to cook for one another, to search bookstores for recipes, to decorate our tables into beautiful feasts for the eye and soul, to dig out our grandmothers' candlesticks and spoons, and to show off craft projects. We never missed a holiday, and we created festive, delicious birthday celebrations four times every year.

Slowly, we began to understand how we were creating ritual and how our attention to the details of our meetings provided times in which the four of us were sweetly and deeply nourished. We knew without research that we were tapping into ancient rhythms. As the oldest of the foursome, approaching retirement, I felt a need for something other than a public party with cakes and jokes about age. My friends had no hesitation when I asked if they would help me create a crone ceremony.

For a year, we devoted part of every gathering to planning the event. Judy offered her property deep in the sacred Black Hills we call home, and we decided to invite enough women to make a circle of twelve. A menu of fruits, nuts, and other whole foods plus red wine seemed to fit the harvest time of year and the coming stage of my life.

The capes, however, took both imagination and time. I wanted three: a white one for my girlhood years, a red one for the decades of motherhood and a business that required considerable caretaking, and a black one for the final stage of my life. Meredith suggested that the white and red capes have see-through plastic pockets in which I'd place photos and souvenirs of my first two life stages. I would pin everything — from cheerleading letters to locks of baby hair — to these capes and tell my story to the circle as I wore the red cape over the white one. Then I'd button the black cape over the red cape. Two friends — well into their seventies — would place it on my shoulders. Each woman would then pin to the black cape a symbol of her wish for my cronehood. My children and others special to me would be invited to send tokens. After the ritual, we would sing and feast and, best of all, visit.

As the scissors slice the satin, pictures of the day to come play through my mind. I feel comforted as these three friends, each a mover and shaker in our community, kneel on the floor to create capes in my honor. I find special symmetry in the fact we are using Meredith's old satin sheet to make the *virgin* cape. Laughter and chatter about pins, about using frogs for clasps, about buttons, flow around the room as we brush muffin crumbs from the fabric.

Soon we'll hug good-bye as we dash off to work, knowing we'll meet many more times to sew, type, and plan logistics. Yet these moments in the basement will live forever in my heart's eye as I recall the realization of a risky dream made possible through this connection among women.

DAWN SENIOR 🦌 Wyoming Mother

How did a lovely, willowy Georgia belle wind up chopping wood and hauling water at a Wyoming cabin surrounded by a thousand miles of sagebrush? She was nineteen in 1941, working the soda fountain at a Macon drugstore. In walked a lanky soldier-artist who'd just rented an attic room up the street to paint in while off duty. They met shortly before her birthday on June 26 and got married on July 15. She left the pecan groves and columned porches, and after the war and years of going with him everywhere — farmlands in the Northeast, desert mesas of Navajo and Hopi country, the Cotton Belt of Texas — they settled in Wyoming. Here she stood swaddled to the waist in drifts, shovel in hand, with elk and antelope and coyotes for neighbors.

Using horses, curved chisels, and lodgepole logs they hauled from the nearby forests, her husband and teenage son had built the cabin between a cedar mountain and a cottonwood draw. Her two older kids had gone off to college, and now the youngest tumbled laughing in the snow like an otter born to the river.

I was that ragged-pants, pigtailed kid, and growing up in a small cabin with a forever yard, you'd think a mother and daughter would get to know each other pretty well. We did, and yet even when I became an adult, my mother remained something of a mystery to me. How did one person give all that homey graciousness that made my friends exclaim, "I wish I had your mom!" How could that fund of helpful thoughts and deeds be so endless and easy for her when I had to think about it, struggle against myself, berate myself for not thinking of it sooner? Why did she worry so much that, even as a grown woman, I couldn't get out the door without her calling after me, "Aren't you going to wear your hat?"

I remember the day I was two and suckled at her breast for the last time. She'd explained to me that from now on I would drink from a glass. Sleepily, I studied the soft expression on her heart-shaped face with the widow's peak. She fondled my hand, and I felt her forefinger with the scarred tip and the twisted-down nail. The fuzzy brown birthmark on the underside of her forearm felt like a mouse. She crooned to me, "There once was a cowboy, who went out a-ridin' . . ."

When I was four, I stole the neighbor kids' rocking horse. Mother sat me on her lap and said, "Buntin', you mustn't steal things from people, because that makes them sad. Connie and Christy's grandpa made that rocking horse especially for them. He's passed away since, and it's important that they have something to remember him by. When they came home and saw their horse was gone, they cried." What greater gift can a mother give her child than the notion of looking at things from someone else's point of view? I never stole anything again.

I still smell grits, cracked eggs, and venison sausage frying on the wood range, their aromas mingling with pine smoke that billowed into the room as Mom thrust in another stick and banged the iron door shut against the wind-driven cloud. She gentled the knots from my tangled mane, gave me bandannas for my bandit chin, high heels for my princess feet, or dishtowel loincloths so I could run moccasined among the boulders with my bow and arrows. To ride with me, she ventured for the first time onto the back of our peppery bay, her voice quavering, "I'm on a moving mountain!" She walked with me in the spring mud when we followed cougar tracks down the creek. She dug worms to feed my baby robin, sacrificed her brother's gift of Georgia pecans so I could treat my squirrel. She not only tolerated porcupines underfoot, rabbits on the rocker, gophers in the sofa, broken-winged larks begging under the table, and baby hawks trying to nest on her head — she sometimes laughed in delight along with me.

I remember weariness in her face, her skin gray as the ashes Dad scooped from the grate.

I feel steam in my nostrils as I recall her squeezing hot, sour-smelling juice from chokecherries and throwing the pits outside for the chipmunks. I hear her squeals as I envision her skimming down the hill on my little sled, while deer stared, stamping, from the ridge top. I see her caught thigh deep in a badger hole, her face red, frowning and smiling at the same time, as she reached for Dad's extended hand.

I see her stumble into the cabin covered with snow and bits of hay from feeding the horse, tottering with two full water jugs, dropping them while Dad, flat on his back with pneumonia, staggered to his feet in time to catch her as she fainted.

She relieved my teenage blues by slowly unfolding her experiences, telling stories that made me see her — and myself — as a woman, a sensuous, thinking, radiant being. When I grumbled at my chores, she handed me a quote she'd copied from Goethe: "It is not doing what you like to do, but liking what you have to do, that makes life blessed."

For years I blocked from memory the time she had a bad reaction to a wrong prescription and locked herself in the bathroom with the razor blades. I heard Dad pounding on the door. "Aileen! Aileen!" He rushed into my room, grabbed me from my bed, and told me to call her. And I, without understanding, yelled, "Mom! Mom, what's going on?" She opened the door.

When I was twenty-five, I saw the glaze on Mother's eyes when the doctor said, "Mrs. Senior, we're sorry. Your husband has died."

One recent summer evening, Mom and I knelt on the sofa, our elbows resting on its soft brown back as we looked out the window at a double rainbow arcing across the eastern sky. Mother said, "Wyoming storms are so brief. Not like Georgia — they can last all night. Once when I was about fourteen, Aunt Doris and Uncle Mac wanted to go to a party. They asked me to baby-sit little Maryanne and Russell. We were at their house all alone when this terrible storm blew up. Lightning lit up the night; loud thunderclaps and big hail were just deafening. I could tell a tornado wasn't far away. Maryanne got so frightened she screamed and cried, but I held her in my arms. I took her and Russell to the safest room, and I held her, petted her, and comforted her till she fell asleep."

Mother turned to me, her smile ablaze with pride and triumph. "I felt like a hero!"

Startled, I looked at Mother with new eyes. All these years, I'd thought her generosity as much a simple fact of character as lichen on a boulder, her hard work and struggles natural as a beaver building a lodge. Now it occurred to me for the first time that perhaps she'd chosen this life and all her actions in it quite deliberately, because she wanted to be the hero of her family and all who knew her.

CANDY HAMILTON ✻ Women in the Rain

Anna Mae Pictou Aquash, a Micmac, was a respected leader in the American Indian Movement in the 1970s. She was killed in December 1975, and her body was found in March 1976. The FBI ordered the removal of her hands "for identification" at a later-discredited autopsy. Pictou's murderers and those who conspired with them have been identified but not prosecuted. Tina Manning Trudell also worked with the American Indian Movement and for improved conditions on her Owyhee Paiute Reservation in Nevada. She, her mother, and her four children died in a mysterious house fire in March 1978.

In Oglala, for Annie Mae

When we buried you
Snow weighed down the sky
with Creation's sorrow.
Wind shoved snow into your grave,
Dug by Lakota women, surrounded by women.
Spindly fingers of winter wrote danger in the snow,
And still the women came, in reservation war's danger,
Tears of fury raced tears of pain, for you who loved the rain.
We knew the FBI threats you heard,
And each woman saw herself in that grave.
The last threat to you:
A gun barrel to your head.
The last indignity:
Those who threaten slicing off your hands.

But not the last of you,
As always greed tried to devour life,
Yet your life flourishes from the grave
As all life flourishes in the rain.
We learn what the rain nourishes
And what the rain erodes.

In Owyhee, for Tina

On another day of keening wind
Full of sorrow's snow
We gather at another grave.
Commit three generations:
    Grandma
    Mom
    Three children
    A baby not yet of this world
From flame to frozen earth.
More children full of future's questions,
More women who protect the earth,
Women who teach us to live beyond survival,
Women remembered, especially in the rain.
This grave does not mark an ending —
Oh no!
Voices for future generations speak your words
As rain falls into the reservoir
You fought to save.

Annie Mae, Tina, Leah,
The children: Ricarda, Sunshine, Eli, Josiah,
Join Cherokee women on the Trail of Tears,
Cheyenne women at Sand Creek and the Washita,
Lakota women at Wounded Knee.
All comforted by the memorial of the rain
And the celebration of life it brings.

Dedicated anew to Angie and Ingrid, two more women
who protected the earth and are remembered in the rain.

DOROTHY BLACKCROW MACK
🐦 Belonging to the Black Crows

When I married into the Black Crow family on the Pine Ridge Reservation in 1977, I soon learned that it was more important to please my sister-in-law than my husband, Selo. In a traditional Lakota *tiyospaya*, or extended family, the matriarch holds the family together. So Catherine Prairie, the eldest of the Black Crow sisters, had the final say. Although Catherine was her legal name, on the reservation all the kids called her Obbi, and all the grownups called her Emma.

Once we arrived in Wanblee, Selo took me to meet Emma in her Lakota-speaking home. We wanted to live in her 1918 "Sioux Benefits" cabin at Camp Lakota out in the country and needed her permission. We planned to fence eight hundred acres of Black Crow land to raise a sacred herd of buffalo. I knew Emma approved of the buffalo herd, but not necessarily the White wife, so I was hesitant to meet her. She already called me *Winyan Tanka*, Selo said — Big Boss Woman.

Selo seemed reluctant to face Emma as well, barely entering the kitchen of her Bureau of Indian Affairs house. It was full of Indian women sitting around a big table, cutting up meat into long thin strips. At the stove, an older woman wearing a large work apron stirred a huge pot of *tanigha*, cow guts. Selo spoke rapidly in Lakota to her and then said to me, "This is my *tanke*, my big sister, Emma," and with barely a pause, said to her, "*Le mitaichu*, Dorothy." He grabbed the enamel coffeepot, poured himself a cup of coffee, waved, and joined the Black Crow men cutting firewood in the back yard.

Emma and I shook hands. Hers were strong and firm. She was hefty, not fat or tall, but broad-shouldered and formidable, like a chunk of iron. Yet her face was fine-boned, sharp and triangular, with deep-sunk eyes and vestiges of a once-beautiful profile. Wisps of black hair curled from beneath her purple headscarf. She didn't seem fifty-five.

Emma handed me a cup of strong black coffee. "*Shkepan*," she said, and switched to English. "Sister-in-law, welcome to Wanblee." She nodded toward the other women, cleared a place at the big kitchen table, and sat down across from me. The other women, ranging from twenty to forty, looked like sisters — long straight black hair parted in the center, high cheekbones, deep-set eyes, straight noses, full lips. They smiled at me but waited for Emma to speak.

"How many brothers you got?" Emma began by establishing relations, the opening of any Lakota conversation, and since I had no relations on the res, she would ask about my family.

"One," I replied.

She leaned forward, peering at me as if I might be ill. "Only one?"

I nodded, thinking of my brother three thousand miles away. He was six years younger than me and had grown up with a different set of friends. I'd last seen him four years ago. I asked in reply, "How many brothers do you have?"

"Four living." She paused. "And one dead, so you married the youngest. How many sisters you got?"

"None." I sipped the thick reboiled coffee I'd been given.

"None?" She glanced around the table at the other women.

It was a painful subject. I should have said, *None living, one dead*, but instead I said, "How many sisters do you have?"

"Eight living, five sitting right here," she said, nodding her head. "Leona, Agnes, Agatha, Betty Lou, and Rena Belle." She paused. "And two dead. How many cousins?"

"One."

Emma laughed. "Only *one? One* cousin?" Her sisters joined in the laughter.

"Jeez, imagine! Only one cousin!" said Rena Belle, the youngest, skinny in tight jeans. "I never met nobody with just one cousin!"

Emma ignored her, continuing her litany. "How many aunts?"

I began to get it. I said hesitantly, "One."

"Uh-huh." She nodded, her eyes wide. "And how many uncles?"

"One." I felt myself flushing, ashamed in spite of myself.

"*Un-shi-ka*," the six sisters murmured in unison, leaning on the "*oon*." I knew from the Lakota prayer *Creator, take pity on us*, that this word meant *pitiful*.

Coming from a nuclear family made me poor in relatives, but I had only now felt the loss. I had grown up as a loner, quite happy in my academic career. Now, depending on one's viewpoint, I was either self-sufficient and individualistic or self-centered and deprived.

Emma reached across the table and took my hand in her iron grip. "*Shkepan*, now you're a Black Crow, you got lotsa sisters." All the women nodded. Rena Belle laughed and said, "Lotsa brothers and cousins and aunties and uncles, too."

I — the outsider, the professor from the big university — sighed with relief. How lucky now to have eight sisters and five brothers! I smiled ruefully. Because I was *unshika*, pitiful without relatives, and practically an orphan, they would take me into the family. Emma would give us her cabin, and we could move in.

My relief was short-lived. Being taken in as a Black Crow made my life very difficult. I had to behave properly, because Black Crow honor was at stake. Thus began many tests.

In traditional Lakota society, men work with men, women with women.

I knew this, but our fence crew at Camp Lakota was so small that I pitched right in. At the university, I'd always worked with men. I heard that Emma didn't approve, but we had to finish the buffalo fence and get the sacred herd before the sun dance in August.

After a month, Emma moved out to Camp Lakota to reclaim her matriarchal role and run things properly. I was acquiring bad habits. I went to the outhouse alone rather than accompanied by another woman. I spoke Lakota using men's vocabulary, not women's. I watched the men's sweat lodge door flap and learned their sacred songs. The Black Crows could get a bad reputation.

Worse yet, I was starving the men. Emma took over the cooking, serving traditional foods with generous portions. I was removed from the fence crew to help her. Each day became a test.

Gather Indian food. Dig wild turnips when the tassel turns blue; use the stems to braid them into long strands to dry. Pick chokecherries when they turn black; grind them fine and make patties to dry. Don't squish the buffalo berries; watch out for the thorns. Boil and can them, and wild plums, too, for berry pudding. Pick only male sage for the sweat lodge, only female sage for women's tea. Most of all, don't be greedy — don't pick them all, and leave an offering.

Butcher with a sharp knife and save all the parts: heart, lungs, kidneys, liver, even hooves. Wash the stinky cow guts clean for soup. Slice the hindquarters into long thin slices and hang to dry. Later pound the dry meat into fine flakes for *wasna* balls. Boil prairie dogs four times to make them tender.

Cook Indian food: fry bread, *kabuk* (pan bread), *tanigha* (cow guts), *wozhapi* (berry pudding), and even *shunka wahanpi* (puppy soup) for doctoring ceremonies. Serve big helpings, not stingy ones.

From Emma's frowning silence, it seemed that I could do nothing right. My fry bread was too small and hard, my dry meat full of holes. Yet as she kept after me with her iron will, I passed test after test. I learned to keep quiet, watch and listen, and laugh at my mistakes.

One day all the other Black Crow women came out from town to take sweat. I ran to get ready, bringing my towel and an armful of freshly picked sage. Emma stared at me, scandalized. "Wrap yourself in a blanket, not just a towel like the men!" While the women scattered the sage around the sweat lodge floor, I found an old blanket and wrapped myself head to foot. Emma, satisfied at last, told me that since it was my first sweat, I should go in last. That way I could follow what everyone else did.

I felt at home inside, as if I were in Mother Earth's womb. I loved the darkness, the smell of crushed sage, the steam rising from the hot rocks. I recognized the sacred songs I'd learned from the men's sweat, so I sang loudly in Lakota to help out.

Emma stopped singing.

"What's wrong?" I asked.

"*Shkepan*, you're singing like a man," she said. "You end everything like a man, with an *o*, instead of like a woman, with an *e*. I bet you sing the men's songs, too."

I didn't say anything. I loved the sweat lodge songs, and my favorites probably belonged to the men. So when Emma began a song that was familiar, I joined in quietly, making sure my endings were *e*.

After the steam filled us and we prayed to the Great Mystery, Emma opened the door flap. In the men's sweats, as cool air rushed in, they would pass around a metal dipper full of drinking water. But Emma had no metal dipper. Instead, she dipped a branch of sage in the water bucket and handed it across to me sitting at the door. I took the dripping branch. Somehow, by coming in last, I had become first. In the steamy dark space, I hesitated and looked across at Emma.

"Take some and pass it on," she said in English. I knew that when people went on a vision quest and fasted, they often chewed a bit of sage to lessen their thirst. So I took the sage tip in my mouth and bit off a piece to chew.

The sweat lodge full of Black Crow women fell silent. No one moved. What had I done? I sat stiffly, wanting to disappear. Finally, Emma laughed.

"*Shkepan*," she said in English, "you sure are a greedy *washichu*."

I didn't get it. I knew that *washichu*, as well as meaning "white person," also meant "takes-the-fat," or "greedy." But what had I done wrong?

"You're supposed to lick off the drops of water," she continued, "not take the whole sage and eat it!"

I choked on my mouthful of sage. No way I could put it back. A terrible faux pas. No word for "sorry" in Lakota. Nothing else to do but join in. I laughed, too.

All the other sisters joined in, dissolving the tension. We laughed and laughed together until our sides hurt and the whole sweat lodge rocked.

"Well, *Shkepan*, you'll be getting a new name now." Emma grinned. "*Peji Hota Yaksa.*"

The sisters began a new round of laughter. I joined in, certain that my new Indian name was better than Big Boss Woman. How fortunate that I'd been able to laugh at myself and stay humble.

Afterward, when I checked in my Lakota dictionary, I knew that from now on my Black Crow sisters would laugh with me, not against me. They would no longer tease me behind my back but to my face — in that open, joshing way. I would hear Emma repeat the greedy-sweat story over and over in Lakota, delight on her face at each retelling. Sure enough, before the day was over, my husband grinned and let me know that my new Indian name was Bites-the-Sage.

♦ ♦ ♦

After the summer powwows and Indian rodeos and Rosebud Fair, in the winter Emma taught me to bead moccasins and sew star quilts. Quilting homes on the res always had four hooks embedded in the living room ceiling, spaced so the quilt frame could be lowered on ropes. We Black Crow women would gather together and sew all night before a giveaway. We'd tell stories and gossip and laugh — and finish quickly, two at each end racing to the center, so we could eat.

One day Emma discovered I had an unusual talent. Emma always took me along to wakes and funerals, sometimes held in school gymnasiums or church basements, sometimes in people's homes. This time we'd gone over to a Potato Creek home for an old lady's wake. She'd been known for her spectacularly beautiful quilts. Over the coffin, propped up on straight chairs in the living room, hung a star quilt emblazoned with an eagle descending from rainbow skies. We all sat admiring it.

"Can you memorize it?" Emma whispered in my ear. "The design?"

"Sure," I whispered back. "Just let me draw it on the back of the funeral card."

"No, no," she whispered in alarm. "You can't draw at a wake. It's not respectful of the dead." She paused. "Besides, that would be stealing. But can you *memorize* it in your head?"

"Sure," I repeated. At wakes we sat up the whole night, out of respect. As we drove home in the morning after breakfast, I drew it on the back of a napkin and handed it to Emma.

"Ah," said the sisters, peering forward from the rear seat. "She got it, without stealing."

Suddenly, I was in demand. My Black Crow sisters dragged me all over South Dakota to wakes and funerals to memorize quilt designs. Stars, stars, stars. All of nature reshaped into the eight-pointed lone star pattern: spread eagles, descending eagles, red-tailed hawks, thunderbirds. Tipis, crossed peace pipes, war bonnets. American flags, Stars and Stripes, End of the Trail.

How I loved to find names for new quilt designs. Names were half the fun. "Now this one's a Coney-Island-Ferris-Wheel," I'd tell Emma, "but this is a Fox-Sneaking-into-the-Tipi." I would watch her giggle like a girl at my fancy. But she was also laughing at my white cultural trait to *name* everything, as if by naming we can pin it down, make it real. I was laughing at myself, too, taking delight in ridiculous names. But no one else among the Black Crow women felt it necessary to name a design; sufficient to call it Emma's.

Under Emma's influence, I began designing buffalo star quilts, then others based on personal Indian names such as Red Horse Woman and White Magpie. Gradually, I became a valuable, creative quilt maker. But I was never in Emma's class. Like a Mondrian or Stella, she had become bored with recognizable images. She experimented with extended-leg and mirror-image stars but remained unsatisfied. Abstract geometries filled her dreams. So Emma, without a compass, began inventing pure sunbursts and novas, pulsating stars with contrasting colors. I named the whole phenomenon Reservation Op Art.

Emma was never a quitter, but one day her heart quit. Matriarch Emma Black Crow Prairie died in 1988. She'd made me a memorizer of stars, so during that year of mourning, I struggled to sew quilts based on her complex geometric designs. And one year later, when we Black Crows celebrated her memorial dinner, I gave away twelve Op Art star quilts in her honor. Black Crow honor. Generosity, creativity, tradition. A fitting end to a tough and tender kinship.

SUE LEEVER ❧ Pink Iron Nails

Dear Auntie Ruth,

One of my favorite gifts from you is the narrow mirror, still in its original wood frame. The gilt and nickel are faded now, but not your picture inserted above the glass. You're dressed in men's tweed knickers, tall wool socks, and your Cheney Normal letter sweater. A rifle rests on your hip, and you're standing in the snowy west pasture in front of Steptoe Butte near Garfield, Washington. Both you and the family Saint Bernard, Jack, are looking directly at the camera. As you so often did, you copied a poem on the bottom of the black-and-white photo:

> Look for goodness, look for gladness;
>   You will meet them all the while.
> If you bring a smiling visage
>   To the glass, you meet a smile.
>   — Alice Cary

I never saw you with a frown.

Somewhere in our family lore, I learned that Great-Grandma Ida regularly took you to the poplar grove for prayers, and more often when Grandpa Vincil was in France during World War I. I love what Ida instilled in you — that matters of the spirit do not only come from church on Sunday.

We never talked about how you lost your leg, but Mom shared her recollection with me. She said you were only thirty-one when they cut it off below the knee. Was that 1934? While you were rounding up sheep on horseback with your husband, Jim, a wild summer storm rolled across the open Palouse country. Your favorite horse, Peggy, spooked at a thunderclap just as you urged her to jump a barbed wire fence. She threw you into the fence. Your leg twisted in the wire, mangling it. Horrifying! You lay there alone, in a downpour, tortured by the wire, in agonizing pain, while Jim rode for help. Forty years later, Grandma Kloma told me that you decided right then and there you had another perfectly good leg and if you had to make do without one, so be it. Get on with it.

I love the names you gave things, living and inanimate alike. Do you remember Dolly Dimple, Duckie Doodle, and Dickie Dandy the geese, and Roosevelt the cat? Your wooden leg was Mehitabel, nicknamed Hittie. Hittie was your constant companion, who gave you full mobility so you could dance, hike, and ride the beloved Peggy again. But I daresay your iron will and sense of humor had as much to do with it as Hittie.

Aunt Anne said it was only two years after the accident that your Jim died, at thirty-six. As she remembers it, he went out to the barn one night to finish the evening chores before dinner. She said you were engrossed in a new issue of the *Literary Digest* while supper was cooking. Realizing that Jim should have been back in the house for dinner, you went to check on him in the barn. There he was, pierced through the neck with a pitchfork. He either fainted or had a heart attack, the doctor said, and fell onto the tines of the fork he was carrying. You must have been devastated, but Aunt Anne doesn't remember you talking about it. With characteristic strength, you got on with it.

For fifteen years, you managed on your own until you met and married Don Knight, the great-uncle I remember. After World War II, you and Don returned to the farm life you both loved, but the county asked you to stay on as a substitute teacher. And so you did. Like me, you never bore any children. You and I never discussed it, but I wish we had. I wonder how you felt about that. What I tell myself is that it wasn't meant to be, and I'm at peace. You and I chose another way to create, give birth, and leave something of ourselves behind: writing.

I love the details of life at the old ranch that you wrote in your family story, *The Tale of Grandmother's Sewing Machine* — how your grandmother's Civil War era Singer sewing machine made the wagon train journey from Missouri to the plains of eastern Washington. Amazing that you sewed with the same machine in 1944 to make clothing for amputees in the Walla Walla Veterans Hospital while you were a Red Cross Gray Lady! I imagine that your sunny disposition and generosity of spirit helped immeasurably with their healing.

You always found ways to bring charm and joy to life. Did you know the name Ruth means "friend of beauty"? Pretty darned fitting, I'd say. Your oil painting called *October Gold* hangs above my bedroom dresser, and each day it encourages me on my own creative quest.

Mom recently gave me a pair of white linen pillowcases that you gave her. The embroidery stitches are incredibly tight and fine. I want you to know those pillowcases are not hidden away in my linen closet. I love how cool they feel next to my cheek on a stuffy August night.

I keep another pillow on my bed that came from you. You made it from an old quilt top that you stitched to a solid pink back. Pink reminds me of you. I remember your pink calico dishes by Johnson Brothers, and I still have the round ceramic trinket box you made for me in 1979. It's topped with roses that you painted pink, and you lined it with pink velvet from Great-Grandma Ida's 1900 scrap bag.

Let's not forget the nails. When the hundred-year-old barn on the homestead had to be torn down before it fell, you had the foresight to save some of the barn wood and many of the hand-wrought iron nails. Thank you for sending me that bit of family history. I still have the nails in the plastic pin box in which you mailed them, and they are still wrapped in the linen hankie — pink, of course — that you used for padding.

You may have had your teaching certificate from Cheney Normal, but what our family learned from you has nothing to do with textbook educa-tion. We learned perseverance in the face of difficulty. You taught us how to make something out of nothing — and, just as important, how to make nothing out of something. You have inspired me to embrace my own cre-ativity. You are as tough as those old nails, but also as soft as pink. The two can coexist peacefully.

Mom has a piece of the Lemon homestead barn wood hanging on her kitchen wall. On it you painted a lemon tree with these words: "When Life Gives You Lemons, Make Lemonade." You certainly lived that motto long before it appeared on a commercial greeting card.

Thank you for all these gifts and more.

With love,
Sue

Ruth LaBounty Lemon McLarry Knight died in 1989 at the age of eighty-six. She was preceded in death by Hittie.

CAROLYN DUFURRENA 🦌 Ghost of April, 1978

Pioche motel,
Formica shelves and orange velour bedspreads
Sticky plastic on the back side.
End of a long drive, spitting rain from Denver.

Copper veins the ridge
Behind the old mining town.

Next morning I climb,
Most of the way up, through sage and stunted juniper
New boots stiff and cold

To a smooth blond ledge in the blustery dawn.
There, a woman's fur coat, black karakul lamb,
As though she had shrugged out of it
Watching the moon last night.
The wool curls brittle, satin lining crumbling into dust,
Its only perfume juniper and thunderstorm.

One black velvet pump
Little silver buckle
Been there maybe forty years?
I set my boot beside it.
Her feet were smaller.

I sit on the cold stone next to her coat.
It is a big valley we look across,
Big and gray in the stormy spring morning.

You must have been
Drunk
Or crazy or in love

To climb up here in those shoes
It would have felt so good to take them off
In the cold limestone sand.

It's not so far from Vegas, a wild night
A romp in the sagebrush,
The realization that you can't go back
To some drunk boyfriend
Or your lockstep life
Waiting for you in that airless pink motel
A half mile down the hill.

You stood,
Raised your hands to the desert sky.
Shimmering in the moonlight,
Rose
Into your future.

I left your coat there when I went down.

DIANNA TORSON 🦎 Joan

we sat in the sun
naked
and stayed for the clouds
letting the sad
sensuous
secrets
riding the coming storm
lick our skin and
seduce our souls

it's hard to be friends with a pecker
you said . . .

but i do enjoy a beer at noon
on a hot day in november
when confused bees hover
around my door

and i did enjoy "wasting time"
in stub's tavern in genesee
rolling pisqueenie squash cigarettes

and i feel enriched by the children
i have

you're right
it's hard to be friends with a pecker
i said . . .

MARY HARMAN 🦎 Some Things Never Change

It was a perfect day to be on the river. The spray from the last wave still glistened on our faces, lingering long enough to make us shiver even while the sun began to bake us once again. Briefly, Carla's eye caught mine, and we exchanged knowing smiles, both of us already anticipating the next stretch of white water. Several minutes later, my daughter Shelly let out a shrill whoop as her dad skillfully guided the raft straight into a standing wave, drenching both her and her sister. Laughing and shivering, the two of them let out squeals of delight as he spun the raft around just in time for those of us riding in the back to suffer a similar jolt of cold, wet reality. Staying relatively dry on his perch at the oars, Sam's smug look of superiority at having successfully drenched us all soon disappeared as Shelly quietly filled the bailing bucket from the bottom of the raft and unceremoniously dumped it over his head.

Sam's reflexive gasp for air, just as a calm stretch of water appeared before us, signaled the beginning of the day's first water fight. A few minutes of screaming and laughing, water flying everywhere, and it was all over, revenge quickly giving way to common sense.

At precisely "ten to," Sam oared the raft toward a sheltered embankment, and Kim jumped out into knee-deep water to pull us from the current and into shore. As in a well-directed play, each of us immediately went about the business of breaking for lunch. Sam tied the raft off to a large fallen log; Carla and Bud collected life jackets and assorted items of wet clothing, which they laid out on rocks and draped over surrounding willows to dry in the sun. Kim retrieved a bottle of sun block and her camera from one of the dry boxes, while Shelly and I opened coolers and began laying out the makings for sandwiches. We were all starving, and lunch, along with a chance to dry out and warm up a little, was wonderful.

Satisfied and relatively dry, Shelly and I lounged on the raft's warm tubes, while Carla and Sam stretched out on small patches of grass near the water's edge. Kim and Bud wandered off, then came back and joined the rest of us in doing absolutely nothing. After a while, one by one, we slowly began to move — putting things away, collecting life jackets, checking equipment — each of us anticipating the next turn in the river.

It was Kim's twentieth birthday. When her dad had asked her what she wanted, she's replied, "I want an overnight river trip, and I want Mom to come." Sam and I had been divorced for three years after a marriage that had lasted for twenty. By then he and Carla had already been lovers for at least fifteen — yeah, I've done the math. And it was by no means the first time we'd all been on the river together, although Bud, Kim's fiancé, was a relative newcomer.

Sam and Carla had met when she began teaching at the same elementary school where he was a third-grade teacher. They seemed to hit it off immediately, frequently attending the same conferences, going skiing on the weekends with the same group, and eventually even going to garage sales together on Saturday mornings. I was very much a stay-at-home mom, but on those rare occasions when I ventured into the social world, somehow Carla was always there. Even that one ski vacation we took as a family, all the way to Silver Creek — she somehow managed to be there.

In the summers, Sam and I operated a white-water rafting business, a pursuit in which Carla suddenly developed a keen interest. Now that I think about it, Carla and I have a lot of similar interests, which, it turns out, was unfortunate for me.

I've never known how it all began — I mean, who seduced whom — and I don't suppose it really matters. I found out years later that students of theirs actually thought they were married. It doesn't take a genius to figure out what kind of vibes they must have been giving off — we're talking third-graders here. The fact is, they were a couple, and they behaved like one. There's no denying it.

I wasn't oblivious. Even though I had no proof, I knew. I even confronted Sam on a number of occasions, only to be treated to protestations declaring his innocence: "Who, me? How could you think such a thing?" Every time I got brave enough to bring it up, he managed to make me feel guilty for daring to make such an outlandish accusation. Sam's a charmer, and I was always easily charmed.

So, anyway, here we were again — all of us, on the river, and it was a perfect day.

We had launched that morning at exactly "ten to" (no matter what time you actually put your raft on the water, it's always exactly ten to). Not surprisingly, lunch was also taken at ten to, and as we headed toward the riverbank at the end of that day, we all knew it had to be exactly . . . ten to. That's what being on the river is all about — never knowing what time it is and not really caring. Not *having* to care — that's the real essence of a river trip.

As though we'd practiced it many times — and in reality we had — everyone set about unloading all the gear, dragging the raft up on the bank, and then flipping it over like a great beached whale. Less than an hour later, coolers had been arranged for cooking and sitting, two tents had been set up, and a fire crackled within a large circle of rocks. Everyone changed into dry clothing, and that timeless ritual of cooking dinner over an open fire began.

There were enough jobs for everyone, and everyone seemed to know his or hers without being told. Wine and conversation flowed freely. With everyone pitching in, even the cleanup afterward seemed effortless. Then twenty burning candles decorating a pan of brownies lit up the face of the birthday girl, and we all joined in singing "Happy Birthday" to our dear Kim.

For a dysfunctional family, we were looking pretty damn functional.

Finally, as the stars got brighter in the night sky and the tip of the Big Dipper pricked the horizon, Shelly announced, "I'm tired. Where's everybody sleeping?" Keeping things light, I replied, "Well, I don't care, but I'm not sleeping with Sam." Without hesitation, Carla chimed in, "Well, neither am I." We all had a good laugh, admittedly at his expense, and then headed for bed — Carla, Shelly, and I in one tent, and Sam, Bud, and Kim in the other.

Snuggled in my sleeping bag, waiting for sleep, I considered the woman lying next to me. I'd often wondered whether we might have become friends had the circumstances been different — two strong, intelligent, outdoorsy, educated, environmentally conscious, self-reliant, dog-loving women. (We'd joked that night that if we'd all brought our dogs along, there'd have been more dogs than people.) We probably would have been friends, I thought, even though Carla, with her smoky sultry voice, is everything I could never be. I've often seen Carla engage total strangers in deep conversation within minutes of their meeting. She's outgoing, laid-back, and gregarious. She can be somewhat promiscuous, practically oozing sex appeal, and is always easy to be with. Carla, I decided, was the anti-Mary.

Somehow I believed our similarities would have been enough to span our differences; would have, in fact, given us cause to explore and celebrate our differences. But instinctively I knew there was one difference that could never be mitigated, could not be forgotten — my children, Sam's children. Carla had never had babies, had no idea, really, what it was all about. And the hard truth is, nothing — no amount of sophistication, education, or intelligence — can ever approach or substitute for the experience of being a parent. This was the one reason we would always be on opposite sides of the universe.

It wasn't so much that our children formed a bond between Sam and me as it was that no such bond would ever exist between Sam and Carla. Although I'd tried to be generous with all of them, generosity wasn't enough. Odd, I thought, as I drifted into sleep, how so often things are not as they seem.

The morning sun rose in a cloudless sky, bringing the first rays of warmth since last night's campfire. As we went about packing and loading the equipment for our second day on the river, I listened to the easy banter between Kim and Carla. They teased and laughed, exchanging light-hearted jabs, challenging each other's daring in the day ahead. Whom would the river gods bless as we tested ourselves against the elements?

I couldn't help noticing how Carla and Sam, in their inexplicable way, acknowledged each other amid the preparation and anticipation — a slight touch, a half smile, a shared glance. Witnessing this familiar exchange was much easier that morning than it had been years before. Now it was merely the natural expression of their closeness, not a bad thing.

We put on the river that morning at ten to, right on time. It wasn't long before we began to feel the welcome heat of a naked sun, and once again the river exceeded our expectations.

MARY LOU SANELLI ✺ Marriage

Fifteen minutes into my morning routine —
the phone rings. Outside, spring blooms sag under rain,
which brings to mind moments of pure joy
I once felt looking out on a garden
I planted in soil so lush and wormy
awe spread through me like electrical current.

Everything changes. Either by winding down
or snaring abruptly. Now, with so much to weed
I'd rather write.

My friend phones to say her husband left her
for a tango dancer with cushion-size breasts. A slap
bores through the buried cable connecting us.
I actually put my hand to my stricken cheek.
I don't know why I'm terrified
as I totter to the couch.

When she arrives, her eyes are reddened by heartache,
and I think I've never seen her like this, not as strong
but more honest with herself and with me. Until now
we've not been close enough to let down.
This infidelity is our first shared setting for grief.

The cat's water bowl is full of ash
fallen from the mill stack, a solid pillar
of asbestos-covered brick no one talks about.
As if shopping at the co-op and eating organic
makes our air clean, makes the odorless gas overhead
breathable. I wipe out the bowl, remember
hearing my cat's sex life last night.
A hiss and growl — the irreverent act.

My friend tries to understand cruelty.
Her eyes fill. Her body
bends toward me, toward a bond
that bears up to this deceit. Then my husband cries,
and the whole room is at half-mast.

I bypass this moist emotion. Head straight for anger.
There isn't enough anger these days. Too often
we call it something else.

SUREVA TOWLER ❧ Up Fortification Creek

A friend is, as it were, a second self. — Cicero

Best friends are hard to come by. They are created as much by chance as by choice. They know your habits, temperament, and foibles, and they accept the whole package. Nothing plays on the relationship. No jealousy. No demands. No guilt. Nurturing them takes time, energy, and lots of chocolate. Losing them is not easy, and replacing them may be impossible.

Amy and I spent forty years together. That's longer than most marriages last. Longer than children remain at home. I decided Amy was OK in fourth grade when she whipped out a water gun and, while Mrs. McPherson had her back to the class, aimed a stream of water at the blackboard. Mrs. McPherson was thin as a stick figure and missing certain body parts, like shoulders and hips, so the shot easily cleared her left ear and dissolved the day's algebra problems. The fractions vanished in a stream of water. Mrs. McPherson disappeared into the principal's office. Amy set the class free, if only temporarily. My kind of girl.

We shared birthdays, anniversaries, adventures: picking up guys at Gilley's, hitchhiking through Mexico, getting tattoos in New Orleans. When we weren't chatting over coffee or cooking sherry, we talked on the phone. We ordered satin sheets from Frederick's of Hollywood to help save failing marriages. We scrubbed each other's kitchen floors and entertained each other's mothers. Our husbands called us "the girls," as if we were an institution. We were joined at the hip.

Our children were grown when the call came: Amy had ovarian cancer. First I cleaned the stove, and then I called the therapist. She said time would help. She was wrong. Amy said not to worry, she'd lick it. She was wrong, too. She died six months later. We buried her at her family homestead on Fortification Creek because she wanted to be someplace, not ashes scattered about a wilderness.

Amy was a Currier & Ives print. She gave them for presents, and she lived them. On Thanksgiving she made sweet potatoes topped with marshmallows, whether you liked them or not. At Christmas she decorated the tree with strands of popcorn and cranberries. She masterminded summer at the beach. She organized "ladies' day out" trips to Sam's Club for groceries or to picnic at a remote lake. She told us where to be and when and what to bring. She rallied the troops, which, more often than not, included dogs, horses, raccoons, monkeys, and people you'd never seen before. And always children.

Amy devoted her life to growing children and flowers. She loved children, anyone's children, and she had an uncanny way of knowing what they needed, whether it was a hearing test, a new book, or a time-out. Just like her garden. She knew what to plant where so there would be life and color everywhere.

She made a million double-baked potatoes and fed our souls. She polished the family silver and made our lives shine. She taught us how to take little naps and make broccoli the kids actually liked. Amy told us when we were "screwing up" and when we "had it all together." And she was pretty near always right.

I've buried grandparents, parents, sisters, and two husbands. Burying a best friend, a real friend, is entirely different. It's more than losing a playmate, soul mate, comrade, and support system. It's an amputation. Part of me was gone. I felt cut loose from the past. No one else remembered people and places and events the way I did, or the way I wanted them to be. There was no one else who could predict how I was going to react, who could complete my sentences.

Best friends see things differently. They know how hard it is to be a wife and mother, mistress and maid, secretary and manager. They know what you mean when you talk about the past and the future. They know why you go to Weight Watchers and why you refuse to drive a minivan. Amy knew why I hated my mom, and I knew she couldn't balance a checkbook. She knew whom I slept with; I knew she drank too much. She loaned me money for groceries when I was poor; I loaned her clothes when she was poor. She remembered my first husband, liked him better than I ever did.

It took months to realize that Amy was gone. I was in a department store dressing room, and no one told me to take off the green one, forgodsake, it makes you look like a musk ox. Suddenly, I knew she was not going to call for my wheat salad recipe. Bring me vegetables from her garden. Make me go to concerts I hate. Tell me not to worry because my daughter isn't going to get AIDS and my teenage son isn't going to total the car. Never again drop everything to do whatever I need done. Listen to me try to figure out what I really think, whether it matters or not and whether she believes it or not. Assure me that I'm not crazy.

Parents die. Husbands stray. Children are supposed to grow up and move away. Your best friend is supposed to be forever. Camaraderie is not contingent on parental expectations or approval. The relationship is not complicated by a blood tie, baggage from childhood, or sibling rivalry. Best friends are there so you never have to explain yourself. They are not defined by your parents, who come with expectations that you may or may not share; by your kids, who think you were put on the earth to serve them; by your husband, who does not have a clue what it takes to keep a man happy and a household running.

It has been two years since Amy died. I still think of her every day. Sometimes I get angry because she left me. I let the macaroni boil over on the stove, walk the dog, drink Irish Cream. Sometimes I look in the mirror and see my mother, and it pisses me off. I see my husband, and it is irritating. But most often I see the fractions in an algebra problem disappearing under a stream of water on that fourth-grade blackboard, and it makes me think of Amy, because she taught me how to grab the moment and turn it into a smile.

BARBARA RINEHARDT ❧ Divas for a Day

Lilac wine washed down dry summer throats
Sea green Buick on a country road
Blues à la Emmy Lou
Blastin' that old radio

Ah, friend, that was a party
Life pursued us lavishly
Without regret
Renamed us High Noon Hayseed Goddesses

I still recall our fearless youth
And laughing challenges for life
Each moment cherished for its gift
Licked clean of all it had to bring

Whole plates of tempting memories
Tickle spasms of laughter
From the quietude
That steals across today

Your face
Struggling for some discipline
The fun just runnin' out your fingertips
To that acoustic guitar

Our voices raised
In harmonies smooth enough for Broadway
Shaped music for the night
Made us divas for a day

Then, with no time left
But that for dreaming
We checked the stars
For good reports

And finding
Some encouragement
Woke up again
And plotted how to make the day a party

SHARON R. BRYANT 🐾 Dear Berry

You are in my thoughts a lot. Your twenty-first birthday was March 21. This year it fell on the first day of spring — how fitting! Remembering how much you enjoyed birthday parties, I just had to jot a few lines in honor of this special occasion.

Can it be over two years since we last hugged and went our own directions? You off to college, me staying behind in the ol' hometown. Phone calls and letters were such a treat! The fun activities, old and new friends, the guys you met, and even the challenges of a difficult "roomie," tough classes, and, as always, social problems of the "young and restless."

The door to your future opened, and you eagerly stepped across that threshold, embracing life and the opportunities that lay ahead. I was so excited and happy for you, but I digress . . . My mission is to meander memory lane with you. We do go back a long way, you know!

I miss the special friendship we shared for so many years. I still have that little note you printed — about second grade, I think. "You are my best friend." I tucked it away, knowing that our relationship would be tested many times and in many ways over the years, but knowing it would come full circle — eventually.

Know what I liked best about you, Berry? You were so resilient, bouncing back from all kinds of adversity. Yup, your "feel-bads" were bruised when life bucked you off, but you got back in the saddle and rode on, a smile lighting your face, wind and motion giving fluidity to that thick beautiful hair, voice lifted in laughter or song. My mind captured those images in a way no camera could. "Tuesday's child is full of grace" — and you were. Even then, you were somehow bigger than life.

Funny how the roughest times are usually worth a laugh or two after the fact. Remember when you were going to run away from home and walk to your grandma and grandpa's out in the country? Arms full of clothes, you finally began the journey at dusk, after long contemplation on the back steps. Teenagers down the block asked where you were going with your stuff. You explained. They suggested that you wait 'til morning; it was getting dark.

You packed your things many times after that: sleepovers with family or friends, then 4-H, dance, and school activity trips to many destinations. You loved to go places — with people!

Remember the summer you visited California with family friends? You had such a wonderful time that your future plans included living there. The sun, ocean, and fast pace appealed to your free spirit. In the many times away from home, I never knew you to be homesick. Were you ever? However, home and family meant a lot to you. Was this the sign of a big and happy heart?

You once labeled yourself a pessimist in a written school assignment. Yet the completed work showed just the opposite. The optimism and encouragement for social change to create "The Good Life," as you saw it, was underscored with the acceptance and tolerance of others that you exemplified in your own life.

Have I forgotten the third- and fourth-grade "girl spats," which were still legend years later? Absolutely not! But we learned from them, didn't we? You and I had our quarrels and disputes, too. Fightin' and fussin' weren't in your nature, though. You were quick to patch things up so everyone could move on to the fun things in life. Who couldn't at least grudgingly admire you for that, whatever your other faults may have been?

I miss those days we shared as we grew up, ever closer, yet moving farther apart. We shared confidences, assessed people and problems, and kept our eyes looking forward. The bittersweet past was a solid meal from which we were nourished and grew. "Dessert" was about to be served. What anticipation!

Then you were gone. Separated by space and time and, finally, eternity ... A month into your dream world of college and career, you were brought home. An empty, battered shell to compare with emotional and paper pictures of effervescence and promise — so full of life!

Your college English assignment became the front page of the funeral program: "A Beholden Day in Paradise." A prophetic piece, it painted a vivid watercolor of a childhood journey to the ocean and back, through the eyes of a maturing young woman. Yes, you did return to the Wild West of Wyoming ...

The victim of a cruel, vicious rape and murder, your blood soaked into the sand and clay of a dark, desolate depression in the prairie. It nourished the sage and native grasses, which in turn nourished the winged and legged wild creatures you admired. Your tears surely watered the wildflowers, which bloom only when there is moisture ...

That freed spirit dances with whirlwinds moving across the vast plains, soars with the raptors over peaks, and glides into valleys below. Songbirds echo your voice, brooks trickle your laugh, tumbling over mossy pebbles. Emerald and golden leaves speak for you as they rustle restlessly.

Your screaming rage is the howl of the wind; his soul is damned in the rumble of thunder. Lightning strikes through his evil heart. The rain of your tears cleanses our wounds, renewing life once more.

Your gentle peace is the face of a garden rose, the sunshine of a mountain meadow. Reborn in new kittens, puppies, calves, colts, lambs — bunnies, too — your spirit is running, bouncing, frisking as you once did. You believed in ghosts. I do, too. Berry, you are everywhere . . . and nowhere.

Lost to so many who loved you so much, out of sight in deep pools and canyon shadows. Touching so many lives in your too-short time. Perhaps quality is to be cherished over quantity. I'm still pondering that . . .

Happy twenty-first birthday, Berry, my best friend — and daughter.

Love,
Mom

WANDA MORGAN ❧ Friends for Life

"Keep dancing," Kathleen hissed. I watched in horror as my beautiful hat spun across the stage, landing on top of the footlights. As we went into our buck and wing, Kathleen grabbed my hand; this gesture was not rehearsed, but she clung tightly. My partner knew I was likely to panic and bolt off the stage, wet my panties, or do something stupid to disgrace Miss Rucker's dance review at the Grand Theater in Douglas, Arizona. The Rockettes we weren't.

Kathleen and I met in the first grade, discovered we had the same birth date — March 25, 1927 — and became friends for life. Kathleen's father, Floyd Biava, worked at the Phelps Dodge smelter dominating Douglas, on the border of Sonora, Old Mexico. Her mother, Emily, was a housewife who had fashioned our dance costumes, including blue satin picture hats. My father was a barber, and my mother was always eager to add to the family income. When I met Kathleen, we lived in a tiny cottage near the airport, where Mom raised turkeys and chickens, sold eggs to the neighbors, and baked pies for a local restaurant.

When times were better, we moved into town, around the corner from the Biavas. Between their back yard and ours was the Mortensons', all three yards simply desert raked clean. My brother, a born leader in devious enterprises — later known as an entrepreneur — thought we should while away the summer hours digging a tunnel from our yard to the Biavas'. Durald knew how to delegate. While he sat in the shade with a glass of Kool-Aid, Kathleen and I took turns digging. The loose desert sand quickly turned into hardpan, or caliche. We didn't go very deep, but we managed to wiggle into the resulting excavation and ladle out coffee cans of dirt until we had a sizable hole straight down. Then we began to tunnel under the ocotillo fence. After a couple of weeks of hard labor, Kathleen and I had tunneled a short distance under the Mortensons' driveway. One evening when Mr. Mortenson drove his Model A into the back yard, the front wheel carriage disappeared into the cave-in with a clash and a clatter.

Punishment was swift and painful — spankings and restriction. After Mr. Mortenson's first fit of anger, being the good Mormon he was, he put in a good word for us. "Kids will be kids. Just put away their shovels." When our mothers eventually relented, Kathleen and I tucked our dresses into our bloomers and did cartwheels, or tumbled head over teakettle on our neighbor's iron rail fence. Inevitably, some vulgar boy called, "I see London, I see France, I see someone's underpants." Once, when snow fell, we raked all the snow in the Biavas' yard into a snowman. As the day heated up, we put the tiny alien into the top of their Frigidaire, where it proceeded to melt into a sludge of dirt and gravel.

Good times were balanced by hard times. The pain in my right side came on gradually during a hot night. My mother thought I was constipated and gave me a good dose of castor oil. My appendix ruptured; peritonitis took over. In those pre-antibiotic days, my condition was serious. After extensive surgery, the doctor packed my body in ice to bring down the fever, then summoned family and close friends to say good-bye.

Kathleen brought games and goodies, and we planned all the things we'd do when I came home. We drew plans for a deeper, bigger tunnel. Meanwhile, the Mortensons' daughter, Clara, the baby sitter who ironed our hair ribbons, was in trouble. The frightened girl put her daddy's gun to her heart and pulled the trigger. Clara's death was our first brush with the ugliness of life. In whispers, Kathleen and I shared our limited knowledge about what happened to girls "who went all the way" at a time when back-alley abortions were the only kind available. Somehow we puzzled through the mysteries of sexuality and worked out our personal code of conduct to avoid our friend's fate.

Inevitably, friendships change. Our family moved to Yuma, and the Biavas moved to Vallejo, California. Kathleen and I became pen pals and have never forgotten each other's birthdays in well over sixty years. In a spurt of patriotism, my family moved again, this time to Richmond, California, to work in the shipyards during World War II. Kathleen lived just a short bus drive away, and our friendship intensified again during our dating years. One of the first boys I went steady with was Carl Maxey, a boy from Douglas. Kathleen introduced us. Our marriage of thirty-seven years produced two children before he died of cancer.

Barely out of high school, Kathleen developed Crohn's disease, an inflammation of the gastrointestinal tract. Hospitalized in San Francisco, she received massive doses of a newly discovered antibiotic, penicillin. For several months, I spent a good part of the weekends traveling by trolley, bus, and then streetcar to visit my friend. We talked about the men we would marry, the good mothers we would become, anything and everything except her condition. We celebrated her recovery with a trip to a ski resort in the Sierras.

Inevitably, we both moved again: Kathleen to Mountain View, California, where she had a long marriage, one daughter, and a successful career in the aviation industry. After several career moves, my husband and I wound up in Corvallis, Oregon, a three-hour drive from Kathleen's summer home in Florence, on the Pacific Ocean. We see each other infrequently, talk once in a while on the telephone, and write letters. At this stage of life, we have shared the passing of loved ones and the slow agony of watching both our mothers develop dementia.

Two little girls grew up in a West that has vanished and enjoyed a lifetime of knowing there was at least one person in the universe who knew us for who we were and are. Kathleen will always be my best friend. In those long-ago years, when none of us had material things, we became self-reliant, dreaming up our own entertainment and creative mischief — after all, our tunnel attempt preceded the Chunnel connecting England and France.

From the cavernlike dressing rooms located beneath the stage, two frightened girls ascend the dark stairway, clasp sweaty hands, and wait for their music.

[handwritten: bj~ buckley — Pay's Public Auction House, Billings, MT 5-5-02]

B. J. BUCKLEY ❧ A Man's Work

The day they called the Leiter Bar
to tell us Norma Malli'd had a heart attack,
Joyce said, "It's 'cause she's done a man's work
all her life." And all the women nodded,
she ranched on her own, did everything
herself, it was too hard, finally might kill her.

All those women nodded, young girls
with faces already going leathery from sun
and wind, from squinting into it to see
some lost lamb in the blue sage or to sniff out
if that was smoke in the wheat or just some boy
in a pickup throwing dust — those women who rode
and branded and cooked the damn testicles and
nursed the kids and cleaned up after everything,
who jacked stuck trucks out of the mud,
who learned to pee from a horse as tiny girls
because if they got off they were too short
to get back up again (and they could be
twenty miles from home looking for some

antisocial heifer who ought to be ready to drop),
those women who mostly did what Norma did,
who stayed and kept the ranches when
their fathers died or their husbands ran off
or their sons left, those women who called it
"man's work," who couldn't, somehow,
call that work their own.

I ran into Norma once on the dirt road
behind Dead Man, she was on her hands
and knees in the roadside weeds and wheat,
her face flushed crimson, pouncing like a cat.
She was catching grasshoppers in her heavy hands
and popping them into a can with a lid, and I yelled,
"What are you *doing,* Norma?" and she said,
"Going fishing, nothing like grasshoppers
for going fishing, half the time the fish
leap out of the water to get 'em before
you can wet the hook!" So I helped her,
while Norma, who never much said two words,
spoke love for fish and her cows and said
she'd never wanted to do nothing else but ranch
even though she was a girl and was
supposed to want other things, and
here she was doing it and how many folks
got to do that their whole lives,
exactly what they wanted?

II

❦

Leaves Speak
for You:
The Nourishing

Western women, often "wed to the land," find pleasure in maintaining diverse friendships; some friends knit and purl with fine thread, others smoke cigars or march "with bloody ax in hand" but have "a belly laugh that pulls you in like a warm hug." All have become "ladies of the circle"; with all we "feel a communion."

In country where "wide-open spaces necessitate relationships," not all friends grow up together. Affinity is sometimes felt when "a stranger spilling longing" walks through the doorway or waves as pickups meet on a dusty road. As strangers become friends, distance can preclude drinking coffee in each other's kitchens, so we may communicate by telephone, letter, or e-mail. In isolated parts of the West, women sometimes tuck gifts and messages into rural mailboxes to maintain contact even though we may not see each other for months.

A visit face to face "is almost as welcome as rain." When Western women are together, we gather laughter and stories precious as jars of jam hidden in our refrigerators. Later, weary and alone, "strung on the sinew of toil," we savor memories that sustain us as they "flicker bright and dark." Sometimes we share secrets with a friend or are refreshed by someone who knows how to sit in "mindful silence" and "how not to fill it with nervous words." Other times comfortable warmth comes from being "clasped in a circle" of women who have measured out "a thousand stitches, a thousand lessons." Always, we are teaching each other the "lessons learned by hand."

The women in the following stories are as tenacious and diverse as sagebrush, as free-spirited as Artemisia, whose name identifies the genus to which sagebrush belongs. A liberated botanist and medical researcher, Artemisia, who may have been named for the goddess Artemis (also known as Diana, the goddess of nature), lived nearly three hundred years before Christ. Artemisia's memory survives in nearly three hundred species of sagebrush growing in temperate regions of the Northern Hemisphere, including the Asiatic steppes, northern Africa, and North America, particularly the American West.

Sagebrush doesn't exist in isolation; it thrives with companions like and unlike it, offering shelter and sustenance to a variety of plants and animals. Similarly, our "hunger for kinship" brings us together in various ways. Some girls may grow up with a playmate who remains a friend for life, or "neighbors by chance" may become "friends by choice."

These women teach us, often by example, to find a way to live well in a harsh and changing landscape, writing a "victorious signature over the grass." From the rough materials of their surroundings, their words weave "the lacy shawl of female friends." Sagebrush, too, provides examples not only of survival in the face of adversity but also of nurturing; it produces soft foliage that native peoples once used to make bedding, skirts, and baby blankets. Like the best of friendships, it is "practical, unpretentious, and richly inarticulate."

Just as the leaves of some plants are bitter and palatable only to certain wildlife, some women may not be companionable with others. A particular woman may inspire you in reverse, making you work to become the woman she is not. Finding "ways to connect" even in the most difficult of relationships is the key to female kinship.

When distance, circumstance, or death separates us from a friend, our "hearts travel on trails of tears and love and laughter." We feel our friends' influence "like the silent steel ribbons connecting the railways across the plains, helping drive us forward." In "one deep and universal breath," the words that follow offer solace, teaching us that "some days rays of laughter" can bridge "the ache of distance." Separate and yet together, we listen as the "wind brings their voices," the leaves whispering quietly, subtle as the blue-green hues of sagebrush.

THELMA POIRIER ❧ chokecherries

this moment in the berry patch
our arms bending the same branch down
your sleeve and mine
snagged on the same burr
I can hear your pain   purple berries
you drop them in your pail
filling it again again

at birth
I was not your sister
now I am

DIANE JOSEPHY PEAVEY ❧ Coming Home

On a warm autumn day, Mary, my eighty-four-year-old mother-in-law, drove her car up to the gate of our ranch house. Dogs and canes spilled out when she opened the front door to pull herself from the driver's seat. What could she want now, I wondered.

Mary and her friend Gertrude were making chokecherry jelly. Already that morning, Mary had driven twice from her rambling green house behind the ranch cook shack to our small log cabin on the creek — each time in pursuit of something to keep the chokecherry project alive.

"Any more jars?" she asked from the front door. She already had every jelly jar I owned. I searched the pantry, then handed her a box of large widemouth pints not really suitable for jelly, but she left delighted.

Mary had come home. It had taken her a long time, but once she had made up her mind to return to her Idaho ranch, no one could deter her. She consulted no one, simply loaded her car and those of several friends with extra furniture, kitchen supplies, old photos, and memories with which to set up house. But then that's her style. Decisions are made, often in the middle of the night, and acted on early the next morning. The best the family can do is get out of her way. Now the real wonder of this day was Mary, at eighty-four, making chokecherry jelly for the first time in her life.

Even though she had spent long-ago summers in this remote place surrounded by bushes heavy with chokecherries, she was only now discovering the mysteries of this fruit at the urging of her friend Gertrude, also eighty-four. Diminutive, gentle Gertrude had arrived earlier in the day with buckets of berries and now led Mary through the delicious steps from fruit to jelly.

I remember this chokecherry adventure clearly because it was the day that I began to understand the friendship of these two women and their gift to me. Although they have each taught me bits of wisdom culled from their varied, long, and productive lives, no message has been more lasting than the one I happened on as the women leaned over a steaming kettle of boiling berries and sugar water: the absolute joy of coming home.

On her visits to Mary, Gertrude has taught me about the landscape of our Idaho ranch country known as Muldoon. Her family homesteaded here when most of the activity in the valley centered on a single sheep operation. The land today is much the same as it was when Gertrude was a child, and she brings those days to life again on our driving excursions.

"There's the old Baptie place, the Marty cabin, and our schoolhouse with eight kinds of wildflowers in the yard." Years later, she is still amazed by the medley of blooms. From this remote, spare classroom, Gertrude learned well, scoring higher than the town children from the Wood River valley on the pre–high school exam.

She points out Thompson Creek canyon. "I'd take a sandwich and a magazine and ride my horse down there and be gone 'til supper." Then she adds, "Two famous bootleggers had stills in that canyon. Brewed up whiskey and beer for customers in town."

"In winter we'd ski those hills," she points to rounded sagebrush hillsides. "The dogs pulled us to the top, and we'd fly down the crusted snow — snow so deep Mother reached out of the top half of the window to hand us cookies and hot chocolate."

Today, if I know the valleys and abandoned homesteads, if I see shadows in these sagebrush hills, hear voices beside the springs flowing below basalt rock ridges, they are Gertrude's memories of this landscape from the early 1900s. It is no wonder she knows the locations of all the best chokecherry bushes.

But from Mary I have learned ranch survival . . . of a sort. A tomboy by nature, she became the son her father, John Thomas, never had, and they roamed the Idaho backcountry together. A banker, Thomas got into the sheep business during the Depression years when others were giving up. He headquartered the operation north of the small town of Carey, just over the ridge from where Gertrude grew up. Later he encouraged his daughter and her new husband to follow him into the sheep business. Despite the proximity of their lives and their intimacy with this landscape, Gertrude and Mary did not meet until years later.

Gertrude left Muldoon to make a name in the field of nursing and as a medical recorder. But she did not stray far from Idaho for long. Mary followed her father into ranching, then also followed him into politics when John Thomas was appointed U.S. senator from Idaho. After the boating death of her husband, Mary moved to Washington, D.C., to be with her father. There she met and married a U.S. senator from Illinois, became assistant chairman of the National Republican Party, and ultimately was named director of the U.S. Mint. Pictures in her home show Mary with *four* U.S. presidents. There was just not enough time to make chokecherry jelly.

Mary returned to Idaho occasionally to keep an eye on the sheep operation, "to hold on to it for her son," as her father had urged from his deathbed. Although she moved easily between Washington politics and ranch supervision, she was relieved when her son took over the operation after college.

Another fifteen years passed before Mary returned to her home state, and several more years before she returned to the ranch. When I came on the scene, she took me under her wing. I was, after all, a city girl, with experience in politics and Washington not unlike her own, but I was hopelessly ignorant of ranch life. She has never been without advice for me, although sometimes it is more insistent than others, such as when I began cooking for the cowboys on our annual spring cattle drive.

I had ridden horseback on a couple of these trips and knew that at noon, when the hands arrived at camp, the cook served up a meal of meat, potatoes, gravy, biscuits, and pie, maybe cake. So when I took over the cow camp kitchen, I knew my role. Then the first phone call came from Mary.

"Now don't you go feeding those boys your gourmet food. They expect meat and potatoes," she cautioned. I was a bit miffed. Did she think I would serve quiche and fruit cups? And then a few days later the second call. "Now remember, feed those boys meat and potatoes, not that gourmet food." The warnings continued daily until I longed for caller ID.

The first day home after the drive, the phone rang. "You didn't give those boys any of your gourmet food, did you?" came the voice over the phone. "Who is this?" I asked just to be perverse. And so it continued for another *six* years until, hearing no complaints from the cowboys, she stopped coaching me.

Only later did this episode make sense to me. At a family gathering, she and my husband began telling of the year Mary cooked for the men during calving season. "I roasted a turkey," she recalled, "and then after a meal or two of cold leftovers, we had soup from the bird for a week. Soup, soup, soup," she said, laughing, while my husband shook his head.

"We lost the entire crew. They just walked out," he said with a sigh.

Mary took up for the finish. " 'Ma'am,' one told me, 'we don't eat no soup.' " And she rocked with laughter again.

Suddenly, I understood her phone calls. I was being schooled in ranch survival tactics in Mary's persistent, if obscure, style. Now I search out the story behind all her advice.

Mary and Gertrude discovered each other soon after Mary's homecoming. In her usual exuberance, Mary arrived home from town one afternoon announcing she had a new best friend. They'd met at a luncheon, and Mary had immediately invited her to the ranch to play cards.

So Gertrude, as gentle and patient as Mary is blunt and impulsive, became her best friend, and the two silver-haired women can often be found playing Spite and Malice by the large window in Mary's ranch house and watching birds at the feeder just beyond the glass. In summer they drive around the open spaces of their childhood checking fields of young crops and pastures of fattening cattle, searching the meadows for sandhill cranes, and picking yarrow, sunflowers, and lupines for table bouquets and for pressing. In autumn, their favorite season, they travel the dusty roads of narrow canyons and creek bottoms to snap pictures of golden aspens and cottonwoods. These adventures are all lived from Mary's sturdy car, her lifeline now that shaky legs prevent her from walking any distance. Her license plate, MTN MARY, chases the faint of heart off the road.

These women have become my teachers through their stories and their vigor and curiosity, which flourish in this landscape they love. Gertrude has taught me the history of this country, and Mary has shared her experiences with ranch life. I have come to see this place through their eyes as they tell me of each pair of antelope and field of camas, each hunter's camp or burst of chokecherry bushes — all the wonders they happen upon as they roam the land together.

Mary and Gertrude, both now ninety-one years old, have brought their lives full circle. They have traveled, achieved, loved, raised families, buried friends and kin, and finally returned to the place that held their hearts safe while they were gone. And through them I have let go of my city ways and opened myself to this landscape and its life, at first so new and strange to me.

I remember the day I first understood their gift to me. I can still see in my mind two friends laughing and pouring sweet, red chokecherry liquid into waiting jars on an autumn afternoon. Satisfied with their work, they sink into armchairs, with their green plastic glasses filled with vodka and settling ice cubes. Mary has turned on her favorite TV show. She claps and cheers as reporters argue over political events, while Gertrude frowns at all the fuss. As the friends relax, one or the other looks away from the screen to sniff the lingering smell of chokecherries now locked tightly in assorted glass jars on the kitchen counter, and each in turn smiles.

COLETTE KNUTSON GJERMUNDSON ❧ Friends Because

Kim and I are friends. We're friends because we live over the hill from each other. Actually, it's at least a mile's trek across windblown fields and prairie pastures, rock-filled ditches, and barbed wire fences — or two miles if I follow the rutted, gravel road from my house to hers.

We're friends because the rest of our neighbors live farther away — five miles in one direction and six or eight in another. Our nearest towns are about twenty miles south. Sometimes wide-open spaces necessitate relationships.

We're friends because our husbands grew up together. My husband, Casey, and her husband, Kelly, attended confirmations together at the same small, country church we now attend.

We're friends because our families help each other with typical ranch-neighbor work — a day of moving cows or branding calves — or respond to a spur-of-the-moment "Help!" when a tractor is stuck in the Knife River or a birthing cow's offspring has one leg down. Our husbands borrow diesel fuel supplement or a shot of vitamin A from each other like I borrow food coloring for cookies from Kim.

We're friends because we have similar values. We both believe that right and wrong are determined by the Good Book. We have similar priorities: God, family, ourselves. We're both involved in church activities. We're both outspoken doers. We enjoy each other.

We're friends because we relate to each other's struggles over losing cattlemen fathers to sudden death, preparing for family holidays and community celebrations, lacking enough time to accomplish all we want and need to do. We both have ranch wife responsibilities that overlap with work responsibilities. We earn outside income to cover "living expenses" while our families work hard to continue ranching, thereby perpetuating a wholesome business and lifestyle. Do other people understand? They don't seem to. While our families produce food for the world, other people dash ahead, never looking back to see who or what is getting run over. They think food comes from a grocery store. Kim and I are friends because we understand the satisfaction of connecting with the land.

We're friends because Casey and I are honored godparents to Kim and Kelly's second child, a boy named Kasey — born on my birthday, September 14.

We're friends because we have developed a relationship and have grown to love and care about each other. We're friends because we live over the hill from each other. We became neighbors by chance; now we're friends by choice.

CHARLOTTE M. BABCOCK 🦌 Letters to Lil

To Lil in August:

These late August days are full of sun and heat, but the mornings are cool, with that unmistakable foreshadowing of autumn — a sprinkling of rime on the picnic table, the stray yellow leaf that hides, ashamed of itself, in the grass. I am frantic with the realization that I have let the summer slip through my fingers. So in spite of everything I think I must accomplish, I've spent two days lounging in the yard trying to store summer safely inside my saddened soul.

Yesterday afternoon I sat very still while the neighbor's cat streaked across the lawn in high spirits with something clutched in his mouth. You remember Porky, Lil, because he was always determined that you should like him, although you couldn't stand cats. He guarded his sparrow treasure with a sharp and mistrustful eye as I went to the rescue. When the sparrow gave a plaintive, wounded cry, I knew death would soon claim another victim. I could do nothing to alter the inevitable, and so I went back to my lounging, once again sorrowing over a death.

The little drama brought you into vivid focus. I miss you very much, Lil. I want the friend who lived across the street for thirty years to be there yet. I want us to be able to discuss the news, our families, our jobs, our philosophies. Was there anything we didn't talk about?

Funny, I remember our disagreements better than I remember our agreements. I think it was Helen Keller who said that one can endure anything if one has friends. I know we were, in some ways, closer to each other than to our own families. I am still angry at you because you died, angry at myself because I could do nothing about it. I'll never forget when you said to me, "This is so hard," after you had been awake all night battling your pain and the fear of the unknown, knowing how short a time you had to live.

I am dismayed at how self-centered I am, but the helplessness I felt watching your struggle to avoid dying was hardly less in its way than your own. I longed unceasingly for a return of our invincible selves, when we knew it all, never admitted defeat, and planned to change the world in two or three years, tops.

Looking back over the months since your death, trying to analyze my grieving, I think I have been afraid that I, too, might die before I need to and not be able to do a thing about it. I realize that amounts to an abdication of faith, but I can't help it. You were so frightened, Lil, and I caught it. Contrary to all that is written about how one comes to an acceptance of death toward the end, you never did. You wanted badly to stay alive, and I think that's what frightened me more than anything else. I'm not immortal, but I guess I never really believed it until you showed me the brutal truth in the only way that cannot be denied. Like the early sailors who feared dropping off the end of the earth, both of us had come to the end of our lives as friends, and "beyond that place, there be dragons."

I've always felt very alive, very young. Now I feel old and used up, vulnerable. I have learned that I have no control. All the polls babble on about life expectancy and how we women can expect to live seventy-six-plus years. You died sixteen years ahead of time.

I've always known what I desire in life — and have realized some of it — but so much more is still out there waiting on me. Can I keep slogging along? Isak Dinesen wrote that the world was made round so we can't see too far down the road. That statement has such great truth and faith that I must try hard to accept it, as she surely did.

You see how I need to talk to you, Lil? But since I can't do that, I've decided to pretend you are on a world cruise and are picking up my letters at each of your ports of call. After all, writing is one of the things I'm *supposed* to do, right?

To Lil in September:

Matthew died this week. I sat through his funeral thinking of you, how the two of you suffered the same catastrophic illness, enduring the same agonies of treatment for two years. You seemed to respond so well to the treatment, while he did not. Yet he lived more than half a year beyond you. I remember how he and his wife wanted to come see you and how you made me tell them you didn't want to see them. They just didn't understand. Some misery loves company, and some misery lives alone.

The other day, I actually dialed your number. It rang, and an automated voice said I had reached a number that was no longer in service, advising me to stay on the line if I needed assistance. I hung up and stood by the phone, heart thumping. Can I begin now to accept what I cannot change?

To Lil in October:

Two or three mild frosts this month have killed the weaker flowers and plants. Apples lie all over the yard. Raking them up and getting them into the trash barrel has not been easy on my old back. I feel unfriendly toward the bumper crop of apples, but the applesauce I made from them was wonderful, tart and tasty.

The huge piles of dry, crisp leaves rustle in the wind and blow around the yard. I have a fierce desire to run and jump into a big pile of them as I did when I was a kid, but someone would see me and send for the paddy wagon. Remember how we used to lie in them and cover ourselves up? It would get very dark, and the sounds of the world would fade into shadows. I loved the smell — dusky, rusty; distinctive, unforgettable. We used to help Daddy rake the leaves all the way out to the curb, where he would set them on fire. The pungent smell of burning leaves hung in the air for weeks sometimes. I am tempted to take a bunch of my leaves to the patio and have my own little leaf-burning ceremony for old times' sake.

It's become a habit to write to you outside, and I've had trouble finding a place indoors that feels comfortable. Everything inside is motionless, inanimate, except for the ticking of the clock, which reminds me of the shortness of time.

To Lil in November:

Winter has come too early. I smell wood smoke in the late-autumn dusk. This year I am angry that the sun sets too soon and that the apples are gone. My fear is that I can't go fast enough to stay ahead of them.

Robert and I knew we must not put off driving up the mountain to see the aspens. Everyone has been raving about their glorious color, so we drove up there Sunday afternoon. They were spectacular, all right.

We drove 113 miles Sunday, Lil — a trip that transformed my anger and fright of this past year into a calmer acceptance of the way this world operates. Maybe I was wrong about the miracles, Lil. We always said we'd admit to being wrong once a year, even if it wasn't true. In case you had a hand in this, I'll say thanks and send my love. I hope my letters catch up when your ship docks at that next port sometime soon.

To Lil in December:

I need you to spur me into the usual Christmas frenzy. It always made me crazy when you put up your Christmas tree the day after Thanksgiving and had about thirty presents wrapped and piled under it the day after that. No matter what kind of insults I hurled your way, you forged right on. But really, Lil, the last straw was when you'd trot off to the post office to mail your packages on December 1. I always felt lucky if I didn't have to send mine special delivery on December 23.

I wrote a Christmas letter to send in the cards. I worked hard on it, wanting it to be funny and upbeat. I finished it just before we went to Denver. We got home Sunday evening, and as we walked in the house, the telephone rang. Just like that, my dad — my bedrock, my vital and energetic link to youth and longevity, the steadfast backdrop in my life — was dead.

We left Monday for his funeral, and once again I found myself struggling to accept something I cannot change. Dad's death has taken my childhood away from me, rekindling and reverberating the fear that autumn had done so much to ease. You and Daddy always had a great time visiting when he was here, and my hope is that the two of you might meet at some point in your journeys. If you do, know that my spirit rises to join you.

I guess I'll rewrite my Christmas letter now, although it is quite likely I won't send it at all. My Christmas star has disappeared, but I will try, Lil. I will remember what I have learned because of you this past year, and maybe the star will rise again one day from an ember's glow.

DIANNE P. ROOD KIESZ 🦌 Time for Friendship

I am forty, my friends eighty-something. Coming to the Manor with Christmas goodies, I find them in the hall between their open apartment doors, a country and western carol blaring in stereo from both directions. They giggle at being caught in their slips. As we hug, I am reminded of college dorm life in the sixties and smile, but I doubt that Hannah and Emma went to college, or high school either. German-Russian immigrant families on the Dakota prairie, unable to support all their children, often hired out teenage daughters to work for their room and board. Emma wistfully remembers longing to go home more often, but five miles was too far.

My friends' lives were shaped by endless hard work, scarcity, and sorrow. Their wrinkled faces and leathery hands attest to those hardships, but their eyes twinkle as they revel in their camaraderie. Widowed and living in these low-rent apartments, they have found time for friendship and have a "best friend" for the first time.

We share a warm pumpkin *plagenda* (turnover) from Emma's kitchen, and Hannah thrusts a hastily wrapped crocheted doily into my hand. Leaving, I glance over my shoulder to see the two women, still in their slips, standing in the hallway, holding hands.

NANCY CURTIS 🦌 La-vin-i-a

Her name was Lavinia Rockfort, and she was built like someone had blasted a hunk of granite out of the ground, blocked out some legs at the bottom, and chiseled a square head on top. In fourth grade, she planted herself in the seat behind me on the school bus and began to make my life miserable.

And if Lavinia — you had to pronounce all four syllables, or she made you pay — if La-vin-i-a wasn't scary enough, she had a big brother and two older sisters to back her up: Max, who went on to become the state heavyweight wrestling champ; Maria, who was La-vin-i-a cloned and enlarged by 100 percent; and lovely Gloria, the oldest. Gloria defied all genetic logic by being both intelligent and beautiful.

And what a suitable victim I was, with hair the color of sewer pipe buried too long and freckles that camouflaged my pasty skin. Worst of all, I didn't speak plainly. Never had. In fact, nobody much understood what I said.

My mother says that the day before I started first grade, she reminded my dad that he shouldn't expect too much of me. After all, I got words all mixed up, my tongue got tangled on things, and I hadn't even learned my colors. He took me upstairs and sat me down, and within five minutes I knew the names of red and blue and all the rest. But he couldn't get me to speak plainly, and he couldn't make me care that I didn't.

Oh, a couple of times I got frustrated when someone didn't understand me. I dashed into school on the morning after Russell's father caught his finger in the auger at our grain bin and got it chopped right off. I told Miss Winslow how we'd searched the ground for the finger, looking in the grain, and kicking up the dusty ground, but we never did find it. "Hmmm, that's good," she murmured. "Go hang your coat outside the door."

Then Russell came in and told her the same story, and he hadn't even been there. He told Miss Winslow how his dad had a big bandage where his finger ought to be.

Miss Winslow asked questions and fussed over Russell. But he hadn't seen the blood in the dirt. He hadn't crawled into the doghouse to see if Remus was gnawing on the finger there. I knew that she hadn't understood a word I'd said, and it made me mad.

And at Christmas I told my parents that I was going to be a Hawaiian Muckletoe in the school musical. They were pleased enough. They seemed unusually interested in my role and asked what kind of a costume I'd need and what kind of songs Hawaiian Muckletoes sang. Then my mother phoned some other mothers.

"Holly and Mistletoe," my mother explained to us. "Some kids will wear red, and others will wear green. It's like a chorus of holly and mistletoe." Holly and Mistletoe, Hawaiian Muckletoe — it sounded close enough to me.

Even so, I was in the bluebird reading group, I wrote poetry, and I learned to write in cursive before anyone else in my class. True, I never knew what phonics was all about, but I did what Miss Winslow asked and didn't cause trouble. And she told my mother that she understood me just fine.

As for me, I knew what I was saying.

But in fourth grade, La-vin-i-a brought me to my senses. She sat in the second-best spot on the bus. The best seats were at the back of the bus, out of view of the driver. Max, Maria, and Gloria sat there. The second-best spot was by the heater behind the right rear wheel well. I sat directly over the wheel well, where no heat ever penetrated. I bundled up with my long red scarf wrapped around my neck and my brother's hand-me-down buckle overshoes over my cowboy boots. Behind me, Lavinia's feet were toasty by the heater.

To entertain herself on the hour ride home, Lavinia asked me dumb questions. "Why do you have all those freckles?" she sneered. "Huh?"

When I didn't answer soon enough, she jerked one end of my scarf. Hard.

"I don't know."

"What are you saying? I can't understand you." She pulled my scarf again and made mush-mouth noises: "I doe unnershan." She laughed. "That's what you sound like." Then she pulled both ends of my scarf, tightening it like a noose around my neck.

When my mother asked me about the red marks on my neck, I said my new scarf rubbed there. "I wonder if you're allergic to it," she said. "That almost looks like a rope burn on your neck."

I decided not to go to school anymore. For almost a week, I convinced my parents that I was sick. On the fifth day, when I recovered from my sore throat thirty minutes after the bus went by, my dad decided to take me to school.

On the drive into town, I curled against the passenger door and alternately glared at him and sniffled. I tied knots in my scarf and then untied them. As he drove up in front of the school, he said, "I tell you what we're going to do. Now don't tell your mother, but I'll give you a dollar for every day you go to school."

My allowance was a dollar a week. I'd have to go to school for only fourteen days to have enough money to buy that Kodak Brownie camera at the drugstore. I took the deal.

School was fine. The teacher kept order in the classroom. But I dreaded the bus ride home, when I knew the driver couldn't watch the road and thirty rambunctious passengers at the same time. I dropped my new scarf in the gutter, stepped down on it with my overshoe, and watched the muddy slush soak into the soft red fuzz. I'd save my neck even if it meant facing my mother when she found out I'd lost the scarf.

But with the warmer weather, Lavinia had moved closer to the big kids at the back of the bus. I'd been reprieved, and I was getting richer by the day.

After a couple of weeks, Lavinia slammed herself down in the seat behind me on the bus. "Why do you talk that way?" she asked.

"I just do."

"My sisters say that in Home Ec they talked about you. They say your mom and dad must talk baby talk to you at home. Is that right?"

"No."

"Is too."

"Is not."

"You saying my sisters lie?"

I looked at Maria and Gloria at the back of the bus. I darn sure wasn't saying they lied. I was a freak of nature. Big girls were warned in class about producing mutants like me. "Don't marry your cousin, or you'll have a six-fingered baby." "Don't talk baby talk to your kid, or she'll sound like that freak in fourth grade."

"Why do you talk that way?" she demanded again.

"I'm just too stupid to learn," I blurted.

La-vin-i-a's eyes narrowed. She was in the blackbird reading group; they read skinny little books with lots of pictures that the rest of us had finished in first grade. "You try to talk right?" she asked incredulously.

"Yes." I wondered if that was a lie.

"Humph," she said. After a minute she asked, "Where's your scarf?"

"I lost it."

"Humph." She got quiet, contemplating me.

My face burned with shame. People blamed my parents because I didn't talk right. I was a disgrace. I'd never thought of it that way before. I didn't want to be an embarrassment to my family. Maybe if I paid attention; maybe if I listened.

Then we pulled into the ranch yard where the Rockforts got off the bus. Max lumbered off first, then Maria, then Gloria. When La-vin-i-a stomped down the aisle, she poked me in the arm. "Bye, Stoopid," she said. "Hope you find your scarf."

Things changed that spring and summer. We played soccer at recess, and my pointy cowboy boots gave me an advantage over the girls who wore low-cut Keds. La-vin-i-a chose me for her team. "Hey, Stoopid," she'd say, "good kick."

That summer I took a cold drink to my dad in the hayfield. We sat in the shade of the haystack, sharing water from the burlap-wrapped Clorox jug. "I've noticed you're speaking a lot more clearly now," he said. "Don't you think so?"

I hadn't noticed.

When school started again, the Rockforts had moved, and I never saw Lavinia again, although occasionally we heard news of the family. Gloria got married. Max joined the navy.

The other day, I read something about dyslexia in *Newsweek*. The article mentioned a type of "speech dyslexia," where sound, language, and speech get twisted up in a person's brain. The symptoms sounded amazingly like the ones I'd had in grade school. The disorder has a name, but I never did figure out phonics, so I can't remember what it is.

That same week, I saw an obituary for Mr. Rockfort in the newspaper. At the bottom it said, "He was preceded in death by his daughter Lavinia."

La-vin-i-a. La-vin-i-a Rockfort. Lavinia was dead.

How could she go and die without my knowing it? Here I was enjoying hating her all this time, and she was dead. She'd pulled a final fast one on me.

La-vin-i-a. I wish she'd had time to poke me and say, "Bye, Stoopid,"
before she left.

I smiled at her memory.

When it came to goading, that girl took the World Cup. "Thanks, La-
vin-i-a. Good kick."

LAURIE WAGNER BUYER 🦌 There Were No Women

Mail came up but twice a week
when the dirt road could stay open
no telephone to salve the stretch
of endless days with a silent man
the nearest neighbor miles away
and there just were no women.

Morning and evening chores to do,
planting and gardening in spring,
harvest and canning in the fall,
no helping hands to ease the load,
no laughing smiles or teasing fights
because there were no women.

In memory my mother's face or
those of sisters, aunts, and friends,
in magazines those feminine dreams
of playing house and beauty shop
turned so lost and left behind
because there were no women.

So I sang to goats, hugged the cats,
conversed with the sad-eyed dog,
whispered words to shaggy horses,
held close a pine tree's roughened bark,
wept silly tears, hurt and harsh,
because there were no women.

Children came, barely conceived,
and cursed before believed in,
dark red rushes slipping away
in wadded sheets and bloodied fear
left me shivering to wash alone
because there were no women.

I was more tired than lonely, more
lonely than afraid, my heart turned hard,
my hands grew raw, my soul dried
and shriveled — near to dying, way past
crying because in all those long gone years
there just never were any women.

I remember sitting on the train en route from Chicago to Montana that early-winter morning twenty-four years ago. So many thoughts and worries scurried through my mind: Would the man I loved, but knew only through his ardent letters, like me? Would he think I was pretty? Would I be tough enough to live in his wilderness world? Would I need money, and, if I did, how would I earn any living eighty-some miles from town? Could I learn to cook, to sew, to split wood, to hunt and butcher? What would I do about tampons and birth control? Could I live without a telephone or plumbing? How would I find books to read? Yet the one thing that never crossed my mind was whether there would be other women in my life.

The first few silent months I lived on the North Fork of the Flathead River on the Canadian border, when I was nineteen, I never saw or spoke to another woman. My mother and sisters wrote to me. My dear friend, Guynn, a wild-running artist-actress whose unconventional ways had instilled in me the personal courage to quit school, wrote and sent me four hand-painted soup mugs and two packets of sweet-smelling bath salts, which I tucked away in my underwear drawer because there was no bathtub and no way to take a bath. I wrote to the woman who ran the post office–grocery store at Polebridge and tucked my last ten-dollar bill in the envelope. She sent me two boxes of tampons wrapped in brown paper via the mail. When the tampons ran out, I folded wash rags and pinned them into my panties. When they soiled, I rinsed them in the icy river, scalded them with boiling water from the teakettle, and hung them over the wood stove to dry.

I counted the days on the calendar carefully, and those times when my period came late, I lived in mortal fear, terrified that I would be cast aside by a man who wanted no children. When the first spots of blood finally appeared, weeks late, I was so relieved that I bore the accompanying pain without complaint. It would be twenty years before I learned from the surgeon who performed my hysterectomy that I had suffered through several early-onset miscarriages.

When folks snow-machined to our door to visit that first spring, I had turned so painfully shy that I went upstairs and hid until they left. When the snow melted and the road dried out, we made our first trip to town in an old pickup, but I felt clumsy and unable to speak to anyone.

The waitress at the diner said hello and smiled at me, but I ducked my head, ashamed of my simple braids, my faded jeans, and my chore coat that smelled like goats and manure. I often thought of the women who had lived in the log cabin on the river before me, and I gained an uncanny sense of strength from knowing they'd survived the isolation.

Though it seems like I never had any women friends during those years, I've found sketches of the women I met in my diaries, and I remember how brief visits and occasional meetings helped me keep my sanity. Pixielike Annie Chappell came with Ken Iddins in April of the first year, and they stayed a week. We formed an instant friendship, then lost track of each other for twenty years. Annie found me again just two years ago, and we resumed our friendship right where we left off. A woman named Jammy lived eight miles away on Trail Creek with her boyfriend, Mark. She signed her paintings with a double bleeding heart, and she birthed her first child one winter night in her remote cabin. A young Mormon housewife who seemed always to be nursing a new baby lived twelve miles downriver. She was exceptionally warm to me whenever we left our horses at their ranch when we made our rare trips to town. The American border guard, Bob Evans, and his wife, Irene, stayed summers in the crossing station only a quarter mile away from our log cabin. I still recall what Irene cooked the times she had me over for meals when I was left alone. Irene and I still exchange Christmas cards, and I cannot eat corn bread with maple syrup without thinking of her. There was Flo, and Valerie, and Lanie, and Noel, and Nancy, and Jean. I have recipes from women whose names I cannot remember, and I have mementos from women I seldom saw but who became friends for life.

The Montana homestead where I spent three and a half years left an indelible mark on my spirit. I returned several times to city life, but I always escaped and made my way back to backwoods environments or isolated ranches. Whenever I was tucked away in some remote enclave, I found sustenance in correspondence, and mail days were holidays for me.

Since 1988 I have lived with my husband on his cow-calf operation only sixteen miles from Fairplay, Colorado, and seldom a week goes by when I do not either receive a letter from a woman friend, talk to a girlfriend on the phone, or meet up with lady friends in town.

Today women create the lace that decorates my everyday rural life — they are fine, delicate, and feminine, but somehow also undeniably strong and enduring. When I search for answers, I ask other women for advice. When I lose my way and can't find the fork in the trail that will lead me home, I seek direction from women. When I fight the constant battle of trying to understand my husband or the world at large, I turn to women for their listening ears and soft shoulders. When I feel sad or lonely or unable to cope, I wrap myself in the lacy shawl of female friends, and I am cheered and comforted. I treasure every woman who comes into my life, because I remember only too well those long, hard years when there were no women.

WANDA ROSSELAND ❧ Because Men Rule

The thing you have to remember about women and the West is that men rule. My brother worked for three years in Oman, a Muslim monarchy. When he came back to the States, he said, "Hell, I didn't have to go to Oman to see women treated like second-class citizens. My sisters were raised the same way in eastern Montana."

So you learn to finagle and go around, get along here and fix there, and when you're desperate enough, you go off either by yourself or with a bunch of other women for the companionship you crave, because the men don't understand and never will, which is all right because that's just the way they are.

Women are naturally nest builders, hens with their wings stretched out, clucking. They need women around them — as opposed to "people," which includes children and men. This is one reason why some women lost their mental and emotional health when they came west to settle. Here there is less rain and fewer trees, rivers, streams, and plants. Grass is tall at one foot, and even raising a garden is a job. It takes a lot of land to support a family, so people can't live close to one another. In the past, visiting with another woman was an infrequent treat. Women friends were treasured.

To a degree, that distance and remoteness is still with us, even though we now have telephones and computers. Face-to-face visiting takes time, energy, and juggling, with dates broken because of weather, work, or other situations.

The other part where men rule is the money. I saw this in my own family with my father, who must have gotten it from his father. Recently, I heard that Grandma had always wanted to write stories for children. (Can't imagine why — she only had eleven!) Well, Grandpa took the stories and threw them in the wood stove and told Grandma that if she wrote any more, he would divorce her and send her back to Virginia. Of course, she would have been penniless, so she wrote no more. This absolute power was common and easily maintained, because women had no way to earn money and thus live independently. Even the schoolteachers had to be single to teach and were fired upon marriage. So women befriending women in the West became a requirement for survival, never acknowledged or discussed, but real nonetheless.

ANNE FANTACI CLEMENT ❧ The Reclamation

Morning light streams in the high east window as I drink coffee. The dogs bark. Who could be here at this hour? A white car I don't recognize eases down the driveway. Diana gets out, calling, "Hi, remember you said if things got horrible with Bernie, I could stay with you?"

My mind rewinds two weeks to a night at the bar in town. Like most people around here, we're regulars, because in this country you socialize either in bars or at church. That night my husband and I had grown concerned because Bernie was drinking too much and being mean to Diana. He wasn't likely to cut back on his drinking; he owned the bar. So we'd told Diana she could stay with us if he ever got violent. Evidently, he had crossed the line.

"Come on in. There's coffee."

"Thanks. I've been driving around all night."

"You feel like talking?"

"Oh, Anne, Bernie got a restraining order against me. The sheriff's deputy came by the bar last night and told me I had ten minutes to pack up and get out. He said I wasn't allowed within fifteen hundred feet of the place until after a hearing. Supposedly, I've been abusing Bernie Junior."

I snort and ask, "Does that deputy know that Bernie Junior is sixteen and stands six-foot-three?"

"I don't think he cares. I'm out of the bar until after the hearing. Since Bernie Junior is a minor, I'll have to prove I didn't abuse him. I don't think he'll testify against his daddy."

My eyebrows shoot up so high they dent my hairline. Everything Diana has is tied up in that bar. "What about your clothes and furniture? Your bike?" One thing Diana and I have in common is motorcycles. She values her Harley Sportster above almost everything else she owns.

"My bike is still at the bar with my clothes and furniture. The deputy said I couldn't go back. He said I was lucky he was letting me take a change of clothes."

I fix eggs and toast while Diana calls the bank. I can tell that the news isn't good.

"Well, Bernie's got a hold on the account just like I thought. I don't even have gas money. Everything except the car and my bike is in Bernie's name."

"I thought you put up the money from selling your house to buy the bar."

"I did, but Bernie said it was better to put the bar in his name. Guess I'm pretty dumb, Anne." Her voice broke.

"No, just trusting." I wanted to hug her but wasn't sure she would welcome it. "Who would have thought that you and Bernie would break up?"

"It's the drinking. Bernie owning a bar is like a kid owning a candy store."

We clean up the kitchen in silence and head for town, not talking much. I drop Diana off at the courthouse and go to Clare's gift shop to wait. I tell Clare what's going on with Diana and Bernie. When Diana comes in looking beaten, her eyes red behind her glasses and her hair looking as if it were combed with a tumbleweed, Clare and I joke around until Diana laughs.

I say, "There has to be a way to get your motorcycle. Who has the keys?"

"Why, I do." Diana looks at me as if she can see right into my head. "Are you thinking what I think you're thinking?"

"If you're thinking that I'm thinking that we can just ride the bike out from in front of the bar, then, yes, I'm thinking what you think I'm thinking."

Clare looks puzzled. "You two are losing me. You're not planning on stealing it?" Diana and I both look at Clare and grin. It's wicked, but I decide to get her involved.

"Stealing it?" I say. "Why, Clare, what a great idea!"

"Now wait a minute. That was just a question." Clare backs away.

"It wouldn't be stealing," Diana says. "It's my motorcycle. The only thing Bernie has ever done with that bike is dent the tank when he was having one of his drunken fits."

Diana's spirit is back; she's not slumping now. Nothing like a plan for action to perk a person up. Even Clare is getting interested. She says, "You know, Diana can't just take the motorcycle. If Bernie sees her, he'll call the sheriff, and they'll get her for violating the restraining order."

"I know that," I say. "Diana's not the only one who knows how to ride a motorcycle."

"You're going to do it?" Clare's eyes get wide. "Bernie will have a fit if he sees you taking it."

"Clare, darling, neither of us cares if Bernie has a fit."

"Well, I don't care either," Clare snaps. "Maybe I'll drive the getaway car."

"Clare, this is not *Dirty Harry*. This is reclaiming Diana's bike. We don't need a getaway car."

"You sure can't walk there from your place," she says, always practical.

"Wait a minute, you two. We're talking about something that could be interpreted as a crime," Diana protests.

"Diana, you worry too much."

"Clare, you don't worry enough."

"Ladies, ladies," I say. "We need a strategy. You two are wasting time arguing."

Diana says, "Now wait, I don't want to be responsible for you two going to jail for stealing my motorcycle."

I shake my head. "We're just *reclaiming* it — returning it to its rightful owner." I am on a roll. I am positively floating as I imagine the look on Bernie's face when he sees Diana's bike is gone. I want a picture of his expression. Diana looks doubtful, so I think the best way to get her behind this idea is to get her mad at Bernie again.

"You know, Diana," I say, "there's no telling what Bernie is liable to do to that motorcycle without you there to stop him. You know how he gets when he's drinking."

Diana treasures that Sportster. It's a symbol of her independence. Hurt her motorcycle, and you hurt her. "I *know* how Bernie gets," she says. "I also know what happens when he's mad. Anne, do you really want him going out to your place after the bike?"

"How's he going to know it's at my place? All he'll know for sure is that it's gone. He won't be able to prove who took it."

"You know how people talk. Somebody will mention to Bernie or one of his buddies that they saw me here. Then he'll be over here raising a fuss. Or he'll call the sheriff and have us both arrested."

Clare waves a hand in my face to get my attention. She reminds me of one of my more unmanageable second-graders. "How's this? We wait until Bernie passes out. Then we take the motorcycle and hide it so he won't know where it is."

Diana says, "We're not talking about hiding some itty-bitty thing. We're talking about my Harley Sportster."

"I know that, Diana, but it's got wheels. We just tuck it into Anne's barn."

"A barn?" Diana whispers. "You want to put my motorcycle in a barn?"

"If we hide it," I point out, "Bernie can't prove we took it. He can't go looking in other people's buildings. He may suspect you took it, but he won't be able to prove anything. Now we have the *where*, but we need to work out the *how* and the *when*."

"What about tonight?" Clare says. "Anne and I'll go to the bar and hang out until Bernie is horizontal. Then Anne can take your bike, and I'll drive off."

"Bernie will hear the bike start up; it's pretty noisy."

"Not if we borrow Earl Dean's orange car with the loud pipes." Nothing will stop Clare now. "I can talk Earl Dean into anything, but paybacks are steep. Last time it cost me a bottle of tequila and a night of listening to his stories about his glory days of stock car racing."

Diana smiles and says, "The things I am forced to do for my Harley."

We know the deciding factor will be how fast we can get Bernie drunk. If the bar fills up with too many of his buddies, it will be a lot harder to get the motorcycle.

I leave Diana at my place and go to Clare's. The first thing I see is Earl Dean's orange bomber parked in front of her house. She's sitting behind the wheel with a small cigar between her teeth, and I just know she sees herself as Bonnie of Bonnie and Clyde.

"Got the keys to the Harley?" she says around the cigar.

"Yep." I shake my helmet so she can hear them rattle.

"Isn't there some kind of law that says you can't wear a helmet while stealing a Harley?"

"*Reclaiming*," I say. "It will just be one more law we're breaking tonight. You sure you can drive this thing?"

"Cake. Climb in through the window. That door doesn't work."

I mumble something about "Dukes of Hazard" as she grins and revs the motor.

Clare is opening the door to the bar by the time I climb out the window. It's pretty quiet. Two of the regulars are on stools at the bar, and two cowboys I don't know are playing pool. No sign of Bernie.

"Hey, Harry, slow night."

"Hey, Clare. Yeah, not much going on."

"You alone?"

"Bernie got an early start," says Harry. "He's celebrating his new freedom. Guess you heard Diana moved out."

"That so? No, I hadn't heard. Bernie out barhopping?"

"No, we put him to bed in the back. What can I get you?"

Clare and I look at each other, holding back grins. This is better than we could have dreamed.

"Two shots of tequila and two glasses of iced tea."

"You got it."

Clare and I make small talk and try not to gulp the drinks down. I keep looking toward the door to the apartment behind the bar, afraid that Bernie will come out before we finish our drinks. I think about starting the Harley and hope that it will catch on the first try, because I sure don't want to spend too much time jumping up and down on the kick starter. Maybe Diana has the battery charged up so the electric start will work. I feel sweaty and hope Harry won't notice.

"You about ready to go?"

I nod at Clare, drain the tea from my glass, and wave to Harry, who is at the other end of the bar talking to the regulars.

"OK, Clare," I mumble, "when you start the car, rev it up and keep revving it until I get the bike started and I'm out of here."

"You got it."

Clare has the biggest smile I've ever seen as she climbs into the orange bomber and starts it up. I pull on my helmet as I walk to Diana's bike. I put her key in the ignition and cross my fingers while I pull the clutch and push the starter. The Harley starts right up. I straddle the bike, kick up the side stand, back it around, and take off.

Behind me I can hear Earl Dean's car roar as Clare pulls out. I have never been so happy to hear loud pipes.

KAREN OBRIGEWITCH ❧ *Who Else?*

How can any female survive without close women friends? Whom does she call when she needs affirmation, when her first-born leaves for college, when the calves don't bring enough cash to pay off the bank, or when her parents die? Who would cry with her?

Who else would sit in silence with her on the sandbar of the muddy river and listen to the sound of water hitting rocks and the catfish jumping as they go upstream, and imagine the history of the bones and the stones strewn in the sand — and give thanks?

Who else would understand that a distant bull sale is a pleasure trip? Or that cows rank in importance before a wife and accept that truth without bitterness or loss of self-esteem?

Who else would go with you to a riparian workshop or a holistic range conference or a xeriscaping demonstration?

Who else would be there in an isolated pasture as you climb over a four-strand barbed wire fence and burst loudly and proudly into song — "Oh, Lord, won't you buy me a Mercedes-Benz" — to join in the chorus?

My best friends all share a love of animals, family, nature, and God — in varying order. We feel a responsibility for God's creatures — including the men! We live miles apart physically, but what we have in common keeps us close and connected. How else would we survive?

KAREN M. BERRY ❧ *Gram's Vegetables*

"Gram, why are you reading up here now?" I asked in a thinly disguised whine. She was at my desk, and I wanted to sit there and write a letter. My Oklahoma grandmother spent her summers with our family. We shared my room in the manner of reasonably good-natured siblings, but sometimes we sparked.

"Reading now gives my mind something good to work on while I sleep," she responded, closing the book. "You like to read, don't you?"

I glanced at the book she was reading — one of mine. "You know I do, but I like the Bobbsey twins and stuff like that. What are you reading that for?"

"Those stories have a place, Karen, but books like this," she lifted the book, *Words to Live By,* "have a place, too. They're food for your mind, just like the carrots and peas at dinner are food for your body. Haven't you read this — or them?" She gestured toward my bookcase. No, actually, I hadn't read some, and I didn't want to talk about it. I'd glanced in them on occasion, but my interest wasn't snagged by any of the words I'd read. They bored me.

"I'm so tired at night that sometimes I can just read a paragraph," she said. A paragraph, I thought. There are times when I read a whole book at once. Just a paragraph? That convinced me. They were boring. Case closed.

"No, I haven't read all my books, not yet." As I pulled stationery from my desk and left the room in a rush, I wanted to add, "I don't want to, either."

The few I'd not read bored me. Why read them? But I was thinking about them even though I didn't want to.

Gram had given me books for my birthday and Christmas on her small income — sturdy hardback books, with lovely pictures on paper jackets and creamy, rough-edged pages with lines of intoxicating words enticing me into them. Some books hadn't enticed me. I hadn't read *Bambi.* Maybe I knew there was something sad there.

Most of my books were bought through the Scholastic Paperback Book Club. A newsprint flyer arrived in the schoolroom every few weeks. We pored over the book titles and pictures of the covers. The featured books were on the front of the flyer and a nickel or dime cheaper for that issue only, down from fifty to seventy-five cents. The regular-priced books were on the middle two pages of the flyer. I hardly ever bought books from the middle pages. Sale books reigned on the back page. A quarter or a quarter and a dime would buy a back-page book. I tried to keep my book total at a dollar with a mixture of sale books and a feature.

I'd bought some I'd never read, some that were called "classics" — one thick one of poetry, another on how to read and understand it, and others that my teacher had recommended. My grandmother's eyes had fallen on these books, too.

The next night, I again found her reading from *Words to Live By* before bed. I sat on my bed, and she began to read out loud. I'm not going to tell you I was overwhelmed or decided then and there to read the book; it wouldn't be true. When she finished, we talked, and she asked me to read for ten or fifteen minutes every night from books she picked out. And because I loved my grandmother very much, I said that I would, and I did. I don't remember all of the books she picked from my shelves, but I do remember *Emma,* and I remember *Words to Live By.*

I loved to read, but I didn't acquiesce gratefully at her opening this great "new world" of different books. I resented them, and as the school year progressed, I wished I hadn't promised I'd read them. I began to think of these as my vegetables. I wasn't crazy about vegetables, but my mother said I had to eat them.

Some nights I honestly forgot to read. Other nights I read a few "vegetable" paragraphs and then delved into whatever fun book I was reading at the moment. I began to think of them as my dessert. Other nights I had my vegetables after dessert. Sometimes I'd read several pages of vegetables before I caught myself. I read my Bible in this manner. (No, I didn't read every chapter and verse.) I read *Leaves of Gold* and finally that book she'd read from that summer evening, *Words to Live By.* I read *The Scarlet Letter,* a gift from my grandfather, long before I understood it. Why a lovely scarlet initial would upset anyone was beyond me. I read *Bambi* and *Treasure Island* paragraph by paragraph.

In one book flyer, there was a Merriam-Webster paperback dictionary for $1.75. I wanted my own dictionary. I needed it to help me figure out some of the words I was reading, but a whole $1.75 for one paperback book. It would be the only book I would get that time. I was afraid my folks wouldn't let me have it, but they did.

This early pattern of reading two books at the same time taught me early to keep them straight. Now I have three or four going at the same time, as well as an audio book for my car. My secret to keeping them straight is that I choose ones that are different. To my vegetable and dessert diet, I've added protein — business books about the work I do — and fruit — mysteries that I like for their character development. I can read these things in snatches, a few paragraphs at a time.

No, I don't read vegetables every night, but on the nights when I do, I think of my grandmother and how she sat at my desk with her hair a pewter shawl over her shoulders, feeding her mind something nutritious before she slept.

Eventually, I might have explored vegetable books and read them on my own. Eventually, I might have learned to read more than one book at a time. But I like knowing that my grandmother introduced me to these books and helped me to differentiate the value of different books in my life. It's a bond with her I will always have.

TWYLA HANSEN ❧ At the Prairie, the Day Before

For Kathleen Claire

The day before you arrived
started much like today, clouded and misty,
a day of celebration and families

near the city on Nine-Mile Prairie
where many gathered in an afternoon of festivities —
poetry, fiddling and guitar, nature hikes,
and the swift-feathered release of raptors;

    the day before you arrived
stirrings already begun — autumnal equinox,
changing of seasons, and you pressing heavy
on your mother's spine;
we celebrated women, women on the prairies,
and prairies, acres of tall grass now but a remnant
of what had once seemed endless,
yet the sky still defining the horizon
on a day much like today — flat, filled with moisture;
out on a section of mowed prairie the effluvium
of sweet, damp hay rose up to greet us,
voices of celebration and of mothers
and of earth — laughter of children playing games,
the clop-clop buggy rides, wings lifting free at last;

    on the day before you arrived
there was yet so much to learn,
too much to touch all at once —
the parting of big bluestem, rough sunflower,
dotted gayfeather, showy-wand goldenrod,
the silk of indiangrass —
we toured the prairie to connect
with what is almost lost,
celebrating women, celebrating mothers,
trying in our very bones to connect
with mother earth;
you were speaking to us even then

    the day before you arrived,
a day that started out in fog,
you stirring your father to nervousness,
in your own manner telling us to listen
though it was yet somewhat early —
the song and dance and celebration
on the prairie was, though we didn't yet know it,
only the beginning —
and surely the women on the prairie
knew deep in their bones that one day,
generations later, you might be here,

that on the day before you arrived
we might be celebrating women out on Nine-Mile Prairie,
and that the love they planted in their homes
would be the planting of the one seed
that would one day be celebrated by your arrival,
passing down as women and men do,
generation to generation,
the seed,

arriving as you did today
resembling the tight, folded bud of the blue downy gentian,
the bright bloom of your skin
against the pastel wrap of our receiving arms,
with your dark hair and eyes and wiggling tongue
and your wrinkled, perfect fingers and toes
that new flower now unfolding into blossom —
rare prairie orchid known as nodding ladies' tresses,
described by the botanist as a delicate spiral of white flags —
and it is you, granddaughter,
that fragrant orchid of the prairie now unfolding
to wave among the forbs and the grasses
as we gather under the sun
on this last day of summer
in one deep and universal
breath.

JENNIFER GREEN ❧ Saying Good-bye to 'Nali

The way you say good-bye to a friend says a lot about your friendship. It is a tough moment to prepare for. You struggle to find the right words, to behave in the right way, to compress all your good times into a single, excellent memory. During the summer I lived on the reservation next to Mrs. Peshlakai, I was never exactly sure about our friendship until the day I left. Out of the two months we spent together, those last five minutes were the most memorable. And we barely said a word.

I was working for the Navajo Election Commission the summer I met her. Housing was tight in Window Rock, capital city of the reservation. After two weeks of sleeping on picnic tables and bathing in the sink at work, I still had no permanent place to live. Finally, someone in my office suggested Mrs. Peshlakai's empty hogan. Sure, I thought, I'll ask her.

Asdzani Peshlakai was about sixty years older than me. Navajo elders are not known for their outgoing nature, and they rarely hurry. It could take a whole summer just to establish a comfortable face-to-face basis for conversation. That's if you speak Navajo, which I don't really. As the Navajo code talkers demonstrated in World War II, it's a very tough language to crack.

It took several trips down a long dirt road to convince Mrs. Peshlakai to rent me the hogan. Her nineteen-year-old grandson Clifton translated. On the first trip, we didn't even get to the subject of housing. On the second trip, we touched on it as a possibility. Finally, on the third trip, she agreed to two weeks' rental on a trial basis.

I moved into the hogan, which consisted of eight wooden walls wrapped around an octagon of dirt. There were two windows and a door, a table, and a cot. Clifton's brother showed up with some buckets for water and loaned me his Coleman stove for cooking. We rigged a closet with broomsticks and baling wire. I bought lots of candles. It was everything I dreamed of and more. The locals wondered what the hell I was doing there: did I want to be a Navajo or something? Really, I just wanted to settle into my new home and make friends with my new neighbor.

Things got off to a slow start. I wanted to express my appreciation in words to Mrs. Peshlakai, naturally, but translation has a diminishing effect on the act of speech. I tried to do good deeds, such as gathering wood and peeling bark off it to keep the smoke down. It was hard to think of gifts. Mrs. Peshlakai mostly sat around carding wool and drinking *deeh* (Navajo tea). She did seem to like things such as the cheese and crackers in little packets or boxed animal cookies from the Fedmart. I brought in some fresh melon once; that was good, too.

One afternoon a cloudburst flooded me into my hogan. After the storm cleared, Mrs. Peshlakai emerged from her doorway, laughing and holding her knees under the fractured sky as I directed the water away from my little puddle island with a camp shovel. I think she was impressed with the way I handled that shovel. It was a big day for us.

There were rules I had to follow while living on her place. I was not allowed to have male visitors or to play loud music. And it was really best if I could be up at a respectable hour, or at least by dawn.

She had me in her hogan a few times. Her dirt floors were covered with rugs. It was smoky and dark, and there wasn't much room for entertaining. A wood stove covered with pots smoldered through a central chimney. Everything had something else stacked on it. Her cupboard was lined with glass jars filled with odds and ends. Mrs. Peshlakai sat on her bed a lot. The door faced east, and she watched the sun rise through it. Clifton had a bed in there. She taught him to get up for the sun, too.

Our social time was mostly spent sitting in assorted lawn chairs in front of her place, watching the eastern sky. There never was much talking. She padded around in tennis shoes, her thin legs shooting out from under a worn skirt. She'd water the clay ground outside her door and sweep it until it was smooth and hard as tile. Now and again, she'd say something in Navajo. Sometimes Clifton translated, sometimes he didn't. A typical conversation went something like this:

"*Ya at eeh!*" I'd call from my doorstep.

"*Ya at eeh!*" she'd call back, waving. Then she'd chant out a long tonal sentence, of which I understood two or three words.

I'd nod and say, "*Aooo,*" which means "yes."

She asked me once where I was from. "I'm from Colorado," I said.

"Oh," she replied in Navajo. "I know where that is. That is up by the sacred mountain of the north."

Aooo.

We became friends in spite of the silence. One day I got the OK to call her *shinali,* as Clifton did; 'Nali for short. It means "my grandma." She usually just called me *ei bilagaana,* which means "that white girl." I didn't take it personally. Navajos are funny about names. They give traditional names in a naming ceremony for use on special occasions. Otherwise, generic names are quite acceptable. It all depends on the circumstances.

These were the circumstances of the friendship between Mrs. Peshlakai and me: practical, unpretentious, and richly inarticulate. A summer went by.

Then one morning I woke to the smell of rain over dry grass. August had arrived; the tribal elections were over. It was time for me to leave Window Rock. I had mixed feelings. I still had so much to learn from 'Nali. I was just figuring out how to spend time, negotiating the minutes of the day as a string of colored beads. I was learning how to use fire wisely, how to walk a long way. I was doing fine without indoor plumbing and intellectual conversation. Most of all, I was figuring out how to live with silence, how not to fill it with nervous words.

I wanted more time to learn 'Nali's language. I wanted her to know what I was thinking when the time came to say good-bye.

The morning I was to leave, I packed the back seat of my car methodically. I postponed my departure by taking a short walk up the mesa. When I returned, Clifton had readied 'Nali for some picture taking. I was surprised, particularly to find her seated by her doorway, dressed to the nines: a fresh skirt and velour blouse; heavy silver around her fingers and wrists; beads around her neck and clasped to her chest; turquoise I had never seen; a blanket folded across her lap and deerskin moccasins. Stuff she kept under that bed of hers. Clifton stood next to her in his usual snap shirt and boots. I dug out my camera, framed the picture, and clicked the shutter on a thousand words.

Then 'Nali invited me in. She patted her bed, offering me a seat. I sat facing her as she turned and reached for a jar on a shelf. From it she sprinkled flakes of dried leaf into a rolling paper. She twisted and licked it, chanting the whole time. She lit it and puffed, speaking Navajo words through a swirl of blue smoke. She took three or four great puffs, with more words in between. I got the feeling she wasn't talking to me at all. She was talking for me. I felt I would make it home safely.

She extinguished the cigarette and pointed to the door. I rose and put my arms around her small frame. I don't recall saying anything. There was, at this point, no need for words.

When I think back on it, I suppose you could call Mrs. Peshlakai and me friends. Friends watch out for each other, listen to each other, teach each other things. Good friends know how to sit in silence together. I never knew exactly what it was she said that day I left. I never saw her again. Writing this, I'm trying to focus on how it went exactly: the sound of the jar lid threading down on the jar, the bluish light, the smell of smoke. This was the way 'Nali and I said good-bye. It holds my memory of us together even still.

PAGE LAMBERT ❧ Backbeat

Blue-eyed, teenage Meg took me into a world of hard edges, carrying with her a hunger for touch born of a motherless childhood.

We literally rode into this world horseback. I dreamed of Romeo and Juliet, believed in undying love, and innocently named my half-Arab mare Romie. Meg rode a proud-cut sorrel gelding who came to her as a four-year-old already answering to the name Blaze. He ran like a wild man, his slightly turned-in front hooves colliding dangerously with each other at every stride. Meg didn't care. She didn't even mind his unpredictable rearing and gnashing of teeth. She accepted fear as part of Blaze's reality and as the reason for his suicidal plunges across ravines or headlong hurls into barbed wire fences. She accepted these things as easily as she would later accept Johnnie.

Spellbound, I watched her hurl herself toward this man's black sexuality. Connected by the cord of our friendship, I passed no judgment nor rendered any verdict. By day we rode horseback through irrigation canals sheathed in canopies of green willows that cut the sun into flickering pieces of sky. By evening, no longer tuned to the tamer melodies of the Beach Boys or Everly Brothers, we listened to soul-bending rhythm and blues. By night, when we were separated by my curfew and Johnnie's needs, Meg danced Johnnie's dance, spoke the words Johnnie wanted to hear, believed Johnnie's lies, and cried "Johnnie tears." As his adult world collided with hers, she slipped deeper and deeper into its mystery. Johnnie plucked on Meg's thin strings like B. B. King pluckin' music from Lucille. Johnnie wooed her with James Brown's "Papa's Got a Brand New Bag" and pledged his faithfulness with Chuck Berry's "Johnny B. Goode." I picked up the pieces.

Meg, barelegged and bareheeled, whipped Blaze on. He understood her fear. Romie and I eased them into slower gaits, trotted with them down miles of river shore, walked through fields of foxtail, and let the hot summer sun temper our mettle. In secret moments, in the hollow of Meg's bedroom with its pink dust ruffles and yellow daisy curtains, she shared with me Johnnie's own private ways of rockin' and rollin'. We heard rumors of other lovers, women full-grown and man-toughened, and she shared with me her jealous despair. We ventured to the north end of town, crossed the tracks and entered the city, peered into the smoke-filled bar joints of Five-Points, saw no white faces but our own, encroached on *his* territory.

Johnnie began leaving bruises on Meg's skin. Like the backbeat of rhythm and blues, they were secondary to her need for him. I held out a hand to Meg but was helpless to pull her from the darkness.

Unprotected, Meg grew round with Johnnie's seed; her belly grew taut and firm like a yearling's. He would no longer let her ride Blaze, yet he rode her still. She looked at me with the eyes of a child lost on her way to becoming a woman. I was but a child-woman myself.

I turned to the safer world from which I had come and sought guidance. My father offered advice to Meg, scolded her as he would scold a daughter, struggled with his own fatherly fears. Meg's father lifted his head from his newspaper, then retreated with a cowardly sigh of resignation. Meg walked away forever from childhood. The cord between us stretched thinner and thinner.

Unwed, Meg birthed a son, adding to Johnnie's brood. Johnnie preened his paternal feathers while Meg dropped out of school, sold Blaze to a rough-stock contractor, and joined Johnnie's harem. The cord between us seemed to snap.

For years, with every half-black/half-white child I saw, I searched for Meg's blue eyes and Johnnie's seductive smile. I rode Romie and thought of Meg — thought of willowed canals and flickering pieces of sky. I married, had children of my own, wrote stories of younger, faster days — but didn't tell anyone they were really *Meg's* faster days and *my* younger ones.

I think of her surprisingly often, especially when my teenage daughter invites me into her own mysterious world of adolescence, and I am reminded of what Meg and I once shared. I am reminded that the layers of my daughter's reality weigh heavy on her shoulders. I am reminded also that the distance between a girl and a woman is but a backbeat.

ARA ANDERSON ⁂ Strung on Sinew

Each iridescing unique soul
Pierced through the heart by life
Strung on the sinew of toil, and
Clasped in a circle by kindred women
Jewels of the West.

JENNIFER GRAF GRONEBERG ⁂ Handwork

It came in the mailbox, which stood watch over the long, snow-swept line of highway that began in Wyoming and threaded its way north through Montana. The mailbox was my rural lifeline, tying me to my neighbors, miles away on roads made impossible with winter, and to my family, even farther away in the Midwest.

I was terribly pregnant that winter — swollen, overdue, miserable, doubtful, and tired, always tired. I'd drive the truck down the snow-packed, rutted country road, first worrying that the bouncing was harmful to the baby and later wishing it would shake the baby loose. At the end of my three-mile journey was our mailbox, where I would invariably find solace and gifts that brought me something close to grace.

The presents were as varied as the women who left them. Raspberry leaves to dry and sip in a soothing tea, from a retired nurse who had seen hundreds of babies come into the world. Back issues of *Country Woman* magazine and a note telling me to put my feet up and read them. A tin of homemade caramels from a woman in her mid-thirties, mother of two young boys. The days turned into weeks, always with something to look forward to at the end of my daily drive. And later, finally, cards and letters congratulating us on the birth of our first-born, a boy who we thought would come in early December but who arrived for the party of New Year's Eve.

"Too bad, a holiday baby," one nurse said. But my husband and I were pleased with our good planning, timing the arrival of the baby to fit the least busy time on the ranch, the long months between weaning and calving. I quickly regretted our plan. I was lost in new motherhood, shaky and alone much of the time with a hungry baby who nursed constantly. Giving birth to my son, who was the greatest joy of my life, also brought me great sorrow, separating me from my husband and the outdoor work I loved. The weather was too cold; the baby was too small; I was too weak. I spent hours awake worrying — the long winter nights pressing in around me — always nursing, it seemed, in the cold draft of a lonely, bitter wind.

The gift came wrapped in the thick brown paper of a recycled grocery bag. I tore open the package and out spilled all the colors of spring sewn into a baby quilt. The brilliant pink of a sunrise, the yellow of a clear morning, robin's-egg blue, and green the color of new grass. With it came a note explaining that the quilt had been a community effort. "The colors should hide some stains," the note read, "so it can be a cape, a tent, a ground cover, or whatever, besides being a baby blanket. Don't baby *it;* baby *the baby* instead."

The extraordinary gift was sent by a woman whom I had known only a short time, yet I valued her friendship greatly. And it was made by women I surely knew, in the way everyone is known in a small, rural community. I knew their stories, the children they'd had, the children they'd wanted but couldn't have. I imagined them building the quilt, the hours spent stitching a reminder of the hours they'd spent mothering in all its countless ways. Everything I needed to know as a new mother was stitched into this quilt, a thousand stitches representing a thousand lessons that my son and I would learn together, just as all these women had done before me.

I think of the many capable hands that sewed this quilt, hands callused from years of chores, strong hands that pulled calves or held bottles for bum lambs. Hands working at jobs in town at the sale barn or the bank. Hands in the soft glow of a night-light, rocking babies endlessly to sleep. When I cover my son with their quilt, I cover him with their wisdom, all of their hands laid on him like a blessing or a prayer.

When my son is bigger, I will find time to join the quilting group and stitch my story into a square. I will use all the colors of my early days as a new mother: deep, dark blue for my postpartum sadness, gray for the loneliness of winter, pink for the creamy perfection of my child, gold for the gift entrusted to me at his birth, and bright green — the color of new grass — for the hope I found in our baby quilt and its promise of spring.

LINDA BOYDEN ✢ *Whatever Works*

I stopped scrubbing bear grease from a blackened windowsill and looked. There in our back yard stood an old pickup, probably broken down in 1962 and forgotten. I think that was the moment I first heard something inside me crack. Not a large sound really. Something small, like the snapping of a twig, but with force enough to jolt me to admit I was completely overwhelmed.

I'd just moved to a dilapidated house in Boulder Creek, Montana, that my then-husband, Dan, bought before I saw it. For days we'd been cleaning out trash bags full of maggot-infested, rotting hides. The move, the cleaning, and the kids — our three-year-old daughter and one-year-old son —

had drained my last drop of strength. I looked out the window at that clunker, my nostrils filled with the acrid aroma of wet bear grease. I tore off my rubber gloves and headed straight out the front door, where I wrapped my arms around myself and contemplated escape.

A car pulled up, driven by a woman I had seen at the market. She yelled at the children in the back seat.

"I will tell you this only one time, so you better listen up." She pointed toward the river. "That there is the Clark Fork River. It is a ten-thousand-foot drop to water icy enough to freeze you dead in two seconds." She snapped her fingers twice for emphasis. "Little girls take even less time, so I had better not see you anywhere near that side of the street, do you understand?"

Then she turned to me and grinned.

"Hey there! My name is Annalee Rogers. Welcome to Boulder Creek." She pronounced it "crick."

"When Erma said she had sold River House to folks from Missoula, I knew I'd have to meet you. Can't believe anyone would buy this dump — no offense, hon."

Annalee stepped from the car and pulled her children out one at a time. "This is Rosalee. This is Emmalee, and this" — Annalee grunted with the weight of her last one — "is Baby T."

The girls followed their mother to my front door.

"I-I'm Linda," I stammered. "Want a cup of coffee?"

"Good Lord, no! This is August, hon — summer? It's too darn hot. Iced tea'd be good. You got some?"

I ushered them in and poured while Annalee scanned the interior and talked nonstop. "Yes sir, nobody's lived here for nearly ten years. That hunter man, Leroy Johnson, he don't count. His wife — if they even were married — she was a Mexican girl or something. They only wintered here to be close to the game."

Annalee stared at the windowsill. "Is that bear grease? Bless your heart, that takes a pile of scrubbing to clean." She offered to return the next day to help.

Her girls and my daughter sat on the couch coloring and munching Oreos. Annalee lifted my son from my lap and fed him his bottle. Her voice softened as his chubby fingers curled around hers.

"This right here is why I keep getting knocked up. Ain't this the sweetest feeling in the whole wide world, hon, holding a baby?"

At that instant of tenderness, Annalee glanced at her own daughters. "Emmalee! Remember what I told you about picking your scabs, girl! You open one up, and all your blood will drain out."

Rosalee, the oldest, nodded. Annalee saw the doubt on little Emmalee's face and reiterated, "Really, Emmie. Then you'll be flat, and Momma will fold you up and put you in a drawer!" Emmalee froze.

Annalee winked. "I still live in the house where I grew up, right here in Boulder Creek. To my recollection, none of the drawers in that entire house has ever been emptied or cleaned. And my kids know it."

She leaned forward and lowered her voice. "Motherhood is a war, hon. One in which we are seriously outnumbered, so we need to use any defenses we have. Whatever works, hon. Whatever works."

I knew we were destined to be friends.

Over the next few years, Annalee taught me about mothering, knowledge that cannot come from a teaching degree. That children will not die from wearing mismatched clothing. That an occasional gooey-bun dinner is good for the soul. That housework will be there every morning, without fail, but our children's precious baby days fade like stars to the dawn.

We picnicked by the river. We pushed carriages in the park. We created elaborate Halloween costumes and stayed up until dawn one Christmas finishing angel robes for the Sunday School pageant. One year we hid ninety-six Easter eggs in the snow for fifteen little children.

We cried. We bragged. We talked on the phone until our elbows cramped. We exiled children to each other's homes when we lost sight of our humor. We laughed: oh, my, how we laughed.

After the birth of our last baby, Dan and I moved our little family from Boulder Creek, pursuing his career. For the first few months, I did not hear from Annalee. I could not understand her silence.

Time passed, and we corresponded gingerly, starting with Christmas cards, then phone calls. Finally, two years ago, twenty years from when we met, Annalee visited my home. We amazed our mates with the ability to pick up old conversation trails right where we had left them, despite the distractions of time and space.

Annalee and Ben celebrated their thirtieth anniversary this year. They still live in the same house, shop at the same stores, wave to the same people. All that security. I am envious.

The last time we talked, I told her so.

"Envious? Good grief! To tell the truth, that's why I stayed away from you when you first moved."

I didn't understand.

"I was envious of *you*, hon! New places, excitement, leaving me behind. It hurt, y'know?"

I did.

"The good thing is, we rode it out and came up on top," she said.

A friendship has a life of its own. It starts out fresh and tight, like shiny new jeans. If worn long enough, it will soften, maybe change as we do, into something new, something different.

All of our kids are adults now. Annalee and I amuse each other long distance with stories of the grandchildren. I remember how she enjoyed hearing that our daughter used the drawer story to stop our granddaughter from picking scabs. I imagined Annalee's eyes crinkling as she chuckled into the phone. "I told you: Whatever works, hon. Whatever works."

BERNIE KOLLER 🦌 Lessons Learned by Hand

Aunt Lena's big hand almost obliterated the stubby pencil she gripped as she drew on the back of an old sale bill. Flowing from the lead, sharpened crudely by a knife, came chickens, kitties, a yard dog, a horse pulling a plow, and all manner of farm animals and objects. Standing at her knee, I ignored the conversation of women and children about who had the flu or how many quarts of tomatoes were put up that week. It was much more difficult to ignore the plate of zwieback, ground cherry jam, and mulberry pies setting on the kitchen table covered with a yellow-and-blue-checked oilcloth. Through the open pantry door, I caught a whiff of sour milk from the separator, the odor that no amount of washing seemed to completely erase. In the parlor, the men sat with their Sunday shoes resting on crocheted rag rugs and attempted not to mess up knitted doilies on the arms of the horsehair sofa.

Aunt Lena's hair was parted in the middle and pulled back into a bun at the back of her neck. Wisps escaped over her ears as she bent forward to finish drawing a goose running after a stick girl.

"Ach, vat a day, ven you got chased. Heh, heh, remember dat mean ol' gander?"

I laughed too and said, "Yeah, I remember, but he wasn't as mean as that electric fence I grabbed. Lucky I had my rubber overshoes on!"

Her coarse complexion reflected the South Dakota sun and wind that had beat on her all of her life. Her homespun dress and brownish stockings suited her tanned face. She never wore lipstick or jewelry. Her hand, as big as Uncle Pete's, added rubber galoshes to the stick girl.

My mother's hands were similar to Aunt Lena's except they were red and chapped from being in water and harsh soap so much. These two pairs of hands lived and toiled on the plains of South Dakota, descended from farmers who were Mennonite Germans from Russia. Both pairs of hands could wring a rag so dry it made me wonder why on earth money was spent on a newfangled laundry wringer with a handle.

Pickle jars quaked with fear when my mother took them off the shelf. Some of them attempted to entomb their vinegary treasures forever by leaking crusty acid around their lids — you know, the kind with the rubber ring with a little tongue hanging out the side. With her Samson-like grip, my mother, the pickle archaeologist, excavated the dull and dilly emeralds from their glassy tombs by crumbling the columns of crust around the cover with a single twist. She didn't even bite her lip or make a face. Meanwhile, my cousin tapped a knife on another crusty jar. Then she took a wet rag and placed it over the top, hoping to get greater traction. When that didn't work, she poured hot water over the jar cover while setting the bottom of the jar in a bowl of cold water, trying to loosen the lid. Finally, the sure-fire solution was called for: place the jar in the strong, trusty hands of my mother.

These women with the strong, capable hands seemed happy with the practical uses they put them to. If they ever dreamed of going to college, or even to New York, I never heard of it. Then I was introduced to the delicate Miss Cotton, whose cheeks were powdered and white, whose hair was soft and light, just like her name. She had attended college. Sometimes chalk dust clung to her delicate fingers when she wrote on the blackboard for her second-grade students. She brushed her hands together to remove the cloudy dust, and a speck of light flashed from her small, sparkly ring. I gazed with delight on the pretty painted fingernails that matched a pink sweater. Her hands fascinated me. Who in the world opened *her* pickle jars?

Diligently, I cleaned blackboards after school to gain her refined attention. I approached her desk.

"Are you finished with your chore?" she asked, knowing the answer.

"Yes, ma'am."

"Did you remember to wash the erasers?"

"Uh-huh." She had within the grasp of her slender right hand a beautiful long pencil with an eraser on top. I fantasized about stealing it and giving it to Aunt Lena for Christmas. But somehow the thought of committing such a sin against the lovely Miss Cotton caused me to shudder, and besides, Aunt Lena didn't have a pencil sharpener. Sharpening that pencil with a knife would be like cutting a sandwich with an ax.

"Are you ready to go home?"

"Guess so." I gazed as she put the pencil down, clasped her hands, and turned her chair slightly toward me.

"Do you have your assignments done for tomorrow?"

"Yep."

"Well, good-bye then." She looked me in the eye.

I lingered. After a pause, she leaned from her chair and allowed me to present her with a farewell kiss on the cheek. The aroma of her perfume startled me. It was the first time I had experienced such a pleasure, and it shocked my nose so greatly that to this day my brain can re-create the scene in glorious detail. That moment was a turning point. I didn't know it at the time, but with a whiff of bottled essence, my mind was opened to the avenues beyond the family unit and the farm. Somehow that lovely aroma got locked up in the cave of my child-mind, right next to Aunt Lena's pictographs, the smell of newly cut clover, straw stacks, earthy barnyards, kerosene lamps, and sour milk. I took one last look at Miss Cotton's hands and left.

Of course, Miss Cotton moved on, leaving behind her particular handi-work crocheted into my heart and soul. I continued to rely on those country hands around me. When I was sick with scarlet fever, they stroked my brow and brought me doughnuts I couldn't eat. These women had their hands full of sick kids and cows, hauling water, cooking, cleaning, separat-ing milk, and doing never-ending chores. I felt kind of sorry for poor Miss Cotton, because her life must have been very dull, stuck in that classroom all the time with nothing but chalk dust on her fingers.

Years passed, times changed, and I went about my schooling, my court-ing, my mothering, living my town life, quite like Miss Cotton's. I worked at a college education instead of on the land, although I occasionally vis-ited these childhood places. Then I began to develop a curiosity about my heritage.

On a trip to Russia and the Ukraine, seeking information about my an-cestors, I clasped the hand of a Ukrainian woman who came out of her humble home to greet the visiting Americans. I could speak no Ukrainian and only a bare minimum of Russian. As I shook this woman's hand, I looked down and stared. Then I took her hand in both of mine. Here was a hand that belonged to the land. Her hand filled me with pictures of the prairie, sun and soil, and priceless memories of stick figures and pickle jars. The old woman looked deep into my eyes and then turned to her neigh-bors, who were looking puzzled. She spoke a few words, and they re-sponded, gathering around as the woman and I matched hands palm to palm. One by one, the women held their hands up to mine, nodding at the similarity in size and strength. They nodded collectively. Yes, I was most certainly a relative. Look at the hands.

Although my hands have had the privilege to be protected from the weather, they recall past labor: shucking ground cherries, pumping water from a well, and shocking grain. Although these hands have been to Paris, Berlin, and Moscow, as well as all over the United States and Canada, they know the security of living on a farm and in a rural town. These fingers have been around fine crystal and in finger bowls. They have been graced with fingernail polish and been immersed in quarts of Jergens hand lotion. However, no matter how much education, no matter how much dreaming, no matter how much money, no matter how much town is in the brain, these hands of mine remain country. There is no way and no reason to hide the genetic gift of these large knuckles. These hands silently represent the generations of women who nurtured and taught me through the lessons learned from the land, the lessons learned by hand.

ELLEN VAYO 🦌 Granma's Gloves

before the evening milking
we scatter   like seed
your ashes onto granpa's grave
we tap them with the flat side of a shovel
weight them with water from our eyes

under a nearby elm   your dog watches
tucks his tail   curls into a ball
he won't eat
hasn't for almost a week
he won't make it
age is against him

behind me   the barn door creaks
pushed by a gentle breeze
eyes of flat-eared feral cats
burn from bales stacked high
they won't come to me even for thick cream
they don't understand but they know

i lift   from the workbench
your gloves worn smooth by hard work
seasoned by afterbirth
ripped by barbed wire
bent like twisted vines into
the shape of your weathered hands

your gloves   several sizes
too large for me

HEIDI R. COUSINS 🦌 Old Ladies Go Hunting

People who meet us think we grew up together, but we met only two years
ago. I love going to yard sales, and at one of those sales I met Elaine.

We are both country gals. Elaine is the wife of a farmer in northeastern
Montana. I have been a ranch hand all over the country, and although I've
had friends, to have a special woman friend was always a dream of mine,
someone to share secrets with and talk about woman concerns that men
don't understand. My dream came true that day at the yard sale. We are

both in our fifties now, and together we go fishing, overnight camping, canoeing; we take martial arts classes; and we go deer hunting.

"You two women go and have fun!" my husband grinned as I slowly departed with a pickup load of camping gear to pick up Elaine for our two-, maybe three-day hunting trip. He knew we'd have fun, camping at the long-abandoned homestead in rocky terrain sprinkled with sagebrush, buttes, and hidden ravines where Elaine had been raised. But he must have thought we were nuts. Elaine's brother had been out there a week earlier and mentioned a skunk had taken up residence under the house.

When I arrived at Elaine's, only a mile cross-country, we loaded all her camping equipment on top of mine, tied it securely to the pickup, and headed out for the hunt. "Ready?" I asked.

"Yep, I think so," she replied with a giggle as she jumped in the passenger's side. I slowly drove out of the yard, saying, "Let's go over the stuff we packed, in case we forgot something, OK?"

"Us, forget something?"

We both laughed out loud and went over the things we'd packed. A mile of dirt road would lead us to the highway, but before we got that far, Elaine shrieked and I slammed on the brakes. "The rifle! I forgot the rifle. Left it on the freezer by the door. Heidi! I forgot the rifle!"

I laughed so hard tears blinded me as I backed the pickup all the way back to her house. From then on, every time we looked at each other, we broke out laughing, and promised not to tell anyone, ever.

No one lives at the old homestead now. There is no running water, and the plumbing is no longer usable, but the outhouse still stands a few yards from the house among decrepit sheds. The place overlooks a creek bottom, where an old windmill pumps water for the cattle pastured there.

We found the kitchen window open and the smell of skunk faint. We had electricity, and the microwave still worked. "And we call this roughing it? Ha!" I shouted. We cooked supper on a camp stove and assembled our cots, then played dominoes and cards the rest of the evening. I couldn't sleep. Our cots squeaked every time we moved. I finally put my sleeping bag on the floor. In the early morning, I woke up Elaine, shouting, "Elaine, Elaine, it's snowing! Yippee, it's snowing! Get up and see!"

"I never saw anybody so excited over snow," she groaned.

"I just hope it doesn't turn into a blizzard like last year."

We bundled up for the zero weather and hunted on foot along Chokecherry Creek, but we saw no signs of game. When we got cold, we returned to the old house to plan another hunt. This time we took the pickup, and I dropped Elaine off at the far end of the south pasture.

"Go back as far as the last open gate and wait for me there, OK, Heidi?"

I drove back while she walked cross-country in several inches of snow on rough, rocky ground. Waiting, I was not alone. A herd of cows ran to the parked truck, hoping to get fed. They pushed so close against the vehicle I felt it move. Every time I pushed the door open, squeezed out, and chased them away, they came back before I was settled back in the truck.

"Didn't see a thing," Elaine said when she returned, sipping the hot coffee I poured for her. "Earlier hunters must have scared them out of here. Let's drive closer to the creek."

We bounced over the frozen ground. The snow had stopped, and the sun was trying to peek through the overcast sky. As we approached a bend in the creek, we spotted a five-point buck and several does feeding below us. "There's my buck," Elaine squeaked.

"Sure thing," I agreed. I came to an easy halt as she slipped quietly out of the pickup and leaned over the hood to take aim.

The instant I shut the engine down, the buck headed for the opposite cutbank, but both Elaine and I knew this would happen. She waited for the proud animal to stop. They always do.

One shot. The buck ran to follow the does, only to find himself slowing down, stumbling, falling. I started the pickup and put it in gear.

Elaine thought I was leaving her behind. "Wait for me, will ya?" The pickup slipped and slid in the fresh snow as we bumped off the trail. "One shot, Heidi!" Elaine announced proudly.

"Yeah, just like last year. One clean shot!"

We walked a short distance to the buck, and, panting, Elaine whispered, "What if he's not dead?"

"Don't worry, I'll cut his throat."

"Cut his throat?" she squeaked.

The buck had gone to his own happy hunting ground. From pure joy, we jumped around him, then stopped to catch our breath.

Elaine said, "Can you imagine going hunting and not knowing how to gut a deer?"

"Gee, some folks would think that of us, 'cause we're women!" I said.

I'd brought a little sled to pull the buck to the pickup. We laughed the whole time we were dressing him out, Elaine wanting to help and me telling her it was a "one-man" job. Then, while I took pictures, she complained, "I walked miles out there, freezing my behind, then find this buck in my old back yard." I looked around and saw that the homestead house was only a few yards away.

I'd filled my deer tag earlier in the season, so our hunting was over for the year, but after washing up, warming up, and having lunch, we bundled up once more and went out to snoop around another old homestead a mile away. We found a few harness buckles, bolts, and nails, right through the frozen ground, and I stumbled over a horseshoe from a workhorse. You know, one of those large, beautiful old horseshoes? I did a little dance around my find and heard Elaine giggle. "Never saw anyone get so excited over so little."

A nasty, cold breeze kept us from more treasure hunting, and we headed back to the warm kitchen for pizza and to listen to *Fibber McGee and Molly* tapes. We played cards and laughed over Fibber's jokes the rest of the evening, then settled down in our sleeping bags on the floor, listening to classical music: Bach, Beethoven, and Strauss.

The next morning, we packed up and tied the buck on top of our camping stuff for everyone to see as we drove home. Call it proud or bragging, we didn't care. Another one of our great excursions came to an end with good friends, good fun, and good luck.

LOIS HART 🦌 Muskrat Ramble

Like Ethel with her loons on Golden Pond,
my mother rushes to the glass to watch her grebes glide by.
"Come see the babies," she calls. "They're riding piggyback."
She points out tiny heads, peeking from the mother's black feathers.

We aren't surprised . . .
have watched her feed our dachshund
the prime bite from her pork chop,
kidded her when she gave a lazy fly
squatter's rights on a sunny kitchen window for the winter.
Her only rule to camping Cub Scouts:
"Don't hurt frogs or snakes."

Now hot August. No rain.
Cattails droop in the drying swamp.
Humped muskrats waddle across the browning grass,
seeking algae green drinks at the lake.
"Poor things," she says, as if she feels their thirst.
Her neighbor sees them, too — rodents, vermin.
He grabs his hoe, is beating at a toddler.
"What are you doing?" We children know that voice,
the one that warned we'd dawdled long enough en route to bed.

What does he think, this gruff and well-known businessman,
when she marches out to plant herself
between his swinging hoe and prey?
Does he know that women — those makers of Kool-Aid,
players of Old Maid, planters of daisies —
can turn intractable? Today my mother is
Rosa Parks unwilling to move to the back of the bus;

Margaret Sanger doling out contraband pamphlets;
Susan B. Anthony boldly casting her illegal vote.

Perplexed by her ferocity, he mutters and retreats.
We tease her: "Are you going to be one of those women
who get arrested for chaining themselves to trees?"
We tease her because we don't know how to tell her
how proud of her we are.

DONNA PARKS ❧ Spider Beside Her

There it was. In the bathtub. A big black spider. I was in the bathroom of my friend after driving for three hours to see her. My friend Margaret is almost ninety years old. She is very tiny and starting to slow down, with several health problems, including a bad heart. Yet she lives alone in her isolated home in the hills. And there was a big black spider in her bathtub.

When I saw it, I thought, "If Margaret sees this, she could have a heart attack." I am not used to killing my own spiders. What to do? The hair on the back of my neck started to rise, but I took my courage in hand and acted.

First, I poured water on the monster to immobilize him, then I grabbed a handful of toilet paper, scooped him up in it, and, shuddering, threw the wad into the toilet and flushed. Breathless from my heroics, I walked out into the room and told my friend what I had done. I was proud of myself. But then I saw the look on her face. She said sadly, only, "Oh." It was then I knew I had killed her friend.

I should have known. Besides being an expert on the habits of birds, she has always been a lover of nature. She has forgiven me, and we are still friends, but I have some guilt left for being so unperceptive as to believe she felt as I did about spiders.

LEE ANN SIEBKEN ❧ The Storm

This is not Nancy's story, but she was the reason I got on that bus. This is not the story of a six-year-old leading me into the bittersweet world of the blind, but she did that, too. It is the story of a storm that became legendary and three women who put my life in perspective.

The storm slammed into South Dakota, spitting ice and spinning snowflakes into eerie sculptures. It stranded ranchers headed home, travelers headed east, and red-faced meteorologists in their cozy TV studios. But my own storm had been brewing since September, when our first-grader, Nancy, went to live on a campus seven hundred miles away from her daddy, her two big brothers, her sister, and me. Strangers would witness her first loose tooth, read her bedtime stories, and kiss her good night. Friends and family gasped, "How could you?"

Sometimes we explained that the South Dakota School for the Blind was noted for "outstanding credentials and a better-than-average success rate," and sometimes we just swallowed hard and whispered, "It's not easy." I dragged through each day as I waited for Christmas break and Nancy's return. When the invitation from her school arrived only two days before her scheduled flight, its words fueled my gathering fury: *"Each and every student will participate in our annual Christmas program. We wouldn't want your child to be the only one without someone in attendance."*

Somehow, someone must make that seven-hundred-mile trip to the school despite the tightly scheduled arrangements we'd already made with an airline to get Nancy home as quickly as possible, and that someone would be me. I would go, attend her program, and bring her home for an abbreviated Christmas break while Duane stayed home to care for the other children and attend their Christmas programs.

Driving to Aberdeen was out of the question. The only travel option available at this late date was to drive thirty miles to the nearest Greyhound depot and take the bus.

The first leg of the bus ride, the 150 miles to Rapid City, went quickly, but by late afternoon the weather had begun to deteriorate, and the twinkle of the city was a welcome sight. When we arrived at the deserted depot, it was crackling cold and snow fell lightly. I was dismayed to find the bus depot closing. A weary gentleman ushered me onto the street, explaining that the depot wouldn't reopen "until the Aberdeen run loads at eleven. You be careful," he warned me. "About this time yesterday, somebody mugged a lady and stole her purse. Better check with us about departure, what with this weather." Other passengers left in waiting cars as I ducked my head into the swirling snow and walked toward the business district with its twinkling Christmas decorations. On a bank sign, the time and temperature blinked on and off: 5:58, −20, 5:59, −20, 6:00 . . .

Following the many partygoers as they traipsed into the lobby of the beautiful old Alex Johnson Hotel, I sat for a while on a soft sofa to wait and people watch. Smiling people dusted snow from their hair before entering the dining room. When I finally slipped into the coffee shop for a light supper, the waitress warned me, "Better keep an eye on your purse. Yesterday some guy mugged an old woman! Got her Social Security money."

Warmed by coffee, I reentered the lobby. An elegant woman sat on my sofa, so I looked for an out-of-the-way place to sit, read, and wait. She smiled. She smoothed her long skirt. She beckoned me to join her, and I did.

We admired the beautiful floor-to-ceiling Christmas tree. She didn't have a Christmas tree at home; this was her tree, had been for years. In no time, I learned that she had an apartment in the hotel and knew everyone who worked there. She called me "dearie."

Mayme Duhamel introduced herself and invited me to go upstairs with her for a chat. It seemed the most natural thing in the world, and for several hours we visited about her hometown and her famous old hotel. Mayme didn't gasp or burst into tears when I told her I was going to Aberdeen to retrieve my six-year-old from the School for the Blind. She just smiled and said, "We've come a long way in eighty years, dearie. When I was growing up, families hid their handicapped children."

Hours dissolved in conversation, and my call to the depot confirmed the bus would be leaving on time. Mayme walked me to the elevator, introduced me to Albert, and squeezed my hand. Before he closed the door, Albert asked, "Where to?"

When I told him I was on my way to the bus depot, he said, "I don't want to scare you or anything, but . . ." By the time we reached the lobby, he'd refreshed my memory about the poor mugged soul. He sighed, clipped an out-of-order sign on a chain he stretched across the elevator door, shrugged into his overcoat, and walked me all the way to the bus depot. He bid me a safe journey and disappeared into the snowy night.

The depot was now lively, and voices rose ever louder, luggage was stacked ever higher, and cigarette and diesel smoke grew ever thicker. Unlike the previous bus, this one was crowded with passengers talking loudly and jockeying for seats. I sat next to an elderly woman, and eventually the aisle cleared and the driver announced a dozen places we'd be stopping. Final stop, Aberdeen.

Nora Christensen was a reassuring woman who was also going to Aberdeen. Soon I found myself confiding in her about our blind daughter, Nancy, the invitation, and the reason I was going to Aberdeen. Our bus passed eighteen-wheelers jackknifed in the median as I went on and on about my family. Cars slid off the road as I lashed out about the unfairness of it all. And we rode on, stopping and starting as some passengers reached their destinations and others came aboard. Finally, with a catch in my voice, I whispered a threat I couldn't allow myself to say out loud: "I'm taking Nancy home, and neither of us will ever return to this school again." Nora nodded and patted my hand. "My husband had a label for protective mothers. 'Mama lions' he called us."

The weather intensified outside, but somewhere along the way I began to control my winds of rage.

We reached Aberdeen early on the morning of the Christmas program, the morning of the never-to-be-forgotten Blizzard of Sixty-seven, the morning when the South Dakota School for the Blind canceled plan A and put plan B in place. The airport was closed, and the highways were closing one by one. The last bus out would meet the Pierre–to–Sioux Falls Greyhound, then go on to Rapid City. No jolly elf here! Santa, in his school lobby workshop, was harried as he handed out Christmas candy in paper bags and called out, "Next."

My own meeting with school personnel lasted only minutes. All previous travel arrangements were suspended, and every effort was made to make sure no students were stranded in Aberdeen for the holidays. Frantic phone calls were made and permission granted for seven children to ride with Nancy and me on the now-departing bus. Would I help the children make their connections? What could I say?

I pried eight blind children, with their suitcases and candy, away from Santa Claus. We boarded the school's van, hurried back to the depot, and began the ticket scramble. The van's driver and I managed to keep kids and coats together, get the right tickets into the right pockets, and gather our little bunch into one corner of the depot. Then I was on my own. I counted those children a dozen times as they clung to each other and those precious paper bags. Nancy was the youngest, only six; Jimmy, the oldest, was ten.

I counted them, three to a seat. I asked them their names over and over. I answered their questions: "Nancy's Mom, where's Jimmy?" "Nancy's Mom, where's the bathroom?" "Nancy's Mom, why are we stopping?" Only Darrell was quiet as he worked the ribbon off and dug his hand into his candy bag. How long since they'd eaten, I wondered.

Donnie amused himself by peeling frost off the window. It made a nice little shower on his upheld face. It made little puddles on the back of his seat and dripped off onto the knees of the lady behind him, who gave me a look. Five little boys, three little girls, and me, the only one who could see. What in the world was I thinking? Why had I even thought I could do this? Not one child cried or fussed, and no one complained of hunger. Maybe I could get cheese and crackers at the junction.

Passengers watched us with pity and expressions of disbelief. When the bus finally reached "jumping-off" junction, where six of the children had to change buses, everyone eagerly helped sort luggage, zip up coats, and hang on to us in the howling wind until six kids were on the eastbound bus, seated and still clutching candy. I prayed that strangers would pitch in to help those six kids reach their destinations.

Darrell and Nancy and I continued westward while the storm raged on. At Pierre I was able to get us a bite to eat, and then we were back on the bus headed toward Interstate 90. We rolled across the Badlands and skirted Standing Rock Indian Reservation. We passed an assortment of stranded vehicles and saw a little group of bedraggled travelers fighting the miserable wind as they walked toward town after abandoning a stalled car. A winter sunset beckoned as we pulled into the depot in Rapid City.

By now Darrell and Nancy were exhausted. The confusion of the depot in their dark world brought tears. We sat. We waited. For the first time today, his blindness frustrated Darrell. Where was his mother? Was she here yet? I reassured, held him in my lap, and watched the clock. At six o'clock, the depot would close for five hours before reopening. I watched the door as seats emptied and the desk clerk busied himself checking the restrooms and jangling his keys. Six o'clock came. We couldn't stay. The list the school had given me had seven names and only six phone numbers, none by Darrell's name. Nancy and I could leave our luggage, but Darrell's suitcase had to go with us. He would need it if his mother arrived and found us before the depot reopened. The paper bag had become tattered and precious, so he hugged it to him with one hand and held Nancy's hand with the other. The walk to the Alex Johnson seemed longer and the night darker than it had just one day earlier.

I don't know how long we waited. We sat, we walked around the lobby, and as Darrell became more and more distressed, so did I. I thought of Mayme's cozy apartment, but I was afraid to leave the lobby for fear of missing Darrell's mother. I didn't even take the children to eat. We munched on snacks, and I tried to comfort Darrell by telling him we'd find his mother waiting at the bus depot when it reopened after a while. What would I do, though, if our bus began boarding before Darrell was united with his mother?

A commotion at the registration desk attracted my attention. A woman accompanied by a child of nine or ten pounded her fist on the counter, fury, like venom, in her hiss. A toddler clung to her stretched cloth coat; frost glittered on straggles of hair poking out around a stocking hat pulled low on her neck. The woman trembled with rage.

The older child caught sight of us before I could go to them. "Hey, Darrell! I knew we'd find ya. Hey, Ma!" The boy came and sat with Darrell, who hid his candy behind his back. I went toward Darrell's mother, my hands extended, but she brushed me off as she jerked Darrell out of the plush chair and cursed him. She shoved his suitcase into the hands of his older brother. Spittle showered me as she screamed, "How did they expect me to find him if they locked up the depot?" Then she knelt down to button up their coats as she cursed the dead battery in her car. "Thought we never would get a ride into town! It's a long way when it's twenty below. You'd think people would stop for a woman and two kids hitchhiking in this blankety-blank cold."

I looked from my sturdy snow boots to her four-buckle galoshes and shivered as she shoved the children through the heavy doors, hunched her shoulders, and stomped away. The desk clerk shook his head apologetically as I called, "Merry Christmas, Darrell," to a jubilant little boy hurrying to keep up with his mama.

Nancy was exhausted. After eating a bowl of soup and a dish of ice cream in the coffee shop, she fell asleep. I tried to read, but a warm sense of well-being filled me. Nancy and I would be homeward bound in less than three hours. Our family would be waiting for us. I even had safe harbors here. Mayme and Nora, the kind woman on the bus, had blessed me with understanding, the hotel was warm, the school had trusted me with a monumental task, and I had handled it.

But what about Darrell's mother? Was there a dad at home, a Mayme, or a Nora? This night there'd been none of that, only bitter cold, a dead battery, hitchhiking in a blizzard, and her lost child. Her plight seemed so hopeless compared to my situation, which was inconvenient, yes, a predicament, yes, but not without hope.

I never saw Darrell's mother again, but whenever I went to Aberdeen, Darrell was there, doing what blind children — all children — have to do to make it in the world: getting an education. He was as bright and cheerful as any other student. When I asked how his mother was and he answered "Fine," I remembered her roar and the mane of frosted hair framing her face.

It took a blizzard and three women to put my life in perspective, but it is Darrell's mother whom I owe the most, and it is Darrell's mother whom I wonder about, pray for, and thank every Christmas Day.

TINA WELLING ❧ Passage

Her name was Genie, like the magic spirit in the bottle, and for a time I secretly wondered whether she manifested only when I summoned her. She was in her early seventies when she agreed to take me on as her student, with the advice not to believe a word she said, unless I experienced its truth for myself.

For fifteen years, she read to me from her ancient books, let me argue with her, watched me veer off on tangents and trot back with my endless questions, soothed me, warned me, loved me.

We met every Wednesday night for three hours. I drove 150 miles roundtrip from my home to her log cabin perched on a ledge high over the Big Thompson River outside Loveland, Colorado. She had built a series of seven terraces from river's edge to canyon top to fortify the eroding slope and to enact, on the physical plane, the teachings of mysticism.

"Seven is a sacred number," she said, "and building, stone by stone, our inner fortress is what our meetings are all about."

Besides renovating her home, she built three other cabins on the canyon slope, one for me to stay in whenever I chose. From one Wednesday to the next, this petite woman in her seventies gathered stones from nearby mountains, tossed each one into her old Jeep, drove to her terraced slope, and laid one stone atop another to make cabin walls that hung over sheer drops. And every Wednesday I saw this labor and wondered what I, forty years younger, had accomplished to match it. Several Wednesdays over the years, Genie greeted me plastered in a homemade cast. No one knew her body better than she did, so she set her own broken bones — a leg, an arm, fingers, her ribs on several occasions.

She had typed from the original some of the rare old books we studied. This was the only way to own a copy before the age of copy machines. She suggested this as a good way to learn, so I did the same, borrowing hers to type copies of my own.

When I arrived each Wednesday evening, we'd settle on one of the seven terraces in chaise longues. She'd read and I'd listen, and we'd both watch the sun go down, a color show on the granite walls across the canyon. At dusk we'd move inside to sit before her fire and continue. After reading, we talked. Genie gave me back to myself. She taught me that I already owned the source of truth. I didn't need to search for it through special teachers or books or churches or schools. Genie taught me that I didn't need her.

"You want to know the mysteries of life," she said. "Ask, be still, listen. Every secret in the world will step out of shadow and show itself to you."

Eventually, I believed her, and we became friends, then family to each other, instead of teacher and student.

Some years later, we moved to homes in opposite directions. One day I received a letter from her. In her nineties, having survived several heart attacks, she felt death was near and wished to warn me. She was saying good-bye. I wasn't ready and cried. But my job was to get ready and to let her know I was. I tried to hurry myself, not wishing to burden her further, but I fell into a kind of stupor, an emotional stall. It took me a month to write her back. Even so, with my reply I enclosed a pin designed from a petroglyph of a turtle. The turtle is the Native American symbol of long life.

Genie's son sent me her ashes. I scattered them in the mountains — places we walked together in Colorado, places she told me about from her girlhood in Jackson Hole.

Now I drive her old Jeep and wear the embossed leather belt that once encircled her waist. The elegant handmade saddle that she used in Jackson Hole rodeos as a girl sits in my living room. Her books line my shelves. But I cherish most the many letters she wrote to me, reminding me of the truth she was so certain I already knew.

SANDIE NICOLAI and NORMA J. KULAS
🦎 End of the World

Sandie: The long bus trip to western North Dakota felt as if I were going to the end of the world. Up until then, my everyday world hadn't expanded farther than 125 miles from where I was born.

Norma: Little did Sandie know she was moving to "the end of the world." I'd thought so, too, when sixteen years previously we had driven into the valley and saw a fast-food sign proclaiming FLEISCHKEUCHLE. I knew then that if I, an English teacher, couldn't pronounce what the local residents ate, I was in big trouble!

The anticipation of seeing Vince — my husband, my lover, my friend for the past twenty-six years — made it exciting. He'd already been at work for the post office there for a few months while the kids and I had stayed behind to finish our summer jobs. The thought of leaving close friends behind and starting over filled me with sadness and dread.

Vince and I are teachers of natural family planning (NFP), so I'd checked a national directory to find out whether there were fellow NFP teachers in Beulah. We had already met one NFP couple when we'd gone to find Vince a place to live. I carried their phone number in my purse, thinking I'd give them a call while Vince was out on his mail route. A cup of coffee with someone might help fill the long hours.

That one phone call was the beginning of a friendship that has spanned thirteen years and many miles. Norma and Arnie's house was only a few blocks away from the efficiency apartment where Vince had been hanging his hat while waiting for us to join him.

I remember that first meeting. I was bent over flowers and bushes that Arnie had left me to water and weed while he went to Montana to teen camp. I was muttering and mumbling about weeds and dry climates when I looked up to see a most wonderful smile and warm, twinkly eyes that seemed to understand immediately that I would rather be reading a good book than weeding and watering.

Two weeks later, when the kids and I arrived permanently, we weren't even unpacked before Norma and Arnie, their arms loaded with fresh garden vegetables, rang the doorbell and welcomed us.

Sandie didn't know that I was most relieved to get rid of the vegetables. With all the gardens Arnie tended, the vegetables created a lot of work. Friendships have many pleasant side effects.

Their three daughters and one son were closely matched in age with our five kids. Potluck suppers together; long walks in the crisp fall evenings; three-handed pinochle for Vince, Arnie, and me while Norma, a non–card player, served as cheerleader, all formed a strong bond in a short time.

Ah yes, those card games. And while I never learned to play pinochle, I did have two hands free for all the snacks. One of my favorite memories of Sandie is "monkey bread." I loved those impromptu Saturday morning calls inviting us over for a warm breakfast. Although I asked for the recipe, I've never made monkey bread. I close my eyes and remember the kitchen, the delicious smell, the laughter, and the chatter . . . I prefer to keep that for Sandie's home. Maybe some Saturday morning, I'll be back in North Dakota.

I felt somewhat cynical when I heard the rector at church each Sunday morning say, "Welcome to our parish," and I thought, "There are only a few people here who are Monday, Tuesday, Wednesday welcomers." But Norma and Arnie were among those who made church believable the rest of the week.

We'd just arrived at Grandma's house after a seven-hour drive with five kids when we answered the phone to learn that our good-natured buddy Arnie had suffered a heart attack at the high school gym that evening and died. He was only forty, and he was gone. And Norma's life had changed forever.

We cut our family visit short to return for Arnie's funeral. The large church was overflowing with family and friends. Evidently, this couple had touched a lot of lives besides ours.

During Arnie's funeral Mass, I looked up at Communion and saw Vince and Sandie coming toward me. The power of their love and the strength of their friendship seemed to surround me at that moment, and I felt almost as if someone had wrapped me in a warm blanket. It was a beautiful message from God, I think, telling us that He would be with us through it all.

Norma's house was wall-to-wall people when we stopped over later in the day and met many family members. Soon all the family went back to their homes, the crowds dispersed, and Norma began the monumental task of raising four children by herself.

I was there when she couldn't get to sleep at night. I was there when she went through the anger stage and kicked the closet door and said, "Dammit, Arnie, why did you have to die?" We walked and talked, talked and walked.

Those late-night, early-morning conversations while the rest of the world slept. The laughter, the tears, the journey. I often thanked God for Sandie's quiet, calm faith and her steadfast belief that God's plan is good. With my friend, I never had to be strong. I just had to be me.

I was there when she went to visit a grave covered with snow. I was there when she started to heal, and I saw her strength and resilience. She remembers my asking if I thought she'd ever marry again. I was also there when she fell in love again. Some thought it was too soon. It was wonderful to see the joy and delight after witnessing the pain and loneliness. Now I was *her* cheerleader!

I am certain our friendship would have remained strong had Arnie lived. But in a mysterious way, what we shared after he embraced eternity bonded us in a very special way and was a gift to both of us.

Her gentle, quiet, caring Roger became our friend, too. We rejoiced as we witnessed their formal, sacred vows to each other in the same church where we'd said good-bye to Arnie.

We moved to greener pastures and better opportunities. Later, they also left western North Dakota.

Now, of course, there is the distance of several states between us. But when we do see each other, it's like we have never been apart. That's because we never are.

There are phone calls, letters, visits, and trips to the weddings of those sons and daughters who once had crushes on each other. Now we're both grandmothers who still do not have empty nests. We're in touch often by e-mail. It's become the new "next best thing to being there."

I am so glad she welcomed the stranger. I am so glad I was given the grace to comfort the sorrowing. We are kindred spirits who laugh and cry together across the miles.

DONNA GRAY ❧ Huddled for Warmth

Before I lived in Montana, I thought that friendships were of a "break bread together" nature. If I hadn't shared a meal with another woman or couple, it wasn't really a friendship. But that's not true around here. Yes, there are those friends with whom I do break bread, but I no longer think of it as a requirement to having a friendship. In the days before Montana, there was less diversity in my friendships. Friends tended to be my age; we were of the same socioeconomic level. Montana changed all that.

Here, where there aren't very many people, we all huddle together for warmth. We used to have a book club here in the valley; the youngest woman was in her twenties, the oldest in her late eighties. Each decade between twenty and eighty was represented. What a rich experience it was. The senior woman in the group confessed to me one day, "I've been boy crazy all my life." I didn't realize that eighty-eight-year-old women felt that way.

RUBY R. WILSON ❧ Mother Love

"Time spent with you, Mom / reminds me how special it is / that life made us Mother and Daughter / but love made us friends." I put the card back and looked for another. "Thinking about you, especially today / Hope you have a wonderful birthday." This one would do.

In our small German-Russian community in north-central South Dakota during the sixties, people were hard working, frugal, and reserved. We didn't meddle in other people's business. Likewise, family matters were not shared with outsiders. Showing affection openly, in public or at home, was not customary. No one ever hugged, kissed, or said, "I'm proud of you," or even "Good job!" I remember wearing my new dress, shoes, gloves, and little white purse in church on Easter Sunday when I was about seven years old, and I leaned my head on Mom's shoulder. When she didn't respond in any way, I sat back up. I was more comfortable spending time with Dad at the car repair garage where he worked.

I didn't know that my father was Mom's second husband until I was about eight years old. "Was Dad glad to finally have a boy after having three girls?" I asked one summer afternoon. She told me that she had been married before and my two older sisters were really half sisters.

"This is what my first husband did to me." She gently showed me how he knocked her to the floor.

She and her husband shared a farmhouse with her in-laws, a turbulent family. My grandmother spoke to me of Mom's first marriage only once, when she told of mending Mom's clothes and finding rips and damage that seemed odd to her. She knew that once Mom had been beaten unconscious and speculated that this had resulted in permanent brain damage.

My mother felt that she was sinning by divorcing and remarrying and seemed to punish herself for this.

"Do we have school today?" I asked her one stormy January morning. She worked the night shift as a nurse's aide and was still in her uniform, sitting in a chair at the kitchen table with her Bible open.

She sat there in a daze. "I was reading, and a pen floated and marked these passages in my Bible." She showed me the unsteady ink marks. Shortly after, she was committed to the state hospital for several months. These "nervous breakdowns" seemed to recur every few years, more often as she grew older.

Mom, when healthy, always worked outside the home, even though it was uncommon at that time. Although she and Dad had only eighth-grade educations, she was determined that all of her children would go to college.

On wages of only a couple of dollars an hour as a nurse's aide and later a cook in a restaurant, she saved three thousand dollars for each of four children for college. Even though I pointed out that costs were higher for me than for my sisters, she was determined that it would be equal. I worked in a bakery as a teenager, and she insisted that every penny be saved for college. When I had trouble rolling out the kuchen dough at the bakery, Mom made dough at home so I could practice. I earned enough to pay for one semester of college costs. With the availability of grants, I didn't have to take out any loans to complete my college education.

"I'm going to buy a new house and new clothes for myself once you kids get through college," she often said. She did both but ended up selling the house and giving the money away, probably to a TV evangelist, when she was not well. When she went into a nursing home, my brother and I had to give away the nice clothes, hardly worn.

I went for a night walk during Christmas vacation last year, on a gravel road in the country where my husband's family lives. As I rounded the corner a half mile from the farm, the road ahead looked so enticing, strange, and new in the moonlight. I felt tempted to keep going but turned around and walked back toward the warm yellow lights of the house. The next day, my family and I traveled the same road, sunlit and muddy, to visit my mother.

Now, two months later, I have learned that she has lung cancer. After talking to her doctor, I read her letter again, which says in part, "The doctor says I have cancer; I have to die." I find myself mourning the only mother I ever had and the mother I never had. As I finish my walk tonight, I realize that the scarf I wrap around myself is hers.

bj buckley — glad to have you "on the line"

B. J. BUCKLEY · **The Woman, Listening on the Party Line**

May 5, '02

There's Eva Dabney, that's the seventh time
she's passed *that* gossip on
in thirty minutes! She's our early warning system —
what's so wild is that she never keeps a story straight,
even when *she's* telling it, even when
she likely made it up. What if I broke in and said,
"But, Eva, last four times
you told it, they only did it *twice!*" —
she'd answer me just like she knew
I'm listening, prob'ly does, there isn't much
escapes her. The line gets
echoey when someone else picks up.
There's Biddy. Good. It's been two days,
she's ninety, glad that she's still with us.
She has eggs, maybe later
I'll call back and ask her, "You got eggs?" —
so she can be happy again
and tell me yes.
Those girls, what cowboy is it this time?
Sandy Vollmer!
Well, they're right, he's got cute buns
(and his head smack up the middle of 'em,
but they'll have to find that out
on their own!).

Now who's that laughing?
Never know what people will laugh at,
could be a tragedy in progress, that'd be
one way of meeting it —
God, I remember when that poor boy
blew the right side of his head clean off
trying to change a split-rim tire and it exploded,
and his father laughing at the funeral,
real laughter full of the warmth of love
and recollection, saying, "I always told that kid
he only had half a brain, and the little son of a bitch
proved me right!"
What would it be like to hear all this
and not know *who* or *why* or *where*, not have
anything to match up with the voices?
Not to know the faces or
whose pickup just drove by —
the one with "no muffler" . . .
Mr. Cyrus. Couldn't be no other
with that kind of noise! — to listen in
and be locked out, to be
a stranger, a stranger spilling longing
down the wire.

GIN SCOTT ❧ Shifting Gears

"Virginia, stay still! I can't watch you and the road," Mother said as she struggled with the stiff steering wheel. The narrow two-lane blacktop was strewn with potholes on this sixty-mile stretch between Grandma's house and our home on the ranch.

I opened Mother's white pocketbook on the seat between us and tore at the wrapper on a roll of Life Savers.

"Here, let me," she said. She pulled off one driving glove and seized the candy. Suddenly, she huffed, "Oh, my God!" and jerked the wheel to the left. The Life Savers flew into the back seat. Our Chevy whipped across both lanes and dove off a steep embankment. Chokecherry bushes flew by the window, and I tumbled to the floor. Finally, the car stopped. Mom's hands clung to the wheel. Her eyeglasses had slid down the bridge of her nose, and her prim hat, like a white enameled pot lid, had tipped forward to her eyebrows. She sat stiff-legged like long johns frozen on the clothesline. I was nose-to-high-heel with her feet, which mashed the clutch and brake pedals to the floorboard.

She stared out the windshield, but her tight, thin words were aimed at me. "You have to scream for help. Don't move fast. Don't bounce the seat. Just stick your head out the window and yell. Loud!" I untangled, crawled onto the seat, and leaned out the side window. Behind me, Mom jabbered to herself in Swedish, her first language. The front tires perched on the edge of a broad irrigation ditch brimming with swift water. Even as a six-year-old, I knew that if the car lurched, we would sink into the ditch, and Mom possessed a perfect lurching record.

"Help us! Help us!" I shrilled whenever a vehicle roared by on the highway. Finally, a car braked and backed up. A door slammed, and a skinny man appeared on the shoulder. His shirt flapped open as he slid down the embankment. He scraped past the chokecherries and peered through my window at Mom on the far side. The man's chest, inches from my face, was bone white and hairless.

"You all right?" he asked.

Mom blurted, "I can't move the car by myself. We'll drown."

"You're lucky, Ma'am," said our savior. "My radio's on the blink, and I had all the windows rolled down in this heat, or I wouldn't have heard ya. In this green car in these green bushes, I couldn't see much of ya either." He carefully lifted me out of the window, his hot, sticky chest against my bare legs, and carried me far up the bank.

He scooted into the driver's door next to my mother. Water sloshed over the ditch's lip. Soon the Chevy's engine squealed like a mad cat. *Ree-urr. Ree-urr.* Black smoke popped out the vibrating exhaust pipe, and the Chevrolet leaped backward up the steep bank.

We reorganized the upturned groceries and two hours later rolled up to the cabin the hired help lived in at a ranch outside Lodge Grass. Before we stepped off the running boards, Mom said, "I'll get you two Popsicles — your favorite, banana — next time we buy groceries if you let me be the one to tell your dad about our adventure today."

I nodded, my throat still sore from screaming. When I whined for Popsicles, she usually said, "We can't afford it."

Mother and I drove into, through, and out of so many "adventures" (her term) in my childhood that I wasted money on my first carnival ride. With her at the wheel of an automobile, we spun circles on ice, were slammed from side to side, were knocked to the floorboard, splashed through pond-size mud puddles and bumper-deep creek beds, rocked in snowdrifts, lurched forward and backward, bucked half a mile, and I screamed plenty of times. She never had a major accident, though.

Mother's marriage to my father, a cowboy, destined her to wrap nervous hands around the skinny steel steering wheels of cars that resembled second-string beauty queens. Mother was somewhat deaf, so to drive them, she relied on bits of information she heard from Dad or me, felt vibrations from the whole vehicle, or watched the amount of fear building on my face.

To start a vehicle, she choked and throttled dashboard knobs and fired up the finicky engine by pushing her toes onto the starter pedal on the floorboard. Simultaneously, Mom pumped the accelerator with the heel of the same foot. When she finally heard the starter's loud grinding or my screeching, "Mother, you're hurting it," she knew the engine had engaged.

To back up the various clunker pickups we owned, Mom pumped the clutch while wrestling the gear stick on the floor, seldom winning the match. So in these stubborn automobiles, Mom drove forward. Only.

Once, between Sheridan and Acme, a rear tire blew out. Our Chevy sedan careened across the highway, but Mom managed to steer us to safety. "You stay in her," she said, and disappeared behind the Chevy. The trunk raised. Clanking and grunting wafted through my open window. The trunk slammed, and she scooted back into the driver's seat. "I don't even have strength enough to get the spare tire out of the trunk," she said. "We'll have to wait for help."

We read. No cars came. Finally, she said, "Well, we can't sit out here all day. The milk will spoil." Mom started the motor and lurched through a U-turn, and we bumped toward Sheridan, flat tire flapping. The Chevy hiccuped. *Ka-fwap, ka-fwap.* I jiggled across the seat, off the seat. Mother's eyeglasses hopped down her nose. Her hat sprang loose from its side clamps and puckered on her head like a bird's nest. *Ka-fwap, ka-fwap.* From my sanctuary on the floorboard, I shrieked with giggles at her new look. My giggles jiggled. Then Mom chuckled.

"We'll probably churn the milk into butter," she said, laughing. Her laugh vibrated. We cackled and crowed and twittered and haw-hawed until we snorted and cried. Mom wiped tears from under her glasses with her driving glove. I laughed myself sick. When I threw up, Mom braked at the side of the road. She had just cleaned up the seat when a cowboy stopped and changed the flat.

"I'm afraid you ruined the tire," he said, wiping his hands on his Levi's. Mom mumbled, "That'll teach me. No new coat this winter."

When Dad drove us to town and the automobile died along the way, he tinkered it back to life — if he could. "Well, the old girl's letting us have another roadside picnic," Mom would say, then slam the vehicle's door. Then she and I would read books on a scratchy wool blanket on the grass in the highway ditch.

Once, when our black coupe spit and hissed at Dad, I tugged at Mom's shoulder. "See, Mother? It smokes like the dragon in my book."

"That car's a dragon, all right. A draggin' me through hell," she said.

✦   ✦   ✦

Years passed. I became Mom's chauffeur after Dad died. On a trip to her cardiologist in Billings, she shook her head and sighed as we passed Lodge Grass.

"Boy, I sure tossed you around like salad when we lived off in these hills," she said.

"Why did you keep trying to drive those old beater cars and pickups?"

Surprise crossed her face. "I had to. If I'd quit trying, I might've lost my nerve."

"Dad could have driven us to get groceries."

"Prying him off a horse and into town was as hard as pushing him into a church. And besides, what if we'd needed help when he was gone on horseback? A bite from one of those big, ol' rattlesnakes would've killed you. Nope. I had to drive." She paused. "We were so alone."

Then she brightened, "Anyway, look at you now. I taught you to drive pretty good."

CLAUDETTE ORTIZ ᴥ Co-Madres

I was doing my usual Cinco de Mayo garden digging when I unearthed two carrots — deep-buried, bright orange surprises with green stems. So, of course, I stopped digging to taste them: very woody but a full-bodied carrot taste.

Chewing on this fascinating find made me think of my granddaughter Alissa's other grandmother, the one who teaches her how to scrape, slice, dice, blend, mash, and puree carrots. If Alissa were here with me now, the only tool we'd use before chomping on the carrots would be the garden hose.

And with the munching came the revelation: kids need both kinds of grandmas. They need a grandma who teaches them to cook and a grandma who will eat anything; one to learn from and one to practice on.

Here in competitive America, the other mother who does everything and does it perfectly can send the less able mother into a not-so-perfect tailspin.

There ought to be a word in English like the Spanish *comadre*; a word that means you recognize the bond, you declare the relationship to your child's mother-in-law. Her hand raised the child your child fell in love with. There ought to be a word in English that kisses that hand, that says thank you for giving all the tools, skills, and love you have to help my child and yours build their life together; the differences between us, the diversity in us, only expand their horizons.

Co-madre. Co-mother. Without a word for her in English, it's easy to feel inadequate instead of grateful. For instance, two of my kids married hometown kids, so I have two *comadres* in town. One of these is a little bitty thing who runs five miles a day every day, rain or shine, snow or wind. She's so tiny I'm surprised one of those sixty-mile-per-hour gusts hasn't blown her to Nebraska. I don't have to walk around with rocks in my pocket, but there we were, shopping together for our dresses for the children's wedding, and I felt huge. *She* didn't make me feel huge. *I* made me feel huge. And grumpy. We looked like one of those before-and-after diet ads. There was nothing left for me to do but buy my dress a size too small and take her out for pie.

Calling each other *comadre* would have been a reminder that we were in this thing together. Over pie, though, I did discover she actually eats. She even cooks big meals, and they have a real mealtime at their house, at 6:00 P.M., an hour when I'm still at work, soon to go straight to some function and get home after nine, only to open the refrigerator and stand there, like a sandwich is supposed to put the mayonnaise on itself.

Here's the kicker: the other *comadre* in town is just as efficient. Remember the one that purees carrots? Well, she also serves regular meals on time, and she plays the piano. No, not at the same time; she's probably saving that trick for her old age. But she doesn't just play; she plays the piano for all four Masses at her church every Sunday *and* sings in the choir.

Lord. If this other-mother thing were competition instead of cooperation, I'd be sunk.

There is one important thing my *comadres* and I share: there isn't a schedule that can't be changed for family. I can see each of us as our children grew, rearranging plans on a moment's notice. We stopped all to swing at the playground before walking our children home — just to let our feet touch the sky.

I know they did this because of the little things they stop to do now. They stop to clip articles I've written and send them to relatives. One *comadre*, on a trip to see her sister, stopped in to see my parents. The little unscheduled stop, to share memories with a great-grandmother on my side, was the meaning of the word *comadre*. I can see her as she shared the pictures of Alissa: "Look, look at our girl."

GAEL SEED ※ Barriers of Silence

My mother and I were not friends. She did not engage in intimate conversation — at least not with her offspring. She took pride in her love of reading and felt no embarrassment at picking up a book in the middle of a visit with me.

She demanded that we call her "Mater," a title apparently culled from one of the stacks of popular magazines in which she took refuge when the burdens and isolation of farm life overwhelmed her. We were embarrassed to be required to pronounce the name with a broad *a* and a broad *e* — "Mah-tehr." The foreign sounds felt foolish and stilted in our rural family, so we tried calling her Mom. A tight-lipped response told us not to try it again. At that time, her friends adored her. My sister and I marveled at that and wondered how we offended her.

I knew things that, as a child, I could not understand. Sounds of crying when our father was away on a fishing trip one summer; her unexplained absence later that month from a family wedding, then her tearful departure for Omaha in the back seat of a 1934 Plymouth driven by one of the local hired men going there to visit family. She returned a few days later, then left on a bus for California, where her cousins and an older sister lived. No one mentioned her to my younger sisters or me while she was away, but every evening our father gathered us for a drive into town after a supper we children had set out. We sat on the bench outside the station, watching in anticipation for the silver Jackrabbit Lines vehicle that drove into town once every twenty-four hours. Scrutinizing the passengers in the yellow light as they surged into the aisle of the bus, we crowded around the tall folding door to watch them emerge. Now and then someone we knew stepped down, and we enjoyed a brief flurry of conversation before a silent trip to our home in the country.

Finally, one evening, Mater emerged from the bus, and we were a family again. We sisters tried to be obedient in washing dishes and doing farm and household chores, thinking we could hold her by being good. Mater didn't leave again, but several years later, after my sisters and I had grown, she was confined to a locked hospital ward for attacking the town grocer with a butcher knife. After a few months of treatment, she was released, and for a while she smiled at us and joined in conversations.

But in time the light in her eyes dimmed, and her animation evaporated. Our father died, and other problems surfaced. Mater developed a debilitating deafness, so that conversation at the necessary level felt like a radio broadcast. I found it embarrassing to converse with her about any but the most public and neutral of topics — the weather, the condition of the roads, or the current illness cycling in our town. My own thoughtlessness denied the devastation she experienced as the deafness exacerbated her growing paranoia. I found it impossible to abide her company for more than a few hours each week, and she seemed to feel the same aversion to me, which both relieved and upset me.

Holidays for my husband and me became exercises in boredom. Refusing to abandon tradition and responsibility, we included her in our dinners, but I was so enervated by her presence, I refused to invite others. We fell into the habit of holidays marked by silent dinners, the three of us seated at our square dining table, spread with the white linen tablecloth her mother had brought west in the early 1900s. I longed for conversation, and perhaps so did she. Every now and then, we both began a sentence, interrupting each other with some labored thought. She could not hear me speaking, of course, so I resentfully deferred to her as silence enfolded us again.

At times she embarrassed me with loud-voiced critical comments ostensibly intended for my ears alone. "Relevant to nothing," she observed one day in the waiting room at the medical clinic, "Bridey Hofer's legs are bowed." I looked around in consternation, knowing that in a town the size of ours, it was likely one of Bridey's relatives, unrecognized by us, sat in the waiting room. Smiles and smirks told me that a few, at least, had noted Mater's observation. On another occasion, Mater informed me that a person passing us in the hallway was wearing "a strange shirt for a man." The tall, rawboned woman wore a flowered blouse and could hardly have avoided hearing Mater's judgment.

I found our times together increasingly difficult. She gave up her home and moved to an apartment. Not long after that, she began to walk with a tortuous shuffle, her breath spent after only a few steps. Food spoiled in her refrigerator, and her blouses carried stains no remover could touch. The situation forced a decision, and we moved her to a private residence where she received round-the-clock care.

One night Mater got out of her bed at the residence and woke her roommate, Josie. "If you'll make the coffee, I'll put in the pills," Mater said. "Then you won't be implicated. I just don't belong here anymore."

"You belong in bed!" Josie muttered out of her sleep.

Another time when Mater couldn't sleep, she called the police to report that the woman across the street was practicing mind control and wanted to poison her. We were appalled and feared her eviction, but the nurses and aides showed only compassion. "She's not nearly as bad as some," they said in consolation.

A few months after Mater entered the home, her grandniece, Margaret, came for a holiday visit. By that time, Mater was well into her eighties. She could no longer walk, and part of the routine included a nap for her before we drove her back to the place where she lived. When Mater awakened, Margaret helped her with eyeglasses and the transfer from bed to wheelchair. She spread an afghan with care over her great-aunt's knees. The three of us had settled ourselves for a talk when Mater startled us by saying, "Well, I made my confession."

"Your confession?" Margaret and I exclaimed in the same breath.

"Reverend Jim came to talk with me, and I made my confession."

I tried to make a joke of this by saying, "*You* had wicked things to confess, Mater?" But I alone smiled.

Tears from Mater. Margaret took her hand. This woman I considered without feeling sobbed. "I had an abortion — I never told anyone," she said to me. "Not even your father. What if it was a boy? He wanted a boy so much."

Margaret cried with Mater as she held the old woman's hand in hers. I sat speechless, though questions whirled in my head. Her torment subsiding, Mater picked at the brown and gold afghan across her knees, a shamed and childlike expression on her face. She seemed about to speak, but the doorbell shattered her inclination to confide. My husband, unaware of the delicacy of our time together, let a visitor in, and the time for confidences evaporated.

On a subsequent holiday, I did attempt to question Mater. I was curious, of course. But more than that, I wanted to know all of the story in the hope it might peel away the years of silence and resentment. And I needed to uncover some compassion in myself in addition to my pity.

"Remember what you told us about an abortion, Mater?" I tried what I hoped was gentle, if loud, prodding. "How did it happen? Did you go away?" I asked, surprised by my own temerity.

"No. Dr. Kent was one of them, and I wish I'd never heard of them." Mater melted again into a human being, vulnerable to hurt and shame, face contorted, tears staining her fresh blouse. Again the doorbell jangled, intruding on this rare display of emotion.

That fragment of memory is the sum of our knowledge. Dr. Kent was the only doctor in our town in those times not so long ago when birth control was illegal and coat hangers and abortion went together. I know, of course, even in my sheltered ignorance, that women have abortions every day. But I could not imagine such boldness in my mother, in spite of her early outspokenness.

For the first time, her life — and, in turn, my life — makes sense. Her judgments, my resentments chafed. But the secret was the fence that separated us. Intimacy is painful, and certain intimacies will be condemned by someone if confided. The risks keep us silent, and the silence grows into barriers too high to scale, too wide to penetrate. The silence kept us apart.

VEE HAGEMAN Majesty

We were young, my friend and I, when we attended the state cattlemen's convention with our husbands. That was a long time ago, before grandchildren and winters in Arizona.

Our relationship has grown richer with the passing years — persistent as a wind-driven tumbleweed, delicate as the first crocus of spring.

Perhaps the miles that separate us have somehow enhanced our admiration for each other. A mountain always seems more majestic from a distance.

KATHY HANKS ❧ Hog Wars

"Hey, how come you weren't at the meeting last night?" Dana asks me over the phone. She sounds out of breath as she announces she's processing her third water bath of strawberry jam. It's late June and seven in the morning.

"What time did you get up to start making the jam?" I reply, ignoring her question.

Without responding to my question, she continues, "Let me tell you it grew tense. We fried the commissioners. Charcoal-broiled, and we ate them for supper! I can't believe those jerks passed the resolution without bringing it to a vote of the people. Do they think there is one person, besides the three of them, who wants a corporate hog farm in our county? Let's get real here!"

I feel tension rising inside of me. One of the "jerks" is our dearest friend. Still, I can't form coherent words quick enough to reply. So she goes on explaining how environmentally insensitive the "mega-corporations" are. How they will ruin our water supply and pollute the air.

"The hog farms will ruin the air quality in our county," she continues, then suddenly realizes I'm not responding. "Surely you're against the hog farms?" she asks, confident I'll agree.

"What are we going to do? Our town is dying. We have to attract new business. Right now we don't even have the tax dollars to fix a pothole in the road or buy a new ambulance. The oil industry is gone, and the cattle market just took a shot in the leg. This particular corporation supposedly has a clean record. If they're closely monitored, surely it will be OK. It'll boost our economy," I say.

"Get real!" Dana hisses her words through the phone. "A hog factory will ruin our community. It will ruin the small producer. I can't believe you're so stupid not to realize this. Just who are they going to get to slop their hogs? Are you going to work for them?"

"I'm not looking for work," I whisper, insulted by the question.

"Do you realize what kind of people they'll attract? Transients — that's who they'll be bringing in. They might buy their food and booze here, but they won't buy homes. The only new job will be for an English as a Second Language teacher in the school." I've heard her this angry only when she's been ticked off at an incorrigible student.

I feel a premonition of warfare as I ask, "Surely you're not mad at me for having a different opinion?"

"Well, how can you be so blind? It's pretty obvious that this is a bad thing," she yells as if we have a bad connection.

"Isn't our friendship more important than corporate hogs?"

"I don't think it is," she states.

I feel wounded as I hang up the phone.

I would never have become acquainted with Dana if we hadn't been neighbors. She certainly doesn't have time to seek people out. But we are neighbors, living four miles apart. We work in the same school and serve on the same 4-H committees. Thankfully, we've had each other to commiserate with through difficult relationships, sickness, and even a death.

Dana grew up working on her family farm in western Kansas. She drove the tractor, cultivated the fields, planted and harvested crops. She learned how to garden and can. All these things she brings to her life today.

I grew up on Long Island, learning to enjoy sailing, art galleries, the opera, and shopping at Bloomingdale's. None of this serves me well as a farmer's wife. So I've turned to Dana for clues on rural living.

Things are changing here on the high plains. Now a difference in philosophy, rather than our backgrounds, seems to be the great dichotomy between my friend and me. If we could have a cup of tea and talk about economic development, maybe we could brainstorm ideas. What business would be willing to come to our community? How will we stay afloat?

Our core values are the same. I don't want to pollute the environment. I want clean air. I want the same things Dana wants. However, we can't ignore that our town is dying, and it needs to be hooked to life support fast. Perhaps she could offer some alternative for saving our community.

I admire so many things about Dana. Take her stamina, for example. She has taught social studies for years in the same rural school (which, incidentally, will be closing its doors within two years because of declining enrollment). From the rural school, she returns home every day with her young children, changes into chore clothes, and then heads out to feed the 4-H animals. If it's good weather, she works in the garden cultivating and planting seeds or gently nurtures her huge strawberry beds.

She lives in a stark but sparkling farmhouse. Flower Garden and Lone Star quilts cover the beds; dozens of strawberry jam jars line her kitchen counter. These are the things that catch my eye.

I haven't heard from her since our phone conversation. The hog war is mounting, and I can see both sides of the issue. But Dana would probably call me a fence rider. I miss my friend, but not her angry words.

I catch a glimpse of her and her family in the county fair parade. They are driving down Main Street in the antique car division; she's a passenger in her husband's sputtering Model T Ford. They are dressed like pioneers, waving to the crowd on the street and throwing candy. Just as they pass me, her head turns to the crowd on the other side of Main Street.

Suddenly, it dawns on me. Dana would be happy to stop the world from spinning forward. Then she and her family could travel back to a fleeting image frozen in time, when farming was a perfect way of life.

DONNA BRITTON HARVEY ❧ Don't Step in the Cactus

I have to think hard to realize the effect other women have had on me. The influence, nonetheless, is there, like the silent steel ribbons connecting the railway across the plains, helping drive us forward.

Many women say that their best friends are men, but having shared my mother's womb with a male, then shared a bedroom with my five sisters, I may be more qualified than most to discourse on female-female and female-male relationships. I admit that I feel a natural affinity for men and boys. Relationships with other women have never been easy for me. I form my impressions of women rapidly and intuitively, knowing quickly whether similar blood flows through our veins. I tend to shun women with whom I do not feel a deep trust and kinship. I was never close to other girls in school. The things they said and did, especially around boys, always seemed silly. I was more comfortable hanging around with my twin brother and his buddies, trying to fit in.

Perhaps sharing the womb with a brother inoculated me with male hormones. Growing up, I was more like a cactus than a rose. A rogue tomboy, I proclaimed loudly on more than one occasion that I could do anything a boy could do. "Even use the boys' restroom at school?" someone taunted. "Yes," I replied, and proceeded to do it. I didn't get caught, and I proved my point. I have spent the rest of my life attempting to prove that point over and over. "I dare you to get on that bull," someone challenged at rodeo practice. So I rode the bull out of the bucking chute. My attempts to be "as good as" men seem to have isolated me from both genders, with the exception of my son.

Becoming the mother to both a son and a daughter has only punctuated my inability to form close female relationships. My son and I are best friends who can talk about everything. How I have longed to have that kind of relationship with my daughter! Until recently, she and I were adversaries. Although we love each other very much, we are just beginning to like each other. I guess I shouldn't wonder about that. She is, after all, her mother's daughter. She probably has as much trouble trusting and respecting women as I do.

Disdain for my mother's attitudes and lifestyle choices pitted me against her until the last fifteen years of her life, when she finally gave up trying to mold me. Or perhaps my thinking had softened. I began to see, after the births of my children, that some gender differences, which I'd previously thought were learned, are actually genetic.

My six brothers often served as my role models, but my sisters all helped shape the person I am today, although they might not admit it. I find comfort in knowing I can count on any or all of my sisters. Our kinship comes from knowing we are bonded by blood. If our relationship also includes friendship, I am blessed indeed.

Perhaps the reason I have trouble connecting with women is because I see in them the things I dislike in myself — sort of like missing the beauty of the prairie because we are so busy trying not to step in the cactus. Maybe that's why it is harder for women to relate to each other — we know our frailties too well and practice rejecting them.

But even a cactus like me occasionally blossoms.

TENA COOK GOULD ❧ The Night

With bloody ax in hand, she marched home up the hill after the kill. Mom had done away with the chicken-eating opossum. Alone — in a nightgown, coat, and irrigation boots. Dad drove up that night just as she headed to the house. His startled eyes filled with questions at the sight of the weapon and the garb, and before he heard the complete rodent-ridding story, he made a mental note to himself not to tick her off too much in the future. As a girl, I thought, "Wow! My mom is a warrior!" Now, twenty-five years later, I am profoundly grateful that her blood flows in my veins.

MARY LOU SANELLI ❧ Trying to Remember She Is Now a Man

Friday, local pub, after-work
friends filtering in, a few close
enough to touch. And one
looking so butch compared to her recent self
a month ago, when I remember
liking her dress, her shoes — strange

especially when she walked
away, the bartender informing me
my friend has been a man all along,
the way the impact of his words
left me speechless, my head a blur,
body immobile. What about her hair
waist-long and windblown,
its crow black sheen
reminding me of my own

womanhood, more evidence of femininity
than a legal certificate?

And now
an oddly familiar man taps my arm
steadied against the bar. In his eyes
the same acceptance
I look for in a crowd, his ease
easing my wobbly way with small talk.
I raise my glass, toast his courage,
put my beer to my lips, drink
too much too fast.

On the horizon
the moon rises and sets
the trees aglow. Mountains
dulled to the color of fog
await the night, none of them
appearing different
from what I can recall.

PAMELA J. OCHSNER ❧ *Vi and Me*

I didn't always like her. At one time, I was sure I hated her. (Oh, hell, why
lie about it. We've walked away, stomped away, screamed away, flung
away, driven away, and wept our way to our own homes many times over
the years. It's become a tradition for family members to decide whose side
they should be on, and our *own* tradition to recruit members for our own
side.)

But there hasn't been a bigger presence in my life or a bigger influence,
or a more loved one, in the twenty years since I met this lady. Not even her
son, whom I married, or my own mother, whom I nursed and took care of
for twenty-five years after she raised me.

You see, I came here a city slicker, with my vinyl boots, makeup, cotton gloves, and pets. I was as green as March grass and as tenuous as a
lilac bud. All I had to recommend me was guts, an Irish grandmother, and
muscle.

But Vi took this city girl under her wing and made a damn good farmer
out of her in twenty years; *she* even says so.

I couldn't say, to this day, where our common ground came from. I suspect, though she would argue, that it was, indeed, somewhere in the middle. After all, if she didn't have the inner strength to bend, she wouldn't

still be here, and if I hadn't learned how, I wouldn't be either. She is unswerving and immovable in her determination to accomplish each day's goals, and from her I learned that I really can do anything *we* put our minds to. From her I learned that a chore shared is one halved and a joy shared is doubled. That a heartache spread out over several unburdens all bearers, and that life, as we know it, must go on.

From her I learned that we gain and lose, love and lose, try and lose, want and don't get, need and can't have, feel and can't say, know and can't admit, see and can't describe, and love and can't keep, sometimes. I learned how to hold on, but I also learned how to let go.

But the most valuable thing she ever taught me is this: There is a state of perfection. It's the ability to keep trying, over and over again, until doing it, and being able to, is all we'll ever really need, and having the choice, and making the right one, fulfills us. We might be covered in slime, in our oldest clothes, and we might have been seen and smelled that way a thousand times, but what really matters is that we did it. We might make mistakes loving our children, raising our cattle, planting our fields, planting our gardens, mowing our lawns, cleaning our barns, caring for our families. Yes, and don't we all?

But we wanted to do it perfectly, and so, like everything else we ever attempted, we kept on trying, and God helped us get through it all. And what, after all, were the "good old days" if not perfect memories of something we already did?

Just like we're making right now.

It's tough economically, it's hard to be social and get it all done, and it's hard to raise a lot of livestock and kids at the same time. A "normal life" cannot be yours if you plan on doing a good job. You belong to the farm, and it belongs to you.

I've become so ingrained by now that I find myself "farming" with other farmers at all kinds of social functions. That once sent me right over the edge when my husband did it. My mother-in-law sat me down and told me that's how farmers keep up on new equipment and practices, that that's how they keep in touch and show interest in each other.

But she didn't tell me that you get used to being alone, that it is good training for learning to get the job done without a boss.

And she didn't tell me that someday I'd be able to hold my own. If she'd told me she was going to train me, I'd have laughed in her face and never heard another word she said. She didn't tell me how hard it was going to be, how rewarded I'd feel when I could fill the whole tank on the tractor by myself, at one time. She didn't tell me that pounding in posts would someday look trivial or that pulling calves wouldn't even merit mention unless it was twins or triplets. She didn't tell me that eighteen hours in the field was nothing or that burying a tractor in a slough was something everyone did.

And she's never told me that she loves me, and I've never told her.

But somehow you just pick these things up, if you do them often enough.

Best Wishes Jean Phyllis Letellier

PHYLLIS M. LETELLIER ✻ *Whistling Girls and Knitting*

My Swedish grandmother was a tough, opinionated old gal, an immigrant from the Old World to whom survival meant a lifetime of backbreaking work. I once heard her tell my mother that many nights when her children were small, she was so tired at bedtime she'd pray not to wake up. Yet her oldest daughter was so ashamed of her mother's life of manual labor that she'd cross the street to avoid introducing her friends to her mother.

During the years Grandma Matilda Mortensen lived on the farm with my family, we clashed regularly. Naturally, she thought I was a spoiled modern brat. She disliked the length of my skirts and criticized the anklets I wore instead of the ugly long brown stockings she preferred. When I whistled cheerfully while I worked, she'd squelch me by snapping in her Swedish accent, "Whistling girls and crowing hens always come to some bad end." She tried to teach me humility and the value of hard work by sending me to the granary after supper for two 5-gallon buckets of barley. I can still close my eyes and smell that barley scorching on the wood stove, because she thought barley for the chickens had to be cooked. In spite of myself, I learned from her, noticing, for example, that women who learned to milk got stuck with the job, so I never learned.

At age eighty, Grandma, barely five feet tall, could still bend at the waist and lay her hands flat on the floor. She bent her knees only to sit down. As I struggle into my "retirement years" with bad knees, I often mutter that I'd have preferred to inherit something from her besides those knees. When I serve guests instant tea or diet soda, I remember she always had fresh-baked cookies and coffee for guests. I keep in my cedar chest the bed sheet she made from six bleached flour sacks to celebrate my move from a baby crib I was kicking the end out of into a real twin bed when I was six. My name is embroidered in a corner in her old-country, hard-to-read writing. Now I understand the sheet was an act of love. When I was nine, I asked, "Grandma, when you die, can I have your shawl?" In a household where we did not speak of death, everyone — except Grandma — was horrified. But when the day came, the family remembered, and the shawl, too, is in my cedar chest.

Despite her harsh words, Grandma patiently taught me to knit when I was eight. For nearly a week, she sat beside me on the old sofa in the evenings and watched by the light of a kerosene lamp, stopping me when I started to make a mistake. She'd explain the problem and show me how to correct it. Years later, she was still there — in my heart — when I taught my young sons to knit. Whenever I start thinking my lot in life is hard, I hear her voice reminding me, nearly sixty years after her death when I was thirteen, that compared to hers, my life is a stroll in the park.

LOIS JEAN MOORE ❧ Sybil Harris

A young girl in British Guiana, South America, became a housemaid in the home of the Shipmans, an American missionary family. She loved this family and longed to come to America to be close to them. A Jewish doctor paid for her passage in return for three years of housekeeping, cleaning, ironing, and cooking.

In the early hours of the morning in New York City, Sybil boarded the subway to Dr. Syfie's house. Her husband remained at home, where Sybil had left the meals fixed and the house clean. In her mind echoed these words, "This is the day that the Lord has made, let us rejoice and be glad in it." On her way home, she hummed or sang songs to bring glory to her risen Lord.

Three years passed quickly. "Now I'm free to live a life of my own," exclaimed Sybil. "I want to live close to the Shipmans." Immediately, Sybil and her husband moved to York, Nebraska, where the Shipmans had agreed to make an apartment for them in their basement temporarily.

On Tuesday after their arrival, Zola Shipman called me. "Can you come over for coffee and rolls? I have a dear friend I want you to meet." I was drawn to Sybil as iron shavings are to a magnet and extended an invitation for her to visit my house later in the week.

Friday a bicycle came zooming into my driveway. On the seat was a joyous personality. "I came to see where you live. My, this place is lovely!"

"Come in, Sybil. Let's have some Red Rose tea while we visit," I said. With teapot, cups, and honey on a tray, we headed to the patio. I wondered what my neighbors were thinking. A neighbor, inquisitive about this black woman's presence in our small town where there were no other blacks, decided to hang some wash on her line. Sybil was eager for new friends. "Let's invite her to join us," she said.

Anna Meyers came over for tea, and soon Sybil had a new friend.

Our tea finished, Sybil had other ambitions. "I know how to garden. May I hoe your garden for you?" I felt embarrassed as I handed her the hoe. "We are partners with God in making this garden grow. I am so happy that you let me share this joy with you," she said.

In no time at all, my garden was beautiful. I breathed a prayer of thanks. "Can you use some of my vegetables?" I asked.

"Yes, I would be thankful for them." I gathered lettuce, radishes, onions, cucumbers, and a few strawberries. "God is good. May He bless you for your kindness," she said as I handed her the bag.

Sybil applied for work immediately, and Epworth Village, an orphanage, hired her. This job gave her the opportunity to show God's love to children and teenagers who had started down the wrong path in life. Some of the children had no place to go for the holidays. "Will you help me give these dear ones some joy for the holidays?" Sybil asked.

"Sure I will, and be happy to do so." Together we planned a Christmas dinner for those who had no one to share Christmas with them. The children responded to Sybil's genuine love, and the day was truly a celebration of the Lord's birthday. I don't know who had a better time — Sybil, me, or the children.

"It gives me more joy than you'll ever know to share this meal with the children and you," I said. "Thank you for helping me to find real joy in giving to others at Christmas."

Sybil's husband was content to eat the food she provided, live in the apartment that was part of the pay for her hire, and demand his special foods fixed after her long hours on the job. She did all he demanded. However, she couldn't help but feel resentment. In frustration she admitted to me, "I wish the lazy bum would get a job."

My husband encouraged Sean to apply for a job at the Nebraska Public Power District. His computer skills were sharp. When his paychecks started coming in, he didn't share them with Sybil. She prayed and asked for grace to endure or deliverance from the burden if that was God's will.

At eleven one night, my doorbell rang. Sybil announced, "God has delivered me from my burden. Praise His name! I found a letter from a woman in New York who has been getting my husband's paychecks. Now my door is locked with a new lock."

I cradled her trembling body in my arms as she let the tears flow. "I suspected he had someone else ever since we arrived in New York. Well, it's over! I'm a fool no more. God helped me find the letter, and He will see me through the years ahead. Glory be to Jesus!"

"Oh, Sybil, stay here tonight. We'll help you get a new start. He was nothing but an expense to you. You'll do just fine without him."

The next morning, Sybil and I went back to her apartment. Nothing had been tampered with. Sean was gone, and Sybil never heard from him again.

The days ahead were lonely. Sybil busied herself with her job and began to look for greener pastures. She was hired as a correctional officer at the Nebraska Center for Women, where she quickly developed a rapport with the inmates. Sybil enjoyed her work so much I decided to try working there, too. For three years, we worked together as correctional officers. Sybil was then hired as the chaplain, and I became the inmates' mother/offspring life development teacher. We prayed on our way to work, "God, keep us safe at our work today. Help us to show forth your love to the women who don't care for you." We took women who had become Christians to church services to put on programs to raise money for a new chapel on the grounds. The chapel is now a reality.

Sybil and I are best friends today. She spends a week at my house every summer. We talk about old times and share family concerns. We laugh until the tears roll down our cheeks. We're good for each other. I stop to see her when I go to York. I always have a place to stay, one where people understand each other and feel at home in each other's presence.

PEARLE HENRIKSEN SCHULTZ
Barbed Wire and Robert Frost

Early June, and my near neighbor tells me
that now's the time to walk our fence lines and
repair the wire or reset the posts
that winter frosts have loosened in the earth.
It is the custom, the tradition in
this high country to mend the lines in spring,
and so we go, each on our own side in new comradeship,
although there are no cows on our five-acre tracts
to keep fenced in, just deer in early morning
and one cannot fence them in or out,
nor want to — this parched earth, already dry
and cracked, yields little food for man or beast.
My neighbor scans the sky and speaks of rain
and of stray dogs that killed some lambs last year
on her son's ranch. The creek that branches through
our land is much too low for June, she fears,
and while she talks we walk along the line
in the established way to check barbed wire.

I am reminded of another day —
long years ago and many miles away —
I watched an old man make a wall of stones,
fitting the coral rocks most carefully
one to the other with strong, gnarled hands,
his white hair blowing in the tropic breeze
that shook blue blooms off jacaranda trees.
The poet was my neighbor, winter months.
"You're mending wall?" I asked the man, and he,
stern guardian of his own privacy,

just scowled, then smiled at me and then he said,
"It seems there's someone wants a barricade
against the next-door avocado trees,
so yes, you might say that I'm mending wall."

Barbed wire again . . .
The arid earth lies sere, the sky's gone dark.
We plod along and find a fence post here
where wire is loose and needs some staples in.
I hear her say, "Strong fences make good neighbors.
Someone wrote something like that in a verse,
I can't remember who. Poems don't last,
not like a real good piece of ranch land does."
I turn to her to quote the famous lines,
then — suddenly thunder, and the rains begin.

GAYDELL COLLIER ✾ Knowing with the Heart

Monique and I have never met. Between us, the Atlantic Ocean spreads too wide a barrier of distance, expense, and time. But we have been writing for more than half a century, and even decades ago, I knew that our friendship was unique.

It began in 1947. I had just started junior high school on Long Island. My French teachers had been sending school supplies and books overseas to help France rebuild after the devastation of World War II. A packet of letters arrived from a school in Cherbourg, and the letters were passed out, willy-nilly, among us.

"Chère Amie Inconnue." Dear unknown friend.

Monique was thirteen, and I was twelve. "What sports do you prefer?" she wrote in English. "I like cycling and swimming. Who are your favorite authors?"

I shared her enthusiasm for Sir Walter Scott and Jack London. Actors and actresses? We talked about Gary Cooper, Ingrid Bergman, Michèle Morgan.

"Have you a garden? We have an apple tree and two pear trees. The pears and apples are excellent, but the little birds taste them before we do." At my home, we still grew tomatoes and kohlrabi in our victory garden, which had been so important during the war. A small pear tree grew in our yard.

We shared school grades ("What do A and A+ signify? We are marked on 20.") and drew plans of how our classroom desks were arranged. After the war, my school life had quickly returned to normal, but Monique wrote,

"Our school buildings were badly damaged during the bombardments on Cherbourg. So we are in another building. Next October we'll reenter our school." During the summer, "on every Sunday I go in the country around Cherbourg. I love to swim and would like to learn how to dive. But the beach at Cherbourg is dangerous, because, at the time of the landing, some of the boats sank, and there remain big holes and some wrecks."

We sent back and forth a stream of newspapers and magazines, post cards and photographs; we both collected stamps. By the time we were well into high school five years later, even my French teachers considered our correspondence long-lived and notable.

Intimacy between us developed in the same way that it grows in a close family: we forget the minutiae but cherish the bond. I know Monique better, perhaps, than I've ever known anyone beyond my own family. We longed to visit each other. Letters frequently included fervent invitations and sorrowful regrets.

Monique progressed to a normal school, and I went on to college. "Now it is cold," she wrote. "The last leaves of the trees in the yard, of the *vigne vierge* along the walls of the school building, are falling; and it seems sad when all is bare at school." I was touched by her attempts to save an injured bird. We shared stories of trips and summer vacations, sympathized over family tragedies, worried about storms and disasters in the news. Monique began teaching school. Our concerns progressed to politics and government, social problems and education. We wrote to each other facilely, if imperfectly. Monique was always far better at English than I was at French, but most of our letters were written in both languages.

We were both married in 1955. I read about the birth of her Cathérine just before writing to her about the birth of our Sam. I had two more children, Frank and Jenny, before writing of our fourth child, Fred, just about the same time her second child, Frédérique, was born.

Monique and Claude moved to St. Cloud, near Paris. Roy and I lived southwest of Laramie, Wyoming, and later moved to our own ranch in Wyoming's Black Hills. Monique and I continued to send information about our new localities, while we shared the problems and joys of raising children and living our daily lives.

"We don't go out," Monique wrote. "With the children, we can't go to the theater, and we don't like the cinema. Now we spend our evenings sometimes reading, sometimes watching television when the program pleases us (which is rare)." I could have written the same. Those evenings she knitted sweaters for her family; I crocheted granny-square afghans for mine.

Eventually, we began writing about our children's marriages and then grandchildren. At last communication, we each had five.

Monique and Claude have retired to the seacoast at Agon-Coutainville. Roy and I still live on our ranch. Monique and I both love the land, the quiet of the countryside — hers by the sea, mine deep in the hills. We both have a small flock of sheep and bees or geese.

"I can assure you that our friendship is a part of the happiness in my life," Monique wrote. "I can't explain easily, but you surely understand." In that, too, we are the same.

Early on, our letters flew back and forth. In later years, as we grew comfortable in our friendship but busy with responsibilities, they dwindled to occasional post cards and long letters written sometimes over weeks or even months, arriving more than a year apart. Now we realize that there may not be many years left to us, and we share more deeply how much this friendship means.

We each write in our own language, but I am slower now in reading French. I have in these letters the record of her life, safe in her own hand, a life reflecting my own. I hold here more than half a century of France, from a war-years perspective to the new millennium. On a wall sconce in my kitchen, a silver candlestick from Monique — with a tall red candle — holds a place of honor. In my bedroom, a small French doll — Bécassine — stands beside the children's storybook *Bécassine enfant*, cherished for five decades. I just discovered that Monique also has kept my letters and photos and all the souvenirs of this correspondence.

The joy of this friendship has colored both our lives in ways we could never have foreseen. Monique writes, *"Cette longue amitié aura été l'un des points les plus positifs et enrichissants de ma vie, et il m'arrive d'espérer que s'il y a un 'au-delà' nous nous y rencontrerons."* Yes, for me too this long friendship has been one of the most beautiful and enriching parts of my life, and yes — surely! — though we may never see each other in this life, we will meet in the next. Whenever it is, then I will light that candle.

When I asked Monique if she would like to add to this story, she wrote:

Since our adolescence, we have certainly changed with the times, but in a nearly identical manner. Even our lives have been parallel. I don't think this is just by chance. The intertwined threads of this friendship, woven through the years, have given me a strange power: sometimes I sense you near me here, and sometimes I run off to your hills. Through joys and trials, I have never felt alone. I always have my friend. She is no longer *"inconnue,"* because we know better with the heart than with the eyes.

Monique D'Hooghe

JODY STRAND ⭐ *Maybe Slower Is Better*

Beulah drinks straight whiskey, smokes Swisher Sweets, still rides her own horses, calves her own cows, and has a belly laugh that pulls you in like a warm hug.

She was sixty-six when I met her, old enough to be my grandmother. I was thirty, newly married and trying my best to learn how to be a hand. Some might say it was an unlikely alliance, but she turned out to be my teacher, mentor, crying towel, butt kicker, and constant source of unending love and strength.

Having just gone to work on the ranch next to hers, we were new to the community and didn't know anyone. Beulah was one of the first people I met, and at the time I had no idea she would be the one to teach me how to smile in the face of adversity and be glad just to be alive.

I met her when our cows strayed into her pasture through a break in the fence and got mixed in with her herd. While I was trying to sort them out, two slipped back into the herd for every one I cut out. I was hot, angry, and calling them a lot of names no lady should ever use, when a rider came loping over the hill. From the way the rider sat that horse, I could tell there had been many long hours spent in the saddle and wrongly assumed it to be her hired man. As she rode up, I could see it was a lady with more than a little age on her. The smile on her face and the "Hi, neighbor" she called to me were more what I would have expected from an old friend than a rancher who had come upon a stranger milling around in her herd.

She said, "I heard I had new neighbors, and I've been wanting to meet you. Do you need any help?"

I allowed as I didn't seem to be getting the job done too well by myself, and she said, "Well, it's such a nice day, why don't we just sit here and get acquainted for a few minutes and let these cows settle down a bit?"

I was thinking we should get after them, but it was her pasture and her herd, so I sat back in the saddle and went to visiting with the old girl. When she decided we'd visited enough, she quietly slipped through the herd peeling back the stray cows, and I pushed them toward the break in the fence. In no time at all, we were done. I couldn't believe how easy it had been. Maybe slower *was* better. When I tried to thank her for her help, she just smiled and said, "It was so nice to have another woman to work with. You come and visit me soon."

After that, whenever I had a day when things seemed to fall apart, I usually ended up at Beulah's house in the evening. I'd tell her all my problems and complain about everything from snorty cows to fights with my husband. Before I left, she'd always have me laughing, and she'd always say, "Aren't we the luckiest people in the world to be out here doing what we love to do?"

Life hadn't been easy for Beulah. Her husband had suffered a stroke at a young age, and she had been left with the responsibility of running the ranch and dealing with an almost insurmountable load of financial difficulties due to poor cattle prices and medical bills. If anyone had ever had a reason to feel sorry for herself, it was Beulah. But feeling sorry for herself was not her way. She was always smiling, always cheerful, and always thankful just to be doing what she loved best — ranching.

When my son was born, she became his "Aunt Bea" and he became her "little man." The sight of those two together out checking cows always brought a catch to my throat. No matter how hard life gets or the curves it throws me, her attitude of "aren't we lucky" somehow sticks with me. Whenever I feel I'm slipping, I hear Beulah say, "Do what you have to do. Get on with life. Life is to live. Don't feel sorry for yourself. That never helps anything." And most important of all, "Aren't we lucky!"

MARY ALICE GUNDERSON ✎ Leah, Bright and Dark

Early memories of my mother flicker bright and dark like film clips. Her telling me I was a copy, that her "real daughter" had died. My running next door to Grandma's when Mother beat my brother with a leather strap.

Some sunny days she sang before breakfast, tossed fresh salad greens for bridge club luncheons, came home with first prize. Once she wrote letters, lightly in pencil, on the white keys of her piano to teach me to play. I hit a wrong note, and she squashed my fingers under the lid. "That's a discord," she said. Her voice was intimate and menacing.

Running through my elementary school years are memories of Mother's rage and euphoria, frantic gardening and baking, grandiose remodeling projects and exotic vacation plans. Days like living on a roller coaster, blindfolded.

My teenage brother concentrated on sports. Dad coached basketball and taught high school history. He drove us to the dentist, the shoe store, hovered in the girls' department aisles as I faced my tripled plaid reflection in the polished mirrors.

Sometimes Mother sat, sorrowful and puzzled, in her red bathrobe, her blond hair lank and unwashed, unable to list grocery items. Tin wires buzzed in her head, she said. She couldn't think through familiar recipes to mix them in order. Then, Grandma cooked and cleaned, lying into the black phone receiver about heavy colds, back sprain, flu.

"Leah was always a nervous girl," Grandma repeated, as if that might end the whispers and raised eyebrows even I sometimes noticed.

I took piano lessons now from Mrs. H., a stern woman with a metronome, tight-rolled gray hair, and watery eyes. Most days I left eagerly for school. I loved the set routine, math following reading every morning, and I slammed our front door hard against my mother's double face.

One summer evening when I was in high school and my brother a sergeant overseas, I sat rocking with our grandparents on their front porch swing. They cautioned me about "overwork and too much studying." I giggled at their joke. Their faces were solemn as they told of my mother's strange letters from college, addressed to them in shaky, looped handwriting. She wrote that her music theory book had become an unreadable, foreign language. When she tried to sing, her throat filled tight with fish bones. She was hungry but too afraid to leave her room to go to the dining hall, she told them.

They brought her home on the train, wrapped in quilts. She rested a semester, returned to earn a degree, taught school, married. There were a number of fairly untroubled years, except for "rough spots" they wouldn't elaborate on.

Beyond my memory was Mother's suicide attempt, which Dad spoke about once. One day, years later, I sat stunned as I heard a new story. My mother's face was remote and expressionless as she told me that she remembered the wrist restraints of shock treatments. Told me, as if it happened to someone else, how they had taken away her belt, shoelaces, and nail file. She stood on top of the silver radiator in the locked basement room, watching through the heavy screen the starched white hems of uniforms, the polished gum-soled shoes and navy blue capes the nurses wore at shift change.

As a family, we had few resources to draw on. Counseling programs didn't exist in rural towns in the Rockies in the years following Word War II. There were few medications other than phenobarbital. Again and again, our pink-cheeked old country doctor, who still made house calls, sat beside her on the couch in a striped shirt. He held Mother's hand. He told her to buy a hat to flatter her pretty face, to walk in the park, to stop this nonsense and get on with life. Over time she did eventually improve enough to spend nearly twenty years caring for her aging parents.

All her life, she was elusive, erratic, sometimes terrified. She had no predictable core personality or consistent behavior. To strangers, she usually showed a cordial, well-educated-lady face. After guests left, she might call them thieves. I didn't know who she was.

One day, studying at the college library, I found her in my psychology book under "S." Schizophrenia. I read about this complex illness, or set of illnesses, that dramatically alters thought, mood, and behavior. Typically, the disease strikes in the late teens or early twenties, I read. That's when it happened to her.

I saw her described in the array of symptoms — fixed, delusional beliefs, the times during which voices and objects sensed were not really there, disorganized speech and bizarre behavior.

A kind of emotional flatness characterized her later years, when she lived alone as a widow — lack of interest in others' accomplishments or needs, sour moods, spurned gifts, requests that I stay away, even after my brother's accidental death. She showed little emotion at either of her parents' deaths. There were few surprises, many disappointments.

When she was in her mid-eighties, I witnessed another month-long manic period following a hip injury. Witches and demons only she could see and hear tormented her, bugged the phone, and poisoned her food.

Who was she? She was the most baffling, the most intriguing person I would ever love. Who might she have been, my beautiful mother, with shining bobbed hair, photographed in a dark silk dress leaning against a tree, that girl in the Oberlin yearbook nicknamed the "Venus of Johnson Hall"?

CLEO CANTLON ❧ The Heart Knows

These are
not
my people, God, I said.
Where is the poetry, the art, theater, music of these women?
They have no travel dreams, fear even the little city where I lived.

They studied me, my odd ways. They did not judge.
But isolated, we were too few to stand alone.
Single, accepting, they barnacled themselves to my heart.

Annie, who could grow leaves on a broomstick,
who, like her quilts, knit a harmonious whole life
from unpromising pieces: an ill child, an unfaithful and stingy husband,
protected and delighted in simple and old people, and children,
who devoured books, took in knowledge and put out wisdom,
who found joy in everything which grows: children, visiting deer, picking
    cactus berries.
Annie, who taught life is not something that is done to us.

Large and penniless Grace,
who came in despair when a kind boy accepted her hopeless invitation
to a prom for which she had no dress.
I didn't know how, but I cut and guessed and improvised;

she rolled into the grand march in blue,
an acre of blue chiffon, a towering monolith of dream fulfilled.

I didn't yet know Rose, my neighbor, separated by my ignorance of sister-
     hood, but I held her
after men pulled me from the tractor to go help tell her he was dying.
Men, poor things, didn't know enough to touch her when they told.
I brushed her hair and pressed on her the purse she would need
when they took her to him.

Mary, child of my heart,
who thrust her weeks-old son into my arms.
He's sick, she said, and I must go.
I don't know how, I said.
Your heart knows, she replied.

They taught recipes and remedies and encyclopedias of virtues: tolerance,
     sharing, silence, and shared joy.
They toil and spin. They plant and harvest.
Like me, they dream.
Unique as fingerprints or ears or snowflakes, we are part of the whole.

PATRICIA ARCHIE ♞ The Sunset Café

Dear Mom,
     You would have loved it today, with the whole house in an uproar and
most of the family there and everybody getting along. But we were divid-
ing up your things! I took a beef roast for dinner. Nancy said, "Patty, your
mother would be proud of you!" You, who were always feeding everybody.
I hope you can always be proud of me.
     We took your bedroom furniture to Laurie today, clear over in Saratoga.
They showed us a video of a church picnic they attended where there was
music and singing. Morgan was dancing at the picnic, with her fat little dia-
pered bottom bouncing along to the music. Then she stopped and looked at
all the people sitting, smiling, and watching her, and she turned to look behind her back to see what they might be looking at. It was so cute! The first
thing I thought this morning when I woke up was, "I must tell Mom about
that video!" And then I remembered.
     I called for help with your insurance today and even got the wrong
place, but I think the lady who talked to me was an angel sent to help me.
She was so kind. She told me to take my time, I had been through an awful
shock. She said we must use this terrible loss to make us better people, to

know how temporary life is, to remember that each time we talk to someone it might be the last time. I'm trying, Mom — I'm trying.

The Schwan's man stopped, and I told him why he hadn't found you home. He said, "That's the trouble with loved ones. They only come with a lifetime guarantee."

Why is it that I am finding it easier to talk to strangers? My family are all back to their own lives, and I seem to be grabbing at help where I can find it. We aren't exactly isolated here on the place, but we do lead a kind of lonesome existence. Would grieving be different if I lived in town? I don't have the experience to know.

It's May. I dreamed last night you called and asked for an *s* word meaning "string beans" for a crossword puzzle. The only thing I could think of (in my sleep) was "limas," which isn't really "string beans" and doesn't even start with an *s*. But you said, "Limas!" in the delighted way you always did if my letters fit. Then I told you, "I miss you so," and I woke up crying. It's been almost a year, and it is still so hard.

It's August. You're really alive and living in Morgan's little body. I feel so bad you won't see her grow and change — you who always wanted to see "how things turn out." She looks so much like you.

It's January. You taught two generations of children in our town. And you did it so well. I was jealous of your students, because you taught them, not me, the constellations. As an adult, I got busy and learned some, too. "That's good; never stop learning," you told me. Each time I see Orion in the winter sky, I think of you.

It is October 1994. I dreamed last night you were at a large table with us at a reception or something. It seemed so real. You said, "I was surprised you didn't ask me to your big supper the other night."

I said, "But, Mom, we thought you died in July 1993!"

It is February 8, 1995. I dreamed I was upstairs in the old house, looking through your bookcase. The books looked so familiar. I thought, "Oh, I wanted some of those books!" There was a big one with a creamy green cover titled *Eating Moonlight at the Sunset Café*. You remember that book, don't you? I know there was such a book.

There was a new book I had never seen before, kind of tall and slender. Opening it, I saw it was a stamp album, with a packet of stamps ready to be used — different varieties but mostly birds. The flyleaf, in your distinctive handwriting, was inscribed: "Bye, Bye, Birdie — For the real girl you always meant to be."

Oh, Mom, this is too real to be a dream. How like you to ease me gently away, to use my lifelong interest in stamps and birds. Is this your good-bye message to me? Are you telling me that I am now on my own, without your presence, free to make of myself what I will?

It is December 1995, two years and five months. I have not had another dream.

JULENE BAIR ⌇ *At Forty-five*

At seven in the morning, dressed for work, I grab the chicken out of the refrigerator, where it's been thawing overnight. I've stored it on a plate, because I'm at that eternal middle age of my mother in all my childhood
memories. That responsible age, when experience has taught us the consequences of carelessness — drying, sticky blood pools on the lower shelf
and drips across the linoleum. I shout through the dining room and up
the stairs to my son, "Jake, get up! You've got twenty minutes before the
bus comes!" At the sink, I cut the plastic wrapper away, rinse out the body
cavity, toss the chicken in the Crock-Pot, and sprinkle it with salt and
pepper.

My mother raised her own chickens. Placed a stick across their necks,
stood on both ends, and pulled. They danced headless among their peers,
blood spurting until they wound down and collapsed. Mom picked them
up before their legs stopped churning. Outside, on the porch stoop, we
grasped their scrawny legs as if they were the stems of squash, some vegetable we'd harvested, and dipped the bodies into a kettle of water Mom
had boiled over the gas range. We plucked their feathers — a tedious,
stinky job. Then my mother took her position at the kitchen sink, where she
expertly wielded her favorite paring knife, the one she'd sharpened so
many times that the blade was no more than a quarter inch wide.

Sometimes my father would walk casually through the kitchen, in from
washing off field dirt on the mud porch, his sun-blackened, hairy arms
dripping water. Spotting her rear, which must have seemed an irresist-
ible target beneath the gathers of her housedress, he would mischievously
swat it.

"Ooh!" she'd yell as if angry. "Har-old!"

He would say things that I didn't know I needed to forgive him for
then, but which I do, without much effort, now. Such as, "What's the matter? I'm just inspecting my property."

Her fried chicken was the best, crusty and amber, never doughy or
greasy. As the youngest, I always got first choice, the wishbone, which
Mom cut as a separate piece. I didn't know then that her style of parceling
chickens was distinctive. I just know now, when I stand at my sink in the
big house I bought because it reminds me of the big house I grew up in, that
my hands look like my mother's against the painfully naked chicken. Our
hands — hers then, mine now — are bony and veined, and beneath our
long fingers, the chicken's wet skin and flesh are the same color as our own.
Their knobby bone ends look like our knuckles would look, were our
knives to slip. When I rub my hands, which are beginning to suffer from arthritis, they remind me of the slick, cool way my mother's hands felt in all
those thousands of purposeful and inadvertent touches between mother

and child. The hands say age to me, age and love and soil and mortality. Soil, because we drew our lives from it and Mom nurtured beauty by way of it, in her immense flower garden. She would stand up while hoeing and splay her hands alternately, working the fingers back and forth. Dad used to make jokes about Mom sleeping with Arthur Itis.

My mother would have called herself a housewife, although there was never an occasion for anyone to ask. Everyone knew that she was just one of John and Lizzie Carlson's daughters, who had married Harold, one of the Bairs. They lived on the farm her parents had built through the typical fifty years of familial perseverance. Jasmin and Harold had three children, two boys and me.

She never taught me, I never learned, how to cut up a chicken. On my visits home, I've never had the courage to admit this, the reluctance intensifying as the years advance. How could I be forty-five, my mother's age when fried chicken dinners were common fare at summer noon meals, and not be practiced in this essential art?

I migrated — spiritually, emotionally, geographically. Yet sometimes, after waking, I murmur as I walk into my cold early-morning kitchen, "Mommy." At night I utter both their names. "Mommy." "Daddy." I plead with fate, because, at seventy-six and eighty-one, respectively, my parents will die soon, and I long to travel now, this instant, the three hundred miles to Kansas. Except after we hugged for a few seconds, after a few enthusiastic words of greeting, the modern house they built in town some thirty years ago would return to silence. We'd take brief comfort from being together. Then I would go home and find myself aching again with the same sense of imminent loss.

I've had this image in my mind ever so long now — her hands, mine, as naked as the chicken; my mother, me, at the sink, preparing a meal for our family. She still prepares a lot of chickens, although she doesn't fry them. "It's the cholesterol," she says. "I have to be careful of Harold's heart." Often when I've visited in the past few years, I've heard her complain while standing at her aqua sink, "These store-bought chickens are just terrible anymore."

"Terrible?" I once asked.

"Yes."

"How? Terrible?"

"It's all this godawful crap you have to scrape out of them, and the fat. Chickens never used to be like that."

She told me a story my sister-in-law Kris had told her about a woman colleague. When Kris had also complained about cleaning chickens, the colleague had said, "Clean what? I just stick 'em in the oven."

"Can you imagine that?" my mother asked me. She stared at me as I sat at the kitchen table, as baffled as Kris's friend had been. I just shook my head in supposed equal disgust.

Since then, I've raked my fingernails over the interiors of chickens while running warm water inside, ripping loose the remnants of kidneys and other gutty things. I've trimmed the chunks of fat that hang loose near the tail. I've done this doubtfully, without much hope that I'll ever understand what a truly cleaned chicken is supposed to look like. Yet I am becoming my mother in the way that we all do — foreseeing minor household catastrophes and taking precautions (the plate under the chicken and a dozen other preventive measures daily), feeling her body aches, her bafflement at the passage of years, the growth of children. I know this for the first full, real time, living in this house reminiscent of the farmhouse, at this age, her eternal age.

Today I'm trying to decide whether to allow a man who loves me to come live with me. My mother could never have constructed such a sentence, although, as I contemplate this, it is not because of the "allow." Traditionally, women have had the upper hand in courtship, their bodies and hearts constituting a fortress whose walls men had to scale. The "live with," though, would have been morally perverse then, and I fear that it may be morally perverse now. Not in the sexual sense people had in mind back then, but because it betrays an unwillingness to give myself over completely. By avoiding vows, do I hope to hang on to authority not only over myself but also over him?

How strange that, at forty-five, I still crave my mother's wisdom in romantic affairs. How did she feel, giving her husband control over her family farm? Did the thought ever cross her mind that she was giving it? It wasn't an option in those days for a woman to run her own farm. But my mother's deeper feelings are mostly inaccessible to me. That means I am also inaccessible to myself. If she could tell me what it's meant to be my father's wife, what she felt when she first met him, how those feelings changed as their marriage matured, then I wouldn't feel like such an amputee, handicapped by the absence of intimate knowledge of the intimate lives of the people I am supposed to know most intimately.

Although my mother enjoys discussing politics, she tends to skirt the personal topics — death, religion, love. If I say something provocative, she says only, "Well . . ." in the manner of all the women of my childhood. I've learned not to wait for the insights that I suspect would follow if only it were OK to express emotion. Was this absenting of herself the reason our farmhouse seemed so airy? How do marriages, how do families, work? Do they function well only if one of the adults (most often the woman) submerges herself, pretending not to feel loss, to search spiritually, to crave appreciation and love?

I am a displaced Kansan, grown to adulthood and then to impossible middle age, the smell of grain dust and summer rain still in my nostrils. No life feels right, no life feels complete unless it's lived the way my parents lived theirs. At eighteen I wanted nothing more than to get away from Kansas, but by the time I was thirty, I began to wish I could have continued my parents' lives down the road in a big farmhouse of my own, cows and sheep in the lot by the barn, in view of my kitchen window. But I couldn't, can't, of course. Got educated, left, met two men, nonfarmers, stayed married to one for eight years, the other for eight months.

If I had married locally, though, I don't think I would be wandering my house murmuring "Mommy" at forty-five. Because in continuing a way of life, we incorporate our parents in ourselves. Wouldn't my mother live on, in me and in my children, if I lived a mirror image of her life down the road? I could look out another window and see their place; my son or daughter would marry and move there. This is the way it is supposed to work out in families, in clans, in tribes. A few miles west, and there would be some other relative living in Grandpa Bair's old place. "Grandpa Bair's," we say, not "Grandma and Grandpa Bair's." This, of course, is only part of why it couldn't work out.

My mother submitted to my father's rule of their household. He was a benevolent dictator whose dominion no one thought to question. The man who plans on moving into my house in December is uprooting himself from California, where I once lived, to come live with me. He loves my son, who has been fatherless since birth. My son loves him. I could not have married a man from down the road because he would have wanted to rule, benevolently, as my father did. I could not have submitted my will to his, deferred to his decisions in the shop and field as well as in the house. That's the kind of daughter my parents somehow raised. But this doesn't stop the longing for the life I've left. *I would dress chickens at the farm sink, the air and light and quiet and expanse filtering in. He would walk up behind me like my father did behind my mother.*

Now, with this man, even if I did learn to cut up chickens, it would be all wrong. He wouldn't deem it his prerogative to swat my bottom as he passed behind me at the sink, and my hands wouldn't extend down through the chicken's guts into the earth of a flower garden. Like almost everyone I've met since leaving Kansas, I am still trying, at forty-five, to invent a life out of the antiseptic remains of history, of displacement. Sometimes it feels as if too many miles, years, and ideas separate me from the past and the people who matter most because they mattered first. But this man has worked his way into my life. A computer specialist who dresses in chinos and silk sweaters, who reads in bed at night wearing half glasses, who fenced off part of my back yard last visit for a place to park his sailboat (in Wyoming!), he often stands with me at the sink. This man respects my other attachments and doesn't wish to rule anyone but himself. I feel an identity taking shape between us. Although shaped by generations of life on the land, our family will have another kind of integrity.

Should I marry him? My mother's voice comes to me, projecting itself

into the void I've always wanted to bridge: *I don't know how to answer your questions, because I never thought of any alternative; I never had any alternative.*
I do.

RIAN CONNORS 🦌 Full Monty

In the ocean, I float buoyant in swells beneath a tropical sunset. My skin awakens to mild salt water, to this light, warm floating that is the one thing I truly miss in the North, my beloved home.

I call to my sister Frances, swimming nearby, "I'm trying the half strip," and pull my swimsuit down to my waist. Ocean water caresses my chest, breasts, belly. "Good idea," she calls, imitating me. We float with the swells in twilight as the sun slips behind towering cumulus clouds, then sinks into the sea. Behind us on the empty white-sand beach, my two sons and two nieces build sandcastles. Earlier they shrieked with joy in their first warm ocean waves in years.

My youngest sister, Stef, swims out to join us. Frances quietly advises her of our submerged seminaked state. "Oh!" she says, and peels down her suit. She and I, with my children and her dog, are frequent swimming companions in the frigid lake at home. There we back float until our toes turn blue. Here, in the Pacific Ocean off Kauai, Stef turns to us and says, "I'm going for the full monty."

We agree instantly, and the three of us float in the sensuous touch of the ocean. We keep watch on the sunset, the rising darkness, and the children on shore. And on our mother, matriarch of this clan, who now enters the waves. Earlier her grandchildren, blissfully unaware of Mom's osteoporosis, begged her to bodysurf. Frances guides her through the gentle waves and out to join us. We swim together, surrounding her, the woman who invited us all on this trip to paradise in celebration of her seventy-fifth birthday.

"We're doing the full monty," I say teasingly, awaiting the reaction we daughters know so well. I am doubly rewarded, for while Mom's eyes and mouth speak the "Oh, you wicked girls!" we expect, she tugs off her own suit. Now we are a discreetly ribald quartet off a peaceful dusky beach, caressed by healing waves, asking nothing more of the moment.

"Sure is warmer than the last time we did this," I say, and we howl with laughter at our memories of Chilkoot Trail in July 1996.

There Frances was first in for a bath after four sweaty, bug-doped days backpacking. When I followed her into a mountain streamlet, my body registered disbelief in conflict with my eye. I saw her floating there, and she was neither frozen nor dead, but my body could not believe life as an outcome of immersion in that stream.

I submerged then and don't remember anything for a while.

Anne, the eldest, came to the stream and stripped. Susan, the fourth, followed. Then Stef and Mom, again the instigator of the expedition, appeared at the streamside. Mom sat on the soft low shore in her "old lady" shorts, plaid shirt, and sun hat. Stef undressed while the afternoon sun, finally free of overcast, poured sideways through the stream clearing. Our white bodies alternated with dark spruce shadows and the bright sunlight. We darted from pond to riffle, trying different spots and leaps, sandbars and logs. Our shrieks grew with the shock of in, out, and into the water, out to the cooling air. We were five Rubens nudes — mature bodies, beautiful at last after years upon years of living, lovemaking, not lovemaking, childbearing, coming out, not childbearing, aging, training, flexing, stretching, marathon running, head standing, accepting ourselves. So much harder than accepting each other, without whom in the hard years of our growing up we each would have died. Our hard times were forgotten, our backpacking blisters, hot spots, strains, and other wounds numbed, reduced, quieted on that sunny cold afternoon on the Chilkoot Trail.

So it is tonight as we float off Kauai, where our holiday comes to darkness. We pull suits back on underwater and rise like sirens from the sea to harbor each other, our children, and our mother in the soft tropical night.

ELIZABETH CANFIELD ❧ Living Without Loneliness

We are all over seventy years old now, the oldest girls among some fifty-five first cousins. The six of us have shared our lives with each other as far back as memory reaches — our triumphs, failures, joys, and sorrows.

We also share Danish immigrant grandparents who came to Wyoming in 1910. We six girls grew up spending weeks in each other's homes, our parents and aunts and uncles cherishing us all without favoritism.

When World War II came along, we were young women. Circumstances flung us apart. We married during those years, moved out of our small circle into places we'd never dreamed of seeing, but we kept in touch, sharing our apprehensions as well as our optimism. When the war was over, several of us had children within months of each other; one cousin and I bore our first children on the same day. The nurturing, caring relationship has never faltered; we know each other well, and we still treasure what we see.

Thinking of these cousins is like counting rosary beads. My cousins and I have been able to see our lives come full circle, to share the memories of all those tumbling years of living. We don't see each other's wrinkles. We remember riding horseback, dancing all night at country dances, each other's first loves. We remember telegrams notifying that someone was wounded during the war, births and deaths through the years. And looking into each other's eyes, we see joy for our glorious days, solace and comfort for the bad times.

The world has never been a lonely place for us.

LYN DENAEYER 🦌 *A Woman's Place*

Mama knew her place.
It was in the kitchen,
at the washtub,
or feeding the hens.
She dressed for town in navy blue pumps
with high heels,
and I would beg her not to wear them out
before it came to be my turn,
but at age thirteen
found them already outgrown.
Learned that rites of passage
are subject to change.

Peggy speaks quietly of breech presentations,
proper application of calving chains,
and baling hay just so
for a man who insists she's "lucky";
unable to credit a woman
with skill in these matters.

Tammy was by today.
"Contracted your winter feed yet?"
"Sorry, Bill's price beat you out.
And you know how the market is."
We discuss weaning weights,
nutrition, and scours.
No hard feelings.
Moms understand about pinched pennies.

Joy reins the colt with a light hand.
Tracy's loop settles neat.
Indignant youngsters emerge heels first
toward Deb's needle and Jan's waiting iron.
Stephanie leans into the lever;
head gate ends careening bovine rush
as she reaches for tagging pliers.

Karen, backing the gooseneck,
fits the chute square,
bails out to give the story
to the brand man.
She rode out at daybreak,
my granddaughter tucked in front.
Eighteen months and mad enough to spit
'cause she's not allowed to have the reins.
Already feelin' crowded by new life
growin' under Mama's ribs.

Hats pushed back,
gloves in hip pockets, we warm hands
on steaming mugs.
Unbuckling spurs,
I ease out of my Tonys,
noticing
they're navy blue . . . with high heels.

NEDALYN D. TESTOLIN ❧ Sky, Grass, Rain, and Sage

"She's a homely woman," I overheard someone say at a Fourth of July celebration. I was astounded. I couldn't accept this cruel observation. How
dare she say that? Francie Miller had a heart so big, so kind, so caring that
the goodness actually shone through her eyes.

I wanted to shout, "She's not homely. You don't know her, and you
don't really see her. She's beautiful. She's like the sky and the grass and the
rain and the sage, all in one."

Instead, I slipped quickly to her side. I knew we would protect each
other from thoughtless remarks.

I was a little girl then, and she was a young ranch woman in her mid-
twenties, recently married to Denver Miller. Francie had received an excellent education before many ranch girls were so privileged. She often said
that her years at school taught her a great deal about a great many things
she didn't want to do. However, she was also exposed to things that she
valued. She found ways to attend an occasional opera or to view an art exhibit, sometimes earning the money by hunting and trapping. She occasionally made time to revel in the fine service and food of elegant dining
rooms or perhaps to enjoy riding a mule to the floor of the Grand Canyon.

Stories abound. I've been a part of many and privy to the telling of
many more.

Her prowess on horseback was legendary, and she rode with the men to help capture wild horses. She was determined to stick with the herd, sometimes galloping over steep ledges and rugged terrain that challenged the best cowboys. And although Francie was quite buxom, respect deterred any man from remarking on her stature.

During one attempt to capture a bunch of wild horses, Francie's job was to head the herd on horseback just as they arrived at a perilous pass along a ledge. All caution thrown aside, she gave her horse its head and plunged on to keep the fast-running mustangs in check. Other riders would join the effort farther along the way. It seemed this time the wild horses would be theirs.

Suddenly, she pulled her horse up, stopping dead still. The wild horses continued on, escaping onto the plains. She had let them get away. This totally bewildered her husband and the other cowboys, who rode up, furious.

Francie drew herself up and looked icily at the men who awaited an explanation. She reached into her shirt, pulled out her broken bra strap, held it in her hand, and with stately dignity asked, "Have any of *you* ever tried to head wild horses with a boob flying over your shoulder?"

Instead of causing her to lose face, this tale only added to her reputation, and she continued to be sought after as a wild horse runner. Few women have been so honored.

Every summer Denver and Francie sought needy youngsters to work on the ranch. They took these children everywhere they went — to ride, to fence, to hay, to picnic, to dance, and to rodeo. They showed them their absolute faith in God and their belief in their fellow man. The children learned to heed admonitions or bear the consequences of their failures. Children clamored to live with them. After the youngsters left the ranch, Francie and Denver continued to provide guidance and funds, sending many young ranch hands on to college.

Francie was comfortable with Shakespearean quotes and biblical references, and she was equally quick to erupt with apt and forthright Western messages. Francie liked effect with its shock value. She created it wisely and with humor, actually enjoying the discomfort her seemingly incompatible interests caused those who knew her in only one setting.

She tells of turning her horse out on a cold spring day and trudging toward the house in her worn work clothes with her old black hat pulled down low in the Wyoming wind. A Bureau of Land Management (BLM) employee awaited her. He inquired whether she had any role in the ranch management. She invited him in without answering, and then silently and deliberately, she washed her hands and set about decorating a most exquisite wedding cake. He didn't know whether to stay or leave. Suddenly, she launched into the ridiculousness of many BLM practices, quoting both statute and regulation with surprising accuracy. The pure artistry with which she created each distinctive confectionery design already held him spellbound, but it was nearly surpassed by his amazement at her knowledge of grasslands and by the sharp rhetoric she had reserved for special use on naive regulatory agents. She had answered his question concerning her role in managing the ranch.

He, too, described this encounter many times. When he told the story, he always included the additional detail that she carried a rifle with her when they entered the house, and she placed it firmly on the kitchen counter between them before she began to decorate the cake.

So many times, when faced with a dilemma, I've asked myself, "What would Francie do?" Gradually, a solution will begin to form. Then I catch my own saddle horse and ride out to work it through in my mind.

What a wondrous enigma. As if still on horseback, she trots briskly back and forth between her faultless manners and her rustic demeanor, always treating all of us with kindness and tolerance. Sure-footed and strong, she continues to give us her love and laughter. Sixty years later, she's still beautiful, and she's still our sky and grass and rain and sage.

JANE ELKINGTON WOHL 🐎 *Daily Acts of Courage*

Bawling calf across her saddle,
she rides through deep and drifting snow,
with hands swollen in old gloves,
on reins stiff in bitter wind.
Beyond fences, cattle clot beneath small trees.
She squints in icy glare to find the cold-numbed mother.

Those were extraordinary times:
unlike those mornings of inner storms,
still black highways, bright indifference.
Her mind swollen with old words,
she faces sage and rising dust,
and drives alone across the plain.

III

New Flowers Unfolding: The Promise

In the often unfriendly landscape of the West, the sagebrushes have extended their habits, learning to reproduce either by scattering seeds or extending roots, or sometimes both. Similarly, the "company of women" represented in these stories may have arrived from somewhere else and adapted to the landscape and culture. Some sagebrush species bloom early, others late. Some women, "still undefined by . . . local roots," may believe that they will "always be foreign in this country" but soon find that their contacts with other women draw them into the community.

Age does not defeat "women of character." Nor does it defeat sagebrush: shrubs forty to fifty years old are common. So the blind mother "heading toward eternity" who says, "I can crochet in the dark," is illustrating more than an interesting hobby; we may need her resolve as dusk begins to fill our own horizons.

Other women in these pages use language instead of a crochet hook, "arranging words against the darkness" as they learn the strength of womanhood from one another. The words we have written, words that matter to some "more than sleep," may inspire others and strengthen the bonds between women everywhere. Many of us spring from generations of women who wrote their lives in grocery lists and hidden diaries, and yet we have found that "poetry [or diaries, letters, or essays] is the rutted road" we must follow. Stories keep us from going "crazier than a rat in a coffee can" and remind us that "we don't go alone," that "communication is the road to sanity." Besides preserving experiences, these stories teach us that "women's journeys are more alike than not" and that we all share the "blood language of this place." If we met our foremothers, our "callused hands would reach" to touch each other as our words have done.

Some of us may have flourished in the shadow of a woman who didn't know her importance, who was not aware of our "hunger for kinship." We might see a parallel in the way Indian paintbrush grows almost parasitically on the roots of some species of sagebrush, displaying its red and orange blooms against the gray-green mantle of sage. The two plants are "friendly neighbors," like many of the women represented here.

Not every story is optimistic, but if our ancestors cursed us, we may turn those curses into blessings and heal "layer by layer." No matter what our situations, we women "find ways to connect," listen to each other's voices, "let the stars and wind wash the tears from our eyes."

United, woven on the wind, Western women form a "beauteous circle of sages." Our written words will teach the lyrics of new songs to children, to the world outside our West. We are the link, drawing strands of kinship from the past through the present to a future none of us can precisely imagine. Listen and you will hear our voices "blow in the wind like wild grass." Listen and you will hear us say, "I am your sister." In this land, forever thirsty, irony flourishes; "tears water the wildflowers, which bloom only when there is moisture," unfolding the promise of new flowers.

These stories can fill us with the joy of knowing one another and create a shield of laughter flung against the darkness of ignorance and fear. Laughing in the night, we call to you: go on with the game, whatever you call it, whoever you are, wherever you live. We call to you to take your rightful place, your seat at the table, in the great tournament of life, and "deal, sister, deal."

LEE ANN RORIPAUGH Oyurushi: Forgiveness

We danced hopscotch squares,
pricked our fingers, blood sisters.
Hiding in the bathroom at recess,
we ate Jell-O chocolate pudding mix
and licked clean each other's hands.
She hid her mother's perfume in a lunch-
box, dabbed it behind my ears, then
gave me a paper cube with a peephole —
I looked inside and saw
You are my best friend.

The other girls taunted us.
She clung to me as I struggled
to pry each finger loose
until I tore away her sweaty palm.
I could not meet her antelope eyes
as she played alone, black hair
leaping the rigid arrow of her back.
She folded another paper cube —
I looked inside and read
I hate you.

She went to live on the Wind
River Reservation. Maybe a drop
of blood gave me courage.
I skipped on another playground
while white girls made slant eyes,
held my back like an arrow.
Mary Running Bull, I'm folding
a paper cube for you —
please look inside and see
I am your sister.

SUSANN McCARTHY The Company of Women

I

When I returned after long absence to the company of women,
my own kind, I was shy at first, ill at ease. I flinched
to hear one say that for years she'd read nothing but books

by women — to free her ear! Fatherly professors whose
teachings tuned my mind to a fine masculine edge
spun in their doctoral robes and turned my picture to a wall.
But gradually, I learned from women to be a woman, at ease
with women, to honor the blood that follows the moon, the healers
drowned as witches, dragged down by their heavy homespun
when I returned from a distance to the company of women.

II

When I had lived awhile in the company of women,
a few of us began to meet monthly, to share a meal, discuss
a feminist book, celebrate a solstice or equinox, and stayed
late talking of help for battered wives and pregnant kids.
We set out together to reinvent womanhood, to bring the
gender balance point back to center. One winter night
as we left, a truck slid off the road. In the circled headlights,
we dragged it out with four-wheel drive and chains —
then laughed to find ourselves so handy at brawn work
when I had lived awhile in the company of women.

III

When I had lived a long time in the company of women,
gainfully employed and quite capable of standing my ground
when businessmen measured me through the reductionist end
of their binocular gaze, or condescended protectively
to the "little lady" I used to try to be, a gray and gold
Odysseus found an attic window of my tower unbarred
and stood, so large, in my delicate rooms as if come home
to unravel my certainties, to drown me in the wine-dark
seas of him, to open me to pains and pleasures I'd forgot
when I had lived a long time in the company of women.

IV

When I had lived a long time in the company of women,
I camped out one June at a silent Buddhist retreat — days
of practice, nights of rain on canvas and flashlight failure.
Friday evening we joined for Sabbath, all stretching to touch
the big, flaky challah or, if beyond arm's reach, to touch
someone touching the bread. After the blessing, a friend
beside me muttered, "Now you can take your hand off my
husband!" — a Joan Crawford line! Was she kidding? Or
warning me? I puzzled long over that in the mindful silence
when I had lived a long time in the company of women.

V

When I had lived a long time in the company of women
and watched a dozen friends get homes through FHA,
I finally yielded to their urgings and applied for a house
of my own. Since then, if I think sometimes about men I
like — might love if we spent time — my little house
grabs my ankles, the loopy Berber rug catches my toes
like silver bindweed. Love stories are dances — someone
leads and someone follows. Owning my own home
took the follower out of me, my feet set down deep roots
when I had lived a long time in the company of women.

VI

When I had lived a long time in the company of women,
a grocery checker called me "ma'am." I snickered! Then
I shuddered. Next it was "Need help with your groceries,
ma'am?" Once — twice? — I was offered the old-lady rate
at the movies! I was disappearing — my face was pulling away
from my mind like a cruise ship from its port of call. I studied it
in my bathroom mirror. It smiled at me. But when I dug out
a dusty jar of face goop, it muttered something droll about
shutting the barn door after the cow's run off down the lane
when I had lived a long time in the company of women.

VII

When I had lived a long time in the company of women,
no longer married and seldom a lover, I remembered a story
I'd read long ago, of a woman who realizes, one night in bed,
that no man will ever choose her — and turns her face
to the wall. That story drove an ice pick into my heart —
anything that jarred it broke a sweat. After years among
women, I noticed that a man wrote it! — and realized it's not
being chosen but choosing that matters. I chose to break
my silence and push out into words, to tell my own stories
when I had lived a long time in the company of women.

LORA K. REITER ❧ She Was Writing

One of my earliest memories is seeing my mother's shadow — huge, gray,
undulating against the dining room wall and wavering on the ceiling of the
McCarthy farmhouse we rented. Mother was writing.

I can summon *her*, too, surrounded by stacks of the *Congressional Record*, Pall Mall cigarette packages, jar lids full of ashes, butts, and pencil shavings. She could whittle a pencil to a more dangerously long, thin point than any sharpener could — the old unpainted #2 lead pencils that would write so smoothly on the blank last pages of the *Record*, whose paper, maybe appropriately, was pulpy.

But I don't see her so much as I see her shadow. It was big and flickering, because it was cast by a gaslight, the kind you pumped up, lit mantles on, and watched the millers get in.

It was late at night, and I was supposed to be asleep because it was Mother's time to read and write. And there she'd be at the dining room table, reading and underlining, frowning and smoking, writing and marking out.

You couldn't erase that paper with those erasers. It would tear, and they would smudge.

But it was better than old wallpaper to write on, because it didn't roll up around the edges, and it was all the same size.

We were poor. No electricity. No typewriter. No tablets for Mother.

The state representative sent her the *Record*, and its final gathering usually provided her a week's supply of scratch paper. We'd catch hell if we colored on it.

So there she was — after a day's gardening or cleaning, cooking, dressing chickens or treating turkeys for the roup — concentrating for all she was worth, writing in her always uphill, tiny script on those pages she cursed because they were unruled and cherished because they were blank.

She showed me writing before I knew it had any content to it. What I knew was that it mattered more than sleep, that it was so intimate Mother did it privately and daily, that it was to be respected without question.

I don't know whether I first wanted to write because it meant sharing something Mother did or because it seemed as necessary as breathing. But I know that writing still means the essential to me, and it is imaged for me by that scene: a farmwoman I loved absolutely battling all odds of education, circumstance, and custom, sitting alone and without encouragement in that smoke-filled room those late nights, arranging words against the darkness.

CAROL BOIES 🦌 The Wedding Shower

The women of the clan, twenty-five of us from age eleven to eighty-something, are seated in a circle around the bride-to-be. She is nervous, and we are overly polite as we balance full coffee cups on our knees and the arms of chairs.

For our part of the country, we are dressed for the occasion. My daughters, reluctant to come, are wearing T-shirts and faded jeans. My cousins and I are wearing not-yet-faded jeans and sweaters, while our mothers have not given up their wrinkle-free polyester pantsuits. Their mothers and the bride's great-grandmother wear dresses.

The room is quiet at first until each woman begins visiting softly with the woman next to her. The volume rises as we converse with aunts and cousins we haven't seen for weeks. When someone invites the bride's mother into the conversation, the talking quiets. We all want to get to know her.

We are put at ease when she says her family has been farming for generations, too. No one will be put off by the faint odor of dairy barn that greets you when you first walk into the porch, and conversation will come easier, because farm and ranch families all have common topics.

Introductions over, we are asked to come clean with our worst kitchen disasters. Let's see, should I tell them about the time I blew up the pressure cooker or the time I melted the kettle on my stovetop because I forgot about it? We tease each other and laugh at our mistakes.

These delicate manners we slipped into for this special occasion begin to slide off, like coats when the sun comes out. By laughing at ourselves, we are sending the message to the bride that each of us has paid our dues and laughter has made the process less painful and more fun. A sense of humor may become her most-used wedding shower gift.

She opens the packages one by one, holding up each kitchen gadget, linen, or casserole dish for everyone to see. Then she comes to the box with no name on the card. She takes the lid off, and her face turns crimson. "OK, who's this from?" A small giggle from one of the guests is quickly swallowed by the roar of laughter from all of us.

"Come on. Hold up all your gifts for everyone to see!" one of the aunts challenges her.

The bride sheepishly holds up two naughty little pieces of lace. The younger girls shake their heads at us laughing "old ladies," most of us remembering a time when we were small enough to sport such things and look good in them. The bride, still embarrassed, laughs with us.

Now we are enjoying the cake that my cousin baked and decorated for the shower. My other cousin, the hostess, made the butter mints and punch. The meal for the wedding reception is being planned and served by one of the aunts.

The party is about over, and we float away, one by one. Some of us stop to exchange recipes or glance at the latest school pictures. I linger over the flowers the hostess has planted in her back yard. No men come up to any of us to say, "I've gotta get home and grind some feed for those butchers. Are you about ready?"

That could be why we like our traditions and stick to them. We're not one of those more modern circles inviting men to the showers, baby or wedding. This is our domain.

We can see that the new bride is a good match for our farm boy. She will not have a problem staying by his side during low prices and calving season. We can also see she won't be afraid to take a few hours every now and then to join our cloistered circle.

LUCY ADKINS ❧ Linda

Big sister, hero,
female in a man's world,
first-born of four daughters,
she drove the Jayhawk at haying time,
mastered gears and levers,
wheeled left to turn right,
topped the stack higher than any man.
Big sister, hero,
walking me to school:
blue jeans beneath our dresses,
wind lashing our faces,
ten below, fifteen,
fingers stinging in blue mittens,
toes turning to rocks;
I cried, but not she.
Big sister, hero,
riding the big Quarter Horse,
the one that toyed with me,
took me under cottonwood branches,
clotheslines.
She tossed the reins to left and right,
cut off the errant heifers,
plunged after the steaming, snort-nosed bull.
Big sister, hero,
she fights with sickness now,
little cells that grow and multiply
in lungs and liver,
threaten all she is;
she looks cancer in the eye
and does not flinch.
Big sister, hero.

KAY MARIE PORTERFIELD ❧ The Legacy

As the snow from one of the last spring storms drifts across my forty-acre back yard, I unwrap the newspapers that cushioned my mother's china teacups on their journey from the storage locker in Arizona to South Dakota where I live.

Seven of them remain intact.

I broke the eighth when I was a little girl lured to touch what was forbidden to me, a trait I still can't seem to shake. That mishap sent my teary-eyed mother to her room for two days, exiting that sanctuary only to use the bathroom. On the way, she would glare at me and ask God what she had done to deserve being cursed with a clumsy daughter like me, or any child for that matter.

Three years ago, when we packed the family belongings to move Dad to a nursing home after his stroke, I asked my brother to cradle the cups in newspaper. Although I told no one, I thought of how if Mom knew I held those fragile beauties in my hands, she would be turning over in her grave, even though she had left them to me ten years ago. Today I alone am responsible for deciding what to do with this legacy.

Each delicate cup is different from the others, uniquely shaped and painted. But every member of the mismatched family is covered with roses, cosmos, cornflowers, poppies, violets, or pale blue forget-me-nots. They remind me of my grandmothers' gardens, planted to distract the eye and spirit from the ugliness of ramshackle houses that could use much more than a coat of paint. The bone china they are made from is so thin they glow translucent when I hold them to the light.

They are the sort of cups special women sip from, women of character who gather on long summer afternoons to share their lives and offer advice in hushed tones over sugared tea and tiny sandwiches with the crusts cut off. As a girl, I spent hours imagining them used at genteel luncheons.

Given to my mother at a wedding shower some fifty-five years ago, these cups never served their intended purpose. They remained preserved on a shelf in Mom's china cabinet like a museum display. Undisturbed behind the glass, they seemed to attain a mystical, almost holy quality. Unaffected by the tight-lipped silences, the tears, and the whippings that marked my family, unchanging and ever beautiful, they endured — a calm display of grace in a home raging with disappointments and unfulfilled promises.

Perhaps they served to balance Dad's muddy and manure-covered galoshes by the door, the brown sofa with springs emerging from the seat, and my brother's and my decapitated army men scattered across the linoleum. Or maybe they served as a mocking reminder of the city life Mother left behind when she married my farmer father. More than that, the teacups seemed a shrine to something my mother longed for but could not bring herself to attain.

She seemed to have no use for the occasional farm wife neighbors who knocked on our door, and even pretended not to be home. She told us that idle conversation — small talk — was the work of the devil. "It's best not to get too close to people," she would say darkly, her voice holding the dire threat that something horrible would happen to my brother and me if we made friends at school. Afraid we might contract some deadly disease through words and laughter alone, we blindly obeyed and became loners until well into adulthood. Today I understand that her fear of people was far greater than any we could muster. She trapped herself in a loneliness of her own making.

While I wash the cups and dry them, preparing to store them away behind the glass doors of my own china cabinet, I wonder what to do with them. Whether by accident or design, my days have been blessed with women of spirit and character who have helped me ignore my mother's dire warnings and take the risk of friendship, women who do not hesitate to share their lives with me and to patiently draw out my own stories of triumph and woe. In their serene constancy, they have given me what my mother could not and in the process have shown me that legacies can be transformed.

Cat, the sister I adopted late in life, finds inspiration and hope in the gloomiest of circumstances and has taught me to accept her nurturing despite my attempts to fight it. My daughter-in-law Amee's warmth, compassion, and humor light her face and her life. Cleo, through her patience and understanding, has encouraged me to trust my intuition and find my own voice. Evelyn shares my love of quilting and has shown me that quiet strength and courage are just as beautiful as any patchwork ever could be. Bev, a survivor, respects me enough to let me learn my hard lessons and refrains from gloating too much when she says, "I told you so." Susie always urges me to keep on dancing, since there's bound to be a better song coming.

Several live in other states; we communicate with phone calls and e-mail. Others are nearby but are often as busy as I am. Nonetheless, when work and weather permit, we visit, meeting in town for coffee or sitting on my porch and watching the sun set behind the hills. It is their presence in my life that makes today a time of quiet solitude rather than loneliness.

As gusts of wind batter the side of my trailer and the driveway drifts shut, I know that my calling is not to preserve the teacup shrine, but to dismantle it. I keep one cup as a remembrance of Mother but carefully wrap the rest of them, sealing each in a tissue-stuffed box labeled with the address of one of my women friends. When the storm stops and the snow melts, I will take them to the post office. I believe my mother would somehow be pleased.

LYN DENAEYER ᢔ Resurrections

"Hello . . . hello?" There was a momentary silence on the line, then strangled sobs.

"Everything is dying!" she choked, dissolving into uncontrollable weeping.

"Brenda? What's up? Take some deep breaths and tell me about it."

A few ragged sentences assured me that no one was literally dying, but my friend continued to weep. "I'll be right there," I said, reaching for a jacket. On the short drive, I cast an appeal for guidance to the Landlord who hung the glittering lights in the late September sky. I care deeply for this friend whose honesty and courage have blazed a trail or two for me. Now I prayed that differences in our backgrounds would not be a barrier to the support I longed to return. Brenda is Lakota. I am *wasichu*, white.

Tears flowed again as I hugged her, and Brenda offered the timeworn woman's explanation. "I don't know why I'm crying."

We usually don't, do we? Men throw up their hands in disgust and mutter, "Women!" while heading for the door to commiserate with buddies over a beer. How could they possibly understand that for so long we've "cowboyed up" — put a good face on a bad deal — that we truly haven't a clue what finally broke the dam?

All Brenda knew was that she felt terribly alone and everything was dying. She was pretty much on her own since Sam had decided to go back to school halfway across the state. He wasn't happy about the separation, but a degree would buy the family a better future, and he was usually able to get home for weekends. Brenda had a good job and was raising some grandchildren, as is often the case with her people. It's an interracial marriage, but Sam participates in the customs and ceremonies of her tradition, and cultural differences haven't been an issue.

I asked Brenda whether she and Sam had discussed her depression.

"Yes, but he doesn't understand why I'm always so sad in the fall," she replied. "I don't either."

Suddenly, light flooded into a dark tunnel from my own past. "You're right," I said. "Me, too. It *is* like everything is dying, and I'm powerless to make it stop. Oh, Brenda, do you think it has to do with boarding school?"

"My God! Of course, but how did *you* know when *I* didn't?"

She had told me about not knowing English and being beaten for speaking Lakota. Support groups on the res call it cultural shame, but some of us whites have it, too. Sometimes we tell others what we need to hear. Most emotional healing begins there. So that night I shared my own story with the one person in my life who totally understood how it is for a country child, sent away at age six, to board in town for school.

Brenda didn't just smile and nod when I mentioned being ridiculed for having braids rather than curls, wearing clothing that was different, and not knowing how to play with other children. She cried with me. She remembered crying herself to sleep every night in the cruel conviction that her parents must not care, since they never came to get her. She didn't find it strange when I described not raising my hand in class or meeting the teacher's eyes, even when I knew the answers. Most important, she nodded vigorously when I said that what I grieved most was the absence from the land, sky, and animals.

"I spoke English quite fluently," I told her, "but we didn't talk the same language."

I remembered my parents' insistence that I buy a high school yearbook and how I managed to lose it promptly. I didn't want a new dress for graduation, didn't want to commemorate the years of sorrow and shame. All the friends I eventually made and the honors I earned couldn't remove the shadow of my separation from the soil.

It was a long night's journey out of that darkness, but we hung on to each other, and we made it to the light. Obviously, summer will always be our favorite season, but neither Brenda nor I have had to descend so far into autumn depression since.

We don't get together much since I've moved, but she walks my mind a lot. She's exploring childhood traumas in therapy, and I find continued healing through researching and writing the stories of pioneer women from various ethnic backgrounds. We're both learning that women's journeys are more alike than not and that we're good at using the rocks we encounter as steppingstones.

A. ROSE HILL 🦌 The Gift

My mother gave a party
to celebrate my birthday
when I turned sixty-five.
She baked a chocolate cake
because she knows my weakness.
She baked some beans, a squash,
a chicken, too,
and called the family in
to dinner.

She gave me antique water glasses,
rimmed in red, cut with diamonds.
Tears brimmed at the second gift,

the one I liked the best,
a simple crocheted potholder,
brown and yellow,
the useful kind.

The beast, macular degeneration,
ate her vision, left her only
tiny windows of sight.
"I can still feel," she says.
"I can crochet in the dark."

SUSAN MINYARD 🔻 word

                word
came to me in deepest sleep through silvery moonlit air from all around
the waiting landscape, where fairy tales still dance at dawn, and *Charlotte's
Web* lay all around, carrying truths, too many, they blurred into dreams.
                word
came to me in stillness, at night
                she's ill, she's gravely ill
I rose up out of bed, a shivering nightgown-clad thick woman did, and
drifted along wise currents to her side. I saw that once again
                nobody came, nobody came.
                                                she
was alone, of an age, seventy-six, on a cotton farm, in a too-empty bed,
king-size with the argued-over mattress, a perfect battleground. Light oak
bookcase headboard, handmade, held all of civilization: grandchildren in
photographs, Bibles, two of his serenity prayer ceramics.

She couldn't sleep. She settled finally in the blue velveteen chair, where
she stayed for hours and hours, with remote control to the snowy television reception, stray wires to the satellite dish out back pushed underneath a brass stand, her favorite spot a throne by morning, with the sun
beckoning and fetching all the birds and stray cats and dogs and lizard
friends and scorpion enemies to the oversize arcadia doors there, to the
dishes of water of all sizes, to her unmoving feet.

Blue velveteen chair squatted beside stacks of unread magazines, store-
bought, for a pioneer who bore five sons in the primitive badlands of
Arizona, who nursed them through pneumonia in deep blizzards, who
nursed herself through fifty years, a lifetime, of doing without. Now, with

electricity and running water and twenty years of dedicated church service and a full pantry and an organized and stacked deep freeze, doing
without again, alone, for
>*nobody came, nobody came.*

But I did go, two months after my dreams of her began, to my mother-in-
law, *Low*-retta, Mom. We sat together, one woman, two women. One awful
belly raged up and up and out and out between us, and the enormous
hanging pendulum on her tiny frame showed now and then through the
threadbare print housedress, her favorite, which matched her forever-
living eyes, shades of sameness I see in my husband and three sons, and
their uncles, too, all of her five sons have shades of perceiving blueness,
but her blue eyes seek me out and do not stray to new horizons and
infinity. I am her horizon, for now. So we sit inside her awfully clean
kitchen with her awful belly, and I feel panic flutter in the sides of my
cheeks
>*what shall I do? what shall I do?*

Chicken little screams at me, that chicken head inside mine, her sad sad
heart still beats beats beats.
>*Others will come, others will know what to do.*
Though this is not the kind of illness that comes with first stage, second
stage, third stage. This kind of illness drives the horses out of control, and
though she pretends to eat the melon she demanded, I see her clinging to
the reins, bouncing around the driver's box, and yelling *It's OK!* to her
passengers.
>*No, no, no!*
I could whine my younger years, *no, no, no!* to my mother-in-law, *Low*-
retta, Mom, and lay my head mostly on her thighbone, diverting currents
of healing intentions toward her awful stomach, which pressed against my
nose, smelling her laundry and yesterday's awkward shower.

Sometimes she would whine back to me
>*why am I so tired? I haven't done a thing, you know?*
>*why? why? why?*
I would say
>*again, no, no, no*
lay my head mostly on her thighbone and weeping willows crept close
around us there along her fire engine red scratched Formica kitchen table,
hand-fashioned long ago by him, and the Constant Comment tea made me
brave the unspoken she wore like a halo. I would say,
>*you're ill, you're gravely ill*
>*that's what makes you so tired*
>*it's OK*

she would pet my hair, and when I raised up off her thighbone to offer a
smile, why she could grin and grin, the biggest grin ever.

I am so glad to have someone young and vital and special
who thinks I am very special, I am so lucky
did you know Rachel and Kelly think I am special, too?

I did ask why, once. Grandma, they said, because of
too much stuff, it's big, very big, and she spread her arms wide
like this
I just thought how wonderful!

My mother-in-law, *Low*-retta, Mom, loved to say that: *how wonderful!*

But then, *nobody came, nobody came*

We ate and ate on three cups of Nancy's macaroni salad, though I am not
sure if my mother-in-law, *Low*-retta, Mom, decided if it was too sharp or
the most delicious pasta salad she had ever tasted, how she would love to
learn to make some pasta salads.

My mother-in-law, *Low*-retta, Mom, is like that, always piping up with
something new to learn to cook, to sew. As far as plants, she wants gardens and greenhouses and scientific inquiry directed to specific questions,
to know everything, and about birds, too.

We had finches and damn starlings and hooked beaks and a mystery fling
tomcat for two weeks, yes, they came to the back yard in split shifts, and a
thunderstorm came, too, and husband Jerry and I and she stood outside
and the wind tore and pushed at her blue housecoat that matches her eyes
and Jerry said
    Mom, you're so tiny!
Nervous laughter began
    you're so small, I'm so big, I'll crush you!
earthquakes
he had held this inside since my dreams began

So we both held her that night out in the thunderstorm weather of the
wind, and all the washes ran that night, the night of the Fourth of July, that
was sure some storm, and she was sure glad to see it all, and Jerry left us
to go back to his cotton, but he wasn't so sure his mother had a flu bug.

teeter-totter
ugh!
true Arizona pioneer woman
with a long, scrolled ethic telling her one thing always,

what's right, be helpful, be prim, don't be loose
we may make do, but we're civilized
we're not barbarians, ban all barbarians from the hearth, from the home,
do it now, lock the doors

why, she could forget all that upbringing and hardness in the feel of wet
clay under her hand, which came upon her like love, sculpt, sculpt
my mother-in-law, *Low*-retta, Mom,

so few people speak heart to heart anymore.

I have her ceramic bells and vases and pitchers now, in keeping, in love,
think about them in the homes of my sons, one day, one day.

No, all people wanted to hear of her was what did you eat, how much,
and did you have a bowel movement, and why not? Their hearts were in
the words, which had meanings and meanings not even discovered yet.
But they still didn't come
    nobody came
    nobody came

She stopped asking
    Why did I let my sister and my husband interfere
    in my relationship with my mom?
    she always only had me to help her
    what did my sister and my husband do to me
    that I didn't go to my mother when she was dying?
    I wish, oh, how I wish I could figure that out.
    My place was with my husband, and I spoke with him,
    but he said oh . . . and then there was my sister.
    why didn't I? why didn't I?

And no one came, nobody came.

And the day they took my mother-in-law, *Low*-retta, Mom, to the hospital,
borne aloft of enormous and tireless elephants on a gold-tasseled padded
couch, to the place she suffered and dreads, to the place, the one place
where everyone will come
everybody
of that day she remembers nothing more than Dianne coming
to help us
pain
laying down upon the floor of the bathroom on the blue blanket
nothing more than simply a laying down

though she seemed awake and virgin modest with all those men, medics,
medical uniformity, objectivity, anonymity,
uniforms
the ambulance didn't run the lights all around town,
for they *already knew she was ill, she was gravely ill*
and they had already not come, already forgotten.

I went aloft the quiet, rocking journey with her, partway with her, she
asked for her teeth at Jackrabbit Road, and I took them out of the hasty
ziplock bag, and she inserted them herself, later she wanted her glasses to
sign her name and read a form.

Then they began to come,
one
then two
children
oh no! my mother is ill, she is gravely ill
she is in the hospital
what shall I do, what shall I do

Those one or two sent out the word, through all the land,
they probably said to everyone just what that one brother-in-law
said to me, what I had been saying, too
    Me, me, me
we were pegged upon a clothesline, next to one another, there in your hospital room, blowing and flapping, uncomfortable. Cuss words passed my
lips, *shitheads!*

I forgot I carried the sword of Damocles, it was in my hands, my hands,
and when your sons said to me
    what shall I do? what shall I do?
    when this happens to me
I swung
hacked away
    perhaps you will do as your father did, die first,
    before your nurse-wife
    she will care for you
    then she will die

You were still teaching me though you didn't hear my dark words,
you are still teaching me,
your pioneer pride in nobody's business but your own,
mother's faith in modern living for modern sons,
no daughters,

only daughters-in-law
we had talked enough, you saw my bent
one female with only sons, households stuffed with men,
you understood them, you understood me, too
you loved them, my sons and your sons, and me
did you know how proud they were that you lived nineteen days longer,
a gentle mother that stirred fond memories and childhood,
not the firebrand and not the sphinx
that you talked and loved them back and down and up until the end,
anger breaking through that one night at hospice,
when Jerry and I bent over your new bed, to press cheeks and lips
all over your still head, when the blue fire ignited one last chiding,
when you told me to write it all, write about an abandoned old woman,
with fifteen hundred dollars cash in her pocketbook
who can't talk her sons into taking her home
to live, to die
and I said to you yes! I am writing it, I am writing it all!

VIRGINIA BENNETT 🦌 Tapestry of Knots

In the quiet-time of morning,
when the moon is going down,
she builds a cookstove fire
with yester-news from town.
And as warmth creeps into the cabin,
measured slowly by degrees,
she sits with pen at kitchen table
with a quilt to warm her knees.

And she writes of thoughts she garnered
during chores of the day before
while she pitched the hay from feed sled,
which she prayed would travel slower.
Upon her pad of yellow paper
dormant words came into life.
Her mind crept beyond the mundane walls,
before she became a rancher's wife.

She could travel (at the speed of ink)
to those places in the heart
when romance bloomed like summer's rose
or a dream broke and fell apart.

She still could see, with clarity,
a dozen years gone past,
when love was new or love was cold
or a spirit had been slashed.

With open, honest invitation
to explore her hidden thoughts,
she scribed haunting, hunted images
like a tapestry of knots.
And she typed them up on linen paper,
so they'd be worthy to be read.
Then she donned her crusted coveralls,
for there were cattle to be fed.

How many more are like her?
We can only guess.
The women who write heartbroke words,
emboldened to confess.
They fold, they stamp, and they mail
their souls from coast to coast
and share their work with all the world
except the one they love the most.

MAURA T. CALLAHAN Pilgrimage

My children were being very patient with me. I was dragging them all over three states with a stack of books and a long list of places to take them one hot August a couple of years ago. I was focused. I was on a pilgrimage.

One of the more remote places we ended up was in a dusty parking lot in northeastern Wyoming. Two houses and a tavern, all there was of the town, sat in the middle of miles of green, gold-tipped, grassy plains rolling in every direction from where we stood. I knew the woman I was looking for would be nowhere in sight, as Gretel Ehrlich had moved away from this state several years before. But she was still here for me. I had stumbled upon Gretel's book *The Solace of Open Spaces* in a used-book store one rainy September in Santa Fe a month after my mother died, turning a tight spring in my heart even tighter. Wyoming.

I picked up the book and read two chapters out of the middle, perched on a stool in the bookstore for so long the owner offered me a cup of hot tea. I was hooked. How could I not be? Gretel made chasing two thousand sheep all over the Big Horn Mountains sound like a brilliant career choice. I was game for it, if not in body, in spirit. I still dream of spending a year, or at least a season, herding sheep up and down the gullies and washes of Wyoming. I can see myself out there learning to breathe thin air with my horse and a dog and a sack full of books.

In Montana, we wandered east of the Rockies until I stood with my girls on the sandy banks of the gently flowing Judith River in the shadow of the Little Belt, Judith, and Big Snowy Mountains, and read them the first chapter of Mary Clearman Blew's *All but the Waltz*. It was magical for me and spellbinding for the girls to see with our own eyes the words made real. The decrepit log cabin where Mary lived until she was three shimmered in the heat off in the distance with the ancient boxelder still standing sentinel at its side. She wrote about the landscape of her family, five generations deeply set in the soil of central Montana. Mary gave me a sense of history I had never felt before. Her graphic telling is so remarkable, I became enthralled with the idea of searching out my own ancestors. I gave my children Mary's to chew on while I mulled over the possibilities.

Her second book, *Balsamroot*, was more personal for Mary and for me. Divulging private thoughts from her aunt's journal written sixty years before, Mary wrote about Aunt Imogene, her mother's sister, and how they were entwined in a beautiful dance, separate but singular lives.

I found myself on her pages in women making hard choices and having to live with them. Understanding how they lived by an uncompromising code of ethics even to the point of pushing away love, having to numb themselves or face the anguish of abandonment. Mary relayed the terrors of being alone in the outer reaches of a hard land and how sometimes it manifested into thousands of embroidery stitches, rooms webbed with the filaments of lacy doilies on every piece of furniture. I was sad when the book came to an end, as if an old and dear friend had moved away.

As we drove on through South Dakota, I dreamed of a life beyond children, a life of horse rides in gray moonlight and walks in loud wind, and conjured up a life like Linda Hasselstrom's *Going Over East*. We ended up in her southwestern corner of the state, and I showed my girls the obvious: the Badlands, the Black Hills, Crazy Horse. But I also tried to relay to them what Linda had given to me in her stories — a keen sense of the durability, substantiality, and order of natural things. She convinced me that we as a race are fast losing a valuable perspective. Those simple things that we overlook or dismiss are integral to our lives, such as cow manure and the sweet and sour smells of the earth's crust and creatures.

Linda showed me an unobstructed view of what I already knew: that life and death are hard, yes, but that there's also an easy philosophy of acceptance to be had here. For someone like me, who sometimes has to look away when I see roadkill, this may be a challenge. But I know the value of a good life, and I see it there on the sun-drenched plains. My friends think I have completely lost my mind when I tell them that this sounds like the life for me. I think Linda and I know better.

It is a grace to be able to share these women's lives. They don't know me, will probably never meet me, would be surprised that I have been so affected by the chronicles of their passions, their weaknesses, their failures and triumphs. I owe them a debt I can't even imagine how to repay. Gretel and Mary and Linda and the many other women authors of the West have opened up the second half of my life for me and made my passage easier, but somehow a simple "thank you" doesn't seem to cover it. How about I challenge myself with adventures, accept the anguish of life's sorrows, not dodge the hard stuff, and always fully participate in the blessed rites of love and laughter, and we'll call it even?

EMILY BOIES ❧ *What Makes Our Lives*

The women in my family have influenced me to hate certain things: the blood-freezing winters, the skin-baking summers, and most of all the mosquitoes. I hate hearing that it's going to be a few months till we sell some calves or some wheat, so things are going to be kind of tight around here for a while. I hate it when heaven blows in sixty-mile-an-hour winds from all directions at once. And I hate it when there's mud on the ground and mud on my shoes and mud on my pants and mud in my hair wherever I go.

Then there are those things I have learned to hate with no outside help. I hate big, dumb, brown-eyed, Black Angus beasts and the flat, desolate land. I hate 4-H traditions and the joys of gardening and the omnipresent haze of pig dust. I hate inhaling ten gallons of water with every breath of air during the month of August and being the only teenage girl west of the Missouri limited to three television channels and people telling my mama I've been growin' like a weed. And I hate wide-open spaces.

The women in my family have also influenced me to love certain things. I love the graceful character of horses. I love seeing my dad so happy after he gets a check for some calves or some wheat or some pigs that will tide us over for a while. I love dark thunderclouds in the sky for hours, and I love it when the grass is so green I can smell it wherever I go. I love feeling connected to my mom and my mom's sisters and my grandma and my great-grandma because I have their prairie-girl blood in my prairie-girl veins.

Then there are those things I have learned to love on my own. The inexplicable beauty of the river hills, seventy-five degrees with sunshine, huge snowflakes falling out of the sky ever so slowly on Christmas Day, and most of all the background music of a thousand crickets. I love my freshman class of fifty and strawberries in June and late-summer nights outside in the dark and the thrilling threat of a tornado. And I love remembering the little girl in me who needs her wide-open spaces.

If there's one thing I've learned from the women around me, it's that my life is mine to hate and mine to love as I choose. It doesn't matter what I hate and what I love. What matters is that I remember it's the things we hate that break our lives and the things we love, no matter how few, that make them.

GEORGIA RICE 🐎 Tea for Two

Supper was finished, dishes were done, everyone had finished watching the *Nightly News and Weather* — it was time for bed. All the lights in the house were off except the one over the kitchen stove that gave a relaxing glow to the room. Quart jars of freshly canned green beans were cooling on the counter, witness to the day's accomplishments.

I knew I wouldn't be able to sleep, so I sat at the long wooden table that earlier had seated ten children and two adults. I thought of the evening meal, all the conversation, everyone having something to share. Most days we had even more people at the table. Blanch said, "There's always room for one more; we'll just add another tater to the pot." The warmth you felt in that kitchen was the true meaning of *welcome*.

I came out of my daydream as Blanch walked into the kitchen and asked if I needed a cup of tea. I said yes, knowing it would be her special Russian tea she hides from the rest of the family. It's used only for special occasions, and our evening conversations were always special.

Somehow Blanch knew when something was on my seventeen-year-old mind. "What are you thinking about?" she asked as she put water in the teakettle. "You seem so far away."

"About our dinner conversations and about my family. It just makes me feel bad that things happen the way they do."

"You need to remember the past," she said, "no matter how bad it was. That's how we learn. You have to remember the good things to keep from going sour. You just can't go around with a chip on your shoulder!"

As Blanch struck the match to light the burner, she began talking about her younger years, when she trained horses on the plains, and in particular about her favorite Thoroughbred gelding named High Pockets. "He was a bugger to settle down but ended up being one of the most dependable animals I ever rode. We entered the horseraces at the fair in the fall, and High Pockets wasn't to be beaten. He won the half-mile race four years in a row. I remember it as though it were yesterday, the crowd yelling us on and the adrenaline rushes I felt by the time we crossed the finish line."

She took four homemade oatmeal cookies from the cookie jar and put them on a small plate on the table between us. We both smiled as another top sealed on a jar of canned beans. The kettle of water began to whistle. It sounded like a train running through the kitchen.

"I know how much you enjoy your horses," I said as she poured the steaming water into the teacups on the counter. "I can tell by the way you handle them and teach others about them. Remember our evening ride last summer? We left the ranch around four o'clock after chores. All six of us kids had saddled our own horses and were ready to ride. You'd packed a picnic supper into the packs on your black and white pony, Babe."

She nodded, and we reminisced while she brought the tea to the table. We had ridden down the lane under the tall old cottonwood trees, across the highway to the irrigated hay meadow, and past the haystack that held the small round bales we had stacked earlier in the summer. The low sun cast long shadows. We rode about four miles and found the perfect hilltop, where we could see up and down the valley. The majestic Big Horn Mountains stood high in the distance — a rose color that only the sun can paint in the evenings. Fall was in the air, but it was a calm evening, and we eagerly ate our picnic dinner. The horses nibbled at the grass.

"Remember how you kids raced up and down the hill?"

I nodded yes, began stirring my tea, and dunked a cookie into the cup. "That's when you told us the horses would take us directly back to the ranch without our help. The six of us decided to see if you really knew what you were talking about, so we gave the horses their heads, and sure enough we ended up at the saddle barn, well after dark. We laughed all the way back to the house. That is a memory that will keep me from going sour," I said as I finished my cookie. "It's one I'll share with my children when we have tea."

We sat in silence for a few minutes. Blanch was staring into her cup. I wondered whether she was thinking of her life on the old homestead. To earn extra spending money, Blanch had gathered eggs, milked the cow, loaded the Model T, and drove to town to deliver the fresh produce to her regular customers.

While she was silent, I thought of other times Blanch and I had spent in the kitchen drinking tea. We talked about my other brothers and sisters, about the prom, boys, and what my future had in store after I graduated from high school. Blanch encouraged me to go to college. "Don't waste your time getting married. You have so much going for you. Do the things you want to do first, like traveling, getting a degree, and enjoying life." I listened intently and pondered her advice.

It was time to turn in for the night. We put the empty teacups and cookie plate in the sink, gave each other a hug, and said good night. I walked toward my bedroom, turning in time to watch Blanch tap the top of each bean jar to see how many were sealed. We retired to our rooms just as the clock chimed twelve.

As I look back, Blanch Wood is my most cherished treasure. She welcomed me into her home, her heart asking for nothing in return. She showed me how unselfish a person can be by becoming a foster parent. She was a foster mother to me for three years, to my two brothers and two sisters for ten. Throughout our stay at the ranch, other foster children were welcomed into this loving home and the ranch way of life. Everyone was treated as one of the family, each of us coming away with a better understanding of the true meaning of love and life.

Blanch has since retired from the ranch. She now lives in town, but her friends and family still gather in her kitchen when they visit. The tea, in its special place, is brought out to welcome each visitor.

PATRICIA FROLANDER Sisterhood

Tonight I finished reading your book, and
before the dream gatherer claims me, I ride east
across the Black Hills
and ask forgiveness for intruding on your solitude.
My callused hands reach for yours in greeting;
in quiet voices we speak of calving and moisture.

Like prairie grass that bows before the wind,
we share our lives . . . so many parallels
urban education
preparing us to claim the land with tears of relief
privilege of good horses, strong calves, full reservoirs
and the love of a man who fit the missing pieces of our souls.

With wind-chapped cheeks and wrinkle lines
proclaiming seasons in the sun,
we laugh at the jokes life has played on us
frown at those who would rearrange our lives.

Those who are not challenged by the seasons
the need to give back a portion of what they have used
to give value to hard work, bring honor to friendship,
cannot understand our need for extremes to breathe life.

As dawn breaks, I warm the bit in my hands
before I slip it into the buckskin's mouth.
With tightened cinch I lead her into the chill air
and turn . . .

The cold air slips beneath my blankets.
I waken wondering if you saw me wave good-bye.

DARCY ACORD ❧ Dear Ann

You didn't like me at first.

Actually, maybe you did. The evening we first met, when I spent an hour playing dolls with your granddaughter, you told Shawn, "You know, not just any girl would do that." But four months later, after we announced our engagement, you seemed to change your mind. Once, when Shawn had an upset stomach, you quipped, "Darcy's cooking getting to you?" And when I showed the family my diamond solitaire engagement ring, you said, "Be careful you don't get that caught on something, it sticks up so far."

My attempts to earn your approval fell short during those first years. When I cooked steaks during one of your visits, you came running from the living room to check them, even though I was standing next to the stove. Also, you never visited without bringing several bags of groceries. Shawn joked that this was your way of making up for the fact that you never called before your visits, but I know you also felt I didn't cook the right kind of food for Shawn, because the foods you brought were things you never found in my cupboards.

You seemed to resent me, or my place in Shawn's life. When you visited two months after our wedding, you became upset with Shawn for sitting with me on one couch instead of joining you on the other.

As I look back now, though, I see that perhaps there was more to your resentment than having to let go of your youngest son, the one you always referred to as "the fun one." You knew that only a certain type of woman would be happy married to Shawn. Once he told me that you wanted him to date a certain ranch girl; perhaps you thought her background matched Shawn's better than mine.

For Shawn is a cowboy, pure and simple. When you and I met, I was a college student working for the summer at a guest ranch. My majors were English and Spanish, my passions writing and foreign cultures, my career goals journalism and international relations. Not exactly the cowgirl you envisioned for your son, was I?

I am a ranch girl, though. I grew up on a small farm/cattle ranch in South Dakota, and the rhythms of agriculture are familiar to me. The critical difference between my youth and the early years of my marriage was that my dad owned our ranch. Shawn and your husband, Butch, have always been hired hands on ranches.

My own mom taught me the skills I'd need to be a rancher's wife. Whether you believed it at first or not, I've always been capable of managing a ranch house and family. Mom taught me how to cook meals, how to tend the garden, how to run for parts, how to watch the sky. She instilled in me a love for the country and for country living and a firm belief that no better lifestyle exists. She showed me a thousand times over how important woman's work is, on a ranch or anywhere, and she gave me the confidence to know that I could be a good wife and mother. Just as important, after my dad was diagnosed with emphysema, she urged me to be prepared to support my children and myself if a husband could not, and she is the reason I have my degree today.

However, prepared as I thought I was, the first five years of my marriage to Shawn yanked the rug of self-confidence out from under me. Mom wasn't able to teach me that being the ranch *hand's* wife means being lowest on the scale of importance at most ranches. My skills meant little in the face of cold suppers lying on the table, newborn calves dirtying my bathtub, Sunday afternoon plans disintegrating in a single phone call from the boss. I think you sensed how much difficulty I would have dealing with these realities.

Even worse than the inconveniences were the feelings of unimportance and helplessness. From those years, I remember waiting by the living room window, peering at the headlights of every passing pickup truck on the highway, hoping Shawn would be home soon. So often, he went out on jobs alone. I learned to memorize where he would be riding each day so I could go out looking for him if he wasn't home by ten that night. As 9:30 and 9:45 passed, I remember desperate prayers that he was still alive, knowing that if I lost him, I would lose not only my best friend but also the home that went with the ranch job.

These frustrations did overwhelm me, especially after our second daughter was born. I still wonder how our marriage survived that long summer when he was so busy with ranch work that he was away fourteen to sixteen hours each day and didn't take a full day off for the first six weeks after her birth. I began looking for ways out of this lonely, bleak lifestyle.

Curiously enough, you and I began forming a fragile alliance that summer. You began to help me with the girls without criticizing, and I began to see that your brusque manner concealed wisdom earned from years of living a life like mine.

Still, Shawn and I decided our marriage would not sustain another summer like that one, and in a move that both surprised and hurt you, Shawn decided to quit ranching. A teaching job drew us away from you to Wyoming; I became the full-time breadwinner in the family while Shawn decided on a new career.

Shortly after our move, the local telephone company hired him to do construction work. Suddenly, he was working a predictable schedule with weekends off, great pay, and good benefits. It was a dream job.

But you probably knew he wouldn't be happy there. He was satisfied for the first year or so, but telephone companies just don't use many horses these days. After two and a half years, a wealthy landowner asked Shawn to manage his ranch. Neither of us considered turning down the offer. He's simply been so unhappy, Ann; not even my anxieties about returning to ranch life will convince me to ask him to stay.

And so, after nine years of a relationship that has been tenuous at best, I am turning to you for advice. You've played the role of the ranch hand's wife with grace and humor as long as I've known you, and probably for all of the forty years you've followed Butch from ranch to ranch. How do you do it?

Do you ever get angry? On our first anniversary, Shawn had to work late to fix a broken-down combine. The romantic dinner I'd prepared turned cold and wilted. I threw a bona fide tantrum, screaming, crying, even throwing a bowl against the wall. I couldn't believe the ranch was more important than even our anniversary. Years after this episode, Shawn told me he remembers you getting all dressed up on your own anniversary, then crying when you realized Butch was working late. Of course you cried, but do you ever rage? Does anger ever completely overwhelm you? Do you ever curse the ranches that take your husband away from you so much of the time?

Did you ever curse the bosses? One boss we had made a regular appearance in church every Sunday. I know, because I watched him from the cry room, where I was struggling with two toddlers by myself. When he hired Shawn, he told us that family and religion were "the most important things." I guess he was speaking about his own family and faith, because guess who was doing the chores every Sunday?

And do you ever grow accustomed to not knowing when your husband will come home? Do you still panic when Butch is out much later than you'd expected? When Shawn and I were first dating, you told me you'd learned not to expect him "until I see the whites of his eyes." How did you cultivate such calm?

I hope you can provide answers, Ann. Most of all, I hope you don't tell me there are no answers. My biggest fear is of giving in, of having to accept the difficulties of this lifestyle because I have no power to change them. I don't believe I am powerless; neither were you. Something — love for a man, for a place — has drawn us both to this life. There are lessons to learn here, and I hope you'll share what you've gleaned from your longer journey.

From my childhood, and from those first five years of marriage, I know this way of life holds more potential for joy and for heartache than most others. Teach me to find the joys, to see the rewards behind the hardships. I expect the best reward will be the look of bliss on Shawn's face as he saddles his horse in preparation for the day's work.

But you already knew that, didn't you?

SHELLY WHITMAN COLONY 🐎 Common Ground

I've spent my adult life trying to find common ground with my mother. We don't understand the choices the other has made, choices that brought us far different lives and made us question how we belonged to each other. I pursued every path as different from hers as I could, and she refused to value any of it. We have been trapped in a war of wills.

We were sitting at the dining room table when she said loudly, as if to banish doubt, that she had given up a track scholarship at the University of Hawaii to marry my father and have me. My mother won the chance to compete in the National Junior Olympic Track and Field competition and narrowly missed a place on the Olympic team. Yet she married before she graduated high school and had her first baby at nineteen. "You married Dad instead of going to college in *Hawaii?*"

"If I hadn't, you wouldn't be here."

That gave me something to think about. My life suddenly seemed tenuous. It would be best, I thought, to take care of myself, to have my own money and no children. This is where our troubles began.

My mother was raised in the Mormon church on a small farm near Bone, Idaho, where girls were expected to marry young and seek fulfillment as Christian wives and mothers.

My choice to go to college and then graduate school flew in the face of everything she believed. My worst fear was ending up in a trailer with several babies and a man who worked at the plywood mill and spent his evenings drinking at the Paul Bunyan bar.

At Montana State University, I fell in love with ideas, with my classes in chemistry, calculus, and music. My love of Greek and Latin words was finally paying off. My pained life as a high school egghead was over.

When I opted for an abortion after I became pregnant the first semester, I didn't tell my mother until months later. She was unusually cold. I didn't remind her that she had told me earlier if I got pregnant not to come home. Our fragile relationship broke. She visited me once in the four years I was in college. I still went home for holidays if I hadn't been invited elsewhere. We were polite.

One spring break, I thought I could interest her in the wonderful practicality of calculus by demonstrating on paper the theoretically most efficient way to lay out a pattern for a duffle bag. "I can do it faster this way," she said, snapping the cloth angrily into a neat fold on the dining room table.

She and my father came to a colloquium I presented to the faculty and fellow graduate students the week I graduated with a master's degree in geology. Afterward she waited while my professors congratulated me and pointed out especially interesting ideas in my thesis, then she said, "I had no idea you knew so many big words. I didn't understand a thing you said." What did she think I had been doing for the past seven years? Wasting time? Her mother told me that graduate school was for people too lazy to work and that I ought to get a job and settle down.

The situation improved last year when I married. For reasons I haven't yet figured out, marriage and moving to Oregon depressed me, and I turned to gardening as a way to reconnect with the land. I visited my mother at our old home a few months after the wedding. The little timber town seemed charming, not the dangerous, sucking, gray pit of my childhood. The beauty of my mother's garden surprised me. Pink dianthus spilled over the native river rock border along the south side of the turn-of-the-century white-clapboard house. The nodding heads of wild columbines danced on the summer breeze, and white spirea billowed like a gown among ferns in the northern border. Nearby, a mountain ash twined around an old mining cart, and around the corner, near the shade beds, a large blue-gray limestone boulder served as a garden sculpture, its cupped side worn smooth by the action of glacial melt water. The old house and grounds had a wild yet genteel demeanor.

We walked the gardens and talked. "I want you to take as many of these plants as you want," my mother said. "The renters won't take care of them." After thirty years in the only house she had ever owned, she was re-marrying and moving to Toston, Montana, a windswept piece of foothills prairie on the banks of the Missouri River.

As we walked through the old orchard, she narrated the history of each tree now lost to weather or time. A graceful arc of border beds rimmed the south and east edges of the property, swooping past the old apple tree, over the site of the cherry tree, and under two junipers. She pointed out the various plants I should take — how to excavate each one, the soil and light conditions each preferred — and admonished me to use horse manure, as much as I could haul.

"I really babied this wisteria. See how rich the soil is?" She dug her fingers into the base of the plant, then stroked the tender vines wrapping themselves around an old wagon wheel and heading for the oak church pew under the spruce tree. "Horse shit, it's the best."

I nodded. I would keep it alive, I vowed to myself, no matter what. Even though I had to drive for two days in hot weather, I would will the wisteria to live. Because it was important to her, and she was important to me.

"This is an old peony I got from our neighbor Mrs. DeFlyer. It's one of those deep red ones. Don't worry about the ants on the buds. The first year I had it — you were just a little thing — I poisoned the ants, and it didn't bloom," she said with a laugh, remembering. "Alice came over and told me to leave the ants. They're good for it."

"These poppies were hers, too," she said, pointing as we walked along the bed that separated Alice's yard from Mother's. "Shake out the seed heads into a paper sack."

Alice DeFlyer was a tiny old lady when I was a girl and had been dead long enough for her house to have sold three or four times, each time to a real estate speculator or a family who lived there for a while, then moved on. Yet her flowers thrived.

My mother gardened to create beauty in the world and to remember and honor other women. By telling me their stories and evoking their memories, she was asking me to join her in the cult of gardening womanhood, tending the flowers and memories of the ones who are gone. And it works. When I look at the white and yellow face of a Shasta daisy descended from a plant Noddie grew, I see her in her cotton housecoat on a breezy summer day — sitting at her kitchen table, holding a long black cigarette holder, and sipping pale champagne from a jelly jar, while pushing a plate of cookies toward me, asking me what I thought of Petey's new perch and had I read the latest *National Geographic*?

All those years, my mother had been trying to interest me in the joys of a woman's life, not mentioned in books, not found in universities or corporations, but growing quietly in the heart and given freely in the garden. I had been so afraid of being trapped by love that I had shunned every practice not useful or economic. And while my way brought me one kind of satisfaction, it was bought at the expense of understanding the role of beauty and honor. Now we have found our common love of gardening and our love for each other.

SISTER HILDEGARD DUBNICK, OSB ❧ Holy Ground

Sitting in a reverie in the darkened chapel after Compline one evening, I watched Sister Angela rise from her choir stall. In her eighties, she was no longer all that agile but still genuflected to the tabernacle to take her leave of our Lord for the night. A real genuflection, even if her knee didn't get quite all the way to the floor. Rising, she turned and bowed her head to the choir, in the customary gesture of acknowledgment to our fellow sisters. Then she stumped off toward the door to the cloister. She could still walk well enough, although she leaned perpetually forward and occasionally staggered to the side to catch her balance.

In 1935 she had vowed herself to God. For more than fifty years, she had worked for His glory, singing psalms and serving her sister nuns and the collective good of the community. I had been in vows for less than ten years on this evening as I sat watching her, five decades ahead of me in the long line of nuns and monks filing along into eternity.

This Barbara Würzburger — Sister Angela — had entered the Benedictine Abbey of St. Walburg in Eichstätt, Bavaria, a strong young postulant in her late teens. She said, in her broken English, "Lady Abbess Benedicta, she bought the Boulder farm, and she needed sisters who know a little bit about farming. I didn't know much, but I came from a farm, and I know a little bit. And so they asked me whether I am willing to go over, and I said yes."

She came to Colorado in June 1935, three months after the first three sisters had come to start the new foundation. The sisters were pioneers at the same time they were political refugees. In the mid-thirties, Europe was forming into armed camps. The four sisters in Boulder had been sent there partly as a safety net. If the German motherhouse was shut down by the Nazis and the building confiscated, the one hundred–plus sisters would at least have a toehold in America.

Mother Abbess Benedicta von Spiegel had found the Boulder land in 1934. A leader of courage and vision, she was "not a businesswoman," says Sister Angela. Her report to the embarking sisters turned out to have been overly optimistic.

"She said, 'You have *sooo* much water. There's a big lake very close to your field, and there you have a *lot* of water.' We could never use the water in the lake: First, no permission. And second, the lake is lower than our fields. And she said, 'And you have the nicest house around. All the others are wooden houses. But yours is a brick house.' She was never in our house. No, she was over in the neighbor's house."

But farming in arid Colorado was a different world for the four Bavarian nuns who formed the new community. Irrigation was a new science to them, and they had no money to buy machines for working their 150 acres. Times were hard all over, but they were blessed with generous neighbors, who lent them tools and machines.

"They put the plow on, just one plow, and then we had to go this way and then that way, and then again, and oh! it took so much up and down, just half. It took long. But we had something. And then when the field was plowed, we need a harrow. And then we went over to the neighbor and ask whether we can borrow his harrow. And he said, 'Yes, for half a day. The next day I will take it.' We did not finish in one day, so we went the next day to another neighbor and asked there, and he said, 'Ja, you can have it for half a day, because tomorrow morning I would need it.'

"And we needed a corn planter. When we needed a corn binder, Mr. Steinbach said, 'Ja, Sister, that's all right. You can pay every month so much, and pay it off.' And so by and by we paid it off, our machines, with the money from the milk check."

A photo from 1937 shows three sisters gathering wheat into sheaves. They pause a moment for the photo in black veils and habits, straw hats on top of their veils. Farming in the thirties meant a lot of hard work, no matter who you were, German or American, nun or wife.

"We kept each penny together. And when Mother Augustina went to town, we had eggs, and she'd sell the eggs. And she had to buy yeast, and she had to buy flour, and what else, potatoes . . . not much. We had our own milk, and our own cream. And vegetables . . . we had one year a garden, and the next year, the grasshoppers ate everything. And we really cried. Ja, Sister, we had no money. We even had some dishes that we kept on the floor, covered up, because we had nothing to put them in. And for little cabinets we had, we made shelves from orange crates.

"Almost every day, Mr. Steinbach would come by. And every eight days, Mother Augustina would have a little bucket of eggs. And she had to go to the elevator, and at the elevator she sold the eggs, so that she could go to the grocery store. She bought once wash pins, a dozen or two dozen. And at the counter, old Mr. Steinbach said, 'Sister, you don't need so many, I bring that back. You don't have enough money.' Right at the counter, in front of all the people! And she told us, 'I was so embarrassed!'"

They did their best to learn English, with occasional lessons from a German American priest or some other neighbor or helper. The superior, Mother Augustina Weihermüller, trained back home as a schoolteacher, was well educated and made quick progress. But the simpler sisters, with little formal education of any kind, formed their own *Walburginisch,* a variety of English heavily influenced by Bavarian German. Sister Angela has always been a great reader, in English as well as German, but she never learned to write English. She knows only the old German script.

Our old building is gone now from the outskirts of Boulder. So are we — the Abbey relocated in 1997. We moved lock, stock, and barrel to a ranch in Virginia Dale, a hamlet on the northern edge of Colorado. It was an advance, not a retreat. We moved to have the freedom to grow (in wisdom and grace, we hope, besides in number). Still, it is always painful to leave behind what is familiar and beloved.

Uprooting the Abbey and moving from Boulder to Virginia Dale was not easy for any of us. Even I, quite a newcomer after only ten years, had to work hard to accept the transplant. How much more Sister Angela, who had seen our place grow from four sisters living in material poverty to a thriving community of more than twenty, with a farm, a retreat house, and a wide circle of friends and benefactors? Where she had helped dig the cellar under the first house herself, with pick and shovel. Where she had nurtured trees through harsh heat and cold, planted and irrigated crops, delivered calves and buried those that didn't make it.

Interviewed for a news article before our move, all she said was, "It is God's will." Life is a pilgrimage. God had led her from her home village to Eichstätt to Boulder — why not on to Virginia Dale?

Lying in bed after a cancer operation, Sister Angela reflects on her situation. She's not happy, surely, to be in pain; still, she is not a complainer — at least not about pain. "I take it as it is," she reflects. "I must. *He* gave it to me," glancing at the crucifix on the wall of her room.

Food is another matter. She continues to be very particular about what she eats, despite all her years of life in common, first with her family and then with other nuns. And she has never been reserved about expressing her likes and dislikes. "That is too expensive," she says when she declines something she doesn't like. Once, faced with a bowl of hearty soup with big chunks of vegetables, she rejected it in the strongest terms she could. "If we would have served such soup at home, the hired men would have got up from the table and walked away without a word!"

Very deaf, she often speaks alone in her room, seeming to carry on conversations, apparently with God. A sister passing by in the hall and hearing her saying "Ja! Ja!" repeatedly went in to see if she needed anything. Sister Angela gave her a none-too-welcoming glance, as though her tête-à-tête with God had been interrupted. Then she waved her dismissively away.

In church, unable to hear our singing or herself, she sometimes sighs loudly or punctuates the prayers of the choir with a drawn-out "Jaaa . . ." But she knows where she is and always acknowledges the Blessed Sacrament in the tabernacle in front of her. And when she receives Holy Communion, her robust "Amen!" resounds throughout the chapel, an eloquent testimony of faith.

A lifetime of praying the Scriptures gives old monks and nuns a way of seeing the deeper significance of things. Borrowing a natural history book from me, Sister Angela said, "For me, that is also spiritual reading — how great God is." When we first arrived in our new place, far from the city lights of the burgeoning Front Range towns, we were all impressed by the darkness of the nights, the vividness of the celestial objects. From her bed, Sister Angela can see the cliffs and some sky. "So many stars!" she says. "How great our Lord must be."

As I sit in the chapel, the long line of nuns and monks stretches centuries in front of me. And as I watch Sister Angela stumping her way after them, I think of her as a young nun, watching her own older sisters heading toward eternity. I rise and follow along in file. Looking over my shoulder, I can almost see more of the long line stretching out behind me.

MARY GARRIGAN ❧ The Concubine

She has a name, of course, but I call her The Concubine so I won't have to say it.

I do this because the pain associated with her name is excruciating. For months, I have barely been able to bring myself to utter it. When I do have to use it, a white-hot rage begins somewhere in my intestines and rises up through my body, as fast and unstoppable as water in a clogged toilet.

One of the reasons I hate to say her name is because it is so beautiful. It's a long name, and the first two syllables of it roll around my mouth like a melody. The last two syllables seem a bit of overindulgent finery tacked on for pure adornment, kind of like a double exclamation point at the end of a sentence. It's not a quick Ann or Sue, Jill or Jane that you can spit out fast and hard, with all the hatred you feel in your heart delivered in one quick verbal explosion. The whole thing takes a bit of time and effort to pronounce.

The Concubine, with its own four syllables, makes a good enough replacement. Plus, it serves my purpose of objectifying and dehumanizing this woman who, I think, has destroyed my life. Much later, I may see that she was only part of God's plan to change it.

I've had little contact with this woman since she slept with my husband, got pregnant, and gave birth to a child she claimed, publicly, is his. I don't speak to her, I avoid her if at all possible, and I certainly don't say her name. All of this is terribly ironic, since, arguably, the most intimate relationship I've had recently has been with her, or at least with the pain she has brought to my life.

Her name is one that I didn't hear very often before she, and the pain that came with her, entered my life. But now her name is everywhere. The book I'm reading was written by an author with the same first name. The movie I go to stars an actress with her name. A hit television show features a character by the same name. I discover a friend I've been calling by a nickname all these years, unbeknownst to me, has the same real first name. Another old friend moves to a new home on a street by that name. There's a play with her name in the title, a musical group whose lead singer shares her name, and a fashion model with a famous face and the same name as hers. Suddenly, my life is full of other people and places, even pets, who have The Concubine's name.

All marital infidelity has the common denominator of pain. Whether it's a one-night stand or a seven-year affair, betrayal is devastating. Infidelity that becomes public knowledge is even more difficult to cope with. And an extramarital affair that results in the birth of a child is a uniquely personal crucifixion — a pain that incarnates into a living, breathing human being. Here is a pain that becomes a beautiful, innocent child whose very existence is flesh-and-blood evidence that everything has changed and the universe will never be the same again.

This pain made me crazier than a rat in a coffee can for a time, and, looking back at it now, I am amazed at just how crazy I got. I was the kind of crazy where I was stricken with panic every time I glimpsed a gray Buick up ahead in traffic because The Concubine drives a gray Buick. Do you have any idea just how many gray Buicks there are in this world and just how many panic attacks you can have driving to work in the morning?

I was the kind of crazy where I had to stop saying the Hail Mary, because the part about the "fruit of thy womb" brought thoughts of murderous rage to my mind, which seemed to defeat the whole purpose of praying.

I was the kind of crazy where, standing in her living room one night at 2:00 A.M., screaming like a banshee, I felt a little hurt when she said she'd just as soon never see either me or my husband again as long as she lived.

Finally, I was the kind of crazy where I stayed married just to prove to some twat with functioning fallopian tubes that she couldn't have my husband.

And then slowly, gradually, the craziness began to recede. In its place, little by little, I found some sanity, then some more. Moving from chaos to calmness was accomplished with lots of tears, lots of prayer, and long talks with people who had compassion for me but not much for my codependency. Much of the time, serenity and sanity were like a slippery eel, something that I could grasp at and hold briefly in my hand before it slipped away.

It took some time, of course, but it took so much more than time. It took every effort I could humanly make to let go of the past and not fear the future. It took confusion and change and crying out to God in prayers as simple as "Help me" or "Do something."

It took reading countless self-help books and attending seminars and workshops. It took hundreds of hours and thousands of dollars of therapy. In the end, it took knowing that all the answers were inside myself, just where they had always been.

As I have healed, The Concubine, this object I created to cope with my pain, is receding from my view, fading from my life.

Standing there now is another human being, a woman who seemed to be the source of nothing but pain, but from whom has sprung a healing that I would never have known otherwise. From the isolating humiliation of this disaster has come a connection to other people that I have never experienced before. Truth has come from lies. Health has come from dysfunction and disease. Love has come from hatred. Renewal and resurrection have come, once again, from a crucifixion.

And for those gifts, I might one day be able to say thank you to her. Maybe I'll even use her name.

SUE HARTMAN ❧ *Anneen*

Anneen has sad eyes. Clear and pale blue as a diluted sky. For having borne such sorrow, she has the sweetest smile. Sweeter, though, with her dentures in. She's funny in spite of herself, despite shadows that threaten to draw her away. Anneen laughs out loud at bawdy jokes, although she's a lady through and through. Never owned a pair of britches in her life.

Anneen plays her harmonica and rocks on the front porch in a squeaky metal chair. We are waiting for G. H. Chaffin, my grandfather, to get back from the ranch. Anneen, my mama's mama, is my best friend. Before I could say Annie right, I called her Anneen, and that name stuck between us; nobody else calls her that. I sit next to her. Normally, I'd be up on her lap, but she can't play harmonica and sing and tap her feet and cuddle me all at the same time. Most people say I'm getting too big and too bony to hold. My skin sticks to the metal seat. Anneen stops playing for a minute to wipe away a stream of sweat sneaking down her forehead. Her pure white hair is thin, fine, and wispy. Like mine. But hers is wavy from the beauty shop. Mine is straight, straight, straight. As on most things, Anneen and I agree on this: my hair is brown as shit brindle. Whatever that means.

An absolutely perfect kind of grandmother was my Anneen, exactly the right size and shape for a playmate. Barely five feet tall and buxom, quite rounded, soft, and warm for snuggling. Better than satisfactory; an E for excellent. Even so, some of the things that Anneen taught her grandkids didn't go over very well in the prevailing Mormon culture. For example, that Brigham never intended the Word of Wisdom as imperative; it was recommendation for moderation. Caffeine, alcohol, and tobacco might not be healthy, but they are not sinful in themselves. This came as a relief to some.

Both of my grandparents were grandchildren of handcart pioneers, followers of Joseph Smith and Brigham Young. A determined lot, they trudged every blessed step from Nauvoo to Zion, a hike of more than a thousand miles, with all their worldly goods loaded onto their handcarts. My grandfather's family was a mixed batch of the devout with Jack Mormons, apostates, and excommunicates — the latter mostly attributed to maternal uncle Johnny Armstrong's unfortunate devotion to his job, U.S. federal marshal. Things might have turned out differently if only Great-Great-Uncle Johnny hadn't accepted the task of busting polygamists as such a zealous calling.

There were more bishops, missionaries, and Relief Society presidents than Jack and Jill Mormons among Anneen's family. One of her favorite nephews was a highly respected bishop and stake president. But Anneen had soured on the church, not just because she didn't like the way my mother was treated when she married a Methodist and converted. Anneen detested the fact that my family was sometimes ostracized in a culture that came west to escape such discrimination. But her problem was much deeper than all that: Anneen had given up believing. God held the number one spot on her permanent shit list.

We are on the front porch, rocking and squeaking, drinking sun-brewed iced tea. Mine is in Grandpa's shot glass, which holds about half an ice cube and two baby swallows of tea. I ask if I can get her harmonica out for her. She keeps it in the top drawer of the buffet in the most beautiful box I've ever seen — tooled black leather lined with faded scarlet taffeta. The best of her few treasures, it journeyed to Utah on one of the handcarts, and from Germany before that. Might as well play, she tells me. First, I must make her a deal not to tell my mother about the tea. I always promise not to rat on Anneen's indulgences — as many milk chocolate stars as we can eat, staying up all hours — but these secrets are usually the first things I blurt out when I go home.

Grandma plays "Annie Laurie," the name she was supposed to get instead of "Annie Lisle." Her mother got so nervous at the baby blessing that when the bishop asked for the blessing name, she blurted out one song title for another. Anneen sighs when she speaks of her own mother, who died when she was ten, so she had to drop out of school to mother her younger siblings. She learned to cook large suppers farm style, scrub floors until they shone, and tat fine lace. Anneen stayed close to her sisters, Viola and Esther, but she doted on her baby brother, Eugene. Years later, he drowned in Bear Lake, and his body was never recovered. By then her internal struggles with God had escalated into all-out battles, even though she was hopelessly outgunned.

She sings rather than plays "Itsy Bitsy Spider," resting her harmonica in her lap so she can do the creeping spider fingers. We wait for G. H.'s new Oldsmobile to roar up to the house Anneen had built for herself and her two children after her first husband, Elias, died.

Annie Lisle Young was twenty when she married Elias Jones Banks, and they were sealed to each other "for time and eternity" in the Mormon Church. She was the mother of two-year-old Louisa and pregnant with her second child when a derrick toppled on Elias, crushing him. Their son, Elias, was born that same night, too early, without a doctor present. You could have fit the baby into a quart jar. So Anneen was widowed at twenty-three, with two years of formal education and two children, including the premature baby. Tables turn. It was up to her father, then, to mother her children while she left Spanish Fork to train as a seamstress. It was 1906.

By 1913 she also became a camp cook and worked at a bridge-building and lumber-transfer site on the Colorado River. There she met George Henry, the line rider for the construction company. He was sent to get things moving. G. H. climbed up on top of the cook wagon and yelled to the crew, "Since you don't want to work, you slowpoke sons of bitches, you just get on down the road!" He fired everyone except Anneen. When the crew seemed sufficiently remorseful, he hired them back.

He couldn't fail to notice my soft-eyed grandma and how hard she worked. He later claimed that he was most impressed by how she kept those polite little kids so immaculately dressed and scrubbed so clean in the swirling red dust. But if you saw the way he looked at her all his life — particularly when they weren't bickering — you knew that there was much more between them than mutual respect and convenience. Their generation didn't speak so openly about love or demonstrate it in public. But after she got ready for bed in her silky pink nightgown and cared for her hair by tucking it carefully into a powder blue hair net, she'd sit at the kitchen table, shuffling and snapping the cards in continuous rounds of solitaire, waiting up for Grandpa when he'd come home late.

It's past dark. George is late again tonight. He's not such a safe driver anymore. Sometimes he yells "Whoa" instead of braking. Grandma doesn't say it to me, but I've seen her worry. I visit them as often as I can finagle it, a week or two at a time, every couple of months. I am seven.

There's a big nest in the cottonwood tree in front where a pair of horned owls have lived for a decade, longer than I've been alive. When Grandma begins to play her harmonica, two curious owlets poke their heads out from under their mother's butt. I squint to make them out in the dim light.

"You can go down there, but don't get too close. We don't want to scare off the mama. Her babies need her."

I go as far as the ditch and lie down. Tons of mosquitoes rise with a million no-see-ums. I hold my breath so they won't fly up my nose. This is when Anneen usually calls me to come in and get ready for bed, but not tonight. She's busy playing her favorite song, "Going Home." When G. H. finally gets back from the ranch, or wherever he's been chasing off to, I am getting sleepy and itching like crazy from mosquito bites.

He carries me through the back door to the screened porch and puts me down while he takes off his dusty boots and trousers. Wearing his long johns, G. H. goes inside, switches on the kitchen lights, pulls on another pair of trousers, washes his hands, and rustles up a late dinner — bacon and eggs scrambled in the bacon fat in his cast-iron skillet. Although we've already eaten, Grandpa makes extra for me and Anneen. While the bacon sizzles, he asks if I want a toddy. I have to fetch him the shot glass. Mine has lots of water and bitter lemon and a dash of bourbon. His is opposite. If Anneen notices, she'll make some comment about seven-year-olds with bourbon breath. G. H. says the song she is playing is about the pioneers being homesick for their original countries. I'm not homesick, I tell him. I never want to go home. It's too sad there since my little sister died last fall. He says that he knows.

That's why Anneen's mad at God and always will be.

I always like waiting up for Grandpa. On chilly nights, we stay inside. I lie down on the couch, sleepy, half watching television with Anneen. What I do mostly is stare at the picture of the lonely wolf on the wall above the couch. He's on a hill in the snow, looking down on the lights of the town below. Yes, I am scared of the mangy old wolf, but it's a good kind of scared, since Anneen is right here and I am warmly wrapped up in the burgundy afghan she crocheted that still smells like violet cologne.

While she snoozes in front of the TV, I snoop through Anneen's velvet-bound album of genealogy charts, crackled pictures of stern women, my mother with a Buster Brown haircut dressed in a first-grade fringed flapper dress. Tucked in the middle is a yellow newspaper clipping with a headline reading, WOMAN DIES FOR FORTY-FIVE MINUTES, SAVED BY PULOMETER AND BRAVE PROVO FIRECHIEF. The woman was Anneen. In 1927, five years after my mother was born, several weeks after a gallbladder operation complicated on her, a machine breathed for Anneen for three-quarters of an hour.

"There is nothing after death, Susie," she insists when I press her. "Nothing but blackness. I know because I died. Only darkness."

I'm not so sure that's right. One of my four-year-old twin sisters came home from the hospital to die at home. Deedee's hospital bed was set up in the dining room, where my mother and Aunt Louisa took turns sitting up with her night and day. Before the roosters crowed on the morning she died, I woke up before anyone came to tell us. The room filled with a bright light — glowing, flickering, then faltering. I thought that meant "Goodbye, Susie." Then I heard my mama slowly making her way up the stairs to tell us Deedee was gone.

What do little kids know about that kind of thing? Enough to ask the right people. Devout or not, Mormons believe in that stuff. In a geography as mystical as Utah's, how can you not? Rock-spire hoodoos. Abandoned cliff dwellings. It's not so strange for a Mormon to gain insight from the extraordinary. So G. H. was more likely to believe a seven-year-old's vision of a sister turned to light. Anneen did not challenge either of us. But until the day she died, she would not forgive God or believe in Him. Her losses piled up on her, Grandpa told me, and Deedee's death was the final straw. She believed that a loving God would not let children suffer and a just God would never have taken that child.

Of course, Anneen's nephew, the Mormon bishop, presided at her funeral when Anneen died twelve years later in 1967. The Ladies Trio sang "Going Home." But being as adept at holding a grudge as my mentor, I would never forgive the bishop, whose ego exceeded his wisdom by tenfold. During the eulogy, he stopped mid-thought to address G. H. "Isn't it a shame, Brother Chaffin, that you were never sealed to your wife in the Church, and since she was sealed to her first husband, Brother Elias Banks, you will never be together with Sister Chaffin for time and eternity?" G. H. wept and squeezed my hand to deter me temporarily from my declaration of war on the bishop. I put my arm around him on one side, and my sister Linda did the same on the other. He whispered, "Now all I've got to live for is you kids and your mother."

Eight years later, when Grandpa died at ninety-eight, resolved that he had enjoyed a good life, his funeral ceremony was conducted by dignitaries from the Elks Club, and a soloist sang his favorite hymn, "Abide with Me."

But what looks like the end is often not, and G. H.'s death was not the end. In 1983 my life was crumbling, my marriage shaky for reasons I did not yet understand. My husband was out of town on one of his perpetual business trips. I had decided to return to school and was ready to study for my Graduate Record Exams, a scary choice at midlife.

My neighbor Sara and I were sitting at my dining room table discussing that night's agenda for the neighborhood block meeting while I typed the minutes from the last session. The air was electric. My dog whined and pricked her ears. The cat hissed. The back door slammed. The lone wolf picture shifted, hanging askew. Outside, the wind chimes banged away, but the catalpa branches did not move. Then my typewriter ribbon split. I would have to go to the mall to get another. Sara had the chills. We agreed to finish later, both of us relieved to get out of my haunted house.

After buying the ribbon, I stopped at a used-book store. Rifling through a barrel of dollar books, I grabbed a thick one from the bottom. It fell open to page 447, "Abide with Me." The book was *Heart Songs: Memories of Days Gone By*, published in 1906, and it contained both "Annie Laurie" and "Annie Lisle." I bought it.

Later, when I sat down at the typewriter again, the damned new ribbon split. Then my eight-track player shot tape across the room, loop after loop. The cat hissed and scooted down the basement stairs, while the dog cowered at my feet.

I would have to have the spookies or listen to the radio, so I turned to a classical station and heard the beginning melody of Antonín Dvořák's Symphony no. 9 ("The New World Symphony"). "Going Home."

I knew my grandparents were reaching through the limitations of time to tell me something with their favorite songs — a warning, to be sure, and the certainty that everything would be all right. The next night, my husband's lover contacted me, meaning I could no longer deny his betrayal. I was devastated, humiliated, then divorced, and I would be all right. It was not their message that so astounded me, but the fact that there *was* a message from them and that they were *together.* G. H., the believer, and the skeptical Anneen had reached me from beyond death, offering comfort and assurance: There is something after. There is more than the dark. And we don't go alone.

THELMA POIRIER ❧ wild roses

coming home late
whiskey-breathed again
he carries roses
to the bed you share, roses
in the morning
        you wear them on your face

and I say,
        leave
but you say, no,
        he brings roses

nights
I cannot sleep
knowing you wait for roses

SOPHIE DOMINIK ECHEVERRIA ❧ My Mother's Moccasins

I come to this house now and then, this oasis filled with paintings, rugs, and comfortable furniture, to soak up the luxury, thirsty from my own life. While I wait for my mother to arrive, I sip orange juice and unwind. I'm loony-eyed after twelve hours on the highway. I spy her treasures. I go through her jewelry, her linens, hats, belts, and brushes. I examine every knickknack.

On the breakfast table is a silver stamp box with a turquoise stone centered on the hinged lid, a wedding gift to my parents. On the bureau is a chipped mug filled with pencils and pens. UNIVERSITY OF ARIZONA, 1944 is painted on the side.

By her desk is a tooled leather waste can. My father brought it back from South America in 1958. Shortly after his return to the United States (within minutes), I was conceived. I have thrown trash in that contraption for most of my life, but until now it has never reminded me of him. He died when I was eleven — jumped on the back of death, grabbed its tangled mane, and rode off into a winter dawn. Now I see him only in my dreams, where black skeleton trees flail the sky and creak in the bitter wind. I miss him.

All around me is evidence of the great sums of money he left to my mother. His legacy has done nothing to dispel the bitterness she feels toward him. I think of all the feuding this wealth could trigger in my siblings. Like Ali Baba's poor brother, who was split into six bloody pieces by forty thieves, we are at the mercy of our greed. All it will take is another good blow from the sword of death and the reading of her will. I doubt any family counselor or lawyer will be able to sew us back together.

"I want the ocean painting!"

"I want the kachinas!"

"I need the leather couches and the BMW!"

I stand at the kitchen sink looking into the solarium at an exquisitely carved hummingbird, and I tell myself, "I want none of this. I won't let myself want any of this."

I wash her dishes by hand to remind myself that I am not a rich lady and that when I go home, I will have no dishwasher, trash compactor, garage door opener, alarm system, gardener, pool man, bug man, or maid. I fold her laundry and deliver it to her closets. Then, while I'm putting away her socks, I see something I do want. Terribly. Enough to maybe even ask for it.

My mother's moccasins. They are suede, dyed rust red with thick cowhide soles. I turn them over in my hands and see that the soles are still very good, even though her footprints are firmly etched on the bottoms.

I used to have a pair of moccasins when I was thirteen. They were calf length. I buttoned the silver conchos proudly on the outside of my jeans. I wore my moccasins through rain and snow, over rocks and fallen branches, through piles of leaves and sweet moist earth warmed by the spring sun.

I felt it all. Every step I took melted and sent a zing to my heart. I knew what I was walking on: summer grass, cornstalks, unrelenting greedy concrete, hot sand, cool creek bottoms, rocks, slabs of primeval limestone worn down by the wind, rain, and my moccasins. Nothing went unnoticed.

I don't remember what happened to the moccasins. I think I put them away at some point as if they were toys I had grown too old for. I remember hearing "wanna-be" and feeling humiliated. I didn't understand then what I know now: There isn't a person in this world whose life is a life I care to live. And I can be anything I please. All is illusion.

"Let us see, is this real, / Let us see, is this real / This life I am living?" A Pawnee poem. One of my favorites.

I want these moccasins. They belong to the part of my mother I love best. It is her wild nature that taught me to listen to the earth whispering honeyed secrets to my soul, to let my hair blow in the wind like wild grass, to dive into the deep thunderheads building from my past.

The moccasins promise me all of this when I hear my mother's car pull into the garage. A breeze whirling past her bedroom patio is captured by a cottonwood and the brass wind chimes hanging outside: church bells pealing Latin hymns, haunting chords from the void left by an abandoned religion. I have yet to find an institution as compelling and mysterious as the Catholic Church.

I quickly place the moccasins back in the oak shoe stand with all of the pumps made from crocodiles and Italian leather. I leave them exactly as I found them. I don't want my mother to know I touch her things and relish how lovely she looks in each carefully chosen silk shirt and starched cotton. I will say nothing of this to her. There is nothing to say.

Finally she arrives. "Sophie! My dear!"

I fall into her arms and squeeze her tight.

"You made it!"

She is exquisite to touch — long, clean blond hair and soft shoulders. I know she loves me. And how I love her. Even though she is tired, bone weary from all of my family's tragedies, I can see she still wants to live, so I tell her that I will take her on an adventure. I will take her to a place that is filled with holy water, more blessed than the most blessed water any Catholic priest could ever give to her.

All afternoon we make plans. I want to travel north — into the moonlight and rainstorms — ride on a flat open railcar with bedrolls wrapped around us, let the stars and wind wash the tears from our eyes, but we decide to drive instead.

In the morning, we get up early and throw our luggage in the back of my truck. We crank down the windows since my air conditioner is broken. We weave through Phoenix traffic and streams of red and green Christmas lights. The signals boss us around, tell us what to do, but not for long.

We escape on the highway. North. North through the desert. We climb the mountains, hightail it for the Indian reservation, and cross the border into Utah. The sandstone monuments laugh at me as we go whizzing by. "Wanna-be!" they yell from the valley floor.

"I used to be!" I retort with a laugh.

It's taken me thirty years to figure out what I'm looking for. It's the love of the land, the magic and mystery I'm after. And I know a piece of it is waiting for me in a cave at the bottom of a distant canyon, where holy water is sanctified only by nature.

I turn left to climb a hidden road up the face of a cliff. I've been here before and reassure my mother that it's safe. We get to the top, drive a little farther, and stop. I jump out and start scrounging around for my hiking shoes, but I can't find them. I look behind the seat, in my suitcase, my backpack, everywhere. We don't have a lot of time, so my mother says she has an extra pair. She unzips her suede leather bag and pulls out her moccasins.

I don't hesitate to put them on. They fit perfectly. I lace the rawhide around my ankles and tie a sturdy knot. I instantly feel the rocks and twigs under my feet and race ahead. I want to scream, "This is too lucky!" She follows behind, older, more cautious, steady.

We descend to the canyon floor. The sand cushions my arches — swish — as it scrapes the cowhide. We walk in the shade along the west rim. I can smell the water. I know we are near. We round a bend, and there it is, the black gaping hole.

My heart pounds wildly. Geese cry and fly into blue sky, all their wings flapping together and singing, "So long! Watch out! Farewell!"

I go right to the edge. A thin crescent of daylight reaches past the cliff jutting from above. The shaft of sunshine casts a half circle on the water below, but the rest of the pool is pitch.

I can't see how far back the cave goes. The darkness is complete. I know there are spirits waiting for me there. I want to strip down and dive in. But this is like wanting to plunge into the pinpoints of someone else's eyes. It's too oblique from the centuries of memories, and I am too frightened to touch the velvety sable hue.

But I knew this was the magic — the undeniable urge to absorb this cave, to make it a part of me — and so I've come prepared. I unhook my canteen from my belt and pour the remaining stale water into dry sand. Then I bend over to feel the cold water with my fingertips. Morning sun warms the back wall, surely, but this is evening, and the cold dark water scares me, makes the hair prickle on my arms.

While my mother stands beside me, I fill the canteen reverently, slowly, wondering all the while what I am imprisoning in my bottle. Whatever it is, is mine forever. It is holy water from eyes and ears and lips and breast. Later I will anoint my pores and know that I have won a piece of the wilderness. I have confiscated the quiet, where few birds sing and only the low hum of the wind can be heard from above, whistling through the junipers and against white rock. Forget the tourist prattle, the background chatter of America. The walls of this cave are lonely. Most visitors touch this place only with the lenses of their cameras, while their hearts wait patiently in parked RVs, vans, and cars.

I wait for my mother to join me, but she sniffs, wrinkles her nose, and says, "This isn't holy water." I stand with my filled canteen, facing her, desperately wondering how to respond. My enthusiasm for the moment is fast slipping away. I am under attack. My ability to discern magic is questionable. She is not going to be bamboozled by me.

She turns away, lifts her head to the sky, and breathes deeply. Her back is straight, full of conviction. She is not going to join me in filling her canteen with this murky, undrinkable water. She is an expert on holy water (having used the stuff for years while practicing Catholicism), a connoisseur of all fine things; she will use only the best.

I'm not sure why she refuses to go along with my fantasy. It seems as if

I'm always trying to figure my mother out. What would be the harm? Maybe she is trying to stay true to herself, but I begin to doubt my wisdom in being here with her.

When we get back to the truck, I start to take the moccasins off, to return them even though I want them. My fingers are thick and numb and seem to take forever to undo the knots. My mother looks down at my hands and feet fumbling together, not cooperating at all. And then she says, "Keep them. They have good memories."

I say, "Oh. You mean you want me to walk in your moccasins?" She laughs. It is a good sound, smart and sexy. I love to make her laugh.

"Not in a million years. I don't ever want you to live my life."

"It's a good thing. I'm pretty busy living my own."

I think about it for a minute, and then I decide to keep the moccasins. I want to wear them out walking when I forget where I've been and life swallows me up. I'm going to keep the water, too, in spite of what my mother thinks. I won't drink it. I'll give a little to my geraniums or my cats when they get bored. Mostly, I'll savor it. I want it to last. I need these symbols to remind me where I've been and where I'm going. These are memory treasures, the best kind of all.

MELINDA STILES 🦌 Her Soul Lives Here

Standing in her driveway, we hugged and cried beneath the gray Michigan sky. "Go. Write. You're my way of living in the West." Our brains knew all the right reasons for my departure. Our hearts haven't caught on yet.

Thinking about Martha, my best friend, confidante, sister, counselor, comrade, soul mate of eighteen years, is easy. Leaving her when I moved to Salmon, Idaho, was one of the hardest things I've ever done. Harder than death. I don't expect the dead to rise and return. I expect to see Martha when I hike, raft, walk, or shop. She belongs here, where her soul is most alive.

The time I used to spend with her, I now spend writing, reading, and communing with nature. I don't find many reasons to socialize or to make new friends. My bond with Martha sustains me in her absence.

Martha throws herself into remodeling her condo and being a grandma. While Martha's waking hours are consumed by a career I left, she finds a respite on her computer screen. Above the monitor on the desk in her classroom, she views thirty seventh-grade bodies in various hormonal-driven positions. Above my monitor, I view the majestic, snowy peaks of the Continental Divide. Our words hurl through cyberspace.

"Sunlight is just hitting Freeman Peak. Can it be more beautiful than yesterday? Stark, rugged, there. You remember."

A year ago, Martha and I scaled Freeman. We hiked five hours, crawled on hands and knees to slurp water bubbling up from an underground spring, and staged a mock snowball fight, wearing shorts and T-shirts. When the last hundred vertical yards looked unclimbable, I scurried up and beheld pristine Upper Minor Lake, nestled in a crater, surrounded by snowcapped peaks. "Get up here now! I don't care how tired you are. You won't believe this."

Ignoring the blisters on her virgin heels, she raced to the top and burst into tears. "Thank you, thank you."

"For what?"

"For making this possible. If you didn't live here, I wouldn't be seeing this."

Martha has visited three times in the year and a half I've lived here. When she was in the throes of a divorce, I insisted that she take her comp days and visit, promising she would return with a fresh perspective. Here she can climb a mountain, stand on top of the world, feel a power she doesn't know in her daily life. Or lie in bed all day and read. Or walk Geertsen Creek Road with me and watch golden eagles soar. Nothing here demands that she do anyone's bidding but her own. When Martha and I connect in the West, our troubles are minimized. The panorama of the Western sky lets us believe that all things are possible.

Breathing in the cool mountain air calmed the fury of Martha's divorce. We drove along the Salmon River. Pulling behind a parked car, we got out, binoculars in hand. A mountain goat stood on the uppermost cliff of the canyon, his lustrous white coat silhouetted against the cornflower blue sky. Martha bawled.

Farther downriver, we saw a herd of bighorn sheep and witnessed what few people ever see: two adult males repeatedly went horn to horn, the impact echoing throughout the canyon. Words were not necessary or possible.

On one of her visits, we drove up Fourth of July Creek Road to the top of Stein Mountain and discovered an outhouse with only three walls. Martha used it and came out smiling. "I relieved myself on top of the world! What a view!"

On a hike in the foothills behind my house, Martha collected wildflowers. The hills were steep, her bouquet large, but she wouldn't put it down. She possesses an artist's eye and created beauty as we hiked. "I love mountain sage. The color, the smell." She crumpled a cluster and held it to my nose. A chartreuse and black caterpillar had attached himself to a lupine in her bouquet. She placed him on her shoulder, and, crawling up and down her shirt, he hiked the four miles with us. We returned and soaked our aching feet in the icy waters of Tower Creek. The bouquet, complete with caterpillar, adorned my back deck for weeks after she left.

MARY E. SCHNELL ❧ Let the Circle Be Unbroken

The phone rang early one Friday morning. "Mary, I'll be by in a half-hour to pick you up for your driver's test. I need to renew my license as well."

A half-hour! My mind screamed in a full-blown panic. "I'm not ready," I stammered.

"Yes, you are," Margie replied firmly with laughter in her voice. "Get ready."

So I did. I passed.

At eighteen, I was a late bloomer. Shy and insecure, I was never ready for much of anything except coming up with reasons why I couldn't or shouldn't. Margie knew this about me. This gentle, patient woman, who would become my mother-in-law in less than a year, had spent the last two years teaching me how to drive. She knew far more about me than I guessed.

We celebrated my victory over a cup of coffee at the local café. "I know you smoke, and you must be very nervous," she said, "so I don't mind if you want to light up." As I fumbled gratefully through my purse for a crumpled pack of Marlboros, it came to me that not only had Margie nudged me through the doorway of a personal freedom most of my friends took for granted, but she also had given me permission to be myself. For the next eighteen years, she was a touchstone of never-wavering acceptance.

She was a North Dakota farm girl who offered no pretensions. She loved beauty in all forms, as I did. Dinner at her house, whether baked salmon or bologna sandwiches, was served on a festive cloth with candles and flowers and her best Red Wing crockery. Coming from a background of cracked Melmac dishes, metal cups, and mismatched silverware, I was inspired. "Where did you learn to do this?" I asked at one memorable holiday dinner.

She smiled wistfully. "I wanted to be a nurse, but my father didn't think that was a suitable profession for a decent young lady. So I went to Minneapolis and became a maid to some very wealthy people. It was there I learned to set a table."

She was a gifted pianist with never a lesson. Unaware of her exceptional talent, she played mostly in church. Her Lutheran faith was an unshakable and integral part of her everyday life. Her Norwegian ancestry showed itself in a mean batch of *lefse* (thin, fried potato bread) and occasional outbursts of "oh for dumb." Stoic was not an adjective to describe her ways but rather a summary of her essential being.

Oh, she had heart! Somehow she sensed the frightened and needy young woman I hid under my cloak of stubborn pride. When the babies fussed and cried and I was all a-jitter inside, she would reach out, blue eyes twinkling. "You are such a wonderful mother," she'd say as she snuggled them in her arms. "I just love the way your babies smell." It was Mennen baby lotion, but I believed her because I needed to, and she knew that.

We weeded gardens together and washed dishes and walls. We compared notes on life over endless cups of coffee. We cooked family meals together, dancing a lively polka of laughter and steamy intimacy in each other's kitchens. It took us eighteen years to get the rhythm down, but it was a dance worth learning.

Her death sentence was cancer, received in the Christmas season of 1990. Her stunned family could not, would not believe that their wife, mother, grandmother, sister, and aunt would ever leave them behind. But she knew and I knew, and it was a bittersweet bond. Finally, it was my turn to do the giving, my time to say thank you and good-bye. I did not want her to walk the last steps of her life alone, isolated in her stoic strength.

So together we packed and labeled china and crystal to be given as parting gifts to beloved daughters and cherished granddaughters. Together we searched her closet for that final dress, her favorite string of pearls. I gave her shots of interferon that didn't work. One day as we were driving home from the doctor's office, she whispered tearfully to me, "I'm not going to make it. I'm not giving up, but I know that I won't make it through the summer."

The moment stretched as far, it seemed, as the road we were on. Finally, I turned to her and said, "I don't want you to go, but I know you're tired and you hurt. So when you're ready, just let go. We'll all miss you so much, but we'll be fine. We'll be just fine." She believed me because she needed to, and I knew that. She died on a beautiful summer day in late July. Just before harvest time.

She is gone now, but only from my sight. She is not so far away. I know this as surely as the weeds grow in my garden and the crumbs gather in my kitchen. In July I became the mother-in-law of a beautiful, spirited young woman of Norwegian descent who makes a mean batch of *lefse*, a nurse who loves animals and fresh garden vegetables and my son. I hope my heart remembers the wisdom I learned from a North Dakota farm girl.

Let the circle be unbroken.

JANET E. GRAEBNER ❦ *Melissa*

"I want you to know I'm a Christian."

The words and tone of voice smacked into the predawn air and literally stopped me in my tracks. I turned to the young woman next to me on the mountain road. Even in the morning grayness, I could see the set jaw, as though she expected an argument. To this day, I can't recall the context that prompted Melissa's statement, delivered with such moral vehemence.

She and her husband and their two toddler-age boys had lived on the property near us for four years before we learned they were permanent residents; we thought it was a second home for them because we rarely saw or heard them. Then Melissa and I met at our mailboxes one day in September and agreed to start walking regularly the next morning, during that last magical suspension of time between darkness and sunrise that brings with it a sense of the holy.

I soon learned that Melissa's Christian upbringing ("I took Jesus Christ as my savior when I was five years old") had another element every bit as dominating as her evangelical faith. She was a radical Republican.

Neither her religious beliefs nor her politics per se disturbed me. It was her absolute conviction that only the Republican Party had a moral core and that all religious bodies but her own had "taken a wrong turn."

Steeped in yoga and various Eastern philosophies, and respecting the Lakota dictum *Mitakuye oyasin* (We are all related), I thought some of Melissa's pronouncements were illogical and hypocritical — often incompatible with the evangelical and biblical interpretations that she professed to follow.

Further complicating our relationship was the fact that I was old enough to be her mother. Neither girlfriend nor mother figure, I wondered how long we could sustain our daily walks. She didn't seem to have any social contacts not tied to her particular belief system, so my divergent comments or attempts to reason with her were like a slap in the face. She seemed genuinely confused when I didn't agree with her.

She really got wound up during the impeachment of President Clinton. There was no stemming her morning moralistic diatribes. At one point, I simply had to declare a moratorium on the subject.

How did I benefit from this relationship? I practiced patience, which is not one of my virtues. And I found myself researching evangelicalism and fundamentalism. I really wanted to understand Melissa's point of view; it was so black and white against my shades of gray. My husband teased me about returning from our walks and leafing through my Bible to verify passages she quoted.

The months of Clinton's impeachment were a difficult period between us, so imagine my surprise when at Christmas we received homemade candy and watermelon pickles from her, along with a card that said, "What a gift it has been to get to know you even better. We are so thankful for you. I can't begin to tell you how much I treasure our walks, Janet. We wish you a very Merry Christmas!"

Are we friends? No, at least not in the close, intimate way that word often implies. We maintain a respectful distance, letting our morning walks be our only contact. But we are friendly neighbors who can call on each other when need be, and that is a treasured relationship in the fairly isolated mountain area where we live.

LOUISE ENGELSTAD 🦌 Reclaiming Mother's World

On a rocky hillside in Glacier National Park, my mother taught me to sit so still that my skull disappeared and the wind blew through my head — so still that my hands joined to the rocks.

We lived with my grandmother, a county home demonstration agent, on the Montana Hi-Line in the 1950s. Grandmother often took me on her visits to remote ranches on the high plains north and west of Great Falls. We sailed over dusty country roads in her blue Ford, up and down washes until I felt that moment of weightlessness as the car came off the top of the hill. Strips of brilliant pale yellow wheat rippled in the constant wind next to strips of gray-brown fields — strip farming was the latest strategy in soil and water conservation on the plains. I learned cattle breeds — Angus, Hereford, Charolais. I learned to sew, knit, crochet, make chokecherry jelly, bake bread, tan hides, weave baskets, and quilt. We made dishtowels from old flour sacks. We made Christmas star balls — we called them porcupines — from foil. At our house, being a girl was no excuse for anything. I didn't cry or miss school the day I fell in the neighbor's vacant lot and cut my wrist on a jagged piece of car chrome. I still have the scar just over the vein. One day, when I saw my ten-year-old girlfriend crying in the street next to her bicycle, I dashed out and pulled her from in front of the huge Montana Power Company truck bearing down on her.

My mother, my younger sister, and I often went camping. Grandmother drove us out to a campground, usually at the end of a rutted Forest Service road. We piled out with our gear, in those days a huge canvas house tent. Grandmother drove off, leaving us for a week. I learned to build campfires, make "squaw corn" in a cast-iron skillet, and roast potatoes in the coals. I learned to pitch a tent, pack a backpack, mend an air mattress, read a topographical map. Forest rangers, once they accepted the fact that we were out there alone with no car, launched into scientific presentations on bears, plants, trails, fires. I learned how to see the wild world with all of my senses.

As far back as I can remember, we went to the woods. We went to Glacier Park, the Marias River at Shelby, and Black Leaf Canyon. After we moved to Bozeman, we went to Yellowstone National Park, the Gallatin Canyon, Chico Hot Springs, the Absaroka and Beartooth Ranges, and Red Lodge. During long Montana winters, we planned trips to Canada. Mother ordered travel folders from resorts in Alberta, British Columbia, and Saskatchewan. She kept them in a magical box under the bed until it was time to pore over the colored pages and maps, planning our excursions. We went to Lac LaRonge, Prince Albert National Park, Banff, Jasper, and the Pan American Games in Winnipeg.

We examined everything we saw and heard — rocks, grass, flowers, birds. We took pictures and developed them at home. In chemical mixtures in the bathroom, slide film turned into flower pictures for me; my sister got the rock pictures. I recorded fireweed, pasqueflower, and monkey flower, using our field guides to read about habitats and life cycles. With the enlarger, I made black-and-white still-life studies of shells, rocks, and sticks on photographic paper.

When my mother was my Sunday school teacher, we grew bean seeds in jars with blotter paper and learned that God is life and living things and kindness — all things are one, and our treatment of all living things is what matters. We didn't go to church on Good Friday because the Crucifixion was barbaric; my mother's God would never have done such a cruel thing.

At the age of thirty, I began to reclaim myself from abusive, alien relationships. At the heart of myself, I found ideas and creativity my mother taught me. Her bouts of mental illness had terrified me as a teenager and closed the door on our relationship. But now I am grown and live in the West she taught me to understand and revere. And I am reclaiming my brilliant and sensitive mother by teaching my urban husband how to read a topo map as we explore the West's remote mountains and deserts, planting milkweed and coneflowers and native grasses in my back yard. Every act acknowledges the gifts my mother gave me.

My grandmother died last summer at the age of ninety-eight. We buried her in a small cemetery in the middle of the Gallatin Valley, where the wind blows through the grass and you can see the mountains all the way around. She grew up there; her father helped the community build the cemetery. She lies next to my grandfather, who died fifty years ago. After the graveside service, my mother, my sister, and my uncle and aunt fixed a picnic lunch and headed to the mountains. We hiked to Paradise Falls in Hyalite Canyon, then built a fire in the chilly evening. Sitting by the fire, I recalled my mother saying once, "This is the world and your place in it."

DIANE J. RAPTOSH ❧ Matrimony

I do, I do. I think you are. I think you are married, yes, my five-year-old answers. But not until after a pause long as the body of dream. To whom? I ask, scratching my thumb pad with my front teeth. *You are married to Karen. You're a bride to your sister.* My daughter's every *s* whistles small births. It's true that my sister does most of the physical work at the house. Hauling the forty-pound bags of coarse salt to soften hard water. Escorting controlled fire around the land's rim. Currying the horses, combing out scurf. She and I hand-weeded half of this five-acre pasture ourselves. With help from our mother. Because weeds were there, because she lives here, too. Because she comes from a long line of Sicilian farmers. Because if I want my daughter to inherit *her* wedding ring, six tiny diamonds shaped like a tulip, we might as well — all of us now — get down on our knees, one way or another, and do it.

GWEN PETERSEN 🦌 The Shell Game

It took forty years to cut Delia out of my life.

Our friendship was a shell game: she kept praise, support, and endorsement hidden like a pea under a walnut shell. Her genius was to shift the pea but leave me sure that the next time, I'd select the right walnut. I was not singled out. That was Delia's style with all who knew her.

We became friends in our freshman year in college, partly, I think, because I felt sorry for her. She was homelier than I was.

I'd grown up in a state of semiconsciousness in relation to other people, because I was more interested in animals. It wasn't until my hormones steamrollered my psyche that I found out I was homely. Buck teeth, thin braids, and wire-rim spectacles, that was me. But shoot, being pretty was outside the realm of my expectations, so I refused to think about it at all. In Delia, I saw someone whose ill-favored mien didn't seem to bother her. The last thing she needed or wanted was protection or rescuing. That summer after our freshman year in college, she invited me to her home in Montana, where I learned just how flawed I was by violating the precise rules for doing tasks in Delia's house. Washing dishes meant immersing the glassware first, and woe to you if you tossed in a soiled fork ahead of schedule. You received a chuckled comment such as "Lose something?" as she pulled the offending tool from the water.

Drying the dishes, washing and hanging clothes — all had to be done in a fixed, immutable order. Determined to please, I vowed to learn the ways of that household, questioning what and how to do the smallest task, until one day, as Delia and I were cooperatively making a bed, I asked, "Do you want hospital corners?"

"Your trouble," she told me, "is that you can't make a decision."

Later, I went back to college; Delia didn't. I married; Delia didn't. For years I escaped her influence over and over by taking up a different life. When twists of fortune brought me back into Delia's neighborhood, I always picked up the threads of friendship. She was like childbirth: once I was away from her, I forgot the exasperation, discomfort, and downright pain. As a friend, she excoriated my soul. I looked up *excoriate*. It means (1) to tear or wear off the skin of; abrade; (2) to censure strongly; denounce.

Delia could verbally maim in a way so understated you didn't realize you'd been flayed till your tissues began leaking vital fluids. I reacted with furious, unspoken defensiveness and a huge determination to "prove" myself, to make her recognize my achievements and abilities. If I got angry or excited, she'd say, "Be nice." My response was a serious urge to commit homicide.

Delia painted pictures; so did I. Delia rode horses; so did I. She wrote stories; so did I. She liked dogs and cats; so did I. You'd think we had a lot in common — except my artwork always suffered from a particular flaw, which Delia was always kind enough to point out.

I'd show her a freshly finished painting I was proud of. She'd chuckle and say, "You have that mountain peak looking like a melting ice cream cone. Too bad you couldn't render it as well as you did in your last painting." She enjoyed mentioning past efforts where I *almost* got it right, and she viewed these demoralizing remarks as "humor."

My horsemanship was always sloppy and in need of correction, and my horses' manners were inferior. Delia personally trained her steeds to the peak of perfection. "Keep that crow bait of yours walking up," she'd say as she lectured me on educating hay burners so they wouldn't dawdle.

In the art of dog-obedience training, Delia was the best. She let you know that at the drop of a dog turd. She taught her canines to stay on the floor of her vehicle, where they gazed wistfully up at bits of sky, like prisoners shut in a cattle car, while my woofer was so undisciplined he climbed right up on the seat beside me, hung out the window, and smiled at the world.

Once she refused to let Mike, my collie-cross pooch, ride in her automobile. "Sorry, your dog will have to stay behind, since you can't make him mind." When I refused to go without Mike, she shrugged and said, "Well, it's up to you," in a tone that let me know how wrong I was.

Delia loved to take fledgling writers under her wing and bring them along, line by line. The disapproval started when a writer had the gall to become independent. Should a writer actually sell a manuscript, Delia would say, "Gads, my ideas, and you collect the money."

Her acclamations, always couched in her humor, came out as slams, especially in front of a group. She often compared one writer's triumphs to another writer's incompetence, especially if the "incompetent" person was present. Sometimes she would say, "This is so bad I don't have anything to say about it."

Sad to say, I'm apparently not only a slow learner; I'm also an incorrigible optimist. I even traveled with Delia, more than once.

An entire ocean of water had to flow under the bridge before I caught on that Delia never giggled with delight, never broke into unrestrained laughter, never actually shared a funny moment. Always she stood back, evaluated (negatively), and passed judgment.

Perhaps the finish for me came when she brought a clock to a writers' group to time the readings, time the response to the readings, and time the response to the response. Naturally, Delia appointed herself timekeeper. When it was my turn to read, I picked up the damn clock and threw it down the hall.

After forty years and several fits and starts, I've cut all ties. I've totally dissociated from Delia, and the relief is grand, like breathing clean air after inhaling smog for years. I feel as if I've been cured of cancer. However, I see blood spots before my eyes if I hear the words "Be nice."

BONNIE LARSON STAIGER ✵ Cycles

For Stacy Jean

Mother and daughter
count the bales
of alfalfa —
it is a time to talk,

You are uneasy
as you wait
for the appearance
of that first
flesh flow
of blood,

While I eagerly watch
for the signs
that mine will cease,

Who is the woman —
who is the child,

Next year we'll
plant wheat
to give the land
a rest.

JO-ANN SWANSON ❧ Alva in the Fields

Different. Was she a flaming begonia between their rows of gentle daisy faces? Dusty field worker, browned from days spent with rows of hard durum and barley and alfalfa, compared to their Tuesday ironing and pea-shelling days. All browns and roses, she glowed with vitamin D and inner sun.

In our part of the country, she put the other farm ladies to shame, with their curled hair and round white faces, work-worn hands denied by rose water lotion. Not for her the tastefully flowered white cottons and lady sandals with discreet snub heels. She wore flaming red or black or green or turquoise dresses and high heels of black patent or moss leather when she and Leo stopped by to visit on, say, a dull Wednesday evening, around eight. Unannounced. This was the late 1950s, early 1960s.

I once heard someone say that maybe she was part Lebanese. But no, she was German, yet she was as brown as well-used canvas, with the high cheekbones and aristocratic face that might adorn some Maya princess. She looked glamorous, in an easy way, wearing red lipstick and Christian Dior–style skirts that looked like ballerina tulle. She was thin, not very tall, and they suited her. Alva was the first person I recognized as having style.

Days, she dressed to work, and she wasn't ashamed of it. Late some afternoon, if she stopped for a cup of coffee or tea, she wore a green or gray tough-tailored work shirt, men's pants, and work boots. How I envied those boots. Were they a young boy's, I wondered later. They didn't make work boots for women then. A few years later, I would have a tough time begging merely jeans. Alva dressed and worked like a man, out in the fields with her husband, Leo — spraying, seeding, rod weeding, cultivating, combining, swathing. She did it all. She didn't swagger. She walked. Like an ordinary person.

Even her manner was different: "How ya doin', Jamie?" She was forthright, open, industrious. And then would follow a list of tasks that needed to be done, the things she had done, and the inevitable litany, like a religious chant, about impending weather, crop prices, early frosts, garden tomatoes. She talked to me as if I were an equal. She did that to children. Of course, she had none herself.

She was the only adult I knew who didn't have children. She and Leo had, imagine it, separate bedrooms. Their house — one of those gracious 1950s white houses, mostly glass to the floor — was serene and spacious with a minimum of furniture, a plethora of large plants. I had never seen a house where the furniture was not herded together like docile cattle. I could imagine dancing in that living room, with its windows on three sides; its south-facing window brought in sun at all hours of the day. I tried to imagine her at the grocery store. I couldn't. Like the bright balsamroot that grew by a wayside ditch or in the midst of our neat rows of registered barley, she wasn't from our world somehow.

In our part of the country, neighbors lived side by side for years, their children after them, and neighbors didn't ask personal things. Most people didn't know what their neighbors had for breakfast. It wasn't polite. Others might cite the strong Irish or Scotch-Irish roots of the earliest homesteaders, a generation back. Given the larger end — to coexist on the tough land for centuries — the means seemed reasonable. Of course, in the long run, it wouldn't work. Nobody then realized that the community might begin to die. I never heard her "differences" used against her.

She was a leader. She and Leo played guitar and musical instruments, staged plays for the community. Her husband turned more religious in later years, more, I suspect, than she. But she took it all gracefully, good sport that she was. She played fair.

So when I heard last year that she had been forced to undergo a mastectomy and I saw her later that year, cheekbones hidden by puffy skin and a roundness coming to that long oval face, I saw an idol's feet trapped in clay. I remembered all of the years she had spent spraying in the Carrot River valley, helping "the men." I remembered all I had read about chemical sprays and their tendency to reside in fatty tissue and to mutate. I mourned a lifestyle as much as I regretted and blasphemed its loss.

As I grow older, my face grows more angular, but I realize I will never look like her. She is now seventy-five or so. It is the idea of her that carries me. She sows in the golden fields of my dreams, and she carries armloads of fragrant wheat. She is smart and rooted in the earth. She lives in her body. She does not fear scarlet. She wades across the fields. Already I mourn the beginning of both passings.

CANDI RED CLOUD ❦ How I Became My Own Woman

My grandma *(unci)* was a beautiful woman. Every wrinkle on her face said something about her. I saw wrinkles of laughter and wrinkles of sadness. As a child, I always liked to run my fingers over her face, touching her wrinkled skin.

Her laughter filled the room — it was strong and giggly. When she laughed, it made me feel very warm and safe inside. Her touch was warm, too.

Always I would see a white cloth wrapped around one of her fingers. I think this was her Band-Aid, because she chopped wood, sewed a lot, and hauled water every day at our house on the Pine Ridge Reservation in South Dakota.

When I was six or seven years old, we moved to the housing area in

Pine Ridge Village. In the evenings, *Unci* often made Jell-O, and while it was setting, we went for a walk downtown. She visited with people on the street, talking and laughing, her hands moving along with the conversation. As for me, I played on the porch of the old Catholic church, thinking it was really cool to jump off from the very top step. Sometimes I landed on my rear end, but it was fun.

When it was time to go home, *Unci* said, "*Leciya huwe, wanna unglin kte, Candi*" (Come over here, Candi; we're going home now). Her main language was Lakota, and this was all I spoke as a child: my Lakota language.

When we arrived home, the Jell-O was done, and she made a bowl for me and some for herself. This always felt like a treat, even though it was something that we did a lot.

My *unci* worked hard, but she also knew how to celebrate each day. She always had food ready for company. Also, I always knew when we were going to town to shop, because she put on her best dress, sparkly earrings, and her red scarf. My *unci* passed on to me her inner beauty, strength, courage, generosity, and, most of all, love for people.

My grandma was my mama and role model from the time I was four months until I was eighteen years old. From then on, I looked to my peers, but the females in my community were very competitive. Jealousy? Man, this is a major issue for the women of Pine Ridge. Now, I am sure that not all of the women are this way, but some are. If it wasn't the way I dressed, it was the job I had or just my way of being me. But all of the negative that came from these women gave me more energy and determination to accomplish my goals: my education, my sobriety, and bettering myself in every area of my life. I turned the negative into a positive.

I still live on the Pine Ridge Reservation. This is where I raised my three sons. God knew what He was doing when He blessed me with my boys.

One of the things I like to do is drive my car. It helps me to think better and to enjoy the beauty: miles and miles of prairie, hills, and pine trees. I like to drive to the lookout mountain on my way to Rapid City and look at the Badlands. The colors are relaxing — tan and pinkish — and the shapes are like piles and piles of colored clay. To the north, I can see the Black Hills with their dark pine trees. The Lord blessed me with all of this creation to enjoy.

I watched an awesome sunset one time driving west from Kyle on the reservation — soft colors of orange, yellow, and red behind the green pine hills. It was so exhilarating that I had to stop my car. I sometimes feel isolated living on the reservation, but on that day, watching the beauty of a Pine Ridge sunset, I felt like the most beautiful and luckiest girl in the world.

Speaking of beauty, this word takes me back to my *unci*, who was a Rosebud Sioux Indian and a gorgeous lady. Her name was Cora Owns The Fire-Iron Crow. When I am parked out in the Badlands, I can almost hear her singing. Every morning at daybreak, she would pack her pipe and sing this song — she said it was the morning star song — and pray. Sometimes, if I woke up, she would let me have a few puffs with her.

I will always be grateful to my *unci*, and I also applaud the women on Pine Ridge Reservation for empowering me and giving me strength to accomplish my goals and be who I am today. All the glory and honor goes to my higher power.

"*Ble hiciya pe*" (Be strong) and "*Ohina wace kiya unpe*" (Pray all the time).

KATY PAYNICH 🦌 Defying Bare Branches

On flat-gray winter days
when wind gusts the snow into drifts
under the aspens, black as skeletons
against the Montana sky,
days when stories of Guatemalan homeless children
await me in the newspaper neatly folded
on my breakfast table,
"Children as young as ten," displaced by Hurricane Mitch,
squat in ghettos, tubes of epoxy held to their lips,
like babies holding bottles,
they breathe the mind-numbing fumes,
sway from the smell of paint thinner on rags, begging,
prostituting, desperate and hopeless.

On the day when the phone call sobs
the news of two promising
and beloved
students who were instantly killed
in a head-on collision with a fire truck,
an accident on any icy highway
that smeared their futures away
and left a ghostly hollowness
where their lives should be.

On days when my heart, heavy with helplessness,
spills out of my eyes,
I'll remember what you said
about this being the best time in our lives.
"Our children are young," you said,
wise about the tyranny of winter,
"Our husbands are still alive, and we are happy,

but this will change," you warned,
the cold blade of winter always in your peripheral vision,
"So we must live these golden moments
while we can."
That same year,
with your shoulders squared against
the unknown future,
you grew a baby in your uterus,
planted a baby
to be born on the cusp of autumn and winter,
a fresh bud, defying
dead grasses, bare branches, and flurries of snow.

On winter days, I'll take out this golden memory of you,
your belly swelling under your paisley dress,
the autumn sun making your raven hair iridescent
as we sat in the park on the warm earth.
I'll remember how we fed you watermelon
in the shade of ripening plums,
lavender-massaged your feet and hands,
scented your hair with rosemary.

I'll remember how the petals
of your vagina opened,
how your fingers wove through mine and squeezed
hard enough to make me grimace
as your uterus contracted and you pushed.

I'll remember the moment
he straddled two worlds,
his wet head out, bundled to the neck in vagina,
his toes still in your womb.
Propelled by muscle and will,
he birthed into this world
riding on a river of amniotic fluid,
blood and stool.

Then I'll remember seeing you, as I looked over my shoulder
one last time, just as I was about to leave
on the evening after you gave birth,
you, propped on pillows, warm and dry
after your wet journey, cozy
beneath your down comforter,
a new baby in the cradle of your arm,

you, with your triumphant smile and
long hair twisted and secured
on top of your head like an Egyptian queen.

On winter days to come, I will open
the locket in my mind where I keep that image of you,
as I opened the door to leave
and looked over my shoulder, the chill
of evening palming my face,
knowing the dead of winter awaits,
but determined to imprint on my memory
the champagne glow of your whole house
and you, Persephone,
having gone on your journey through darkness
and returned,
bring with you,
Spring.

LAURA HAWKINS GREVEL 🦌 Dear Quilting Sisters

My new friends, I write an ode to you. Who welcomed and accepted a
stranger in your midst. A stranger whose eccentric family actually homesteads. "My my," you say, eyes glinting humor yet approving, "chickens,
pigs, draft horses, and milk cow in this day and age!"

I am a very pregnant stranger with a small child. One for whom your
expectations have to be oh so patient for any real contribution of quilt and
craft and time. One for whom you already predict the long wait for significant progress to come.

And that is exactly what makes you the beauteous circle of sages you
are, the circle of faith you are. You teach patience with each stitch. You teach
gentleness with needle and thread. You teach love with callused finger.

You who at ninety-three are as strong as Hercules. You who are so kind
despite frailty and infirmity. You who are so gracious despite experience.
You who are so cheerful despite bereavement. You who are so steady facing
the long, rough road ahead.

There you are, Hallie, born 1906. You lean on a walker to deliver a meat
loaf for the usual potluck with a smile fresh as your yellow tulip pattern,
pieced at home alone. And Willie with your stroke-stricken face, eyes half-
closed, tongue lazy, recounting details of ranch land and history as exact as
a cathedral window coverlet. There you are, Lydia, born one of fourteen
yourself, seven children rested in your womb. At eighty-five, quiet and
fragile, you steadfastly wove nostalgic joy during my husband's horse-

drawn wagon ride. There you are Verba Lee, refusing therapy against the hostile growth within and welcoming the crazy quilt life each day still offers. And you tottering Rita, a widow still in love, pulling calves on 105-degree summer days, living out the scraps of your dear husband's retirement dream. And there you sit Ethel, Era, Hilma, Jim, May, Clara, Elizabeth, Polly, and too soon the next, a sampler of widows hard and heavy as black brocade on broken silk hearts, your staring lined faces grieve lost husbands — children and hard-worked farms scattered seeds to the wind — a cheater's quilt it seems. There are — how many of you with cancer, arthritis, other laments — who always come, eager souls, to help with luncheon and love, your eyes and hands resistant, your tiny stitches an art lost to other times?

Ah, and here I sit, with an infant bulging like a dinosaur egg in my belly and my girl toddler hanging at my knee, enjoying a baby shower of brightly wrapped packages, tiny boy clothes spilling off lap and table. I tear open paper and ribbon, amazed at your optimism and generosity to a fetus and family still undefined by gender and local roots. We will always be foreign in this country. Yet there are even toys for my daughter. And she and I keep opening the endless gifts sewn by shaking thought and speckled hand, encircled by a tradition and confidence as old as motherhood.

Under the rustle of paper, I hear the circle whisper, "You have to carry on."

SUSAN VITTITOW ❧ Jean

Jean kicked me out of her rental house in the middle of winter. It was one of the kindest things anyone has ever done for me.

I suppose I should back up a little. I refer to this stage in my life as the time I ran away from home. Things hadn't gone so well since Brian and I had moved west together. I drove off one day with all my possessions in my pickup, promising to return if I felt like it.

I found a job editing a small weekly newspaper. I needed a place to live and heard Jean's bed-and-breakfast guesthouse was available for the winter.

Jean was a beautiful woman still, despite sixty years of sometimes-tough living. She was petite, with short white hair, brilliant blue eyes, and a trim attractive figure. She flashed her bright smile at me, declared me wonderful, and said she'd love to have me live there.

She showed me the house. We sat in the rental living room while she talked ten words to my two and smoked multiple cigarettes. She said I could have a kitten, I said I'd take the place, and all was agreed in a haze of nicotine.

I had no idea what she saw in me. She was a fourth-generation rancher, while I was a transplanted and poorly rooted Easterner. She had once been prominent in her community and well-to-do, while I had scrounged and drifted since leaving home. We were thirty years apart in age and a continent apart in politics.

Jean didn't just take me under her wing; she put me in a headlock and dragged me into her world. She'd sit, light a cigarette, and let loose a string of memories and struggles and feelings. She told me how her first son, now a tall strapping man, had been a terribly sickly child. She admitted that her still-fine figure had breasts bolstered with silicone. She told me how she met her husband, Dick, when they were both about ten, and he threw her in the creek (repeatedly) so he could pull her out. She told me about the time he was terribly injured, with his liver kicked nearly in two by a horse. She told me how one woman who had been hired to help for the summer had a thing for her married son. Jean told me she packed this woman up and shuttled her back home to Kentucky. She told me of roots grown deep and love of family and struggles and heartaches. I don't know if it ever occurred to her not to tell me something.

I wasn't Jean's only stray. There was Wally, who lived with his young girlfriend in another of the buildings and helped out on the ranch. There was the Border collie pup Rodeo, better known as Rodeo-do-do. There was always a cat or kitten seeking handouts by her door.

Dick had once been a breathtakingly handsome young cowboy. She showed me an old photo of a tall, well-muscled man used to hard outdoor work, leaning against a truck in faded blue jeans. He had lived with multiple sclerosis and other severe health problems for nearly thirty years. Still tough as nails, he walked with a cane and struggled with daily tasks. Their money had gone to medications and doctor's visits until they were at risk of having to sell the ranch. Dick loved Jean more than oxygen.

They were used to ranch living. I was not. The first few nights the boxelder bugs nearly drove me out of the house. I knew they were harmless, but in silhouette they look like cockroaches, and in flight they remind me of wasps. They are drawn to warmth and light, so I left the lamps on in the bedroom and slept in the cold on a thinly padded bench next to the fireplace. I finally came down from my antichemical soapbox and sprayed cheap insecticide in every window.

The coal furnace seemed to go out constantly and proved nearly impossible to relight. They showed me how to use paper and cardboard and candle drippings and a few muttered prayers, but I never did get the hang of it. Sometimes Dick made a semicontrolled fall down the rickety stairs to relight it, using cane and handrail to complete the trip without injury. I held my breath and bit my tongue, knowing that to show my concern hurt him more deeply than a tumble down the steps would.

A strange smell in the refrigerator would not go away, and I could not pull in a single radio station. The ranch cat I acquired was a neurotic and uncompanionable companion. I was unused to muddy roads and isolation and the complete darkness at night.

My new job required that I be both the editor and staff of the paper. My office was in a converted storage room of a small restaurant, space the owner granted in exchange for advertising. I scraped out whatever revenue I could, covered town meetings, and stayed up until all hours of the night completing production.

I tried not to complain, because I did not want to be the uppity city girl who moves to the country and complains that it's the country.

Jean was there when I was tired and frustrated and needed an ear. She invited me to dinner often. She rarely stopped smiling.

I still saw Brian. He was where I had left him, thirty-five miles away in another small town. Brian came out to the ranch a few times, and Jean seemed to fall in love with him immediately. He and Jean could both talk to beat the band. He was on his best behavior, hoping I would come back.

Between all the tasks of running a newspaper, I found myself making the drive to see Brian late at night on bad roads, leaving the cat to fend for herself. In the mornings, I'd drive back to the ranch in hopes that I could fill the coal bin before the fire went out. Next, I'd head to my office and try to sell enough advertisements and write enough stories to make a newspaper for another week.

Jean caught me on one of those rare occasions when I was home. "Am I the only one here who can tell you're in love?" she asked. And then she told me, "You have to leave."

That was it — she was sending me to my real home, with Brian. She said Brian and I deserved each other — and she meant that in a good way. I wanted to reconcile; she was wise enough to give me a push. She had known true love in her lifetime, and she recognized it in us.

I didn't expect my deposit back, but she promised to return it. Money was tight that winter, so she repaid it in part with a used washer. Brian purchased a house closer to both our jobs. We moved in on a snowy Christmas Day. I purchased the newspaper about a month later. I didn't have any other job prospects, so I had little to lose if I couldn't make it work.

I still ran into Jean at the post office and the local grocery. She sometimes called me unexpectedly when I was working late and brought me a plate of home-cooked food. We'd talk, and then she'd help me proof pages before I did the final paste-up. Occasionally, I stopped by the ranch to visit when I needed a break.

One night Jean called me at the office and told me she would come by to proof pages. I unlocked the door and kept working. She never showed, but Dick called wanting to know where she was. I didn't know, but I added my worry to his.

I saw her the next day. She told me she had spent the evening in the

262 · WOVEN ON THE WIND

company of a man she had known many years ago. She didn't feel like a bad wife; she felt like a young girl.

Somehow I felt that whatever happened, it did not diminish her love for Dick one bit. I did ask her not to use me as her alibi again. Jean landed herself in the hospital that fall, crashing her car after having too much to drink. I heard of it, both from friends and from the police blotter — which I ordinarily published. I couldn't single her out, leave her name out of the paper because she was my friend. I added her name to the page and printed the paper.

The first day I went to see her in the hospital, I almost didn't recognize her. She was asleep, pale and wrinkled. I had never seen her look so old. I didn't wake her. The next day, she was in better shape — awake and alert. I told her what I had done. Never have I been more ashamed of my livelihood than that day, watching my friend broken, bruised, and pale, crying in a hospital bed because I had printed her name as a drunk driver.

I followed my own policy. I hurt my friend deeply. And she understood.

Another December rolled around, and I prepared to sell the newspaper. I had worked literally night and day and had taken little more than my mileage expense. It was time to pull the plug.

Jean entered the hospital again, this time with pneumonia. I don't think she had fully recuperated from the auto accident. I stopped by after a couple of days to see her. I had almost talked myself into the intensive care unit (ICU), even though visitors were supposed to be restricted to family, when there was an emergency. I was told to wait in the lobby. I waited far longer than I expected, then decided to try another time. I called her daughter-in-law to ask how Jean was doing. She started crying. Jean had been recovering when she unexpectedly had a massive hemorrhage in her brain stem. The family was struggling with letting her go, disconnecting the machines from her still-breathing body.

That had been the emergency that had kept me out of the ICU. I had been sitting in a vinyl chair, impatiently thumbing magazines, while my friend died in the next room. I was half an hour too late to say good-bye. I hung up the phone, curled into a ball on the wood floor in the hallway, and cried while Brian held me.

I ran the obituary in the next edition.

Brian and I both went to the funeral, but he didn't stay long. After five minutes, he walked out crying and hiked the mile or so back to his office. I gutted it out. The minister talked of how she would be made perfect in heaven. I wanted to scream, "Isn't it enough that she was here and that she loved with her whole heart? Can't we be thankful for that?"

I ran a memorial poem the next week. Two weeks later, the paper sold.

Jean's family told me I was welcome out at the ranch anytime. Once Dick called to tell me how much he missed her. I couldn't imagine. I had shared just over a year with her and felt as if my lungs had been ripped out. He had shared a lifetime.

Several months later, Dick disappeared for several days, prompting statewide news stories before he was found dead. He had had a seizure at the wheel and driven off the road into an area that concealed the vehicle.

I still find it hard to think of Jean and not cry. Although I miss her, I feel her presence when I wake next to Brian and remember her gentle push out the door.

DONNA APPLEGARTH MENTINK ᐟᕐ Come Home

"No matter what you ever do, I'll always love you." I don't know if my mother ever actually said these words, but I knew how much she loved me.

I knew it most when I was twenty-two, expecting a baby, and unmarried. What I had done would be such a disappointment to my parents. My mother said, "Come home." I went home and sat on the end of her bed. Mother asked me, "What do you want to do?" I didn't know what to do. My mother's feelings were expressed by a simple statement. "I can't bear to think of my grandchild being raised by strangers. We'll work something out." And we did.

My daughter and I lived with my parents on their ranch for almost seven years. My mother never once judged me. She was never embarrassed that I was a single mother. She said, "Come home," and gave me the most precious gift, my daughter.

And Jenny . . . my mother paved the way for a bright and beautiful little girl to grow up happy and secure. She helped me raise a baby to become a loving, sensitive young woman. And now I say to her, "No matter what you ever do, I'll always love you."

Thank you, Mother.

MAUREEN TOLMAN FLANNERY ᐟᕐ Before She Left

for Maggie Hopkin Tolman

When I was a girl
Grandma didn't go to the mountains anymore.
I couldn't understand it, and I'd call her every time,
"We're going to the mountains, Grandma. Wanna come?"
She was gracious in declining, and her voice sloped away

like the rutted road toward the creek.
"Naw, honey, you go on. Bring me down some lupine, though."
I asked Daddy and all the herders if they knew why.
It seemed to me a place
so pieced of the fabric of her soul.
Her blue flowered apron
hung on a nail by the cabin back door
and the plank by the water in the springhouse
was smooth from her knees
and her quilts
covered every mouse-eaten mattress
that covered squeaky springs
and her red checkered oilcloth
was still on the table
and her whistled gospel tunes
blew through the windows with the smell of pines.
And in the granary,
where she stayed that first spring
before there was a cabin,
the door still hung on leather hinges
she had made in desperation
(by cutting up a harness) one doorless dusk
to separate her children
from the hungry timber noises that come out with stars.

Something of her was everywhere on the homestead.
She birthed on its table
and corseted herself behind the cabbage rose curtain
hung on a rod over the doorway to a tiny bedroom,
year after year, in a world of men.
The cabin's comfort was her plumpness.
Its bread was of her kneading.
Hers was the taming of its wildness,
the endurance of its harshness,
the proving up on its acreage.
She gave it her youth and its next generations
and was somehow content not to go back.

Her modest house in town had running water,
sweet peas snaking up the siding,
and thin teacups in a china cupboard
so unlike the dipper
hung over the rim of the galvanized metal bucket.
Did her curly willow fingers

recall decades of diapers washed in icy creek water?
Did her memory leap like a sheepdog
at the sound of an old pickup
that went to town and didn't hear the train?
Had her weakened pelvic floor
too many times
endured bouncing up washed-out roads,
first on horseback, next in wagons,
then in the rattly army truck
brought back after the war
when her boys came home?
Maybe she had no need to return,
carrying it all around with her
in those mountainous breasts,
no longer corseted.

I know, at least,
before she left
she crocheted onto meadows of lupine
the ecru sinews of her youthful strength,
taught forget-me-nots to whisper their names
from the tiny yellow centers of pastel blue and pink,
tatted the ridges of pines with her joy,
and planted for us on hillsides of wildflowers,
the seeds of her fullness.

HILARY BARTON BILLMAN ❧ How the West Was Won

How the West Was Won — that's the title of the painting. A cowboy stands in the foreground, arms crossed, chaps flapping in the wind, hat tilted to keep the sun out of his eyes. Behind him, a woman hangs his laundry on a line, apron tied around her waist, hair in a bun, everything in order. The painting used to hang in the Fossil Country Museum before I became the museum director. Now it hangs in the old Methodist Church on Sapphire, where my husband and I live. Our artist friend Mick and his wife, Pam, gave it to us as a wedding present.

My husband and I have different ideas on the significance of the title, his idea having something to do with the cowboy as protector. Mick stays out of the argument, but Pam agrees with me. My view has to do with women as the backbone of the West and men as pretenders, trying to appear as if they are in control. The painting reminds me of the Mormon women who survived treacherous wagon train journeys and miners' wives who had to take in boarders and do extra laundry just to get by, not knowing when there would be another mine explosion that would take their father, husband, brother, or son. There is a strength in Western women that is inherited through remoteness, weather, and circumstance. The West is different. Relationships are different. They have to be when the elements are the controlling substance of life.

I came to Kemmerer with my husband, who loves Wyoming, the high desert, the snow, the remote life, the low population. The weather, like everywhere in the West, is unpredictable. One year we had six inches of snow on June 17, and once snow on July 4. I've seen photographs of past snowstorms where the wind blew so hard a four-inch-thick layer of snow rolled up like a jellyroll. In the winter, sagebrush sticks out of the snow like a three-day-old beard. In the summer, the surrounding ridges look like a moonscape. In any season, the wind always blows. But this place is beautiful, and I am surprised to find myself missing the wind, the sagebrush, and the dry air when I am away.

Kemmerer is a rough town and always has been. It is not Jackson Hole, but it is not quite Rock Springs. It is a working-class community with a coal mine and a power plant. The gas industry is beginning to become a bigger player in Wyoming, but at the moment Kemmerer mostly sees the well pads as intrusions on its landscape.

Before I moved here, my husband, who was then my boyfriend, told me that the West is different. Friends are harder to come by, he said; people tend to stay in their own circles, are wary of strangers, don't be offended. Everything he said made sense, but I was offended. I was used to making friends easily, to being surrounded by people my own age with my own views. The West can be a lonely place. To enjoy life here, you have to appreciate the wildness in the landscape and the long winter months.

Mick and Pam are our closest friends in town, and they are old enough to be our parents, although we forget that when we are together. The West is ambivalent about age. That doesn't mean people don't look old, because the cold and dry wind are unforgiving. But age doesn't matter as much when it comes to friendship. People get Pam and me mixed up. We don't look alike, but we are often together, walking in the morning before work in a town where many people do not walk anywhere, and I suppose we are associated as one and the same.

With my job as museum director, I have to deal with our volunteers on a daily basis. All of them are women, and most of them are old enough to be my grandmother. They know more about the history of this place than I will ever learn in my daily research. If I had to name my friends in town, all of the volunteers would be on that list.

One of our volunteers is a Mormon, and she is a lovely woman. She is honest and reliable and extremely nice and sensitive. She claims not to know how to do certain things because she has never had a job, never "worked," as she says. But she has worked, does know how to do almost everything, and is strong — a good wife, mother, grandmother, and friend. I wish she realized that *work* does not mean a nine-to-five job.

Most of the volunteers at the museum are widows and have been for quite a few years. Some have had bad marriages, a few have never been married, some don't have children, some have great-grandchildren, all consider each other friends and often stay after their shifts talking to the next volunteer. They share a history in a coal-mining town past its prime and in between booms. Most of the volunteers are former professional women — bankers, secretaries, and teachers — and I love to sit around and drink coffee with them and listen to their stories.

Their close friendship makes me jealous sometimes, makes me long for the city, where I always had a close group of friends. I think they forget the reasons they have formed their bonds: their husbands have died, their children have moved away, their parents and siblings are gone, and they share a harsh history that they don't realize is so harsh. These are the women in the painting who have held the West together, who are still holding the West together. They have the key to our history, but they are living in the present. I wonder what they think of me and my husband, living in an old church, my husband working at home as a writer, me almost thirty with no children. Whatever they think, they don't share it with me. Instead, they ask about my museum work, my husband's writing, recent town gossip. I don't enjoy the days I don't get a chance to leave my office and talk with them for a few minutes, find out what's happening with them, get a friendly hello, sometimes a hug.

We are buying a house, leaving the church behind, doing something permanent, staying in Kemmerer. The volunteers are excited for me because they know the house. It was the first house in town to get electricity and was owned by a notable family for a long time. Now the volunteers know I am not a drifter like so many other Westerners. I am going to stay in this hard town, try to make it better, help make its history part of me.

We are hanging our painting on a wall in our new living room. It will be the prominent piece in the house, and every day when I look at it, instead of feeling lonely, I will find comfort in the strength behind the woman hanging up laundry.

MAUREEN CAIN 🐾 Car Pool Friendship

My teaching job takes me twenty-five miles to the west every morning and twenty-five miles back in the afternoon. To save gas and money, I car-pool with a fellow teacher. Kay is the same age as my mother and has been teaching since before I was born. She is intelligent, generous, and kind. But we wouldn't have a relationship if we didn't both live in a small rural town and work together at a remote school about half an hour away. We are different in almost every way: religious and political beliefs; hobbies and entertainment choices; dress and hairstyle preferences; age and income.

We live in the old mining-turned-art-gallery town of Bisbee, Arizona, where most of the homes were built in the early 1900s and art cars with plastic toys or huge suitcases glued to them drive the streets while tourists stare. Kay lived in Bisbee when the mine was open, and she laughs at the "weirdo" artists, but the art teacher in me loves them. She attends Mormon church services and women's meetings; I meditate in the evenings and go to yoga class twice a week. Her husband is retired from the Phelps Dodge Mining Company; my longhaired husband works at the local food co-op. Her advanced education and teaching experience have made her one of the highest-paid teachers at our school; I've taught for only a few years, and I'm still paying off my student loans.

If it were up to me, we'd leave for work at about 8:00 A.M., eat breakfast in the car, and show up thirty minutes late. But Kay likes to finish her bulletin boards and straighten out her desk before her students get off the bus. I get up early and take a long walk in the desert. Kay gets up as early as I do, but she curls her hair, fixes her makeup, and usually takes the time to iron a dress and put on nylons before she picks me up at 7:00 A.M.

During our occasionally uncomfortable time in the car, these differences sit between us with our tote bags of papers to grade. I often wonder what would happen if I mentioned how different we are, but talking about it would create more tension. Does Kay feel the same awkwardness that I do? More than anything, I wonder why it's so important to me to try to form a deeper relationship with her. Something in me wants to connect with Kay in a meaningful way. As we speed through the desert, I see our relationship slowly building.

Some mornings when I get in the car, I'm sure that today our conversation will turn ugly. Of course, we keep our talk polite and our topics safe. She tells me what her students are doing, and I talk about my weekend plans. But every once in a while, Kay will give a commentary on the state legislature, and by the time I get to work, I have a swollen lip from biting on it for the last seventeen miles.

Some days we move a bit closer to an authentic relationship. The highway we drive on is about three miles from Mexico and runs parallel to the border. One Tuesday afternoon, about ten miles away from school, we saw a Mexican family illegally jumping the fence into Arizona. Parents were handing babies over the barbed wire fence and running to a truck waiting nearby. An older man was half-hidden behind a tree, keeping a lookout for the light green Border Patrol vans that guard the border. Kay almost drove off the road watching the scene. I turned my head and looked out the side window because my eyes were filling with tears and I didn't want her to see me crying. I could tell she was upset, but we didn't say much. We didn't discuss the politics of illegal immigration, for I'm sure we would have disagreed completely. We commented on how sad the whole situation is, but mostly we were silent for the rest of the drive home.

Driving past the same row of telephone poles every day, the same scraggly desert trees, the same few houses reminds me that some things will always be the same. I know that when we cross the San Pedro River, we're about five minutes from work. I know that we will see at least three hawks every morning along our way. I know that when the wind is blowing, I have to maneuver the handle of the car window just right so it doesn't whistle so loud we can't hear each other talk. I also know that Kay won't change to see things my way, and I most likely won't change to see things her way. But spending an hour with her every day has taught me that even with the vast differences between us, women find ways to connect. It is not the small talk, the shared recipes, or the helpful teaching suggestions that have formed a bond between Kay and me over the years. Unspoken respect for each other's views, and the struggle to form a relationship in an awkward situation, has created a connection between us.

LOUISE STENECK ❧ Circled in Shadows

I sit here by the campfire, and you are circled there in the flickering shadows. The wind sighs in the grass, and the embers pop and drift, and somewhere in the far, far distance a coyote sings. Listen. I will tell you a story about women and all they know and all they share. I know the story like the curve of my husband's back and the smell of rain on dust. I know it like my mother's touch.

But no — I cannot tell it, for my words have a terrible power, and to use them would be an act of betrayal.

Friendship, like all forms of love, is based on mutual trust. In my lifetime, I have earned but a handful of true friends, women from whom I have no secrets and who have, in turn, shown me their deepest selves, flawed as they may be. I can pin them upon the page, glorious wings spread wide, so you may see their beauty and take flight among the flowers of our friendship. If I choose, I can turn them over to show you their dark underbellies where the softest touch leaves a bruise. With my sharp pen, I can dissect the pulsing heart of kinship, touching the places where tears and laughter form, where all that we love and value and share sustains us.

I choose not to do this, for the story holds too many risks. I have no shame when exposing myself through my writing, stripping myself bare, fervently hoping the reader sees not me, but the essence of our shared humanity. But I dare not take the same liberties with my friends. How do I tell you of the friend who rocked me like a child in a time of terrible loneliness, offering up my need for comfort without exposing hers as well? How do I show you my grief for a friend I turned away without cruelly displaying her vulnerability? How even can I replay the contented clucking of my women friends as they lean over a cradled newborn, or their breathless chatter as they primp in front of the mirror, or the soft ramblings of our conversations as we do the dishes after a shared meal? It seems innocent enough, but would I ever hear those sounds again in the same way if they feared I hoarded them not just for myself, but to show the world? They have taken a terrifying leap of faith to befriend me, to trust me with their secret selves. Writing must remain one of the flaws my friends forgive me.

And so there is no campfire tale tonight.

Listen to the crickets in the sighing grass. Watch the shooting stars. Let your mind drift with the embers.

I will hold the love of my friends silently, for in truth, friendship is not art — it is life.

MAUREEN HELMS BLAKE ⅍ To Breathe on My Own

Dear Sharon,

You know me well enough, Sis, to know that I claim only a handful of friends. This probably stems from a lifetime of using the word *friend* sparingly, out of respect for all it entails. A moment in my senior year of high school gave critical definition to a budding sense of what it meant to me to both have and be a friend. I'd handed Mom a book I'd been given as a gift from a classmate, and she'd just read the inscription, something loving and lighthearted. Mom got very quiet, her eyes reflecting life passages I had yet to experience. "You know," she murmured, "friendship also means holding someone's head while she throws up and then cleaning up the mess." Her solemnity sobered me, and I filed away her observation for further reflection.

Remember the day I left Kentucky for South Dakota? Weeks of packing and cleaning had finally come to an end. Larry piloted a twenty-six-foot, sunshine yellow moving van, towing a blue Toyota pickup. I drove the beige Toyota van, filled with three kids and a great-aunt. Two households overflowed the three vehicles. You and Jim and the kids were there to see us off. A photograph I snapped out the car window as we pulled away captures the sadness on your face. But only my heart recorded the ripping that reverberated inside the van, unheard by anyone but me.

For the first few hours on the road, I focused on controlling the tears enough to drive safely. Then the inner pep talks started. "C'mon, Maureen, get a grip. Of course you'll miss your sister, but it's not like you're moving to a brand-new area. Lots of Larry's family is waiting for you there."

Well, Sharon, that rationale got me across the plains and into my new home, but that's all. Only days after our arrival, I sat upstairs in my still unfamiliar bedroom, face wet with the loneliness and desperation I'd been able to hide for a week behind the busyness of unpacking. But that morning the fragile façade crumbled, and there stood The Question, demanding an answer: how could I survive without you?

Being sisters was an effect caused by our parents, but we chose to be not only friends, but also close neighbors — first in Kentucky, then in Nevada, and then again in Kentucky. We both found ourselves developing and defining our roles in ways society considered nontraditional: living on less money, having our babies at home, feeding them from our bodies, schooling them at home, making every possible effort to have our marriages last a lifetime. For support, we chose to relocate near each other. And you may not know it, but that physical closeness we shared has probably been the key to my survival in traveling these different paths. I had you, someone outside my nuclear family yet still inside my heart, to go to with complaints and frustrations and come away from with support and encouragement.

For ten years, we were together. Threads of shared daily experiences and cords of common values wove our lives double strength. When world weights crashed in on me — a car accident killed two family members, substance abuse ensnared others, repressed memories of childhood incest broke through, severe depression paralyzed — when these emotional meteors hit, resilience, born of our togetherness, saved me.

But now I sit alone, a thousand miles from you. Much careful thought and prayer precipitated this move. So a part of me — at the moment, a very remote part — knows that I am right where I need to be. But my stomach knots. I feel as though I have been disconnected from my life-support system. I'm not sure I can breathe on my own.

We talk on the phone, cry together long distance. Fat envelopes stuffed with a dozen handwritten pages fly back and forth between us. An inner balance has been developing these past ten years, and now that the guy wires of our physical friendship have been cut, I surprise myself by remaining upright. As I let it, my new hometown begins to nourish me. The window where I often write frames Spearfish Peak and Crow Peak. Never having lived where I could see such sights from inside my house, I look out at them and see past the problem of the moment. Sweet healing inches through me.

This summer I realize I've made my peace with living here, away from you. As I drive across the prairie toward Spearfish one day, on my way home from a trip, it occurs to me that I am truly home. Something in me is finally settled, grounded, here in the Black Hills.

I still miss our next-door-neighborness, but I refuse to whine anymore. We stay close through letters, e-mail messages, phone calls, and physical visits. It astonishes me that in five and a half years, we've seen each other only five times. But haven't we pushed the definition of *together*? Sometimes just knowing that I can pick up the phone and count on your thoughtful, openhearted sympathy vaporizes the need to do so.

So basically I'm OK with me out here in South Dakota and you back there in Kentucky. I'm glad I was willing to let go enough of one season of our friendship to be able to wrap my arms around this new phase. We've refused to let geographic miles be a barrier. Hearts travel on trails of tears and love and laughter, and these know no bounds or limits.

Love,
Maureen

JANE ELKINGTON WOHL ❧ **Below Zero — December**

For Cherry

Today the ski slope's shadows
fall long and blue at 10:00 A.M.
By noon, the sun will hang
inches above the southern rim
and shine straight down the lift
as my children, beyond my sight,
experiment with increasing speed.

In the car, on the way up the mountain,
my son says, "I wish you had seen me wreck."
But then, on that below-zero day,
tears frozen on his face,
amber goggles blurred,
he would not let me close.

And I think of Cherry,
whose children decide this year not to drive with her
to see Christmas lights.
So she goes alone
through snow-packed, rutted streets
where white lights spell out MERRY CHRISTMAS
and stars send multicolored rays from rooftops.

In cold so deep the side windows never clear,
she drives into the tunnel of night
until at midnight at Wal-Mart
she buys two parakeets,
one blue, one pale green,
and a white steel cage.

In the parking lot, the steel sticks to her fingers,
birds huddle in the far corner of the cage,
too small, too tropical for below-zero December nights.
Each bird fits easily within her palm
as she places them beneath her coat.
Two heartbeats play a quick counterpoint to her own
as she drives home with fragile birds against her chest
and draws small warmth from pale soft feathers.

The habits of mothering are worn
like rutted streets within us.
We seek small creatures:
the infant who lies easily along one arm,
frozen tears to wipe away,
small birds' hearts against our own.

Deep blue shadows fill these well-known routes,
which we must learn again to travel for ourselves
as our children leave us with increasing speed.

VANESSA HASTINGS ❧ Cultivating the Iris, Dawn of Change

That spring day, I attributed my chaos to a seemingly failed love affair with a long-time friend and coworker. Through my confusion and anger, I could see only that I had reached a breaking point, that the walls of indifference I had built during the past few days were crumbling to reveal a weak and wounded woman.

I began to sob uncontrollably in the newsroom around the time my grandmother, sitting in a lone chair in the basement of her house two hundred miles away, placed a .38 against the roof of her mouth and pulled the trigger.

Later, the coroner would place Iris's death at around 3:00 P.M. — the time the clock displayed when I walked into my apartment and fell on my bed, praying for a few hours of deep sleep to compensate for recent endless nights of sleeplessness and eerie dreams.

I didn't know then that tragedy sometimes becomes the piece that completes the picture.

Iris

As a girl, Iris lived in Edgemont, a small railroad community, when it still thrived in the southwest corner of South Dakota. With sparkling eyes and deep dimples, she led the student body in cheers for the school's sports teams, the Moguls. As a young woman, she taught children in that same school, perhaps never noticing her eldest daughter, Veleare, standing on tiptoe to catch a proud glimpse of her from outside the window at recess.

Not long after that, Iris moved to Arizona with an alcoholic husband to raise Veleare and two other children. She divorced, worked to pay the bills, married again, and returned to Edgemont in 1990 to spend her "golden years" with Harold, her second husband.

I often passed through what's now a ghost town on trips to the ranch of my father's mother, thirty miles to the south. Sometimes I forced myself to make the turn after empty storefronts and drive the few short blocks to Iris's home.

She was a kind, quiet woman, whose low, sultry voice belied her mousiness. Most who knew her loved her. But I did not know her, not enough to give what grandmothers deserve.

Each time I stepped out of the car, I dreaded going in, not because of the woman, but because of not knowing. We forced conversations as her husband sat in the background, as they both smoked slow, brown cigarettes. Their still shadows seemed to have left permanent marks in the hardwood floors, and discord hung in the corners like faint fog.

Iris and I tried to love each other in the half-hours we shared no more than two times a year. More often than not, I passed this woman and Edgemont and instead sped down the highway toward the grandmother who hugs me like her own child.

Sorrow visits when I remember Iris telling me I was the only one of her grandchildren who wrote or came to see her.

I can still see how her will to live quietly faded as the silence of all the empty, run-down houses and streets grew louder every day.

Veleare

My mother and I were on the phone that evening when the police officer knocked on the door of her Colorado Springs apartment. Veleare put down the receiver, and I waited four hundred miles away in front of my computer screen at work, thinking of encouraging things to say about her search for a job.

She picked up the phone and said she had to go — her uncle had called the Colorado Springs police from Edgemont in an effort to find her, to tell her there was an emergency. I asked her to call me back after she knew more and waited. The phone finally rang.

"Mom's dead," she said, tears warping her voice. "It was probably my letter that killed her," she mumbled as I began to cry.

"No," I said, sensing the unbearable burden of her regret from hundreds of miles away. "No, it wasn't. I'm going home to get ready to drive over there. Call me when you hear something new."

"OK."

"Mom?"

"What?"

"I love you," I said.

"I love you, too." Click.

At home the message machine blinked insistently.

"Mom shot herself. I guess it was my letter after all," Veleare's oddly calm voice echoed.

The next day, driving like mad toward the east to beat a storm raging its way behind me, I hoped also to outrun the postal service.

Veleare had read the letter to me the weekend before. I encouraged her to send what seemed like an angry — but not brutal — cry for help to her mother.

"You need her support, Mom. It's OK to ask for what you need," I said, believing that for the first time in almost fifty years, this letter would open a line of communication between the two women.

I remembered watching my father trying to keep his arms around my mother as she leaned over piles of paperwork, the way she stiffened at his touch, physically unable to return his affection. Even then, I — an only child who had the open love of the women in my father's family — wondered what had happened to her.

After they divorced, Veleare moved to Colorado, where she tried to take her life. A junior in college then, I came to believe that my increased phone calls would help save my lonely mother.

We became friends and learned to share everything. She pushed me to succeed in winning the attention of the editor of the newspaper where I work. When downsizing eliminated her job at a publishing company, I called repeatedly, trying to shove the image of her still form and an empty bottle of pills from my mind. She admitted to depression but denied the will to die.

And that was why I thought a chance still existed for her to enjoy the same kind of closeness with her own mother and why I encouraged her to mail the letter.

Crossing the state line into South Dakota, I prayed that Iris had never received it and that Veleare and I could cling to each other with diminished guilt.

At the Crossroads
My aunt Bobbie had something to tell me as we lingered in the house where Iris died, the house my mother and I entered with trepidation. Bobbie's eyes widened as she stood in the middle of the living room, and as they drifted from me to a desk near the window, I suddenly saw it: the address in Veleare's perfect handwriting, the crisp white envelope standing stiffly in front of other correspondence, the neatly slit opening.

Though we remain strangers, Bobbie and I moved like choreographed dancers at that moment, dropping delicately but quickly into our places. Her petite body managed to hide my outstretched arm as I sidled up against the desk. The letter whispered as I slid it into my coat pocket, and she took that as her cue to move away. Veleare noticed nothing.

That moment and her lack of questions told me all I needed to know about Bobbie. Dread soon overtook my gratitude; the letter weighed lightly on my person but tugged insistently at me.

That night my mother and I lay facing each other beneath old orange bedspreads in the darkness of our antiquated room, one of a dozen the town's old hotel housed. We talked about her family and past, the twilight zone that Edgemont had become, the local cops' ineptitude, and Iris and her final wishes.

"I just wonder if she got the letter," she said.

Silence stretched invisibly from my bed to hers. She deserved to know.

"I have the letter," I said.

I told her that Bobbie had spotted it and helped me steal it, and that it appeared that only Iris had read it.

The lamp from outside the room cast a silver outline on Veleare's thin shoulder and hip, and she looked frail. Later she told me she cried in the mornings, but I would not see her grief throughout the rest of our surreal trip — not during a secret and private viewing of Iris before cremation, not when we parted ways, not even at that terrible moment.

My mother used to sit on the edge of my bed each time a migraine put me there, trailing her cool fingertips across my sweaty forehead, nose, and cheeks until I fell into a sleep that would chase the throbbing away. That night I wanted her to spread her long, gray-streaked hair across my lap so that I could attempt to work the same magic, wiping away the mask that concealed her hurt. But I was paralyzed, afraid of failing her.

"Please destroy it tomorrow," she said steadily.

"I will."

"I'll never put you through this again."

As her pain gouged me, relief soothed the wound, and I had never felt such freedom. I wanted to weep, but I could not. My vulnerable mother needed a rock to grasp.

Erosion

We said good-bye to Iris and heard our lives calling us back. Veleare struggled to contain her panic over her unemployment, and the wreckage of my own life lay in wait. But we decided to drive to the ranch to share dinner with my dad's mother before turning our backs on Edgemont.

Exhaustion wrapped around me as I navigated the familiar gravel road that led to the countryside. My mother followed me in her car, so she did not see what I could no longer hold back.

Marcelene

My only remaining grandmother greeted us at the door of the old ranch house with firm, warm hugs that softened Veleare, and then she hobbled toward the kitchen to check on her chili.

At seventy-four, Marcelene is the toughest woman I know, making weekly two-hour drives to Rapid City for supplies despite two hip-replacement surgeries and bone spurs along her spine.

Although she no longer cries at the loss of a lamb, she would do anything for anyone who hurts or needs. The respect that shines in the eyes of the many people who know her humbles and inspires me. "She's a great lady," they always say.

"Have a seat," she said, smiling sincerely at the woman who divorced her son. We talked plainly about Iris's life and death. We relished Marcelene's chili and some of her pie, and then I walked my mother to her car, uneasy and unwilling to see her go.

As I stood next to the driver's side of her silver Buick, she looked up from behind the steering wheel, her eyes dry behind the thick lenses of her glasses. "Thank you for being there for me," she said, and I could see the shadows of Iris's dimples on her cheeks.

"I wouldn't have it any other way."

My worry faded with the taillights of her car. I knew this changed woman had the strength to face her tremendous grief and she would come out all right. I went back inside, ready and willing to let Marcelene mother me.

That night she gave me the lighter she had used when she drove truck during the war and made me try on a flared spaghetti-strap dress she had worn to the dance halls. We talked about husbands and boyfriends. We made tangible our bond by encasing it in words, and my heart began to heal.

"You are who you are," she said when I revealed my recent inability to talk to "friends" who complained I was too emotional, when I told her how much energy I expended trying not to feel, about the resentment that threatened to blow me apart when people failed to read my mind.

Crossroads Revisited
Sleep eluded me again that night as I stared out at the stars through a huge picture window. In the absence of confusing city lights, everything became clear.

The next day, I would meet Marcelene's bright blue gaze and promise my return. I would get in my car and drive away from Iris's choice, from the brink from which my mother veered, and toward myself.

DORIS BIRCHAM ❧ The Waiting

Rags of snowflakes settle against the window.
My friend and I look out across the field
where his cows heavy with calves
stand backed against the wind.
I hope, he says, *my bale stack*
hangs out 'til spring.

The handles of our cups bruise our fingers,
our thoughts white whispers
we move toward the room where his wife,
drowsy from morphine syrup,
lies curled between the sheets.

I've memorized this room:
the log cabin quilt she stitched,
this year's school pictures of her children,
her night table piled with dressings
and syringes I have brought, today
a fresh bouquet of crocuses
beside her bed.

Through the glass we look past snowflakes.
The buds on your tree are getting fuller.
She turns, we hold each other with our eyes.
Maybe, she says, *once I make it*
past this snow, I'll get to watch
the baby calves and see the leaves
get green again.

CINDY BELLINGER ❧ To Smooth a Mountain

Working my way through a crowded hardware store, I noticed a woman fingering a cabinet in the kitchen department. Something about her — the way she stood, the way her hair fell — made me pause. I couldn't place her and continued on.

In the gardening aisle, I passed her again, just as a grimace crossed her face. A twist of muscle under her high cheekbone sent ancient sparks through me. It was Carol, the woman who had once stood on the sidelines while I tried to tame a wild horse. The woman I had once considered a friend.

I could easily have stepped forward. Enough time had passed. We would have chatted, and I know she would have said, "Come on over, and we'll go riding." I stood in the aisle and imagined trailering the horses into the high country and riding side by side, talking of everything like we used to. Then I turned away.

Days and months went by, but thoughts of Carol remained. Twelve years had passed since I'd last seen her. We'd met when I interviewed her for the local paper while she was shoeing horses. The string of horses she trained needed exercising. "Come on over and go riding someday," she said after hearing I'd grown up with horses but hadn't been around them in years.

I live on the other side of the valley now, a mountain range between us. To say our lives went separate ways is kind. We split down the middle, ripping a friendship to shreds. I thought we were through. So why this pulsing insistence to think about her? One night, while warm water runs over my wrists as I do dishes, I let myself drift back and begin to understand. The pain is still tender. But instead of searing anger, I find a new feeling. I realize I want an apology. I turned away in the store because I was afraid of not getting it.

In the beginning, training Sadie, the wild high plains mustang, was easy. At the adoption center, the blue roan eyed me no matter where I walked. My first horse fresh off the range, she was easy because her curiosity pushed her forward. Smitten with this new exchange, we took each step in the gentling process eagerly, making up after mishaps. Three months after the adoption, I mounted Sadie; Carol was ponying her off Taco. That evening, when we put the horses away, Carol and I hugged and hugged. I can still hear her praise: "You've done a real good job with that horse of yours."

Carol was my guide, staying on the sidelines through the steps of the enormous project, buoying me on the rough days — before her own rough days began. Her marriage broke up, her kids ran wild, she took a lover. Many days her face turned dark and fierce; her mood swings frightened me.

While replaying the days — the day she didn't speak, the day she was too busy to ride — I saw a change. After all this time, my view had widened. I'd always said the demise of our friendship was her fault. But no longer could I say Carol turned on me. I had to face my own contribution: I also had something to apologize for.

When Sadie began refusing to move unless she followed another horse, I asked Carol for help. Not completely understanding how stranded I was — literally on a horse that wouldn't move — Carol announced, "You're on your own now."

Through ensuing days, the tension rose. Through the years, I told and retold the same story: how the day her son showed up drunk at school, the day she kicked her husband out, she also told me, "Take your horse and get off my land."

In each retelling, I failed to say what I didn't yet know: that our needs were clashing. She needed to be free, and I needed her too much.

I found a new trainer who easily brought me and Sadie together. I moved Sadie to another ranch, began working cattle, and pushed Carol into the past. Yet I often found her memory close, important and unforgotten. Now, not only do I want an apology, I know I need to give one. I'm sorry for needing her so much when she couldn't have anyone else pulling at her.

As I go about my chores, I can feel myself moving to give Carol a call. Maybe I'll drop by someday and try smoothing the mountain between us. Maybe we'll go riding.

A. ROSE HILL ❧ Barefooting Summer

We barefooted summer, Sister and me,
shed our shoes at the schoolhouse door,
scrambled up the willow limb,
dangled our feet in spring-cold water,
chased the cows to their evening milking.

We played house, Sister and me,
under the hedge, osage orange,
pulled thorns from our toughened toes,
punctured our soles with rusty nails,
watched grimy skin heal layer by layer.

We gathered eggs, Sister and me,
forgot the muck when the pullets cackled,
slipped in the rain through barnyard ooze,
screamed when a blue racer streaked our feet.

Grandmothers now, Sister and me,
we still kick off our shoes at the kitchen door.
When the last call comes, I know for sure
we'll leave our shoes at heaven's gates.

SUSAN AUSTIN and LAURIE KUTCHINS
The Field Road

Laurie: A half-mile field road joins our two places. Days want to be simple, without phones, without power, up here. Nights want to be black oceans of starlight lapped by the monthly moon. Nights and days, the road across the wide curvature of this ridge is the one line between us, and we walk, bicycle, drive, or ski it when we have something to share. Baby lettuce fresh picked from Greg and Sue's garden, planted in the used-up tractor tire. Thimbleberries my son and I gathered and whisked into muffins during the Sunday storms. A book, a topographic map. The earth here is patterned with our dogs' paw prints, with the wheelruts and bootsoles of our comings and goings.

In high summer, the road is two strips of deeper-than-ankle dust across 160 acres of rolling barley. Flash rains slicken it so that we know how quickly the hillrise becomes an edgewise slide into the grain furrows, and wind churns it back to dust faster than the Laundromat in town can dry our sheets and towels. In winter the road is whatever a pair of skis makes it across the undulant silence of the white slopes. Over and over, snow and rain and wind erase this road between us.

Susan: The half-mile road between us can be short or long, mudruts or snowdrifts, dust deep as our bootlaces by the dry end of summer. The polka dot pockmarks left by a light rain remain for days in that trail of dust, my boot prints a measure of my hunger for kinship, but just as often the wind stirs things up, teases anvil clouds into lightning and thunder, a river of rain making the road a slippery muck, flash floods spawned in the tire ruts.

The road has no name, no sign to announce it. First-time visitors have to make notes and pay attention to find their way in. We like the road unruly. We prefer it simple and secretive, that it sleep long winters under the unplowed snows. More intimate than next-door neighbors who share a driveway, a lilac hedge, or a fence, we have forged our friendship out of its drifts, its dust and mud and shadows.

When the county road thaws out, we cross the fields in mud. We wake to the cold wind out of the valley, carrying with it the smell of dirt: earthy, pungent, succulent, a good smell after a long sterile winter. The thin green necks of spring beauty push their way through drifts on the county road. But the field road and the fields are still thawing out. The unshaved face of winter begins to show: last year's brown barley stubble zippering across hilltops and south slopes. Islands of bare ground emerge, atolls in a wet white sea, the volcanic soil now satiated pitch-black sucking mud.

The first time we spoke, we stood on the road getting acquainted. Late August morning, I had stepped onto the porch and latched the door tightly, having gathered the last of my things from the homestead's small frame house I turned into a study in summer. The windmill creaked on its old footings. I whispered thanks to it, and I thanked Miles and Karl, the Hollingshead brothers who had built over decades each of these homestead structures, and who still keep after the place, although they are buried in the family plot back in Missouri.

I thanked the pair of Douglas firs I'd taken to calling Miles and Karl for their brushstrokes of shade outside the south window on hot July afternoons, the only two trees on the whole shadeless ridge. Beyond them, the barley rippled green-gold and healthy in the breeze, and my dog raced across the grown-over furrows, yipping after low-flapping blackbirds.

From the porch, I saw the glint of her hair, a Pacific color, above the tall grass near the low-slung cabin where Greg had lived by himself for as long as I could remember. She was carrying water from a disheveled white car while a pup ran a gleeful trail around her in the scratchgrass. Her hair was like the silk of the milkweed when it breaks open at the end of summer, so sun-bleached it was white.

My bootprints met hers in the road dust. Her red puppy bounced back and forth between us, bumping against our shins, stirring the road powder into clouds around our ankles. She was soft-spoken, shy. She'd wintered here, her first amid such silence, such unbroken white space. I understood. We hardly shared two sentences.

The summer of the Yellowstone fires, I was sick with mono and the smell of smoke. I had fallen in love and then fallen asleep. Moments faded by the hour, but what I remember are smoke plumes big as mountain peaks from the Huck blaze, the sun shrunk to the glow of a kerosene lantern in a window in the fog, and Laurie making her way along the field road fenced only by barley stalks. Her hair was the red of some lichen I've seen on rhyolite boulders down in Bull Elk Creek. She said she was a poet. How long had it been since I'd made a word? I had just spent my first winter in the homestead cabin. I kept tripping over "snow" while we shooed away deer flies and licked dust from our lips, the sun beating down, as if I had been the only one ever to overwinter, my awe that great, but she listened anyway, and nodded, because she knew all about awe and weather. I must have talked on, the way shyness sometimes does, about snow and whiteness and quiet and how many pans of snow it takes to make enough water, the two of us standing at the edge of the field road among whispering dry grass, the dogs running circles around our feet.

The dogs. They were a scrappy bunch, one from a mother notorious for chasing snowflakes, the other rescued from a pack of marauding town dogs in Tetonia. My Betsy was a Chesapeake Bay retriever, and so I had two things to remind me of the sea that first summer: the dog and the barley stirred up by the wind. Betsy was big and pawlike, but Laurie's Ellie, a Blue Heeler, was fast. The two dogs ran tight circles and figure eights, goading each other into a chase, tousling dust and trampling the young barley stalks. It was like giving up a child to first love, the way Betsy trotted off down the field road in the morning, after her breakfast, toward Ellie's cabin.

The dogs brought us together years before we realized it was the road and the ridgetop in all its weather, before we began to share meals, recipes, books, walks, and writing. All that summer, they were like a tight braid a girl refuses to wash out of her hair. They romped, roamed, ate, peed, slurped, and napped in the aspen shade around our cabin. Or they'd trot the field road to wrestle around the homestead cabins where Sue and Greg lived. There was something downright erotic in the way they twisted and flopped against each other and tongued each other's mouths. Their boundless frolics made me understand in a whole new way the expression "puppy love." Often at twilight one or the other of us would go on roundup to claim her missing dog. These were our first exchanges, simple and radiant, the dusklight spreading shadows across the fields, the dogs spinning a gauze of summer dust around us, our maternal marveling over them, our first real bond.

My partner, Greg, made Betsy a sled out of a yellow plastic toboggan and aluminum flashing. I made a harness out of webbing cut off a retired backpack and fleece from an old pair of mukluks. That first winter, often as not, Greg ended up lashing it, and the laundry or groceries loaded on it, to his backpack and skiing, sled and all, home. Betsy was boundless with energy and not too smart about the knife-edge drifts. She simply forgot the sled was following behind when she loped down a steep slope of snow and chokecherry brush after grouse.

I tried to teach the dog not to sleep where I dug snow. And then I gave in, because the drift where I shoveled made a natural shelter for her. She brought me home out of blizzards, her black nose smelling the ground four feet below the snow. And when the world became maddeningly white, the same white that drove prairie women crazy, that brown dog would sit there in that patch of snow I used for making water, the only thing not white as far as my eyes could see.

Greg wasn't home that first day I drove up Pinochle Road, the clack of yellow aspen leaves muffling the sound of the gravel road. The old Scout bucked up the last hill to the top of the ridge, and there was the homestead, gray logs and splinter chink, dwarfed by the mountains and snow coming on, the galvanized windmill blades creaking in the wind. The barley fields were barren, cyclones of dirt in the fields. The cabin was planted low in the center of all that ground, cold, its shoulders turned in a little to brace itself against the coming winter. I looked in the window. A table and two chairs. Jars of dried beans on a rough pine shelf. A suit quilt on the bed. A simple pine wardrobe. A postcard from Hawaii on the drop-leaf table under one small sash window. A lineage of backpacks hung on the walls. A pair of sandals set square at the foot of the bed. There was no sign of a woman.

Unlike me, Sue is a "year-rounder," living with Greg on the ridgetop. From Thanksgiving to May, they ski the three miles back and forth, up and down, from truck to home and back. Their ski tracks make another road most people can't fathom: it begins at the graded slope on the county road just beyond the Reeces' barns, where the snowplow stops to turn around, and it ends three miles up the white dugway on the windswept bench, beside the smooth pine-limb door handle of their log cabin. They ski their laundry, groceries, and trash back and forth in packs on their backs. They keep an impressive woodpile and a year's supply of oil stored for the lamps. In the two-room cabin, they keep their stove going day and night, and on the top they melt snow heaped in tin basins. This is a sound they probably grow so used to it becomes, literally, their white noise: the continuous hiss of snow melting against the dry wood heat.

They are deeply partnered, to spend their winters in such solitude, in such close quarters. Their marriage is made of so much weather — long bitter nights that begin in the afternoon, the incessant push of wind and snow against the cabin's small windows, the daily sweep of dust and crumbs and snow tracked inside on the soles of ski boots, hurled back out over the simple threshold. To emerge after the winter months and still look lovingly after the other is no small feat. And they do. They emerge intact, deepened, both singularly and as a pair.

When I return in May or June, winter is often still receding from their bodies like the bowl of snow high up on Rammell Mountain. Sometimes when I first see them, I can hear the snow still whispering about their ears. Like perennials slowly unfurling from dark frozen earth to spongy grass and abundant sunlight, their spines are still straightening from the downhill windward tuck of the three-mile ski from cabin to truck. I can hear the winter I've missed in Greg's voice as he and my husband share a beer at our table. I look into Sue's eyes as I serve her mint tea by lamplight, and I glimpse remote, shadowy patches where the snow isn't all gone.

There are things he had to teach me. First, how to bow my head so the glare of my headlamp did not blind him; how a storm can bend you in circles, like a dog chasing its tail; how to stand a log on end and aim the ax blade between buried knots; how a piece of cardboard set over the outhouse hole keeps frost from forming on the seat. And before all that — how to ski.

How many words do the Eskimos have for snow? They make poetry of it. We add to that edible words, as if we could subsist on it: champagne, sugar, mashed potatoes, and corn.

He had to teach me how to make water because the leathers on the old windmill wore out long ago. Maybe ten times a day, we packed snow into four metal pans and then set them on the wood stove to melt. There is a recipe of sorts. Add a little water, or the snow burns. If the weather comes out of the north across the Yellowstone Plateau, the snow falls light as feathers; no good for making water. The temperature bitter cold. January and February are the hardest months; the snow made more of air than water. It's the wet stuff, the rotten snow, that's easy. It is full of water already. During January thaw and spring melt, we have enough water to waste.

I am seasonal only. As a teacher, my migrations to and from my family's place on this ridgetop follow the school year. I'm like the sandhill cranes that return each spring. Reluctantly, I leave for milder winters in late August, as the school calendar beckons, around the time when the barley is two weeks from harvest and the first flicker of yellow in the aspens announces another summer's gone. That dawn I'm not awakened by the cranes' thin-throated cries, that certain dusk I no longer see them flapping low across the fields to bed down among the creeks, I know it's time.

All school year, I live with the ache of distance, the twist of not being able to resolve love of place with love of what I do for a living. I've slipped gradually, unwittingly, into this paradox, and my challenge has been to embrace it as my life rather than to solve or resolve it. I see that poetry is the rutted road that led me away in the first place, and yet, time and again, it is my tongue, my words, my voice that anchor and pull me back. How many times have I fallen asleep elsewhere and wakened with the blood language of this place on my tongue: aspen, sagebrush, chinook, elk, outcrop, snow?

Silence is only sounds muffled by the pop and hiss of the wood stove. One day while I was melting snow, a cow moose and her calf dropped down off the four-foot drift to the shoveled path. They must have stood there on the frozen ground for a minute, feeling their legs solid beneath them. A cow moose stands nearly as tall as the old cabin. When I opened the pine door and stepped outside into the cold, I scared them into the deep snow. The cow looked back at me, steam puffing from that unimaginable nose, then she bounded away, post-hole after post-hole. To her, I did not look like I was made for this country, standing outside in my long johns and T-shirt. I think she took bets whether I would make it a winter.

In winter I miss the snow like a lover. I miss my family's cabin, its smell of old sunlight in its logs, its strong masculine arms, the family tracks of three generations. I admire Sue and Greg, how intimately they live with winter, quietly going about their business inside its cold skull for so many months. I admire, and at times envy, their tenacity, their choice. To live that closely and succinctly with your partner. To live that alertly within a portion of the earth and sky, and in humble accordance with elemental rhythms. But could I ever succumb to winter on their scale?

The snow is always tidying itself up. And I'm left to find my way back to words each new season, a kind of practice, an oiling of old hinges. I write words in the snow that a stranger might read before the wind catches me talking to the sky and erases the slate. It's just air, really — words. Too long left to myself, words fall apart from their meaning.

The wind is chattering outside my window. I see her walk over the crest of the hill, the sun a globe of fire descending behind her. From here, a half mile away, she still looks pregnant, her baby bundled so close. They are drinking wind and alpine light, shadows. I hear her talking softly to him. The wind brings their voices to me.

One summer, as fast as they spiraled into love, our two dogs butt heads and turn into bitter rivals. Irreconcilable differences. They've both come of age. Both dogs assert an alpha energy; neither will back down and accept second fiddle. Our summers are turned topsy-turvy — how to go about friendship and keep these two dogs from each other's throats?

Their cabin is warm and smells of *tamari*, fresh ginger, roasted sesame and garlic on this day of storms. Without dusklight in July, the dark comes early, and when we arrive, the kerosene lamps are already burning. Sue has covered her round garden under a plastic tarp to help it survive another hard frost. The dogs make their unfriendly overtures, then curl into separate protected nooks against the cabin. My husband is gone. Eager for adult company, I've trudged the half-mile road with my two-year-old son bundled on my back. He curls up on Greg and Sue's bed with a stuffed bear and a bottle of milk.

We sit down to an Asian feast. The wicks in the oil lamps burn steady and slow. Two tin basins of hot water wait on the cookstove for the dirty plates. My eyes roam across the shelf of grain jars, coarse teas, and books, taller than my child, stacked on the foldout desk. The meal is elegant, delicious, and artfully simple. As I dip one more *nori* into the *wasabi* and *tamari* sauce and float it into my mouth, I think of the complexity that lives within such simplicity. I marvel at the time she must have put into tracking down these ingredients (not to be found on the "exotic foods" shelf of the valley's grocery) and into preparing this labor-intensive meal: hand-chopping every sliver of carrot, avocado, gingerroot, zucchini; cooking the rice until soft, chewy, and moist; rolling the rice and vegetables around the seaweed papers into tight, colorful rolls; cooking the vermicelli so that it's silky, not clumped and sticky like mine would be.

For dessert we drink hot green tea and eat fresh berries. My black rubber boots are mud-caked with the field road beside their door. The meal, the snug cabin shadows in the glow of lamps, the company, the hot tea fill me with a warmth and drowsiness. I don't relish the thought of pulling the boots back on, bundling my sleepy child on my back for the cold walk home across the slippery darkness.

Over time, as our friendship's taken root atop this dry ridge, I've come to think of Sue as a keeper of the homestead, the field road, the whole ridgetop world from the Bull Elk to the Swanner drainages, a gem patch of hundred-mile views in most directions. She is a woman presence who watches over it, goes on breathing into it for much of the year when I am gone. Over time she and I have patchworked our friendship out of summers and winters, proximity and distance, road dust and snowdrifts, mud and change. Love brought her inland from the ocean and up here in the first place, and love brought more love, as it's prone to do. But love's also brought change and heartache, as it's prone to do.

The nineties have been a ruthless decade on this place. We've watched the change creep closer, from south to north, from valley floor to ridgetop, in annual increments. I used to blame the creeping storms of change on the valley's proximity to Jackson Hole and Yellowstone National Park, but now I know it's not that simple. This place is just one small dot on the contemporary map of Western conquests. What's happening here is what's happening all up and down the Rocky Mountain spine, anywhere you have mountains in your retina, powder snow under your feet, blue skies, disposable income, a lean ranching economy, and a Bigfoot called resortism.

Together, often walking side by side, Sue and I, along with our husbands, have learned how to hold our breath through the summers. We begin the supernatural inhalation each spring, as the snow melts, as the white hills give way to brown mud, which dries and gives way to the trucks and plows and the new crop of barley, a squiggle of newborn green by the summer solstice. The gravel road opens, dries, we hear the slur of stones each time a vehicle passes, and we brace ourselves for the Landcruisers and Outbacks we don't recognize turning onto the unmarked field road. The flash of those new vehicles, the sound of a strange engine idling, the doors opening and slamming shut fill our mouths with a dryness no meltwater slacks. "Nope, nothing up here for sale," we say, shrugging and turning away even when we know the dirt we're standing on is for sale. "There's lots down in the valley. No access up here anyway in the winters, and winters up here are a damn lot longer than summers."

Summer up here used to be almost as solitary as winter, but it's become the growing season not only for crops and tourists but also for land seekers. Folks who, just like us, want to love a patch of dirt and call it their own; earth lovers who, just like us, want to swallow an enormous sunset each night, want to watch moose chew aspen leaves outside their windows, want good neighbors at some distance. But unlike us, they also want access all year, electric power, ease, convenience. They won't love the field road rough and simple in its dust and hibernations. They want asphalt, a subdivision, a basketball court. Their dreams-come-true turn our heartache up a notch until it's at an unbearable pitch.

But summers always end. Sue and I say good-bye. The aspen leaves turn and fall. The first snow blows in from the west. The road closes. Greg and Sue bend their backs to another winter. We can breathe out and easy again, but for how much longer? Trying to fend off year-round access and electricity on this ridgetop, we've had to accept we're no longer remote. We've had to admit we are powerless to keep it powerless.

I am a vigilante, snapping skinny sticks over my knee, making kindling of real estate signs. I have silence in my mouth, snow melting from the corners of my eyes, wind carried in the canals of my ears. I am only the sow bear protecting her cub; the killdeer faking a damaged wing. I chase hungry coyotes off the road and brush mountain lion tracks from the dusty trail. I kick berry scat into the barrow pit. Autumn, I yell for the deer and elk to hide. I want nothing to change. Or is it that I want everything to change? I talk to a windmill. I stand under its creaking metal and ask what the old boys would have done. Why Karl refused electricity when the rural cooperative came to town. Do the carrots I grow in the tractor tire taste as sweet as Miles's? The last brother died the year I was born. They teach me that white is not the absence of color and silence is not loneliness. They hold us up winters, bundle us in their cabin, whisper through the windows, leave drifts of snow across pillows. What was it that brought the windmill down on the day the surveyors arrived to section lots out of the old homestead? While they hammered skinny sticks into the brown soil, the windmill just spun on its base and walked away. Tall tale, some say. Coincidence. I believe the brothers had a hand in that microburst of telling wind.

Strange how it could make a difference to know that a place is cared for, watched over, attended and listened to, as if the place were a helpless thing in need of our care. But the place is harsh. The relationship of this place to *its* neighbors — wind, sky, weather, us — is ruthless. Does it matter to the place that Sue and I have loved it? Did it ever matter to the place that Miles and Karl loved it? They chose its harshness long before Sue or I ever laid eyes on their old windmill. Isn't our shared heartache our own reluctance to go with the drifts of change, our inability to roll forward into development and neighborliness, rather than ski backward into a roadless, millennial midnight?

Until the windmill fell, I believed Miles and Karl were the keepers: steadfast, invisible, ever present. But something happened that day the windmill vanished from our horizon view. "Go now; you must go on now," I whispered out to them all that summer, as if I were trying to shoo a pair of pesky bears away from the garbage before someone came near with a shotgun and a sense of entitlement. Was I crazy, telling those brothers to leave their home, believing I might spare those two old homestead ghosts the heartache of what would fall next in a place lacking well water, a windmill? And even if they listened, where else would they go?

Once the windmill went down and the land all across the ridge fluttered with fluorescent orange strips on wooden stakes, I understood something in a new way. Long ago we entered an apprenticeship, Miles and Karl, Sue and me. This is probably the gist of our kinship, although neither of us has ever spoken of it. I know she speaks to the grass, to the aspen trees, to the road ruts when there's not a human voice other than her man's in her ear for months. She knows I've trained myself to listen back, regardless of distance, attentive to their various voices. I know she bows down to the wild tracks in the buried road dust, brushes them away with her hands, whispers, *Don't be seen.* She knows I've studied the sky, over and over, how it pulls dusk over the Bull Elk drainage, so that I watch that passage of dusklight even thousands of miles away. We both know how the wind clicks across the emptiness where the windmill once shirred its constant song of home into the brothers' ears as they went about their daily chores. Like them before us, we are learning to hear winter coming long before it shakes its white body out over the bare and lovely hills. And to fully welcome it.

JEANNE ROGERS ᨒ Community of Stones

They spoke to me in a dream
these Women
with grief closing up their eyes.
And the Women's voices
became one
became Everywoman
so I wrote a poem:

> Prairie Winter, 1838
> She kneels
> Her swollen breasts a testimony
> of a journey too long,
> a winter too hard for growing
> babies, the work too much.
> She gently touches stone after stone
> after stone, the small mound of a scar
> on frozen earth, as her mind tells
> her she must go, her heart tethered
> to a newborn silence.

And Everywoman
became the woman in Miles City
who, after hearing the poem,
whispered through her tears
hugged me

and thrust a note in my hand:
    It's been thirty-three years
    but I was that Woman.
These Women
they speak.

MARJORIE SAISER ❧ My Old Aunts Play Canasta
in a Snowstorm

While there is time I must read the wrinkles
under each faded blue eye, related to my
father's blue eye, related to me. I must ride along
in the backseat; the aunt who can drive will

pick up each sister at her door, six in all, will keep the Pontiac
chugging in each driveway while one or the other
puts her overshoes on and steps out, pulling
the door shut with a click, the wind

lifting the brown fringe of her white cotton scarf
as she comes down the sidewalk, still pulling on her
new polyester Christmas-stocking mittens,
right hand, left hand. We have no business being
out in such a storm, she says, no business at all.

But the wind takes her laughing cracking voice
and lifts it and she sinks into the backseat or
the frontseat. On to the next house, the next
sidewalk, the heater blowing to beat the band.
Get in, old girl, before you freeze us all.

It is a good canasta day, the deuces wild
even as they were in childhood, the wind
blowing through the empty apple trees, through
the shadows of bumper crops. The cards line up

under the long finger bones; eights and nines and aces
straggle and fall into place: long-time habits or well-
behaved children. My aunts
shuffle and meld, the discard pile frozen,
the wind a red trey to be remarked upon, remembered,

and appreciated, because, as one or the other says,
we are getting up there in years; we'll
have to quit sometime. But today,
today,
deal, sister, deal.

Contributors
Acknowledgments
Credits

Contributors

DARCY ACORD *(page 223)* writes and lives with her husband, three daughters, dogs, and horses near Ucross, Wyoming.

LUCY ADKINS *(page 206)* was raised on Nebraska farms and taught junior high and high school English before settling in Lincoln.

ARA ANDERSON *(page 136)* was raised on a ranch near Elk Mountain, Wyoming, and is a Campbell County reference librarian.

PATRICIA ARCHIE *(page 134)* lives with her husband on their ranch on Horseshoe Creek near Glendo, Wyoming. She's a ranch wife and grandma.

SUSAN AUSTIN *(page 281)* lives in a house that overlooks the field road. She is pursuing an M.F.A. as a Michener Fellow at the University of Texas and also is a wildlife biologist.

CHARLOTTE M. BABCOCK *(pages 34, 111)* is the author of *Shot Down!*, a book about crime in early Casper, Wyoming. She is a past president of Wyoming Writers and is an Exemplary Alumnus of Casper College.

JULENE BAIR *(page 186)* grew up on the family sheep ranch and wheat farm near Goodland, Kansas. "I considered myself a tomboy and resented my brothers' comparative freedom." She now lives in Laramie, Wyoming.

JUNE FRANKLAND BAKER *(page 6)* grew up in New York and moved to Colorado and Kentucky before settling in eastern Washington, where she has lived for more than thirty years.

MAY H. BAUGHMAN *(page 28)* was born in the Nebraska Sandhills and lived on farms in northeastern Colorado before retiring amid mountains and farmland near Fort Morgan.

CINDY BELLINGER *(page 279),* of New Mexico, says she's "done it all — wrangled horses, taught ballet, worked as a waitress in a truck stop, modeled for artists, painted houses, tended gardens, taught school, and worked as a secretary." She is a freelance writer.

VIRGINIA BENNETT *(page 216)* has worked on Western ranches since 1971, alongside her husband, Pete. She has written two books, *Legacy of the Land* and *Canyon of the Forgotten.*

KAREN M. BERRY *(page 127)* is a "daughter, sister, mother, friend" who lives in Denver, Colorado.

HILARY BARTON BILLMAN *(page 265)* was born in England, grew up in St. Louis, and lives with her husband, Jon, in Wyoming.

DORIS BIRCHAM *(page 278)* has been partnered with, she says, "the same man, same ranch, same wind for over thirty years" in southwestern Saskatchewan.

MAUREEN HELMS BLAKE *(page 270),* of Spearfish, South Dakota, is a "freelance writer, alive woman, amateur actor, committed wife, full-time parent of three, and home school educator since 1982."

CAROL BOIES *(page 204),* born on a farm in Gregory County, South Dakota, "hightailed it out to Wyoming," where she met her husband. She worked with him on several ranches before returning to South Dakota, where they raise daughters, cattle, wheat, corn, and hogs.

EMILY BOIES *(page 219)* has called South Dakota her home for more than half of her life. Now focused on being a typical teenage girl, she plans to pursue a career in journalism or advertising.

LINDA BOYDEN *(page 137)* taught in western elementary schools for twenty-six years before moving to Maui, Hawaii. She draws on her Native American mixed-blood heritage as a writer and professional storyteller.

SHARON R. BRYANT *(page 96)* says, "This anthology project has broken a painful two-year writer's block following the rape and murder of my daughter. We have a story to share with humanity. It begins here."

B. J. BUCKLEY *(pages 100, 158),* of Lolo, Montana, has worked as a writer in Plains states schools for nearly twenty years. In 1999, she was selected for the *Poets and Writers* Montana/New York Writers' Exchange.

STEPHANIE PERSHING BUEHLER *(page 19)*, of Big Horn, Wyoming, says she plays in their vegetable gardens with her husband, daughter, and two dogs because they like the feel of dirt on their hands and paws.

EVA POTTS WELLS BURTON *(page 20)* grew up on her parents' homestead and raised six children on food she hunted, gardened, canned, and froze, while supplementing the family income by teaching.

LAURIE WAGNER BUYER *(page 119)* is a ranch wife and poet who lives with her husband, Mick, on the South Fork of the South Platte River near Fairplay, Colorado. She was the recipient of a 1999 Literature Artist Fellowship from the Colorado Council on the Arts.

MAUREEN CAIN *(page 267)* taught art in rural Arizona for ten years. She now lives in Tucson with her husband and two children. She enjoys yoga, hiking, and beautiful sunsets.

MAURA T. CALLAHAN *(page 217)* says, "The prairie calls to me and I have answered . . . Soon. My heart has resided smack dab in the middle of the West for as long as I can remember."

ELIZABETH CANFIELD *(page 191)* and her husband ranched, owned a farm equipment company, and raised three children near Sundance, Wyoming. She now writes a column for the *Sundance Times* and has published a book of poetry, *When the Heart Is Reached*.

CLEO CANTLON *(page 183)*, of Minot, North Dakota, and her husband, Ed, ranched from 1965 to 1999. A combine-operating, calf-delivering farm wife and former teacher, she is also a freelance journalist who loves theater, reading, writing, art, fishing, and travel.

DEB CARPENTER *(page 20)* teaches at Oglala Lakota College on the Pine Ridge Reservation in South Dakota and lives in rural northwestern Nebraska with her husband and two daughters. With Lyn DeNaeyer, she performs a program of original poems and songs based on women's journeys across the plains.

ANNE FANTACI CLEMENT *(page 123)* was born in New York, grew up in northern Virginia, and headed west when she left home. She spent nearly thirty years in rural Colorado before settling in Montana, where she has lots of room to ride her BMW.

GAYDELL COLLIER *(page 177)* lives with her husband, Roy, on a small ranch in Wyoming's Black Hills, where she runs a mail-order bookshop.

She writes by the creek, on a hilltop, or in the pines, nudged along by her dog, Penny.

SHELLY WHITMAN COLONY *(page 226)* is the author of *Landforms/ Lifeforms,* a permanent exhibit at the Museum of the Rockies in Bozeman, Montana. She lives with her husband in northwestern Oregon, gardening and writing about solo Western journeys in her van, Javelina.

RIAN CONNORS *(page 190)* was born in the North and currently lives in Edmonton, Alberta, where she is a freelance writer. More than anyone or anywhere else, she loves her sons, her mother, her sisters, and northern lands.

HEIDI R. COUSINS *(page 143)* says, "Self-sufficiency is the most important thing in my life." She cooked, hayed, and cleaned barns — "whatever had to be done" — on farms and ranches in the West, then drove a semi around eleven states before settling in Montana.

NANCY CURTIS *(page 115)* runs a book publishing company, High Plains Press, from the family ranch in Wyoming. She also teams up with Gaydell Collier and Linda Hasselstrom to compile books written by Western women.

LYN DENAEYER *(pages 192, 209)* grew up without siblings on an isolated Nebraska Sandhills ranch and writes, "I gave my best years to the locusts, but I'm finally walking toward the light." She insists that constructing one's own bio is "the most difficult writing assignment that exists."

SAUNDRA DEREMER *(page 52)* teaches, writes, travels, and gardens in Nebraska. She nurtures her students, herself, and her flowers, and often travels the path back to the old home place.

BETTY DOWNS *(page 53)* was raised on a wheat farm in North Dakota. Married for forty years to a construction mechanic, she is now widowed and lives in Black Hawk, South Dakota.

SISTER HILDEGARD DUBNICK, OSB *(page 228)* was born in 1961 near Chicago, where she could see the Big Dipper on a good stargazing night. She entered the Benedictine Abbey of St. Walburga, forty miles from Fort Collins, Colorado, in 1987.

CAROLYN DUFURRENA *(page 86)* writes about the desert in northwestern Nevada, where she lives with her husband, Tom, and their son

Sam. She came to Nevada as a geologist and now teaches in a one-room school seventy-five miles from the nearest town.

NORMA NELSON DUPPLER *(page 35)* won the 1997 Heritage Writing Contest at the North Dakota State Fair. She has worked as an emergency manager, coordinating Federal Emergency Management Agency (FEMA) programs through nine presidential disaster declarations, and enjoys exploring her family's ranch.

SHANNON DYER *(page 17)* came to the Nebraska Sandhills because of love for her husband. After eighteen years, the sand has sifted into her veins, and she has grown to love the hills, too.

SOPHIE DOMINIK ECHEVERRIA *(page 239)*, of Colorado, says, "All my politics is based in art and agriculture . . . the bedrock of complex civilization." Her large Basque sheep-ranching family is spread across the West.

LOUISE ENGELSTAD *(page 248)* was raised on the high plains and mountains of Montana and has been a librarian most of her professional life. Her passions are nature writing, outdoor adventures, yoga, and enjoying her wildlife habitat yard filled with native plants.

MARY PEACE FINLEY *(pages 43)*, of Manitou Springs, Colorado, says the same spirit that drew her great-grandmother to Colorado Territory drew her to northern Nicaragua and to kinship with Rosario.

MAUREEN TOLMAN FLANNERY *(page 263)* was raised in a ranch family but moved to Chicago. She returns to the West every summer so that her children can trail sheep and know some of the life she loved.

JEANNIE FOX *(page 50)*, of South Dakota, whose essay describes an encounter she had while working at a domestic violence shelter, believes that rural women face greater adversity in abusive relationships than urban women because of social and geographic isolation.

PATRICIA FROLANDER *(page 222)* was raised in the city but came to a fourth-generation ranch in Wyoming as a young wife and mother. Now, after more than thirty years of ranching, she feels more privileged than ever to work the land.

MARY GARRIGAN *(page 231)* is a South Dakota native who lives with her daughter and writes essays, columns, newspaper stories, magazine articles, and long letters to her three grown sons.

COLETTE "KOKO" KNUTSON GJERMUNDSON *(page 110)* grew up in western North Dakota and now lives there, in the Knife River country, with her husband, Casey. She writes for agricultural publications, covering the beef industry, history, and rodeo.

TENA COOK GOULD *(page 170)* lives in Chadron, Nebraska, where she works for Chadron State College, writes, collects family history, and takes photographs.

JANET E. GRAEBNER *(page 246)* moved with her husband to Conifer, Colorado, after pursuing a freelance writing career in southern California. She now writes fiction, essays, and book reviews.

DONNA GRAY *(page 156)* was born in Illinois but has lived most of her life in the West, first in the San Francisco Bay Area and for the past twenty-three years on a small ranch in the heart of Montana's beautiful Paradise Valley.

JENNIFER GREEN *(page 131)* lives on a ranch near Trinidad, Colorado, where she teaches school, raises horses, and writes children's novels.

LAURA HAWKINS GREVEL *(page 258)*, raised in Austin, Texas, homesteads with her husband, ranching and farming organically with draft horses as they aim for a self-sustaining life.

JENNIFER GRAF GRONEBERG *(page 136)*, a ranch wife and mother in Polson, Montana, gives thanks to Kathy Mosdal O'Brien for sending the quilt that inspired her writing.

MARY ALICE GUNDERSON *(page 181)* is a fellowship recipient from both the Wyoming Arts Council and the Wyoming Council for the Humanities. She is the author of the book *Devils Tower: Stories in Stone.* Her nonfiction, fiction, and essays appear in magazines and anthologies.

MARY HADLEY *(page 7)* grew up riding jumping horses, married a cowboy, and moved with him to Nevada, on to Oregon, and finally to Wyoming while raising their seven children.

VEE HAGEMAN *(page 166)* divides her time between Arizona and Wyoming after spending many years raising livestock and children on the family ranch.

CANDY HAMILTON *(page 77)* is an English instructor at Oglala Lakota College and has won national awards for her poetry and journalism. She has lived and worked on the Pine Ridge Reservation for many years. She worked in the American Indian Movement (AIM) with Anna Mae Pictou Aquash and Tina Manning Trudell, the women she writes about in her poem.

KATHY HANKS *(page 167)*, raised in New Jersey and New York, lives in Pendennis, Kansas, population 6 — "a census would uncover more ghosts than living people." With her husband, she runs a cow-calf operation and raises wheat and milo.

TWYLA HANSEN *(page 129)* was raised on a small Nebraska farm and has worked as a horticulturist and arboretum curator. Her books of poetry are *In Our Very Bones* and *How to Live in the Heartland*.

MARY HARMAN *(page 88)* says she holds "a bachelor's degree and two declarations of independence." She has lived in Wyoming or Colorado for fifty-one of her fifty-three years and calls nature "the source of my spirituality; the mountains are my church."

LOIS HART *(page 146)* teaches literature at Mount Marty College in Watertown, South Dakota. Active in the antiwar and civil rights movements in the 1960s and the struggle for gender equality in the 1970s, she hopes her writing will promote peace and understanding.

SUE HARTMAN *(page 234)*, a descendant of Mormon handcart pioneers and a once-and-future resident of Utah, now lives and writes in Colorado.

DONNA BRITTON HARVEY *(page 169)* was reared on a ranch with eleven brothers and sisters, worked for newspapers, and now works for Conoco, while raising Quarter Horses on her Lance Creek, Wyoming, ranchette.

LINDA M. HASSELSTROM *(page 45)* writes nonfiction about plains life and conducts summer writing workshops for women in her former home, Windbreak House, on the family ranch in western South Dakota.

VANESSA HASTINGS *(page 273)* grew up in South Dakota but considers Wyoming home because it always draws her back. She works for the *Casper Star-Tribune*.

A. ROSE HILL *(pages 210, 280)*, mother of three adopted children, has lived in Wyoming since 1947 and in the same Sheridan house since 1955. She has kept the books for her husband's — now her son's — business since 1959.

JOYCE BADGLEY HUNSAKER *(page 17)* is an award-winning historical interpreter who has achieved national acclaim for her living history portrayals. She was born in rural eastern Oregon in the shadow of the Blue Mountains and lives there still.

KATHRYN E. KELLEY *(page 42)* is an enthusiastic collector of oral histories from her large extended family of early Dutch and Irish settlers. Her interests include landscaping and flower gardening.

DIANNE P. ROOD KIESZ *(page 115)* grew up on the South Dakota prairie and wandered for twenty years seeking her fortune. Back home after working as a college speech and theater instructor and owning a thrift shop, she is now a pastor.

BERNIE KOLLER *(page 140)* is a retired teacher who works as library director for the public library in Freeman, South Dakota. She is involved with her German-Russian ancestry, conducts tours to Hutterite colonies, and lectures at the annual Schmeckfest festival.

NORMA J. KULAS *(page 153)* grew up in Sykeston, North Dakota, studied in Bismarck, and taught in Beulah. She and her husband, Roger, live in Gladstone, Michigan, where they are the parents and guardians of ten children.

LAURIE KUTCHINS *(page 281)* lives near the Idaho-Wyoming border when her work at James Madison University allows. She was raised in Wyoming, "where the incessant wind and the vast sky sculpted my writerly eyes and ears at an early age."

PAGE LAMBERT *(page 134)* lives and writes on a small ranch in the Wyoming Black Hills. Her collection of love stories about land and family, *In Search of Kinship*, is now out in paperback. Her second novel, *Confluence*, is nearing completion.

SUE LEEVER *(page 84)* was born in Michigan, studied in Boston, and lived in Washington, D.C., before moving to Colorado, where she's an executive assistant for a telecommunications firm. She likes to travel, garden, hike, and read.

PHYLLIS M. LETELLIER *(page 173)* lives with her husband, Henry, in the country east of Greybull, Wyoming, where they farmed for eighteen years. A farmer's daughter, she wrote rural humor for twenty years before the family farm was foreclosed in the 1980s farm depression.

ROBIN LITTLEFIELD *(page 61)* has spent the past thirty-five years caring for, training, and enjoying the company of horses. She has a twenty-acre horse farm on a rural island in the Pacific Northwest, where she practices and teaches the art of dressage.

DOROTHY BLACKCROW MACK *(page 79)* raised a sacred herd of buffalo, taught at Oglala Lakota College, published many reservation stories and poems, and now is writing her memoirs.

JANELLE MASTERS *(page 57)* was born in Niobe, North Dakota, population 35, surrounded by farm and pasture land. After a stint in the Peace Corps, she lived in several other states before returning to her home state, where she lives on a hill overlooking virgin prairie.

SUSANN MCCARTHY *(page 201)* writes from Taos, New Mexico. She has been honored by the Santa Fe Recursos Discovery project.

HELEN APPLEGARTH MCCONNELL *(page 13)* grew up the oldest of five children in a Nebraska Sandhills ranching family that shared work and play in the house, hayfield, and barnyard. A children's librarian, she lives with her husband in Albuquerque, New Mexico.

DONNA APPLEGARTH MENTINK *(page 263)* wrote her bio as a snowstorm moved through Nebraska, with both calving sheds full of first-calf heifers and their babies, older calves shivering on the wrong side of the windbreaks, and older cows getting ready to calve a week early.

KAREN N. MILLER *(page 73)*, the granddaughter of four South Dakota homesteaders, is a retired clinical social worker whose essay is her first attempt at creative writing since college.

SUSAN MINYARD *(page 211)* moved to the Sonoran Desert when she was twelve. She and her husband, a cotton farmer, raised three sons. She returned to college in midlife and is now a writer and media/installation artist.

LOIS JEAN MOORE *(page 174)*, who lives on a ranch in northern Nebraska near where she was born, raced through school and began teaching at age fifteen in elementary schools and the state prison. She now directs a puppet team and teaches church for children.

WANDA MORGAN *(page 98)*, a freelance writer for thirty years, writes a weekly newspaper column in her hometown, Enterprise, Oregon, as well as historical essays.

LORRIE MYDLAND *(page 48)*, of Kingsbury County, South Dakota, writes about a friend her husband sent to the penitentiary when he was a circuit court judge.

SANDIE NICOLAI *(page 153)* grew up on a farm near Breckenridge, Minnesota, but has been a North Dakotan since her marriage in 1961. At age fifty-five, she returned to college and currently does social work at a small rural hospital.

KAREN OBRIGEWITCH *(page 127)* lives near Wibaux, Montana, where her family "raises cattle and manages grass and battles for the right to continue our chosen lifestyle." The grandchild of homesteaders, she was raised on a ranch in the Little Missouri River badlands.

PAMELA J. OCHSNER *(page 171)*, at the time of her essay, "was going through a tremendous battle with the family's addiction to alcohol and the damage it does to everyone it touches." Now, though single and no longer farming, she is "still, and always, influenced by this lady's [Vi's] approach to life, addiction, and love."

CLAUDETTE ORTIZ *(page 162)* says, "You can do two things with hurt: you can pull that scar off and whittle it into a knife or make it into a key." She is a poet, columnist, and letters editor for the *Casper* (Wyoming) *Star-Tribune*.

STEPHANIE PAINTER *(page 26)* writes and paints in Wyoming; studies at Vermont College, where she is pursuing an M.F.A. in creative writing; and belongs to WordBand, a trio that performs choral poetry in spoken words.

GINNY JACK PALUMBO *(page 44)* is a third-generation Wyoming native raised on a sheep ranch near Hiland. She lived all over the rural West while raising her three sons. At forty, she returned to college and now works with Alzheimer's support groups.

DONNA PARKS *(page 147)* married and moved away, had three children, and in due course came home to South Dakota. She is a lifetime student, picking courses on a need-to-know basis, observing and absorbing, and loving the process.

CAROLINE PATTERSON *(page 24)* lives in her hometown of Missoula, Montana, with her husband, daughter, and son. She has published award-winning fiction and nonfiction.

KATY PAYNICH *(page 256)* lives in Bozeman, Montana, with her husband and son and teaches high school English. She also volunteers as a doula, providing physical and emotional support for women during labor and delivery.

DIANE JOSEPHY PEAVEY *(page 107)* writes about the family sheep and cattle ranch in the foothills of south-central Idaho and about the changing landscape of the West.

GWEN PETERSEN *(page 250)* is a humorist, novelist, poet, and playwright who keeps computer keys afire when others are filling the nights with useless sleep. Her latest novel is *The Whole Shebang,* an audio book.

THELMA POIRIER *(pages 107, 239)* ranches in southwestern Saskatchewan. Her books include *Grasslands,* a poetry volume; *The Beat Pot,* a children's story; and *Rock Creek,* a reflective prairie journal. She is the editor of *Cowgirls: 100 Years of Writing the Range.*

KAY MARIE PORTERFIELD *(page 207)* wrote this story in a little house on the prairie near Rapid City, South Dakota. It won first place in the creative nonfiction category in the 1999 Laura Bower VanNuys contest.

C. L. PRATER *(page 29)* is a full-time wife and mother and also has several part-time jobs. She grew up on the Rosebud Sioux Reservation in South Dakota but crossed over the border after she married and has lived in Nebraska since then.

DIANE J. RAPTOSH *(pages 14, 249)* is of Czech and Sicilian descent. Raised in Idaho, she has taught literature and creative writing at Albertson College since 1990 and is the mother of one daughter, Keats.

CANDI RED CLOUD *(page 254)* was born and raised on the Pine Ridge Reservation, where she has raised her three boys. She is a sixth-generation descendant of Chief Red Cloud. She works as a social worker, dedicated to helping the women of the reservation become "whole women."

LORA K. REITER *(page 203)* is a professor of English at Ottawa University in Kansas, not only because she loves books and teaching but also because the "wide spaces" give her a place for horses, a big dog, and "plenty of breathing room."

GEORGIA RICE *(page 220)* lives with Kelly, her husband of twenty-five years, on the Nisselius/Rice ranch twenty miles south of Gillette, Wyoming. She works as a secretary at 4J School, eight miles farther south.

BARBARA RINEHARDT *(page 95)* has spent much of her life in small towns or in the country, where her friendships with women have both supported and challenged her. Married with three grown children, she lives in Washington.

JEANNE ROGERS *(page 289)* is a wife, mother, grandmother, sister, daughter, in-law, and friend. She lives and works in a small Wyoming town. Her women friends are of immeasurable worth.

LEE ANN RORIPAUGH *(pages 59, 201)* was raised in Laramie, Wyoming, and now lives in South Dakota. Penguin Books published her poetry book, *Beyond Heart Mountain*, when her manuscript was selected for the National Poetry Series.

WANDA ROSSELAND *(page 122)* is a farm wife and freelance writer from Circle, Montana. "My grandfather's ranch taught me that most of what we live with is extra and unnecessary. All that really matters is water and sky." She and her husband, Milton, have three children.

ECHO ROY *(page 41)* writes to pay tribute to and preserve her family's ranching heritage. As a fourth-generation Wyoming rancher, she raises cattle in partnership with her brothers on ground homesteaded by their great-grandfather in 1876, and she farms with her husband, Rick Klaproth, near Shoshoni.

MARJORIE SAISER *(page 290)* lives in Lincoln, Nebraska, with her husband, Don. Reared on the Nebraska–South Dakota border, she waited tables and fried burgers in the family café and says her hometown had a population of 190, except on Saturday nights, when it doubled.

PEGGY SANDERS *(page 20)* writes full-time when she is not going for parts, holding wrenches, or taking snacks and meals to the field on her family ranch in southwestern South Dakota.

MARY LOU SANELLI *(pages 92, 170)* teaches poetry workshops and is artistic director and founder of the Moving Arts Dance Company in Washington. Her third collection of poetry is *Close at Hand*.

MARY E. SCHNELL *(page 245)* lives on a ridge above the Piedmont Valley of the Black Hills and works as a bank teller in Rapid City, South Dakota. Married for twenty-five years, she has two sons.

FAYE SCHRATER *(page 55)* was born and raised in the West, moving fourteen times between the first and twelfth grades after her father lost the homestead. She's worked in a hospital, with the Peace Corps in Guatemala, as a research scientist, as a teacher, and as a technical adviser for the World Health Organization. She's been homesick in Massachusetts since 1968.

PEARLE HENRIKSEN SCHULTZ *(page 176)* was born in rural Montana and grew up in Wisconsin, where she married the boy next door. Now retired and living in Big Horn, Wyoming, she likes small towns, country roads, quiet evenings with her husband of fifty years, and "books! books! books!"

GIN SCOTT *(page 159)* spent her early years in Montana without plumbing, electricity, or discipline. With her husband, she lives at the edge of Dayton, Wyoming, neighboring with deer, wild turkeys, horses, and vultures.

GAEL SEED *(page 163)* is the pen name of a South Dakota writer who grew up on a ranch. After rearing a family and experiencing years of part-time job-hopping, she feels a compulsion to write.

DAWN SENIOR *(page 75)* lives in the family log cabin in the Snowy Range foothills of Wyoming, where she enjoys riding horses; working on bronze sculptures, oil paintings, and woodcuts; and cooking and eating meals with her eighty-year-old mother.

SHERRY SCHULTZ SHILLENN *(page 10)* is a retired deputy county treasurer and former telephone office manager with six children and eight grandsons. Born in Montana, she will return there when her husband retires. Her life has been dedicated to animal welfare.

LEE ANN SIEBKEN *(page 147)* writes and operates a preschool in Douglas, Wyoming, where she and her husband devote themselves to promoting literacy in their community. Their daughter Nancy, who appears in "The Storm," is now a program specialist of technology services for the Nebraska Commission for the Blind and Visually Impaired.

ANNE SLADE *(page 23)* ranches with her husband, Robert, and her son Brett in the Cypress Hills of Saskatchewan. She has been writing since she was a schoolgirl and joined a writers' group eighteen years ago.

BARBARA M. SMITH *(page 37)* writes about people "caught up in living the boom-and-bust life of the contemporary West." The granddaughter of Norwegian immigrants to Nome, North Dakota, she has taught English at Western Wyoming Community College in Rock Springs, Wyoming, for the past thirty years.

BONNIE LARSON STAIGER *(page 252)* lives near where her ancestors homesteaded, west of the Missouri River in North Dakota. "I'm a city girl who is rooted in the short-grass prairie." She owns a small business specializing in management and lobbying for professional organizations.

JUDITH MCCONNELL STEELE *(page 63)* says, "The story of the rural West is also the story of those of us one generation removed from the farms and ranches, who grew up with a sense of both belonging and loss," with the land "with us and within us." She lives in Boise, Idaho.

LOUISE STENECK *(page 269)* has worked as a mother, journalist, marina owner, librarian, and hog farmer. She now owns a meat processing plant with her husband, Gus. She is looking forward to whatever adventure comes next.

MELINDA STILES *(page 243)* taught high school English for twenty-one years in Michigan and Wisconsin before moving to Salmon, Idaho. She quit before she burned out so that she wouldn't drag her students through her ashes. Now she faces the Continental Divide every day and writes.

JODY STRAND *(page 180)* has spent twenty years in the northern plains doing what she loves best, ranching. Beulah still rides her own horses and continues to inspire.

JO-ANN SWANSON *(page 30, 253)* was raised on a farm in north-central Saskatchewan and has lived in Montana for twenty years. An associate professor of English at the University of Great Falls, she has organized historical conferences on women.

SANDRA GAIL TEICHMANN *(page 38)* is assistant professor of English at West Texas A&M University in Canyon, Texas. Her poetry collection, *Slow Mud,* was published in 1998. She has written two other books, *Woman of the Plains* and *Women on Trains.*

NEDALYN D. TESTOLIN *(page 193)* has "been fortunate to always have her own saddle horse, pitchfork, and shovel, with ample opportunities to use them all," building her life around horses, cattle, and kids. She belongs to the fourth generation of six involved in Wyoming agriculture since territorial days.

EILEEN THIEL *(page 70)* walked out the front doors of a convent finishing school in Oregon and straight into the arms of an Idaho potato farmer. She lives in Joseph, Oregon, and finds rural people genuine and unencumbered by false manners.

DIANNA TORSON *(page 88)* works for students in higher education in South Dakota, where she has lived since 1967. She owns Cottonwood House Bed & Breakfast near Lake Campbell and has been a farmer and beekeeper.

SUREVA TOWLER *(page 93)* began collecting outhouses, sheepwagons, and stories when she moved to Steamboat Springs, Colorado, thirty years ago. She credits altitude sickness for her publishing a small-town weekly and writing regional histories.

ELLEN VAYO *(pages 66, 143)* was born in Seattle and raised in Colorado but settled down only after moving to Wyoming, where she lives with her husband, Frank, in a high-mountain basin near Casper.

LILLIAN VILBORG *(page 64)* grew up in the city but spent summers on the farm where her mother was raised. Her father told his children they were luckier than children who spent summers at the beach. "I didn't use to believe him," she says, "but I do now." She lives in Manitoba.

SUSAN VITTITOW *(page 259)* lives in Cheyenne, Wyoming, with her husband and two dogs. A former newspaper reporter, columnist, editor, and publisher, she freelances and works as a public information specialist for the Wyoming State Library.

SHEILA VOSEN-SHORTEN *(page 21)*, a native Montanan whose ancestors homesteaded on the Hi-Line, is rooted to the land, culture, and spiritual qualities of her home state and people. She lives in Bozeman with her husband, Perry, and makes pottery.

ELLEN WATERSTON *(page 72)*, a New Englander who moved to the ranching West, writes poetry rooted in both cultural and geographic landscapes. Her work has appeared in numerous anthologies and reviews.

TINA WELLING *(page 152)* lives in Jackson Hole, Wyoming, and has published essays, fiction, and poetry. With her husband, she owns a resort business and conducts guided hikes with journal writing, passing on Genie's teachings.

JANE WELLS *(page 5)* says she works part-time at the Jim Gatchell Museum in Buffalo, Wyoming, full-time on the ranch she shares with her husband, and overtime in the house.

KATHLEENE WEST *(page 6)* grew up on a family farm, then taught and worked as a poet-in-the-schools in northeastern Nebraska. She now lives in Las Cruces, New Mexico, where she is poetry editor of *Puerto del Sol*.

AGNES L. WICH (page 11) was born in Colorado, married a farmer, and lives on a piece of the farm her two sons' great-great-grandfather settled more than 110 years ago. A registered nurse, she also works in the family business.

RUBY R. WILSON (pages 156) graduated from South Dakota State University with majors in German and geography. She lives near Brookings, South Dakota, and enjoys writing, photography, gardening, woodworking, and church work.

JANE ELKINGTON WOHL (page 195, 272) teaches full-time at Sheridan College and in the Goddard College M.F.A. program. She directs the Sheridan Young Writers Camp and has been published in many anthologies and small journals.

LUCY L. WOODWARD (page 67) was born and reared in Wyoming, Ohio, but never felt at home until she came to the state of Wyoming as Tom Woodward's bride, settling eventually in Casper. She senses an integrity and freedom of spirit in the West "that I never experienced back east."

CHERYL ANDERSON WRIGHT (page 33) was born in 1944 in Iowa, studied Wyoming geography in sixth grade, and decided at once to move there and raise dogs and horses. In 1979 she moved with her husband and three children to Cody, where she is assistant manager of a bookstore, takes long walks with her dog, and writes.

Acknowledgments

We thank the readers who supported our first collection, *Leaning into the Wind*, for their enthusiasm. The kinship felt among contributors and readers of *Leaning* surprised us and inspired us to try to define that most cherished bond: women's friendships.

We also thank the women who contributed to *Leaning into the Wind* for making the process of compiling and promoting that book so fulfilling that we undertook this second collection. And we thank them for their devoted promotion of *their book.*

Woven on the Wind has been shaped by the hundreds of women who submitted their writing. Even though we couldn't include all the work, we thank them all for trusting us with their thoughts on friendship and relationships — and for their patience and generosity of spirit.

We thank the men in our lives for putting up with grouchiness, distraction, and neglect — and for sometimes even cooking dinner so that we could keep on working.

Special appreciation goes to Marc Jaffe for accepting this work for Houghton Mifflin and guiding its inception; to sagebrush authority Kendall Johnson for providing information on *Artemisia* and checking the introductions for accuracy; to Monique d'Hooghe for adding — from France — her words to "Knowing with the Heart"; to Tamara Rogers for her skill and her dedication to keeping us organized; and to Tracy Eller and Mindy Keskinen for their assistance.

And finally, special appreciation also goes to Susan Canavan, Larry Cooper, and Barbara Jatkola of Houghton Mifflin for their cooperation and care in preserving the integrity of the writing — and especially to Susan for her cheerful good humor.

CREDITS